LANTHREA

A novel by

Lindsay Jaye Nesheim

Table of Contents

Dedication

To my sons, Aric and Britton, my 'chosen' daughter Emma and husband Michael—the beloved ones of my heart.

Acknowledgement

Thanks to Claudette Spear for the pencil sketch at the end of the book, Michael Nesheim for his word-smithing, Aric Nesheim for his editing and literary expertise, and Marcel Lanahan, who (whether he knows it or not) helped inspire this manuscript.

About the Author

Lindsay is a mom and wife, teacher and musician. She spends her time (when not writing) exploring the endless trails of the Pacific Northwest in Washington and the wide open prairies of Montana— often on the back of her beloved horse Gandalf, and always with her dog Luna.

CHAPTER ONE:

The Dark

She closed her eyes, held her breath, and pretended as though she were invisible. For all the good it would do. Her terrified glottin kept trying to help, whispering incessantly in her ear. She clapped her hand over its mouth to quiet it down.

"Miss, they come for us. Miss…" it repeated for the umpteenth time.

"Quiet, Tenk" she mouthed back, putting her finger to her lips….*they will* hear *you."* She tried to calm her racing heart by reminding herself that it was doubtful anyone would try to break in. For her small home, made of mere mud and straw, adorned by only one tiny window, and situated in the poorest of neighborhoods, almost assured no one would bother her for riches. Anyone looking could tell that no coin would be found here. Rarely was her home a target for theft.

But it wasn't always coin they wanted. Not these men. They cared for nothing but fulfilling their bent desires and cared even less for those they used in fulfilling them. Shuddering, she remembered the time a group of them had cornered her in an alley. She was just a young girl at the time and had been digging through a waste bin for food. Had it not been for Tenk scurrying in amongst them and biting at their ankles (adequately distracting and confusing them) she never would have escaped.

The little glottin peered up at her once again and whispered, *"they come for us."* She pressed her hand over its mouth again and hoped they had not been heard.

And so, as it was every night, breathless in the dark with dear Tenk tucked into her chest, she waited. Waited for the angry shouts and terrified screams outside to lessen. Waited for the morning.

After what seemed like an eternity, the shouting and mayhem quieted—leaving a heavy silence in the streets. Her heartbeat began to calm, and Tenk squirmed its way out of the bed and scurried over to sleep by the fire. Myka let her body and head fall back onto the bedding.

She rolled over on her side and tried to pull the tattered muslin cloth that served as a blanket over her aching shoulders. Having no coin for a wooden bed, she made do with a pile of hay covered in cloth. It was hard on her old frame; her body having long since lost its elasticity and ability to recover easily from a day's labor. Thankfully (if one could be thankful for such a thing) the years had done much to thicken her calloused feet and hands, making them, at least, somewhat impervious to the cold of her dwelling. She reached up to run one of those calloused hands through her long gray hair in a meager attempt to soothe herself to sleep, only to find her hair so thickly tangled that even this small comfort was denied her. Sighing, she let her arm fall back to the floor and began to hum. At night, especially, she liked to sing. Since she was young, music had helped her drown out the street noise and calm herself. In her imagination, it had also helped transform her from the girl that she was— unshapely, with the fair skin and blue eyes that were quite undesirable in Drymac—into one of the lovely courtiers with their skin the color of chestnuts, deep brown eyes and shining black hair who were chosen to sing for the court. She thought of those women now. Those who lay their bejeweled heads on impossibly soft pillows at night. Those, unlike herself, who were lovely in both form and feature.

She mused only for a moment on these thoughts, then quickly tossed them away. She was old now. And to be honest, she was one of the lucky ones. There was a roof over her head, a fire in the hearth, a glottin curled up snug and warm, and no men of the court to impose themselves upon her. Withered she may be and broken of body, but just as her callouses helped keep her feet from freezing, so the curses of age were, in fact, blessings—keeping her safe from the eyes of the marauding gangs or Lord Bythim's men.

She hummed a song until her eyes fell heavy, and the pain in her broken body at last slipped under the gentle blanket of sleep. Her glottin had long since drifted off by the fire, its quiet snoring lending a certain contentment to the small dwelling.

Outside, in the alleys and side roads of Cenecal, evil of every sort continued to ravage the unsuspecting and naïve under the blackness of night. For some, this would be the last night of their innocence: an initiation into reality. And reality proved that Drymac was a kingdom replete with violence and treachery, all encouraged by Lord Bythim and oft rewarded by the same. For if the lawless citizenry weren't bad enough, Lord Bythim and his court were always on the prowl for the successful and beautiful in the kingdom with the sole purpose of using, then bleeding them dry—both literally and figuratively. He paid his men for this scouting (and often for thievery and mayhem) to both increase the court's treasury and terrify the people. He enjoyed terrifying people. It kept them in line. Predictably, every so often a resistance to Bythim's reign would be secretly organized by some brave souls. These were met with complete and utter domination by

Bythim's men. The Uprising of N'een was one such event. It was met not only with death of the insurgents and their leader, N'een, but to every one of their wives and children.

The uprisings did not often occur.

Cenecal itself was a large city, smack in the center of Drymac. The entire place was designed like a wheel with the streets as spokes and Lord Bythim's palace smack in the center. Surrounded by the preternaturally sharp and imposing Circacian Mountains, Cenecal was almost entirely cut off from the rest of Drymac save for the logging roads that led down to the Outer territories of the south. The town itself was dusty, dark, and smelled bad even to the citizens used to it. It had four well established sectors, each serving a different purpose, with most people living in the ramshackle, tightly packed Market Quarter. It was here that Myka had spent her entire life amongst the waste and makeshift huts.

She, an impoverished orphan, had lived on these streets alone since the age of five. This made her quite vulnerable to the many dangers of Cenecal, but in a strange irony, her circumstances also offered a form of protection: that of invisibility. Her five hard decades of poverty along with the inevitable ravages of age had only punctuated this invisibility. And so, age, like her station, had become her Friend.

Never the less, when the marauders or court soldiers had enough drink in them, even an old woman was in danger. In that, this night was no different. The screams, the scuffles, the soldiers in blue capes ravaging anyone they wished, the drunken mayhem spilling from pubs into alleyways, and, as tonight, right outside Myka's door. Any victim would do. It was a miracle she ever slept at all.

An insistent tapping on her arm awakened her from an uneasy slumber. "Miss…get up!" Tenk's voice was urgent, and she bolted upright, attempting to clear her head of sleep. The glottin was staring at her, eyes wide with fright. Heart pounding, she pulled the small creature to her and held it close. "Tenk, what is it now?" The little creature buried its long nose in her chest and breathed heavily. "Danger, miss…something *here.*" Her eyes darted about the small room. The fire had died down but it was early morning, and the sun had risen just enough for her to see there was no one else in the room. "What danger, dear Tenk? I see nothing here." The little furry creature pulled its leathery snout from her chest and glanced furtively around the room. "Something was here…*danger*…" it whispered, burying its head in her chest once again. Fully awake now, Myka knew there would be no more sleep for either of them.

Setting Tenk gently on the floor, she forced herself to get up; gnarled hands supporting her lower back as she hobbled over to the fireplace and stirred the embers to life, adding a new log. "What on earth did you see?" She patted Tenk on the head. "You scared me, small friend." Tenk pulled at her nightshirt. "Something was *here*," it whispered quietly in its squeaky voice. "Gone now, methinks." It was still glancing nervously about the room but soon settled back down by the fire as the new log erupted into flame. Myka sat down in her only chair, a comfortable rocker made of twisted twine and sturdy branches. The one thing on the planet she had left from her childhood, back when she still had a family. Her mother had once rocked her to sleep in this chair… back before she had died. Back before Myka had been left alone. Back before…

She couldn't remember the last time she felt safe. Or at peace, for that matter. The town was dangerous enough by day, and Tenk was always awakening her to remind her of imminent dangers at night. She looked around the room as the dawn illuminated the space and reassured herself no one was there. Not this time, at least.

***

The marketplace was going to be busy today. It was only ten days until the Festival of Ciracus, loosely named for the mountains surrounding the kingdom and in celebration of the Spring plantings. The exchange of goods and services would reach a rather fevered pitch until the Eve of Cirac when all shops would close at dusk and not reopen until the day after the celebrations ended. Depending upon Lord Bythim's whims, this could be anywhere from one to three days. Although Myka remembered once, as a young woman, when The Festival was cancelled entirely because Bythim was in a particularly petulant mood; a Courtier had summarily rejected his advances. She, of course, had been publicly executed, and he had publicly pouted—punishing the entire kingdom for the sake of his bruised ego.

Myka gathered up her items, patted Tenk on the head, locked her door, and shuffled the mile or so to her place in the town square. Her space was just a small indentation in the city wall which acted as a booth—with a butcher on one side (who brought in tremendous business) and a purveyor of religious statues and trinkets on the other (who had practically no business at all). It was a safe spot, clean and close enough to the Constabulary to be relatively free of theft and assault. People would come for the butcher's rich quail thighs and salted porks, then linger at Myka's booth—the women often talking their husbands into a new piece of cloth for use as a scarf or table covering.

Myka's cloths were well known in the town. She had a certain artist's touch and could paint the loveliest designs on any piece of fabric—making even the most utilitarian of materials literal works into works of art. This talent had kept her in food and clothing since the day she discovered she had it. It had also kept her from digging in the waste bins and begging on the streets for coin. In fact, when times were hard, and no good cloth could be afforded, Myka would paint on old grain sacks found in the trash—rough and worthless bags—which, under her touch, would become lovely place mats or wall hangings.

Upon reaching her booth, she set out her designs in the most enticing display possible, then straightened her skirt and spine, pulled her matted hair up into a lumpy, thick bun and secured it with a rusty hairpin. She then pinched her cheeks for color, and waited for the mayhem of the marketplace to begin. What began as a trickle of customers soon swelled into a crushing wave of commerce. People were pushing and yelling, elbowing in front of each other to get to the best items—often coming to blows over who got there first. Myka watched sadly as a grown man pushed a small boy down and snatched the tiny bag of sugar from his hand. To these sorts of infractions the constables would not attend, and most people knew better than to even bring a child to market. The officials only got involved if a knife or other weapon was brandished, which, because of their proximity to the Constabulary, rarely happened to Myka or her butcher friend.

Myka's cloths were completely sold out by mid-day, and, tucking the hard earned coins into her pocket so as to keep her hands free and money hidden, she thought to take a new route home. Normally it would be a dangerous and silly thing to do, but Myka had learned to be quite savvy over the years. Only that one time as a child had she been cornered. She had learned much since then. And outside of a few things stolen from her home and a piece of cheese or two taken from her by force in the Marketplace, she had fared quite well in Cenecal. Of course, like everyone else, she lived in a constant state of terror. But there was nothing to be done for that.

But this day seemed different. Mild, lovely and *soft. S*pring had come early this year. And today, with the streaming sunshine, people smiling at one another, and the life of a new season in the air…it felt almost *safe*. She took the chance.

Aside from being tussled about a bit as she weaved her way through the crowds, she was able to get out of the Market Quarter without incident before dusk descended and found to her delight that she had wandered straightaway into Old Town—the loveliest (and least visited) section of Cenecal. Here, hanging gardens still graced the brickwork lattice doorways of the homes, and flower pots provided glorious offerings of color and fragrance to the otherwise drab and often dirty town. It was mostly the very aged that lived here, as they were the sole keepers of happy memories and civic sensibilities like gardens and flower pots. For there had been a time, before Bythim and his handful of despotic predecessors, that Drymac had been ruled by good men and women. Kings and Queens born of royal blood, not bloody conquest. These had been times of shared prosperity—of colorful homes painted lovingly and the well kept gardens that surrounded them. A time where neighbors cared for one another, when learning and the arts were valued and sought after. A time when kindness was a priority, and a woman could walk in the cool of the evening through a hanging garden unaccompanied and unafraid. Most in Cenecal had no memory of this time nor interest in it. But here in Old Town, the elders cherished these memories and did what little they could to perpetuate the values underpinning them.

The ravaging hoards and blue caped soldiers left this Quarter alone. Somewhat inexplicable, it was as though the very colors of the place and life of the gardens somehow repelled them. It made the place seem almost magical, as if the gardens were guards and the flowers within them protective talismans.

In truth (more than likely) it was the fact that the elders had few belongings and even less coin to steal, and everyone knew it. Most were old as well—*very* old—and had nothing to offer Bythim's men who hunted down beautiful young women for the court and able bodied men for the corps. Still, the fact that these homes weren't plundered and the gardens destroyed amazed Myka. Something about this place was simply a mystery.

These Old Towners had very little food, and lived communally, hand to mouth, sharing what little they had amongst each other and their animals. Unlike the Market Quarter, where the only creatures to be found were glottins, here a large variety of animals and birds were plentiful. Bluejays sang in the manicured trees, dogs or cats were curled up on almost every doorstep, goats and sheep in every field, and the occasional horse and cow could be seen grazing contentedly in the larger pastures. Interestingly, for all the varied animal life in Old Town, Myka didn't see a single glottin scurrying here and there under the boardwalks or in their preferred waste bins near the buildings. She thought it odd, but then again, perhaps it was too clean and tidy, lacking in outdoor bins or dry basements within which glottins were most comfortable. Perhaps the surplus of dogs and cats frightened them. Or perhaps glottins just preferred the more densely populated areas (and therefore food opportunities) of the Market

Quarter. Either way, she saw none, and this saddened her— making her feel uneasy.

Of all the talking creatures left in Drymac (most had been hunted to extinction), glottins were the most prized. Soft brown fur, little round little black eyes spaced a bit too close together, and sporting long, leathery snouts—they looked rather like a hybrid of a pudgy mole and an anteater. Quite irresistible when mature, and completely when young. Everyone knew that to take in a glottin was good fortune, indeed: a gift from the gods. 'Taken in' was actually the wrong phrase. Wild, skittish, hard to catch, and impossible to keep by force, you rather had to be chosen by them. She had been chosen by Tenk when she was five, on the very day her parents died. It had bounded up to her, begging food, as she sat crying on the stoop of her home. The home that had been her universe for the entirety of her five years. She had taken the baby glottin into her life that day, naming it Tenk because of the chirping sound it made when content, 'tnk, tnk, tnk.' Never had there been a day when she had regretted that decision. So, to not see any of these helpful companions here made her a bit suspicious of this place. Normally, such uneasiness would bother her greatly, but the sights and sounds of the this old quarter brought back such a flood of happy memories that she overlooked her disquiet.

For even though Myka hadn't been here since she was a very young child, she remembered it well. Her grandparents had lived here long ago, and she and her parents had visited often. It was her grandmother who had taught her the joy of reading before she died, giving Myka a beautiful primer when she was but three. She closed her eyes for a moment and remembered—sitting on her nona's lap in front of a roaring fire and devouring the words on the pages. Smiling at the memory, she found herself wandering in the direction of their house, vaguely remembering both its location next to the fountain in the center of the Quarter, and the odd shape of the little place—a rather oval hut of a home—made of straw and mud, smoothed over with clay and painted a bright blue. She recalled her mother calling it the Robin's Egg, for so it appeared. It only took her a few minutes to find it. No longer painted blue, but was still the same egg shaped little hut. The sun was just setting now, and a welcoming fire could be seen shining brightly through the windows. Myka felt as if she could simply open the door and make herself at home. She stood, hands on hips, just staring at the place. The wooden door had been painted bright red, and the hut itself was now a lovely cream color on which the setting rays of the sun cast an amber glow.

A voice from behind her startled her from her reverie. "Can I help you, ma'am?"

Myka whipped around to see an elderly man—twenty years or more her senior—leaning on a colorful, intricately carved cane and smiling at her.

"No. I, uh… My grandparents lived here…once, long ago…" her voice trailed off as she turned and faced the hut again.

"Mykealla and Daneeb, I remember them well." The old man nodded. "After they died, the home was to have been given to their children, but they never came to claim it. The house has been sold many times over the last four decades."

Myka turned around again. "Mykealla, yes…how did you know?She is my namesake." She reached out her hand to the man, "My name is Myka. I live in the Market Quarter. And you are?"

He grasped her hand firmly with both of his. "Petrul. I live there (and here he nodded toward the next block) in the red brick house on the corner."

"Petrul. Nice to make your acquaintance." Myka looked around slowly. "It is so…so peaceful here".

Petrul nodded. "The last place in Cenecal to be so blessed—the best of the Four Quarters, if you ask me. Under the protection of the king, you know." He smiled at her and winked. She wondered what he meant by this but had no time to inquire before he let go her hand and tapped his cane on the ground. "Have you had evening meal yet? My wife would love a visitor…she is a grand cook."

Myka laughed. "While I no doubt her cooking ability, I do doubt her love of an unexpected guest at this hour."

Petrul tapped his cane again softly in the dust. "It's getting dark. And I see the weariness in your face. Please, join us for evening meal, Myka."

She sighed, unused to such unsolicited kindness and generosity, finding herself reluctant to accept them from a stranger. But she *was* tired, her feet *did* ache, and her stomach had been growling since the noontime bell.

"It is a kind offer," Myka finally succumbed, "and I can help your wife with the preparations."

Petrul waved off her words as they turned to walk, arm in arm, to his little brick house. "'Tis not necessary, friend. Your company will be gift enough for us tonight."

"Kind, again," Myka smiled softly as they walked. "Pray tell, how did you know my grandparents were Mykealla and Daneeb? There has been a full generation of people in that house since then."

"If you don't mind me saying," Petrul cleared his throat, "*you* gave that away. Most of the inhabitants of that house have been too young to have a granddaughter of your…your…"

Myka laughed. "I forget my age sometimes," she sniffed and rubbed her aching shoulder, "but I am reminded often."

They reached the little house—both laughing about their aches and pains—only to find a lovely old woman standing on the porch, perhaps ninety years of age, round of body and with a smile as bright as the stars.

"And isn't it just like my husband to bring a guest for evening meal."

Her sarcasm was betrayed by the smile on her face.

"Yes, I see Petrul has found another stray." She reached out and grasped Myka's hands with both of hers, as Petrul had done.

Myka was immediately set at ease by her humor and her warmth. "He has indeed. I take it this is not an unusual thing?"

The woman laughed, her laughter hearty and authentic. "No, my friend. It is a regular occurrence—especially around the high holidays. We have more people wandering into Old Town during the Festival of Ciracus than any other time of year."

Petrul interrupted.

"Marinda, this is Myka. Her grandparents lived in the Egg House many years ago."

Myka was taken aback, "That's what my mother called it! The Robin's Egg."

Marinda laughed again. "Well, it looks just like one, doesn't it?" She stepped aside and opened the door. "Come in, come in. Food will be ready in just a few minutes."

Myka entered the house and was immediately set at ease. The brick walls were all painted a warm yellow, and a huge fire was burning in the stone fireplace. Colorful plates, two particularly beautiful stone mosaics, and a variety of cups lined the walls, displayed proudly on open edged wood shelves, and the overwhelming smell of bread baking was wafting from the kitchen.

A large overstuffed chair was prominent next to the fireplace, and two small wicker rockers sat on opposite sides of the room, with a small intricately carved table set between. The carvings reminded her of something familiar.

"Petrul, the table…it matches your cane!"

"A good eye, Myka. I made them both myself. If you'll look carefully, you'll see the the carvings represent many of the stories of Palem."

"Ahhhh," Myka intoned, leaning over to inspect the table more carefully. In truth, she had no familiarity with whatever Palem was or *any* of its stories but didn't want to appear ignorant. "They're lovely."

It was at that moment that Marinda appeared in the doorway to the kitchen, wiping her hands on her apron and announcing in a loud voice, "The food is ready if you are!"

The little kitchen had a lovely nook where a table was set for evening meal. A candle burned brightly in the center, with a wreath of jasmine in full bloom laid about it. There were three plates, with bowls atop, made of heavy earthenware, and three delicate glass goblets next to those, etched with what might be a family crest. The forks, spoons, and knives looked to be made of real silver, and there were beautiful, lacy napkins folded under each set. A steaming round loaf of rustic bread was already on the table, along with a hunk of what Myka was sure must be butter. It was the most inviting and lovely table at which Myka had ever been a guest, and she found her eyes glaze over with tears.

"Sit, sit," Marinda sounded like she was reprimanding children. "The stew will cool if we don't get to eating!"

Petrul and Myka sat down, whereupon he tore a piece of the hot bread and, dipping it in the butter, handed it to Myka. Marinda next appeared with a pot in her hand and ladled out a hot, thick stew into each bowl. The smell—of onions and barley and garlic and carrots and vegetables Myka couldn't even identify—enveloped her. Her mouth was literally watering, and she felt her stomach lurching in hunger as she waited for Petrul to pour the deep red wine into the goblets.

Thus finished serving, Marinda sat down at her place, and after Petrul broke a piece of the loaf and handed it to her, the two of them bowed their heads. Petrul cleared his throat and spoke before Myka could discern what was happening.

"El-Gudan, we thank you for this food, this day, the sun and the moon, the stars and our breath. Make our arms strong for our labors and bless our new friend, Myka".

They then both looked up, smiling as Myka shifted uncomfortably in her chair.

Marinda winked at Petrul and broke the silence.

"Eat that bread before I do, Myka."

"I'm sorry, I…I don't hold with any of the gods. I've never seen people….pray before."

"Oh, not a worry, not a worry, dear," Petrul said as he tore off a hunk of bread and dipped it in his bowl. And we don't hold with the gods, either—at least not the ridiculous ones people buy statues of in the market. We honor only the High King El-Gudan in this home."

Myka nodded as though she understood, but in fact, she felt that one god was as good and as mythical as the next. While she knew many who dabbled in magic (who didn't need help surviving the harshness of life?) she had never before befriended anyone who actually held to a god. It was a new experience for her, an uncomfortable one. She tossed off the discomfort and picked up her spoon. Digging into her stew, the very first bite overwhelmed her. She pushed back from the table for a minute, head back, eyes closed.

"Oh, Marinda. This is exquisite."

Marinda grinned sheepishly and waved off the complement. "Just some old vegetables from the community garden."

Myka had another bite. "Well, maybe so, but you have some sort of magic with vegetables, then. I haven't had food this good in years."

Petrul slapped his hand on the table in glee. "I told you, Myka. I told you! Marinda is the best cook in Old Town, maybe in all the four quarters of Cenecal!"

"Petrul. Stop," whined Marinda coyly.

They ate their dinner together in good spirits, and Myka felt they might quickly become good friends. She had so few in town. People were not…safe. The talk turned easily from topic to topic: from the upcoming festival to the early warm spring, to the politics of Old Town itself. Myka discovered that living here was like living in a completely different world from hers. In fact, it was. The people here, most of them much older than Myka, still cared about each other. They grew gardens together, dividing up the bounty, took turns milking the goats and their one shared cow, helped one another in sickness, and shared in grief upon death. And many of them, in fact, most all, believed in, and honored a god name El-Gudan. Most curiously, though, was that the main topic of the evening was of a place called Palem. Both Marinda and Petrul talked on and on about it, telling stories back and forth across the table excitedly. Comments like, "In Palem, where the rivers run with healing waters…" and "Bythim, ha! The Good King will one day show him what true royalty is." And most curiously and most soothing to her ears was, "Of course, there is no fear there…the True King sees to that!" Myka listened intently but purposely withheld her ignorance of the topic. She felt somehow foolish not knowing these legends, as they seemed so important to them.

She thought to bring the subject up again as they retired to the living room; Petrul in the oversized chair by the fire, Myka and Marinda in the wicker rockers by the carved table. It was the table that allowed the subject to arise easily.

So, these carvings, Petrul, they are stories about this Palem?"

He nodded, blowing on his hot tea. "Uh huh, each carving represents one of the Solemn Memories."

Myka sniffed. "The Solemn Memories… of course."

Marinda was looking at Myka strangely, with an almost imperceptible smile on her face.

"Tell me, Myka," she said as she sipped her tea, "Which is your favorite to consider?"

Myka, aware she had just been discovered, smiled sheepishly and set her cup down.

"Alright. I've been found out. I've not heard stories of this place, or the Memories, or *any* of the legends you have spoken of until tonight. Is this a legend only the Elders here in Old Town know? By the stars above, I have lived for over five decades, and I have never heard these stories before."

Petrul chuckled. "Oh, we knew this from the moment you mentioned that the carvings on the table and my cane seemed similar." He motioned to the table. "Anyone knowing would have simply said something like, "What wonderful carvings of the Memories" or "Lovely images of Palem" or something of the sort. And, you, being from Cenecal's market quarter… well, we wouldn't have expected folks there to know of Palem and the True King.

Myka sighed in relief, the gentle jibes Petrul poked at her making her feel more like family than ever.

"Well, you speak of this myth with such warmth and appreciation. It must be very important to you both."

"Oh, dear friend," said Marinda, almost giddily, "Palem is not a *myth*. It is quite *real*." Marinda's resolute expression was very unsettling.

Myka cleared her throat. If there could have been a more deflating moment in the evening, she could not think of one. These two otherwise lovely old people had given up their sanity. They not only held to a god, but they believed—actually *believed*—in some sort of mythical place as well. A wishful place where the horrors of reality did not exist. They were not just religious, they were, in fact, deluded *by* their religion.

If Myka knew anything after fifty nine years of life on the streets of Cenecal, it was that religious people were blind, naïve, and sometimes dangerously fanatical. Had it not been a group of religious zealots who followed the god Plenor that had slaughtered a group of merchants two years ago during the Ciracus Festival? All because they were selling statues of several other competing gods as well? Her neighbor at the market (the seller of religious trinkets and statues), was very wary to come to market for months after that event, and when he finally did, he made certain statues of Plenor were featured prominently in his booth.

She smiled at Marinda and Petrul, fully aware that her expression suddenly held less gratitude than pity.

"Well, then. It is getting late. I should be getting back. My poor glottin must be starving by now. I can't thank you enough for the dinner and the company."

Miranda made an odd face, paused for a moment, then responded. "Are you sure you can't stay? Petrul's chair makes for good sleeping.

And we all know what happens under cover of darkness in the Market Quarter.”

Myka stood up, her back and shoulders suddenly aching again.

“No. I couldn’t. Your kindness has been too much already. My stomach has not been so full in many, many years. Speaking of which, would you mind if I took a crust of bread for my glottin? I have little in my house for it tonight.”

What happened next only served to solidify the warnings Myka was feeling in her heart. Upon hearing her request, Marinda observably bristled. “Oh, I hate feeding those things,” she muttered, “perhaps you should put it out of your home, Myka.”

Myka’s heart almost stopped. She felt anger rise like bile in her throat and thought it best to simply not respond. Her dear Tenk, how dare this woman even suggest? She was no different than every other religious person she had ever known: imposing and judgmental.

They all stood, and Petrul reached out to grasp Myka’s hands again warmly in his.

“Please, please come again, Myka. We are just getting to know you.”

Myka forced a smile, “You are so kind. Perhaps I shall.” She said this, full knowing she would not be visiting again any time soon.

***

Miranda and Petrul stood on the porch, arm in arm, and watched as Myka disappeared into the dark.

20

Slowly they turned and walked back into the house together. Petrul spoke first.

"I do not think that we shall see her again."

Miranda sat down in her rocking chair, head in hands. "Oh, Petrul. I should not have said what I did about her glottin. And we spoke too much of Palem. Too much. I knew it as we were talking, but I could not stop myself. Oh, Good King, forgive us."

Myka walked as fast as her old legs and aching body could carry her, not looking back until she had reached the outskirts of the Merchant's Quarter.

The warm, welcoming lights of Old Town were long gone. All she could see around her was the black of the night.

CHAPTER TWO:
The Book

Myka slept fitfully but not of her own accord. She had fallen into an exhausted sleep, and it was actually Tenk who had awakened her three times. Annoying, yes, but she was thankful for each interruption. The first time there had been voices outside her dwelling, and Tenk had pulled her out of slumber with a frantic reminder that she had forgotten to latch the door. The second time he pestered her until she got up and took a tincture for her back pain, which she had also forgotten. "Milady will be in pain tomorrow, too much to bear," it warned her. Myka had just fallen back to sleep when, for the third time, Tenk's frantic tugging at her nightclothes roused her. It had been certain someone was trying to break in through the window, and sure enough, Myka found scratch marks on the windowsill. She shivered from the knowledge of it and simply could not get back to sleep after that.

She made herself a cup of tea, using the pot that hung over her simple fireplace, and thought longingly of the lovely roaring fire with the stone mantle at Petrul and Marinda's house. Sighing as she sipped, she felt a sudden sadness that such good people had given themselves over to superstition. How could intelligent people fall prey to such nonsense? An imaginary place where a good King ruled and all is well with the world? She shook her head. Religion ruined people for any sensible purposes. Kept them bound by wishful thinking and gave then nothing but empty hope. She stirred the tea with her finger. Perhaps she could attempt to dissuade them of their beliefs? They were, after all, very *kind* folk. Maybe she could help them break from their bondage to such utter futility.

She shook her head. No. She simply wanted some kind people in her life, that was all. She was just lonely enough to try and think she could attempt to change them. No. There was no parting a fool from their folly. Even a kind fool. Tossing the fantasy of friendship out of her head, she dove into the reality at hand.

Today was a painting day. She had sold every single cloth yesterday at market and needed to design some new ones immediately. Dressing as quickly as possible, she piled her hair on top of her head and bound it with her pin. She had to take another sip of her back tincture as she was already hurting, just as Tenk had predicted. Good Tenk. He was the only creature on the planet that truly cared for her.

Rummaging about in her one cupboard, she found only one small piece of cloth. She was certain she had more in her inventory. Careless. She was getting careless in her old age. This meant a trip into the heart of the Market, fighting the crowds and spending a considerable amount of the coin she had earned just yesterday. Sighing, she slumped into her chair. It never ended. The cycle of working hard just to spend what one made in order to work hard again. There seemed no gain to this cycle, this exercise in futility.

Tenk crawled up on her lap. "We will have no food, Miss, if no new cloth." It sniffed sadly, and she petted its head gently.

"Don't worry. I'll take care of it today." Setting Tenk down, she took the coin bag out of her cupboard. Counting out her earnings, she proceeded to take half of them and tuck the coins in her pocket. The others she hid under the one piece of cloth left and locked her cupboard—double checking the lock.

She had but one piece of hard cheese left in her larder, and this she split with Tenk.

"I'll be back before noon bell," she said soothingly to her friend as it nibbled on the cheese rind. "You take care of the place."

Wrapping a shawl around her shoulders against the light spring breeze, she remembered to latch her door as she left. While glottins were rarely stolen (because they are almost impossible to catch), good coin *was,* and she couldn't afford any more loss this week.

Having thoroughly enjoyed her diversion to the Old Town quarter yesterday, she decided to take a more circuitous route to the inner Market today. The Forbidden Quarter stood just outside her part of town and would make for an interesting distraction on this lovely spring morning. Ominous in name only, it was the most ancient part of Cenecal—some said in all of Drymac. Basically, a collection of crumbling dwellings, with but a few buildings yet standing and a temple ruin or two dedicated to the old gods of the land, it was more an architectural oddity than anything else. It came to be known as "forbidden" several centuries prior when looters were routinely stealing artifacts and anything of value from the ruins. One of Lord Bythim's predecessors, wanting any such bounty for himself, had declared the place 'forbidden' and imposed large fines or even larger punishments for anyone going near the place. But that was hundreds of years ago, and now it was 'forbidden' in title only.

Myka always enjoyed walking through the ruins, imagining what it might have been like—wondering about the people who lived and worked there. Today was no different. A few other wanderers walked along the dusty roads beside her; remarking on 'that broken turret,' or the 'size of that temple ruin'. She enjoyed hearing the discussions, plus her aching bones felt better than usual today, probably due to the double dose of medicine she had taken but also because the warm sun was promising a lovely day ahead.

About half way through the Quarter, she saw a small alleyway she had not noticed before in earlier trips through. Pulling the shawl off her shoulders (the sun was too warm now) she wrapped it around her waist and decided to explore.

The alley looked as though it had, at one time, functioned as a livestock run—perhaps for moving cattle and sheep through town without blocking the main routes. There were little stone divots carved into the buildings, which most likely served as mangers for grain, along with much larger carved troughs made for water storage. She thought it a grand idea, proving once again that the ancients were more clever than people assumed.

Continuing on through the little alley, she saw a small building, most likely serving once as an individual dwelling, standing alone at the end of the lane. It looked to be almost completely sound: four walls, roof still intact, and windows on two sides. It was made of stone, and one could see (if one looked carefully) that it had at once been painted with bright colors and delicate designs that had long since faded with time.

Intrigued by the very fact that is was so intact, Myka thought to enter the little dwelling to see what it might have been like to live here a few centuries before—perhaps watching the sheep being herded down the lane or baking bread in the fireplace on a lovely spring morning such as today.

To this end, she lifted up her skirt and stepped over the door frame, which was piled high with centuries old dirt and mud.

The little home had nothing remarkable about it once inside. Four stone walls, gray of color, and smooth to touch, a small indentation on the floor where a fire pit may (or may not) have been, but nothing of any note otherwise. Long since picked clean of any pottery, wood, or reliquary that might tell a story, the stone walls themselves spoke very little of the past. Myka sighed, then gave a half hearted chuckle of resignation. Of course there would be nothing here to inspire her imagination. How silly of her to think otherwise. Turning to go, she felt her right foot give way a bit and, thinking she was having ankle problems again, looked down. There, in the hand hewn stone floor, she saw a panel of wood. As though someone had covered a hole in the rock so as to level out the floor. Thinking this an odd solution as stone was cheaper than wood, she bent over to inspect it further. It was a hardwood, a panel about the breadth of her hand and as long as her foot. Knowing she would pay for doing so, she dropped to her old, creaky knees and pulled at the plank. Surprisingly, it released in a cloud of dust, and, waving it away, she found herself looking into a hole in the floor. But the hole wasn't what caught her interest. It was the item that lay within. Heart racing with the excitement of such a find, she gently pulled it from its resting place and dusted it off.

It was a book. The rarest of commodities in Cenecal. Leather bound, inscribed with a some words she could not read, and with a picture of a tree etched into the leather cover. Excitedly, she opened it. The pages were of some sort of thick, waxy substance—perhaps dried leather pounded thin or reeds woven and compressed into a writable surface. Certainly not the more fragile papers they sold at the market today, made of pounded fibers mixed with glues.

Each page had a lovely drawing on it, she noticed this first because the artwork was exquisite and delicate. She could not come *close* to painting designs such as these, and it drew her to the pages immediately.

The words, however, were unreadable. The language looked like ancient Drymacian (a long dead language), but no one spoke it any longer, and the words were undecipherable. She couldn't make out a single character on the first page nor the second. But, as she turned to the third page, she gasped. For there, as clear as day, jumping off the page in the midst of all the other strange letters and symbols was the word '*Palem*'.

She blinked, thinking it her imagination because of her conversation last night in Old Town…but there it was. Standing alone amidst the undecipherable words of the ancient language was one she *could* read: *Palem.*

She squinted and looked again. The unfamiliar characters and letters danced across the waxy page, all but for that one word. She was not imagining it. Shutting the book, she thought for a moment to return it to its dusty tomb—letting it sleep with the ghosts of the past in peace. But she was far too intrigued at this point, and instead slipped the book into her waistband, replaced the wooden plank, covered it over again with dirt and dust. Then, paying the price for getting down on her old knees, she managed to pull herself up by grabbing at the wall, cursing her old body as she did. She headed back out into the alley, dusting off her skirt.

The Market Quarter was almost too crowded to navigate by the time she got there, and had she not known the cloth seller—a friend of hers named Patrice—she would never have made it through the lines to get what she needed. But as it was, Patrice saw her, beckoned her to come around to the back of the booth, and helped her pick out what she needed. Paying her friend for the cloth and a bit extra for her trouble, Myka headed home—her arms holding the new cloth and her waistband holding a new treasure.

Opening the latch, she was greeted by an exuberant Tenk flying into her arms.

"Oh my!" Myka exclaimed, hugging her little glottin tightly. "You missed me today, then?"

"Tenk misses Miss," was all it said, burying its pointed little snout in her chest.

Smiling, she carried Tenk over to the fire and, stirring the embers, tossed on another two logs. She set Tenk down in front of the hearth just as the fire leapt back to life and pulled the book out of her waistband.

So excited was she to look at her new treasure that it took Tenk to remind her she had completely forgotten to pick up some food at the market along with the cloth.

"Food, Miss?" It insisted, pointing at its mouth, "food?"

She rolled her eyes as she took off her shawl, tossed it onto a hook by the door, and set the book down on her one table next to her chair.

"Oh, Tenk. I forgot. Let me…let me…" she stood, spinning in her one little room of a home, looking for food she knew wasn't there. "Let me go back to market for us. You stay by the fire, but if it goes out before I get back, you mustn't worry. The day is heating up nicely, and in a few hours, we will have no need of the fire."

She unlocked and opened up her cupboard, grabbed her pile of newly purchased cloths, and shoved them in while grabbing a single minat from her coins. She then shut the cupboard, locking it carefully again. A minat would buy them bread and cheese for two days if the market was not gouging prices for the Festival. She could only hope.

Tenk had settled down again (glottins are, by nature, lazy creatures) and was sleeping by the time she had locked the latch on her door.

It was mid-morning now, and the sun was surprisingly hot for this time of year and this time of day. Glad she had left her shawl at home in her hurry, she thought to try the nearest purveyor of breads, meats, and cheeses. He was not her favorite (he sold day old breads as fresh) but he was close by and relatively inexpensive. It was only three blocks to his shop, and she was in fine spirits with the sun at her back. There was no warning at all as they jumped on her. She felt a thud in her head and then felt her body buckle. There was laughter, and she could see a blur of feet running away as she hit the ground.

When she next opened her eyes, there was a small crowd gathered around her, though not offering help.

"Is there any coin on her?" One was saying.

"No, they got that alright," was an answer from another.

"Ho…leave her be then. We don't want no trouble," said yet another, and the little crowd disappeared altogether.

Myka moaned and sat up slowly, her head pounding. Her dress was ripped, her knees bloody, and her coin gone. She touched her head only to find her hand covered in blood.

She stumbled to her feet and turned to limp back home. There would be no food for them today.

Opening the door to her little house, she found Tenk jumping up and down excitedly. "Food, Miss? Food?"

Myka shook her head, wincing at the pounding as she did, and collapsed in her chair.

Tenk leapt onto her lap and sniffed her head. "Hurt, Miss…hurt. Tenk help. Tenk help. Miss might die." It snuffled its nose on the wound, making her wince again.

As always, the little glottin's assessment added to her concern, but she had no energy to consider anything right now. She rallied just enough to address its hunger. "I'm sorry Tenk. There is no food. I think I just need to sleep, little one. Sleep."

Whether from the blow itself, or just sheer physical exhaustion, she drifted into a deep sleep before Tenk could even respond to the revelation that they would go hungry again tonight.

Her eyes fluttered open sometime during the night. The fire had long since extinguished itself, and the moon was shining brightly through her window. Her head was throbbing, and her knees stung badly. She was having trouble arranging her thoughts, and her memories of the day were jumbled in her head.

Something about Patrice…buying cloth…a little stone house in the Forbidden Quarter…no food…back to the market…knocked down…pain….and a book….a book she had set down somewhere. Her table, that's right. Before she left the house, she had set it down on table.

Confused still, she reached over to the table and felt about in the dark. There was nothing there.

Perhaps she had imagined it or set it down somewhere else? Had it been stolen, too? Her thoughts were too jumbled to make sense of it, and she really didn't care that much.

She rose from her chair stiffly and shuffled over to the fireplace. There were no embers left to even light a lamp. Tenk was sleeping next to the cold hearth, snoring loudly. For some reason, this irritated her, but she didn't want to awaken it. The hunk of cheese she had fed it yesterday was hardly enough for a full grown glottin. She would let it be, allowing the mercy of sleep to mask its hunger.

Too tired to start a fire with flint, she sighed, picked up some kindling from her wood pile, and walked to her door. Opening it, she held her kindling up to the oil lamp affixed to the outside of her dwelling until it lit. These lamps were most often kept oiled by the town officials in an ever increasingly futile attempt to stop thieves. She was lucky the lamp was lit tonight. Cupping her hand over the tiny stick so as not to extinguish the flame, she shuffled back inside and over to her bedside lamp, carefully lighting the wick. The little lamp threw a soft glow about the room. She then tossed the still burning kindling into her fireplace along with some moss and other twigs from her log pile until a flame leapt forth. She only had one log left and added it hesitantly—but the warm spring day had turned into a bitter cold night, and she knew she needed the warmth. Her injuries weren't life threatening, but she knew she wasn't altogether whole.

Thankfully, she had filled her urn from the well earlier in the week, so had plenty of water. She dipped a cup into the cool liquid and drank deeply. Plopping back into her chair, she looked around her home.

Where was that book? Not seeing it with a cursory glance about the room, she laid her head back in her chair.

"I'll look tomorrow. Tomorrow…"

And with that, she fell back into a deep sleep.

CHAPTER THREE:

The Mystery

When Myka at last awoke, she had been sleeping on and off for the better part of two days. Her body was heavy and stiff. She felt as though she had become one with her rocker, and her head still pounded when she moved. But move she must.

Tenk, bless its soul, has mercifully left her alone for the past few days sensing her need of rest. But today, its hunger had removed all restraint, and it was now bounding about the room, excitedly begging for food. Every now and again, it would stop, check on her and ask, "Miss better now?" Then back to the bounding.

There was no way around it this time. She had to get to the market and get something for their stomachs. She had cleaned her head wound best she could, but her knees were stiff and scabbed over. It took a handful of ligament oil to even bend them without excruciating pain. But bend them she did, and after another long drink of cool water (and one for Tenk) she had coin in hand and was out the door.

It was now only six days till the Festival, and although it was yet early morning, the market place was awash with patrons. Even so, she was able to secure a loaf of bread, a round of soft cheese, and remarkably, a piece of salted fish without incident. She wrapped these items in her shawl, safe from view, and walked back home, this time acutely aware of every movement around her.

Tenk was jubilant when she arrived and presented the bounty from the safety of her shawl. They both ate more than they should have, but

they both needed it. It was as they were relaxing after their meal—
she in her rocker, rubbing her bruised temple, and Tenk curled at her
feet, rubbing its full belly—that she remembered the book again.

Sighing deeply, she was too comfortable to get up and look
anywhere. Besides, she was certain she'd put it on the table.

"Tenk, did you see a thing here? On the table? When I got back
from market with my cloth? A thing? We call them books. Did you
see?"

Tenk ignored her and rubbed its belly again.

"Ah, well. You probably didn't even see it, little one." She patted
its head, and it curled up into a little ball and fell fast asleep, drowsy
as it was from the big meal.

But the thought of that book gnawed at her, and she got up at last,
careful not to awaken Tenk, and poked around the room. She checked
the hearth, the fireplace, her locked cupboard—even pulling each
piece of cloth out individually and shaking them to see if she had
absentmindedly shoved it in with them without remembering. Re-
locking the cupboard, she stood, hand on hips, surveying her little
dwelling. It was at that moment she saw a bit of something in the
kindling box. Walking over, she felt her heart leap. There it was! The
book had been stuffed in amongst the kindling and moss. She pulled
it out gently, blowing the off the moss, and noted that the cover had
been practically chewed to bits. In fact, there was only a little part of
it left. All the writing on the binding had been chewed, and only a bit
of the tree that so gracefully adorned the cover remained.

She whipped around. "Tenk!!"

It opened its eyes sleepily, only to see the book in her hand, whereupon its eyes flew open wide. Jumping up, it scurried under her chair.

"Tenk. Why did you do this? It was not yours!"

The little glottin was shaking. "Tenk…Tenk…was….hungry, Miss. No food in house, Miss."

She sighed. Of course. She had practically starved the poor thing the past few days. The leather cover probably tasted good to the little creature. She bit her lip in order to stop any more words of anger.

"It's mine, Tenk. Do you understand?" She said in measured tones. "Mine."

The glottin skulked away and hid under the chair, refusing her eye contact, its back towards her.

Her head began pounding again, and she had work to do. If she were to sell any of her designs before the Festival of Ciracus proper, she had to paint them today. She eyed the book in her hand. But perhaps a few minutes looking through this antique might be worth a bit of procrastination. Smiling, she sat down in her rocker and flipped through the waxy pages. Thankfully, Tenk had only managed to eat through the leather cover, and each page was intact, right down to the lovely artwork. She thumbed through the pages thinking that these designs might just be the inspirations for her cloths today.

It suddenly struck her that, though Tenk had only chewed the cover, that it had also lied to her and hidden the book in the woodpile, presumably to be burned accidentally with the wood to cover its crime.

Glancing over at her friend (its back still towards her) she decided to address this.

"Tenk. Why didn't you tell me you knew where the book was? Tenk…answer me."

Without turning around, its voice sounded pathetic and small as it answered, "Tenk hungry, Miss."

"Yes, I know. And I'm sorry I had no food for you, dear one. But, Tenk. You've never *lied* to me before."

Tenk shifted its weight but did not turn to face her. It also did not answer her.

Myka sighed deeply. *It must feel terribly guilty about chewing the cover, enough to lie about it.*

"Tenk," she said at last, unable to remain angry at her only friend. "I forgive you. Please, dear Tenk, you don't have to hide. It's alright."

The little glottin finally turned to face her, peeking out from under the chair.

"Miss no longer angry?"

She shook her head and smiled.

"No. I'm not angry. I'll just remember to bring food home next time we're hungry."

With that, Tenk fairly leapt out from under the chair and bounded into her lap, settling down and making its namesake sound. "*Tnk, tnk, tnk*" it chattered happily as it preened its fur.

She petted it absentmindedly, putting her attention back on the book in her hand. She flipped through it again, landing on the third page where the word Palem jumped out at her again. It could be none other than the 'Palem' Petrul and Marinda spoke of the other night. It was doubtful the word had two meanings. *So. The ancients were superstitious, too.* Continuing through the book, she couldn't see one other word or letter that was any more decipherable than it had been the other day in the Forbidden Quarter. Just that one word. "Palem". *Worthless,* she thought, flipping through the pages once again. *But the designs on each page* are *lovely. These I can use.*

She set the book gently down on her table and went to her cupboard. Taking out the new cloths she had purchased, along with her paints and brush, she brought them over and set them down in front of her bed, then went to the urn and fetched a cup of water. Easing herself down to the floor, she sat cross legged on her bedding and spread out the various cloth in front of her. Choosing the bright yellow one made of a thick cotton, she pushed the others aside, smoothing it out in front of her on the floor. Reaching up, she pulled the little book from the table down to her lap and thumbed through the pages again, stopping when her eyes fell upon a lovely design of a what looked to be a small deer—a doe—with a tiny silver crown upon its head. Such an interesting idea and so delicate. Perfect for this bright cloth.

Dipping her brush in the water, she mixed it with a jet black paint and began the outline of the deer on the coarse cloth.

I wonder if this was a taking beast? There were many before the age of Lord Bythim... he and his relentless determination to make trophies of them. Mostly only glottins are left now. It must *be a talking deer. Why else would it have a crown on its head if it were simply a wild beast?*

Her thoughts wandered as she painted, filling in the deer's outline with browns and tans, creams and blacks. She added in a forest background with trees in fall foliage, thinking it well complemented the yellow cloth.

Once finished, she sat back and contemplated the finished piece.

Perfect. Unique. Lovely.

She then set that cloth aside to dry properly and chose another — this one a soft blue made of a wondrous silken fabric. She opened the little book to the fifth page, where the illustration was that of a waterfall. The way in which the artist had drawn it was lovely: spilling down the page from the top right corner to the bottom left, the water drawn so realistically it looked as though it was actually sparkling as it tumbled down the page. This one would be hard to replicate, but it was so beautiful, and this cloth would so well represent the water.

She inhaled deeply as she dipped her brush into a white paint and began.

The water looks alive, as though it could tell stories of the places and wonders it had seen in its wanderings. It gives me a strong feeling...what is it? It is quite unfamiliar, an old emotion.....Joy! I actually feel joyful painting this!

Once finished, she lay down her brush and looked at her work. Although not as magical as the illustration in the book, this was indeed worthy of the silken cloth. It would sell well at market. And she was certain it would bring joy to whomever purchased it.

On it went for most of the day, choosing the most lovely and interesting designs, then attempting a reasonable facsimile of them on her cloths, until near dusk when Tenk snuffled up to her begging a meal.

"Has the day got away from me, dear Tenk?" she mused as she ruffled the fur on its head. "I do suppose it is well past time we eat."

She pushed herself up to her feet, moaning as she did. Her legs had gone quite numb from being seated in one position so long, and her knees needed more ligament. As she went to her cupboard, she noted that her headache was gone. She hadn't realized what a relief that was. That fact perked her up, and she happily pulled out the bread and cheese remaining from the morning's feast (the fish had been long gone since then) and cut a piece of each for Tenk—laying out a bowl of water for it. Then she sat down to her own meal at her rocker.

"And stay off those wet paintings, Tenk," she reminded it as she chewed on her cheese. From her chair, she took inventory of all the paintings she had done today—six in all. Each one an amazing and unusual piece of art. No one in town had seen drawings such as these for probably well over a century. Tomorrow could be her best day yet at Market!

Besides the doe and the waterfall, the other four paintings included a beautiful, long haired maiden, a lacy forest scene complete with a quiet pond, an odd creature with the wings of an eagle and the body of a horse, and a tree—similar to the one Tenk had almost chewed right off the cover.

After supper, she picked up her cloths, paints, and brushes, lay them out carefully in front of the hearth to dry completely, applied ligament to her knees (which had scabbed up nicely by now), and fell into bed.

Tenk was there by her side in a moment, shaking her. "Miss. Lock the door. Miss. *Miss! Danger!"*

She moaned, looking over at the door that was most certainly unlatched. What would she ever do without her little glottin? She patted her little friend, then forced herself up, shuffled to the door, and, surprised to find it latched already, checked it twice before returning to bed.

By the time the moon shone through the clouds, Myka was sound asleep, her dreams full of waterfalls and shining maidens. She didn't even hear the tussles and fights in the street that night.

Morning, and a brilliant spring sun was already shining brightly by the time Myka's eyes fluttered open. Although still stiff and sore from her treatment at the hands of the thieves, she felt as though she was truly on the other side of her injuries now. And she couldn't remember such a remarkably sound and comfortable sleep. After a quick breakfast of cheese and water, she rolled up her new paintings, now completely dry, tied each with a ribbon (she kept a roll in her cupboard amongst all her other treasures), kissed Tenk on the head, and left for her booth at the Market.

It was only five days now until the Festival of Ciracus, and this fact, combined with her new paintings, would almost certainly ensure a good day of sales. She patted her waistband. The book was tucked in there nicely. She just didn't trust Tenk with it, and the drawings were certain to be her inspiration for quite awhile to come. She needed the book.

She found her way through the crowds to her booth in the city wall and nodding to her neighbors, the butcher and the purveyor of trinkets, she unrolled her cloths, laid them on the table so each design could be seen, and waited.

She hadn't been there but a few minutes when they came. Women from every quarter of the town, most dragging their husbands from the butchers, and all with plenty of coin to spend. Her new designs were sold before the noon bell, and at a premium, as two or three women at a time had been haggling over each cloth. She had simply taken the highest bidder and sent the others on their way empty handed.

Having more money than she had ever made in her life, she wandered over to her friend, the butcher. She and Tenk had never been able to afford his choice meats or sausages. That was about to change.

She waded through the bustling crowd surrounding his booth, their hands pointing and gesturing, voices yelling out the goods they wanted.

"Maruk!"she called out, waving at him until his eyes met hers. "Maruk!"

He smiled widely and made way for her through the crowd. "Move it now, take it over there, sir," he directed them as he reached out and took Myka's hand to pull her through.

"A good day for you, then?" Maruk grinned.

"Never one like it," she said breathlessly. "And I'd like to buy some sausage....your finest."

He nodded. "I have just the thing for you, wait here."

Disappearing behind a curtain at the back of his booth, he reappeared with a small package wrapped in paper and tied with coarse string.

"Spring sausage," he grinned. "My best. Not enough to sell to a family, but for you…"

Myka dug in her pocket for her money. "Is five minac enough?"

"For you, four."

She smiled gratefully and handed him the coins.

"Do you mind if I sit here for a minute?" She said, eyeing a stool. "My feet are not holding up well, and it would be nice to sit with you for a moment."

"Please. Sit!" He turned and called to someone behind the curtain. "Banum! Get out here! The crowds won't wait!"

A young man, about sixteen years of age, appeared from behind the booth's curtain, tying on an apron as he emerged.

"And don't forget to give them a fair cut for their coin, son".

Banum nodded, turning to face the flurry of gesturing hands and demanding voices.

Maruk sat down on a stool next to Myka.

"So. Your best day yet, eh? To what do you owe this? The good crowds this year for Festival?"

She nodded. "That, yes, but mainly it is the designs I painted last night. I had some inspiration."

"Inspiration, eh? From where?"

She rummaged about in her waistband, presenting the little book proudly.

"This. It has the most unusual and delightful drawin…

She never finished her sentence. Maruk's eyes widened, and he fairly slapped the book out of her hand onto the ground.

"*Where* did you get that?" He hissed.

Confused, she bent over to pick up the book before it was trampled by the crowd.

"Put it away," Maruk looked positively desperate, his eyes darting about wildly into the crowd. "*Now, Myka…put it *away*!"

Tucking the book back into her waistband, she stared at her old friend in utter disbelief.

"What is *wrong*, old friend?"

Grabbing her hand, he pulled her off the stool and behind the curtain.

Pushing a few boxes of cut meats aside, he led her to sit on one. 'Myka…where did you get that?"

"The Forbidden Quarter, I found it under a floorboard in an old house."

Maruk inhaled slowly, composing himself.

"Do you know what this is," he whispered, "the book…do you know…?"

Still reeling with confusion, Myka shook her head.

"No, it is…it just has the most lovely drawings. They were my inspiration for my cloths today…"

He let out a small noise like a moan. "No, Myka, no …you didn't use pictures from the book for your designs? You didn't sell them, did you?"

She shifted her weight on the box. "Maruk. What is wrong?"

"No one can know you have that book, Myka. It is…it is *unsafe*. The words written there are forbidden. It would be best if you simply put it back where you found it, or better yet…burn it."

"But Maruk. It is not decipherable. No one could possible read it. And the pictures are so lovely."

"No, no, no!" he repeated the word emphatically. "You do not understand. Just *having* it is dangerous. If Lord Bythim's men…" And here he stopped. Banum had poked his head behind the curtain.

"Sorry to interrupt, father, but we need more cuts of lamb. The people are going to riot!"

Maruk blew out his breath softly, puffing his cheeks as he did. "Let me take care of this," he said, nodding at the crowd. "But Myka, if anyone knows you have that book, or if anyone recognizes any of the drawings you just sold….you could be a grave danger. Get rid of it, old friend. This is my solemn advice to you."

With that he grabbed a box filled with cuts of lamb and mutton and went back out to face the hungry hoards.

Myka felt an uneasy creeping fear in her veins. She could feel the book in her waistband—suddenly, it felt heavy and uncomfortable. She thought that perhaps tonight, she could simply burn it in her fire. But it made no sense. What harm could this book possibly hold? What was written in it that was so dangerous?

She made sure it was completely hidden in the folds of her garment before standing and pulling back the curtain of the booth. The crowd was still there, arguing over lamb chops and quail thighs: Maruk and Banum hard at work negotiating prices. She slipped out from the booth, keeping her head down, and started toward home.

A certain ruckus was starting a few yards in front of her, at first, she thought it a group of marauders, but as the crowd moved, she caught sight of three of Bythim's men. Hands on swords, one of them was waving a bright yellow cloth in the air and screaming into the crowd. He had a young woman by the hair and his dagger to her throat.

"Where is she?" He was screaming at her. "Where is this old woman who sold you this…this…*travesty*?"

Myka's blood ran colder than before. The yellow painting of the doe. She had just sold it to that young woman an hour before.

The young woman was pale and limp. She was terrified beyond her capacity to bear, and the guard finally realized he was getting nothing more from her. Letting her drop to the ground, he stood and addressed the growing crowd.

"Does anyone know where this came from? Speak now, and receive a reward from Lord Bythim's court."

It only took the reward to bring forth about a dozen hands, all pointing in the same direction, towards Myka's booth.

Shaking in terror, Myka drew her shawl up over her head, concealing her face, and walked past the growing mob toward her house. She had no idea why the book could be so dangerous or desired by Bythim. All she knew is that her sweet Tenk was home alone, and someone was certain to know where she lived. It was just a matter of moments.

She made it to her dwelling as fast as she could get there. Throwing open the door, she breathlessly whispered (although she wasn't sure why she was whispering), *"Tenk. We must fly. Tenk.... Tenk!"*

Her little glottin poked its long snout out from under her bedding where it had been nesting.

"Fly, Miss? Fly away?"

She was madly grabbing things out of her cupboard as she answered.

"Yes, Tenk. Get a blanket. Grab the bread and cheese. Hurry, Tenk, *hurry!*"

By the time the Guards rounded the corner to her little home, they found it quite empty but for an unlocked cupboard with some dry paints and brushes and a bit of ribbon. They kicked the bedding around in fury, and, finding nothing else, they set fire to the place using the very oil lamp the town provided to prevent crime, and left the place to burn.

Myka and Tenk were already up the hill on the outskirts of the Merchant Quarter as the smoke rose from her home. The only home she had known for the past forty years. She watched it burn, tears pouring down her cheeks, then dried her eyes and inhaled deeply. Wrapping Tenk soundly in the rough muslin blanket, she set it upon her hip, turned her back to Cenecal's Four Quarters, and headed South into the Foothills of the Ciracian Range in the Outer Territories.

CHAPTER FOUR:
The Foothills of the Ciracs

Myka was grateful for the midday sun. The early spring was indeed glorious, and, had circumstances been different, this could have been a lovely hike. The old logging road leading out of Cenecal was wide and well worn, and even though it cut directly through the lower part of the Ciracian Range, not too steep, either. She found the sun seemed brighter the further she descended, finally realizing that it was because the dense forested areas—replete with hundred foot trees that blocked much of the sun's rays—were gradually giving way to the more sparse, scrubby trees of the foothills. Whatever the reason, it felt like she could breathe easier, and after about four hours of walking she rested on a grassy knoll, setting Tenk down beside her.

It had remained quiet for the entirety of the journey thus far, and Myka assumed it had been sleeping. But when she unwrapped it from the blanket, Tenk's eyes were wild with terror, and it seemed rather frozen with fear.

She pet its head and tried to soothe it.

"It will be alright, dear Tenk. There, there, little friend, it will be alright," she cooed as she surveyed the path before them. It widened about a mile ahead of them into a proper roadway, winding down from the foothills to a flat, open plain. Pulling out a piece of bread, she broke it in two and handed Tenk a bite.

"Here, this will calm you…eat," she urged.

Tenk just shook its head, refusing the bread, eyes still wide with terror.

"Danger, Miss. Go back. Go back home."

Myka sighed. "We can't, Tenk. I don't know why the paintings from the book are forbidden, but they know I made them, and Bythim's men have no mercy for transgressors. Besides, our home is gone, Tenk. There is no home any longer."

She nibbled on her crust of bread, wishing for a drink of water. That would be their next priority—to find a stream. Scanning the plain for a river or lake, she finished her crust and thought to pull out the book, still tucked in her waistband. *What on earth makes this book so threatening?* Thumbing through, the illustrations seemed only to soothe her nerves. The waterfall page felt the most calming, probably because of her thirst. She stopped on that page and admired the artist's ability again. The water indeed looked *alive*. It was remarkable. Her own rendering of it on the silken blue cloth had done it no justice. Here, under this unknown ancient artist's hand, she swore she could see the water moving across and down the page, sparkling and bubbling in joy. As she was scanning the page, suddenly her eyes fixed on one of the words midway down in the text. She could not explain it, but suddenly the word was legible. She could *read* it. How had she not seen this before? Had the lovely, sparkling waterfall simply pulled her attention away? She blinked, squinted, and looked again. There it was, clear as day, the word '*alone*'.

Not knowing why, she was suddenly pierced with an overwhelming sadness…no, more like sorrow…no… *grief.* It was grief. It welled up inside of her until she could hold it in no longer, and she began to weep uncontrollably. Something about this particular word was piercing her heart. 'Alone'. She *was* alone. So alone. Out here, in this wilderness, yes, but even more so for the past five decades of her life. The word seemed to reveal what she had been hiding in her soul for a lifetime. The word she could now read seemed to be *reading her*. Sobbing, she held the book close to her heart and wept until she could weep no more. When at last her composure returned, it was dusk, and the sun was setting over the wide plain below her. Looking around, she couldn't find Tenk anywhere and began calling frantically.

Some rustling in a small bush next to her caught her attention, and she sighed in relief as she saw a leathery little snout poke out from amongst the budding leaves.

"Tenk. Get over here. You frightened me."

The little snout just shook back and forth.

"Tenk scared. Danger, Miss."

She walked over and picked it up from the bush.

"We are fine, Tenk. We have some bread and cheese. There is no one here but us. The evening is calm."

"No water, Miss. We will *die*."

Its words charged her nerves a bit. Water was something they did need to find. Brushing away her apprehension, she tucked Tenk into her shawl, wrapping it in the tattered muslin blanket, then tying it like a sling over her shoulder so she could keep her hands free.

"We shall find water, Tenk. Down *there*." She nodded at the wide flat plain below them. "There are trees down there, and that means there is water."

As she tucked the book carefully back into her waistband, and just as she bent over to brush the dust off her skirt, her eyes fell upon a stone. A small faceted rock, only about the size of a thumbnail, but literally sparkling in the setting rays of the sun. Brilliant blue, it was irresistible. Had she seen it in Drymac, she would have thought it a jewel fallen from a Courtier's crown or a merchant's trunk. She picked it up, rolled it in her fingers, and admired it as it sparkled in the sun's rays. Tossing it in her pocket, along with the coins she had taken from her cupboard, she smiled. *A good omen,* she thought. *For a journey I never dreamed I would have to take.*

Hiking Tenk up on her hip (with most of its weight resting in the shawl) she began the descent into the plains below, hoping the crisp spring afternoon would lead to a forgiving night.

***

It was about midnight when Myka's aching feet and back informed her she could walk no further. The moon was a waxing crescent and had offered just enough light to traverse the road without difficulty. The air had remained crisp, but a merciful bit of cloud cover had kept the frost from setting in and the temperature bearable. Even so, she was shivering against the cool air and fighting exhaustion by the time she found a grove of squat, scrubby trees within which to take rest.

Setting her aching bones down on the coarse grass, she gently unwrapped Tenk, shook off her shawl and wrapped it around her shivering shoulders. The glottin's thick coat of fur would hold it well enough against the elements, although it would miss the warm fire and hearth tonight, of that she was certain. Shivering under the crescent moon, she realized she would miss them too. She smoothed out the muslin blanket, lay down on the grass, and covered herself as best she could. Tenk curled up by her side and nestled in for the night.

She looked up and watched the clouds moving across the moon, which slipped in and out of sight capriciously, winking at her. How she longed for flint with which to make a fire. It would be her first acquisition upon finding a village. Water had to be the first priority, though. She swallowed hard, her throat was so very dry. Trying not to think about it, she gently touched the book at her side and remembered. *Alone.* So very alone.

She fell asleep easily and slept hard—not stirring until the first morning light.

Tenk was already up, chewing on some of the nascent buds on the trees in the grove. Had it been later in the season, there might have been berries on some of those trees, but although spring had been early and warm, it couldn't force fruit yet.

Every bone and muscle in Myka's body hurt. The hard, unforgiving earth, her parched, dry throat, and the cold of the night had all coalesced into one unhappy crescendo of misery. Grunting in discomfort, she sat up, envying Tenk his breakfast of tender green spring shoots. A thought occurred to her. Was there any dew on those leaves? Pushing herself up to standing, she arched her back, hearing the bones crack, and literally waddled over to the trees and shrubs. Her feet screamed in pain with the first steps, making her gasp audibly. She hadn't ever been on her feet for as long as she had been yesterday, let alone carrying a twenty pound glottin the entire time.

Her instinct proved right. On each little green leaf was a droplet of dew, glistening in the morning sun. Carefully, she held her hand under the leaves and shook the precious water into her palm, and drank. Repeating this process—leaf after leaf, bush after bush—she at last felt refreshed. Pulling out the cheese and what remained of the bread (now just a tiny hard hunk and crust), she found a rock on which to sit and ate them both. Tenk would do fine with the vegetation, and she had no idea how far it would be until they found a village. She needed the food.

Calling to her glottin, she decided today it could walk on its own four feet for a bit. Her back ached too badly, and her limbs were simply too stiff to carry it. With its usual apprehension, Tenk stuffed a few more leaves in its mouth, then bounded up along side her, but not before murmuring, "We must be careful, Miss."

Myka actually brushed off its warning this morning. There was no danger anywhere in sight, the day was proving to be clear and bright; the road was open and wide before them with the portend of good fortune.

"Nonsense, Tenk. There is no danger here today. Can't you try and enjoy the walk?"

"Where, Miss? Where we walk today?"

Sighing in frustration, she snapped back.

"I don't know! I don't…know. But we cannot go back, and so forward we will go. Besides, I've never been on a journey. I've not been out of Cenecal in all of my fifty nine years. Maybe it's just…time, Tenk. It's time."

They walked until about the noon hour when Myka first saw the village. Just a blur of something standing against the horizon initially, but as they approached the distinct outline of small, rounded huts could be easily seen. Each hut had a hole in the top, where smoke was wafting up from several, and the unmistakable smell of bread baking could be detected, making Myka drool. If she had been a religious woman, she would have prayed that the inhabitants be friendly, but instead, she simply hoped for the best, swept Tenk away into her shawl (perhaps they'd never seen a glottin before), and walked straightaway into the village.

As it was, she needn't have been a bit apprehensive about these people. As she entered the little circle of huts, a group of children greeted her, chattering happily and offering her their hands. They looked to be near cousins of the Drymacians—the same lovely brown skin, big brown eyes, and long black hair adorning both the boys and girls. Except for the colorful dress and notably better health, these could be the children on the streets of Cenecal. The children led her to the center of the village, where the women were outside pounding grain on flat stones, and the men were tanning hides. All turned to see her arrive, and all (save a few of the youngest of children) had broad smiles on their faces.

A tall man with a long grey beard and a handsome face browned and leathered by the sun stepped forward.

"A wanderer!" He bellowed, clapping his hands together. "It's been long since anyone has entered our village. Welcome, welcome!"

He grasped her hand with both of his, reminding her of Petrul and Marinda, and smiled sincerely. His brown eyes were surprisingly penetrating, and with them, he took inventory of her face.

"You do not have to be frightened," he concluded. "What is your name, friend?"

"Myka. I've come from Cenecal. I had to leave….rather, I'm on a journey." She said this last part quite sheepishly, the first part being the real truth.

"Well, whatever your reason that brings you to us, we welcome you. I am Neruk, and this is the village of Glanèt." He motioned her to walk with him as he turned and gestured at various points of interest along the way, narrating as they went. "This is the home of Nanut——she is the best seamstress in all of the foothills. That is our well, it has never run dry in over four centuries. Over there is our gathering place—where we meet, eat and hold ceremonies." On he went, Neruk narrating the salient parts of the village proudly, and Myka not really hearing anything past, "that is our well…." Her mouth had grown dry again, but she was trying to be patient before she asked anything of Neruk.

Suddenly stopping up short, he turned to Myka. "I have not asked you if you need anything after your long journey. Forgive me, we have so few visitors…I get carried away. Is there anything you require?"

Myka licked her lips. "I could use a good drink of water if you don't mind."

Neruk's face broke into a wide smile. "Of course, friend. I should have thought of it when we first saw you!"

Taking her arm in his and turning back to the well, he accidentally nudged and awakened Tenk, who had been sleeping inside her shawl. Its long sharp snout popped out, little brown eyes wide as saucers, staring at Neruk.

He visibly flinched. "Is that…is that a glottin you have in there?"

Myka laughed. "Yes, it's…it's my….yes…its name is Tenk. Perfectly kind little creature…of course, you know that if you know glottins."

Her calming words seemed to have no effect on him. He backed away from her, still obviously distressed, and called to a woman outside a hut near him. "Tanbè! Water for our guests!" Then, he simply bowed once at Myka, turned his back, and disappeared into a large hut near the well.

A tall, graceful woman wearing a long skirt embroidered with delightful, brightly colored flowers and animals went to the well, drew a bucket of water, filled a leather pouch, and brought it to Myka.

She whispered to her as she handed the bag over, "Neruk has strong…opinions on things. Don't worry about him." Her smile was warm and sincere, and Myka drank the water gratefully, handing it to Tenk, who squeezed the cool water into its mouth happily.

"I didn't mean to startle him," Myka explained. "I would have told him that Tenk was in my shawl had I thought of it."

Tanbè shook her head. "It's not that. Glottins have not been…welcome here in many decades."

Myka instinctively held Tenk a bit closer.

"May I ask why?"

Tanbè pursed her lips. "I think the question might be, rather, why do *you* have one?"

Head spinning with the question and feeling quite defensive, Myka took the water pouch from Tenk and had another long drink.

"It found me. It *saved* me. I invited it into my home when I was but an orphaned child and have been glad every day since." Tanbè stood quietly, listening. Myka rambled on defensively. "It has kept me from harm and danger for all my many years. You may not understand this, but the place I am from—Cenecal—is full of danger and death. And I was so alone. Without its help and friendship, I could never have survived."

Tanbè smiled but in a reserved manner that looked strained. Her eyes appeared to hold something more akin to pity than understanding.

"Come," she said at last, swooping her long black hair behind her, "let's find you two a place for the night. I assume you will be staying with us?"

For a moment, Myka considered moving on. That Tenk would not be welcome here made her both angry and anxious. But sensing no animosity from Tanbè and no real malice from Naruk, she decided to stay. She could learn what might lie on the path ahead, or perhaps this could become her new home. All was new to her, and nothing was known.

Squeezing Tenk tightly to her chest, she nodded and simply said, "We will stay the night. Thank you."

The afternoon and evening passed uneventfully. Tanbè found a family who offered to host Myka for the night. They had a midday meal already prepared and invited Myka to join them. She sat on the floor of their hut, on a large pillow (which seemed to be their custom), and had her first proper meal in days. A bowl of hot grains, with a bit of oil drizzled on top, a piece of flat, unleavened bread of some sort, and a plate with dark, leafy greens, served hot with a delightful spicy sauce. It was completely different than anything she'd ever had in Cenecal and, at the present moment, seemed the best meal she had ever eaten in her life. Tenk wouldn't eat the greens with the spices but gobbled down a small bowl of hot grains, the oil splattering all over its snooty little face.

The children of the family had laughed at Tenk, and it scowled at them, oil dripping off its nose.

After midday meal, everyone in the village took a nap (they called it a *paridiso*), and Myka took advantage of the time to rest against the wall of the hut on a pillow and pull out her book.

Tenk was taking advantage of the nap opportunity and was making its happy 'tnk, tnk, tnk' chatter in its sleep as it nestled next to Myka.

Stomach full and as comfortable as she'd ever remembered being, she flipped through the pages slowly, letting her eyes soak in the lovely artwork again. Stopping again at the waterfall, she smiled. Never would she tire of looking at it tumbling down the page like a shimmering ribbon. Her eyes fell to the word 'alone' still legible on the page, but it didn't seem to impact her as much today. She turned the page to find the drawing she had called 'The Courtier' when she had painted it the other day. Dressed like one—in flowing satins and silks with a lacy gold crown atop her head of long brown hair— this maiden was almost as lifelike as the waterfall and far more beautiful than any of the women in Bythim's court. She had had trouble painting her, not because the image was difficult to replicate, but because drawing the maiden had pierced her heart. Myka had never known any beauty in herself and had yearned for even one moment of it. As a young woman, she had thought that perhaps a suitor might come, perhaps someone might see her at the market, selling her lovely cloths and be attracted to her. But her face was uncomely, boy-like and toothy, and her figure in her youth had been like a dead tree, bone thin and with no shapely form. And, of course, no suitor had ever come calling. As she had painted the maiden, Myka cried. In that beautiful image, she could almost imagine herself mirrored as if the maiden's lovely form were her own. She felt she could almost appropriate the image's beauty for herself. But of course, this had caused her nothing but pain, for reality told her the truth, and no amount of staring at a lovely image of another could change hers.

She traced the image on the page with her fingertips, letting the disparity between it and hers fall heavy on the floor. Never would she know beauty or love or family. For her, that life and hope was over. Wiping a tear, she reached down and ran her fingers through Tenk's thick brown fur. *At least I have always had you, dear friend. Whatever would I have done without you?*

Letting her eyes fall back onto the page, she scanned for any new clues or words that she might have missed before. Nothing was legible. She slipped the book back into her waistband, tucking it in carefully, the piercing longing for beauty lingering long after she had closed the book.

The rest of the afternoon, after paridiso ended, was a flurry of activity in the village. All the women gathered, sharing foods and cloth and gossip, while the men worked together building a hut for a newly wed couple. Myka left Tenk in her host's home (it was happy on the pillows) and wandered freely amongst the people, asking questions, helping with a baby or two, watching the men pound straw, water, and earth into a thick paste, then slap it onto the curved wooden frames of the new hut.

It was evening meal that was the most engaging part of her stay. It was a communal affair, each bringing an item from their homes to the gathering space and setting them on long, wooden tables in the center thereof. Myka sat next to her host family and was joined by Tanbè, Neruk and his wife, who all seemed happy enough to be with Myka as long as Tenk wasn't by her side.

The foods, again, were foreign to Myka's usual Cenecalian fare, and she enjoyed every single dish. Strange spices, unfamiliar fruits and vegetables and grains, and not an ounce of meat or cheese to be found. Even so, the meal was filling and sated her hunger; the conversation sparkling and easy.

She learned that Neruk was indeed the leader of this group, having come from a long line of benevolent overseers called *manteem*s. Most of the villagers had never been into the Ciracs— and none into Drymac, let alone Cenecal. The tall, sharp mountains seemed to frighten them. Almost to a person, all of these souls had lived in the village of Glanèt their entire lives, outside of a handful that had come from the more southern regions of the Prathian Desert and been grafted into the community. Stories of past harsh winters and happy springtime plantings came from the villagers. The children told of brave men who protected the village from wild animals and giggled when whispering of weddings and beautiful brides. Myka took her turn to share stories of Cenecal: of Lord Bythim and his evil, of the Market Quarter, the crowds, the festivals, and the violence, of Tenk's good friendship, and of finding the book. All sat still, captivated, as they listened, and Neruk often shook his head, remarking, "so blessed are we, so blessed are we", peppering his sincere gratitude of their simple lives throughout her stories as she spoke. By the time she finally finished—telling them about the night she left Cenecal— almost everyone in the village had stopped eating and was staring, mouths agape, at her.

Neruk was first to speak.

"They burned your *home*? For painting on *cloth*?"

Myka nodded, swallowing her last bite of spiced vegetables.

"I think that, more than the paintings, it was because of the book."

Tanbè spoke quietly. "Do you think it good if we see it?"

Myka nodded, pulling the little book from her waistband and handing it to Tanbè. She felt no compunction to hide it from these villagers. None had even been to Cenecal, let alone had any experience with books or Bythim.

Tanbè flipped through the pages gently, running her fingers over the illustrations.

"They're lovely. I see why you wanted to paint these."

The book was passed gingerly through the village, each family admiring this page or that drawing, and eventually, it made its way back to Myka, who slipped it again into her waistband.

Neruk had examined it last and was shaking his head again.

"You have no idea why this book is forbidden? You know of no reason why they reacted in such a fearsome manner?"

Myka shrugged. "I only know my friend Maruk the butcher told me that it was forbidden. He seemed to understand how they would react. Had I known, I most certainly would not have painted the images and sold them openly at market!"

Neruk sucked in his cheeks as if in deep thought. "This word, '*Palem*' you said you could cipher…does it mean anything to you? Anything that would frighten people?"

Myka shrugged again. "It is a mythical place. A legend told centuries ago in Cenecal, from what I can tell. I met an elderly couple just a week ago who spoke much of it. But they were superstitious and much older than I. It seems the Elders in that part of town hold mightily to this tale. It gives them hope in their dying years, I imagine. As far as I know, this story of Palem is unknown by anyone outside of the Old Town Quarter."

Neruk fiddled with his food, pushing the remaining bits about his plate.

"But why would Bythim not want this myth to be known? What could be written on those pages that so inflamed him?"

Myka bit her lip. "I cannot possibly know that. Except that sometimes legends can incite people to action. I know of a time, for instance, some ten years ago, when the story of Banthus circulated in Cenecal. Rumors began that a giant—named Banthus—came to the outskirts of town that fall harvest. And if he were not appeased by gifts of food and drink, he would exact vengeance on those who refused. It caused a great upheaval and disruption in goods sold at Market, for many were hauling their foods and wines in great amounts to the edge of town as offerings to Banthus—leaving them there to rot in the fall sun. Bythim was unable to collect tax on those unsold goods that year. Legends can have power in that manner."

At this, Tanbè, who had been quiet for a while, spoke softly.

"Or perhaps this legend is true. Perhaps there *is* a place called Palem."

"You might as well just say there is a giant who eats meat and drinks wine under the Harvest Moon," retorted Myka with a sniff. "I listened to the two Elders talk of this place—of rivers with healing properties, of peace in every season, and of a king who rules justly. I have lived in Cenecal for fifty nine years. I have seen the way the rulers treat their people. I have seen death by violence and by plague. No. There is no such place. These are the tales told by the weak to engender hope in a hopeless world. These are the fantasies told by old fools and children."

She was surprised by her own vehemence and drew back a bit, softening her tone. She saw the pain in Neruk's eyes and realized suddenly that he, himself, was a *good* ruler—something she had never known, and therefore denied existed.

Stammering, she tried to take back her biting words. "I'm…I'm sorry, I'm certainly not speaking of you. You obviously treat your people well." Finding no good way out of the moment, she at last simply muttered, as though it excused her words,"I must be holding more apprehension for my journey than I know."

Neruk waved away her apology. "Not at all, not at all. No need of apologies. You've endured a life none of us have. It would be hard to imagine anything *other* than darkness and pain had we been you."

His words struck Myka's heart like arrows. She had never once considered her life 'darkness and pain', nor something to *endure*. She was one of the *lucky* ones. Had she not a roof over her head and a glottin at her feet? To hear her life characterized in such a way shocked her. Hurt her in a way to which she was unaccustomed. Revealed something.

Smiling weakly, Myka gave her thanks to all around her and excused herself from the table. Leaving the gathering space, she felt a sudden sorrow. The families were still seated, laughing and hugging and enjoying each other - free from the oversight of Bythim. Free from the nightly marauders and drunken revelry. *Free.*

She suddenly felt the ache in her feet and the pain in her back as she lumbered back into her host's warm hut. Tenk darted up to her, "Food, miss, Food?"

She sighed. She had completely forgotten to bring something back for it. Spotting the pot hanging over the fire in the center of the hut, she walked over, lifted the lid, and behold! Some of the grain from midday meal was still there. Scooping a bit out into her hand, she took it over and plopped it in front of Tenk. It sniffed at the cold grain a few times but ate greedily enough.

She lay on the pillows given her (enjoying the luxury) and rubbed her aching shoulders. *Endure? Is that what my life has been? Simply an attempt at a miserable existence?*

She pulled the book out from her skirt and opened it to the maiden again. Her flowing hair, the twinkling golden crown on her head and lovely smile. It was at that very moment, as she was thinking how welcoming that smile was, that she heard a voice. *"Wounded"*. Jerking about to see who had entered the hut, she saw no one. Shaking her head vigorously, she wondered if she'd had one too many glasses of wine at dinner when she heard it again. A gentle voice. A woman's voice. *"Wounded"*. It was coming *from the book*. Slamming it shut, she tossed it across the room, completely unnerved. Shaking, she sat up, attempting to run her fingers through her impossibly tangled hair, and tried to think. *The wine. Perhaps they poisoned me, and I'm not in my right mind. But why would they?* Checking herself, she found her thinking to be clear, and no dizziness or weakness. It was not a potion that had caused her to hear a voice. *This place, maybe it is enchanted. Perhaps the people had put a spell on her, a curse to make her mad. But they seemed so kind.* Heart pounding, she called Tenk to her side and held it close.

"*Danger*, Miss," it whispered in her ear. "There is d*anger here*. Something *wrong*, Miss."

"I know, sweet Tenk. I know. We will leave in the morning."

She left the little book where it had landed, afraid to pick it up, and began to wonder if Bythim's men weren't right. Perhaps the book was dangerous. Over and over again, she considered the word the book had spoken. *Wounded.* What on earth could that mean? She slept fitfully, terrified she might be slipping into insanity.

CHAPTER FIVE:
The Taking of Tenk

Myka awoke to find her host family already arisen and out the door. Shaking the sleep from her head, she sat up, rubbed her eyes and saw that someone had set the book neatly by her side. Somewhat nervous to even touch it after last night's events, in the light of this new day, she thought to simply erase yesterday's experience from her mind and move on quickly from Glanèt.

Calling out for Tenk, she got up on her feet, finding that the luxury of sleeping on soft cushions greatly eased her morning aches and pains. She tidied up her space, fashioning the pillows neatly against the wall, tucked the book into her waistband, rolled up her muslin blanket, and wrapped her shawl about her shoulders.

"Tenk. Let's go. Tenk."

No little snout popped out of either blanket or cushion. Neither did she see him in the center of the hut by the fire.

"Tenk! Where are you? It is time to go. Not a good time for hiding."

No response from her little glottin. Her heart began to squeeze a bit. Tenk had never once left her side except to forage for food. Perhaps that was the case this morning, as no doubt the leftover grain last night had been less than filling.

Ducking out of the small door into the bright spring sunshine, she was greeted by a few villagers who were already up and working on their tasks for the day.

She returned their greetings absentmindedly, instead focused on searching about the village square for Tenk. She checked every waste bin (although Glanèt was so tidy, there were few to be found) under every box and in the abundant and thick bushes on the outskirts of the square. It was nowhere to be found. Panic rising in her throat now, she suddenly thought to check the Gathering Area. No doubt a few scraps of food had fallen after evening meal and enticed a hungry glottin. Jogging as fast as her old, stiff legs would carry her, she came upon the space, only to find it swept clean and no Tenk in sight. Her panic was now visceral, she was finding it hard to focus, and everything was swirling about her. If it had gotten out on the road headed south…if it had become dinner for one of the wild beasts the children told tales of last night…if it had fallen into the well looking for a drink…the well! Whipping around, she headed to the center of the village, where three women were already drawing water for the day. Practically pushing them aside, she peered down into the well and called out for Tenk. Seeing nothing at the bottom but water and no glottin struggling in it, she slid down against the well and wept.

One of the women gently touched her shoulder.

"It's hard to put one out, friend."

Myka blinked though her tears.

"What?"

"Glottins. They are hard to let go," the woman clarified.

Myka sat bolt upright. "What do you *mean*? Do you…do you know where Tenk is?"

The woman looked at her companions, and they all turned and nodded sympathetically. "We *all* do," she said plainly.

Myka fairly leapt to her feet. "Where is it? Tell me now!"

The women all pointed to Neruk's hut simultaneously.

Myka felt her blood begin to boil. Neruk. Of course. He had made his stance on glottins quite clear upon her arrival. But to *take* it from her? Not even a marauder in Cenecal had done anything so cruel.

Lifting up her skirt, she hobbled on aching feet to his hut and pounded on the door, screaming his name, not caring about the curious eyes of the villagers upon her.

The little door opened, and Neruk stood before her, tall and calm with what could only be called a concerned look on his face.

"Where is it?" Myka demanded. "Where is Tenk?"

Neruk stepped outside, shutting the door behind him.

"Myka. Listen to me. I know this is hard for you, but it is for your own good."

"*What* is for my own good?" she shrieked, barely able to control her panic, "What have you done with Tenk?"

"Tanbè told me she informed you we do not allow glottins in the village. There is a reason for that, Myka."

"I don't care what Tanbè said or did not say," her voice was bellowing. "Give me Tenk now. Where is it?" She attempted to push past him to the door, but he blocked her.

"Myka. Listen to me. It is best that you let it go. It is not your friend."

Myka's face turned bright red, and she drew back in shock. "It…it…how would *you* know what is my friend and what is not. Were you there for the past fifty four years since Tenk came to me? Where was any help or companionship in my life but from it?" With this, she fairly threw the entirety of her weight at Neruk, pushing him aside as she practically fell through the door into the hut. There, in the corner, in a small cage, was her beloved Tenk. Crouched down and whimpering, it looked up and, seeing her, began to whistle—a sound only made when in great distress. Running to the cage, she let it out, holding it close, although she needn't have, for Tenk had already grabbed onto her with all four paws and buried its nose in her chest. Neruk was behind her, imploring.

"It is best for you to leave it. Glottins are not what you think, Myka. You have to believe me."

Myka stormed past Neruk, slamming the door behind her on her way out, and ran as fast as she could past the well, past the women pounding grain, and past the scrub bushes on the edge of the village. She didn't stop until the village was no longer visible behind her. It was then that she finally collapsed on a large rock by the side of the road and sobbed.

Tenk crawled down from her side and nibbled on a few leaves of dry grass. "Danger gone now, Miss." was all it said.

Wiping her tears, she nodded haplessly. "I'm sorry, Tenk. I would never have stopped there had I known."

Tenk crawled back into her lap, chewing on a twig. "Tenk Miss's friend. Tenk keep Miss safe."

She hugged it and breathed deeply, resetting her emotions. It was at that precise moment that she saw something red protruding out of the dirt at her feet. Reaching down and dusting it off, she found a bright red, smooth stone. About the size of a small robin's egg, and shining in the morning sun, it felt as irresistible as the blue rock she had found the other day. *Another good omen,* she thought, *a good reminder of our escape from Glanèt and a promise to keep Tenk safe.* As with the blue stone, she tossed the smooth red one in her pocket with her coins and wiped the road dust from her skirt. She turned to Tenk, "I'll not let you out of my sight again, friend."

Having not had any time for a morning meal and quite unable to eat prairie grass or twigs, Myka felt her stomach growl and noted her throat was far too dry to walk much farther today without finding water.

Making matters worse was the fact that she had been told by the villagers that the road south led straightaway into the Prathian Desert. If she were to find water, it would have to be here before she came upon the desert proper.

Being that Glanèt had a deep, fresh well, she assumed that there was a river or lake somewhere from which it was fed. Her job was to find that before nightfall. It was this thought that brought a sudden frustration. Nightfall meant cold air again. And she had not thought to borrow flint with which to make a fire. It had been her first priority, and she had forgotten completely.

"I'm afraid we are no more prepared for our journey than we were before," she bemoaned to Tenk. Sighing deeply and saddened greatly by her disappointment in the people from Glanèt, she rounded her shoulders and bade Tenk walk beside her as they turned south and headed toward the desert.

With a stroke of good fortune, they were on the road in the early morning before the sun was high or too hot. But Myka had heard from the villagers that the Prathian Desert was a brutal place even in the springtime, especially in the midday heat. There were no two ways about it—she must find water before long or turn back and take her chances at Glanèt again. Watching her little glottin leap and play along the road, her heart squeezed with affection. She would find water. As good and kind as the Glanètians were, they couldn't be trusted with Tenk.

The road had narrowed a bit as they left the foothills; scrub brush and squat trees being seen less and less frequently, whilst new plants such as cactus and tall spiny yucca made their appearance. The dirt was noticeably giving way to a more sandy topsoil, and the sun was also noticeably more intense. Turning a corner on the road, Myka almost cried at the sight before her as she came around the bend. For there, amongst some very tall, sturdy cacti, was a small pond adorned with reeds and lily pads, complete with several waterfowl lazily floating about, diving now and again for bugs or algae below the surface.

Breathing a sigh of relief, Myka made her way to the edge of the pond, and both she and Tenk drank deeply of the sweet water. Satisfied and their thirst quieted, they plopped down by the edge of the pond. It was at this point that Myka had to make a plan, for she had no canteen nor leather pouch with which to carry water. She lay out her belongings one by one. A shawl, a muslin blanket, her two new stones, a waist pack (in which was her money), a hair pin, and the book.

Looking at the entirety of her possessions laying there by the pond's shore, she began to laugh. And once started, she simply could not stop. After over half a century of life, and this was all she had to her name. This and a glottin that sometimes proved more trouble than it was worth. She laughed until tears came, and once that happened, the tears became those of sorrow quickly. Perhaps Neruk was right. Perhaps her life had been nothing but a burden to endure. Gathering her senses, she stuck the hairpin back in her tangled gray hair, wrapped the shawl around her shoulders, tucked the book into her waistband, and looked at her waist pack. It would have to do. Large enough to carry enough water for one, maybe two day's journey, it would suffice. Although made of supple leather, it would need to be waterproof. Scanning the pond, she suddenly had an idea. Wading in, she gathered up several waxy lily pads and lay them in the sun to dry. She then emptied her waist pack of her few coins. Taking the lily pads, she carefully lined the pack with them, overlapping them so as to ensure no holes. She then dipped the pack into the pond, filling it with water. Holding it up in the sun, she could see no appreciable leakage, and satisfied, she tied it off and set it gently on the ground.

Her coins and stones could be stuffed again into her skirt pocket.

"Tenk, I believe we can move on," She hollered at it, busy as it was chasing a duck (that was quacking angrily) around the pond.

Smiling at its antics, she tied off the blanket at her waist, ensuring no coins could slip out of her pocket and started back down the road.

"Come if you're coming, Tenk!" She hollered again, feeling a spring in her old step.

***

The Prathian Desert came upon them fast. In a matter of an hour, they had left the foothills and any semblance of vegetation, trading them for the hot sun and endless vistas of sand. Tenk wouldn't walk on the hot ground for long, constantly jumping up and riding in the sling-like shawl with Myka. The extra weight was killing Myka's back, and the heat of its body against hers was getting unbearable. It was now midday, and Myka was wondering if they had not made a terrible mistake. The villagers at Glanèt had told her that, once past the forbidding parched lands and salt flats of the desert, they would find the more welcoming Dunes of Martauk. There, the rise and fall of the dunes would often provide shade, and (even more hopeful) there would be the occasional oasis with fresh water, trees bearing fruits and the wandering nomad or two with whom one might trade or at least find company. Her mouth parched, she would take small sips from her pack and offer the same to Tenk, always being careful not to let it grab the bag and spill any water accidentally.

Had she been a younger woman, this would still be a rigorous and dangerous trek, but as it was, at her age and with her aching body, this was, in fact, deadly.

The fact that she had taken in no nourishment today was another confounding factor. Myka was used to being hungry, but how much could an old body take without sustenance?

By dusk, they had drunk all the water in the pack, and she could hardly put one foot in front of the other. Stumbling every other step, her lips were chapped, the sweat stinging her eyes and tasting like salty metal in her parched mouth. The unforgiving sun beat relentlessly on them, and her footfall made dents in the sand that the wind erased in mere seconds. It seemed that perhaps this would be her demise; the journey coming to an ignominious end under the screaming desert sun. She felt her legs buckle and slumped into the sand, the wind blowing the shawl off her head and shoulders, Tenk scrambling underneath her to find shade. Her main impulse was to sleep, so dizzy and disoriented was she. Chills kept running up and down her spine, and if she could just rest her eyes for a moment…

When she, at last, opened her eyes, she couldn't focus them. Someone was pouring water in her mouth and wiping her forehead with a mercifully cool cloth. Confused, she tried to sit up, only to hear a voice say, "Lay back down. Just rest."

Reaching out, she felt the comforting fur of Tenk and, relieved by that, let darkness swim over her again.

CHAPTER SIX:
The Dunes of Martauk

It was dark when at last, Myka awakened. She was lying on her back, staring up at a jet-black sky punctuated with the brightest stars she had ever seen. A palm tree waved in the gentle breeze above her, partially obscuring the moon, and a robed figure was hunched over a fire just a stone's throw from where she lay.

Hearing her stir, the figure turned around. "She awakens at last." It was a woman's voice—young, from the sound of it—and she rose from the fire and walked over to Myka's side. The figure was wrapped from head to toe in a loose-fitting, flowing robe and face covering. Myka could see only the woman's brown eyes but yet could sense in them a certain warmth, kindness and intensity. The young woman spoke.

"My name is Cla'neen. I found you just a few yards from here." She pulled down her hooded robe, revealing her long black hair and lovely smiling face. "You'd almost made it here to this oasis," she winked, "Only a few more yards and all this would've been yours." She gestured with her hands broadly as though showing off a fine dwelling or a temple square, then laughed merrily. "Well, so it's not so grand, but there *is* fresh water here and a few date trees. Here, let's see if we can sit you up." With that, she reached over, supported Myka's back, and helped her up, leaning her gently against a tree.

Returning to the fire, she stirred the flames to a brighter intensity. "What is your name, friend? How long have you been traveling through?"

Myka found it hard to speak; her throat dry and her cracked lips pulling and stinging as she formed words. "Just a day. I'm Myka. From Cenecal."

"Cenecal?" the young woman seemed surprised. "That is in the mountains, is it not?" That's more than a day's journey from here."

Myka swallowed hard, wanting to explain, but all she could say was, "Water, please."

Cla'neen nodded, "Oh, of course, of course. But try taking small sips rather than gulps. Your stomach will be glad of it." Handing Myka a small pouch of water, she plopped down, cross-legged, in front of her and nodded to the left. "You have a creature tagging along with you…did you know that?" Myka looked over, and there, curled into a tight little ball, was Tenk, snoring away under the moonlit sky. Smiling weakly, Myka nodded. "My glottin. Its name…Tenk." she rasped, taking another sip of cool water.

Cla'neen looked puzzled. "Glottin. Never heard of 'em. Not a desert animal, by the thickness of that fur." After the episode at Glanèt, Myka thought it best not to respond, so stayed silent, pretending to sip the water. Noting the obvious avoidance, Cla'neen changed the subject. "Soooo…. I'll wager you've not had anything to eat for a good while. How about we get some food into you?" Getting up, she walked over to a cluster of date trees and pulled some low-hanging fruit from the cluster at the center of the tree. Placing them into a palm frond she picked up off the ground, she took her fingers and mashed the sweet fruit into a kind of paste, bringing it over to Myka.

"Here. This will nourish you. But, as with the water, take tiny bites, or your stomach will reject it."

Myka dipped her fingers in the dates and licked off the sweet paste. Never had anything tasted so divine. Even the meal at Glanèt the other evening couldn't compare. Resisting the temptation to swallow the whole lot at once, she took sips of water in between to slow herself down.

"Thank you," she finally muttered softly, "Can you tell me where I am?"

Cla'neen tossed her long, black hair behind her and leaned against a tree, her brown eyes sparkling in the firelight. "These are the Dunes of Martauk, in my estimation, the most beautiful place on the planet. Oceans of white sand and wind blowing sparkling crystals into the air, oases of palms and blue waters, the rising sun clear and steady, and the setting of the same casting a glow over the sand like a golden blanket."

Myka smiled at the girl's certain poetic description. "Lovely it may be, but your sun is brutal as well."

Cla'neen nodded. "Agreed. But most don't attempt crossing the Prathian Desert with a pet, alone and with little water and no food. Especially at your age."

"Fair enough," Myka responded, dipping her fingers in the last of the date paste. Her head clearer now, she thought to check her belongings. It was at that moment she realized her muslin blanket, which had been tied around her waist, was gone and her pocket empty. Worse, the book was no longer in her waistband. Bolting upright, she glared at Cla'neen.

"And is it the people's custom here to take a stranger's belongings?"

Cla'neen let out an understanding sigh. "Ah, I'm sorry. I should have shown you your things right off. Here." She pulled the book out from her robes and handed it to Myka.

Taking it, Myka responded. "And my blanket and money and water pouch?"

Cla'neen looked confused, then reached under her robes once again. "Right, I almost forgot. Here you go," she said smiling, handing Myka the two small rocks. "They took your water pouch before I found you, I'm afraid, and your blanket must have blown away in the wind."

Myka stared at the two stones in her hand. Her red smooth, and blue faceted stones. She looked up, panic rising in her throat. "No… my coins. Did you not find them as well?"

Cla'neen shook her head, nodding towards the stones. "I thought those *were* your trading currency," she said slowly. "There was nothing else laying in the sand beside you when I found you but this book and those rocks."

"But who....." began Myka as Cla'neen interrupted her.

"Salastans, most likely. Desert thieves…nomads. Rather merciless, in fact. Had you not already been left for dead, they most surely would have made certain of it."

Myka leaned her head back against the tree in resignation. How would she ever make it any further without coin to trade along the way? How could she possibly secure food and water?

Cla'neen spoke softly. "I'm so sorry, friend. As it is, you are lucky to be alive. Nor did they kill your animal, which they are known to do. Meat is a luxury out here. You are indeed fortunate."

Myka felt as though she'd been punched in the stomach, not fortunate at all. Perhaps it would have been best had she simply perished in the desert. Why was she on this journey, anyway? Just to escape Bythim's men and whatever punishment they might mete out? To see new things? To simply leave for new horizons because she had no home any longer to which she could return? Whatever her reasons were, they were fast fading in this journey's harsh realities.

She tumbled the stones in her hand. Whatever her situation, it was not for lack of this girl's kindness. "Thank you, Cla'neen. For everything."

The desert girl stood up, brushing the sand off her robes and twisting her long black hair into a braid.

"Now. Let me hear your story, Miss Myka. And I shall bake us some bread."

Myka, feeling she had nothing to lose, and deciding she could trust this young woman as much as anyone, told her of her life in Cenecal and of the happenings in the past week. Having produced a small bag of flour and a pouch filled with oil from her knapsack, Cla'neen listened as she formed and then baked a lovely flat bread on a hot stone. They sat and shared it between themselves until Tenk awakened at the smell of it and bounded over, begging for food. Myka gave in and introduced it to Cla'neen, who seemed completely mesmerized and entertained by the hungry little glottin. Strengthened by both the rest and the simple (but hearty) sustenance, Myka spent the rest of the night inquiring about what lay beyond the Dunes and how long it might take to get through them. Cla'neen was extremely helpful. Born of a nomadic tribe that had inhabited the Prathian Desert for centuries, she not only knew all the surrounding territories but all the pitfalls of the Desert itself. She was living out here, alone for now, for her father had offered her hand in marriage to a man from a neighboring tribe in exchange for several head of goats, and Cla'neen was having none of it, finding both the man and the arrangement despicable. She had escaped out here to the Dunes of Martauk to avoid the union.

Before they bedded down for the night, Cla'neen continued to press Myka on her desire to go further, reminding her of the harsh challenges of the journey ahead.

"I can travel with you though the Dunes for a time, but it would be best if you found another companion after that. I can give you a water bag, flint for fire, and you can pack dates enough for a few days, but the sun and the wind are merciless, as you now know. Without understanding the desert… where the water and date trees hide, a person is quite realistically dead out here alone."

Myka finished the last of her flat bread, ripping it into small strips and chewing it slowly. "The truth of it is that Tenk and I have nowhere to go. I have no one that is concerned for me, and I have nothing much to live for any longer." Thinking of Neruk and his comment about 'enduring life', she added, "I'm not sure I ever have." She stared up at the stars for a long moment. "So, then. This journey is something I just have to take. I am not sure why."

Cla'neen nodded in understanding, then slapped her thighs with both hands. "Well, then. We shall begin at morning light. You'd best sleep well. You will need the rest. Does your pet need some bedding?"

Myka smiled. "No. It will make a bed in the sand by the fire. But thank you for your kindness."

They both settled in the warm sand, Myka using her shawl as a blanket and Cla'neen pulling her robe around her tightly. They let the cool desert night air and the gentle lapping of the water lull them to sleep; the unusually bright stars and moon twinkling above them in bright benediction.

***

When Myka awakened the next morning, it was already hot. Every bone and muscle in her body ached, and her head was pounding like a blacksmith on an anvil.

Cla'neen was already up, protected head to toe from the sun in her robe and hood. Handing Myka a water bag, they filled them both, then picked as many dates as they could carry. Cla'neen showed Myka how to cover her head and face in the manner of the nomads against the elements with her shawl, and, as an added kindness, she wrapped Tenk's feet in soft leather, tying them securely with strips of palm frond to protect it from the burning sand. Myka put her entire life in her pocket: her book and two stones, then grabbed her water pouch and looked toward the south. According to Cla'neen, somewhere out there, past the Dunes of Martauk, was the K'olach Range, marking the end of the desert and the potential promise of a new life if Myka so chose.

The two women walked steadily south all morning, careful to ration their water and eat a date every so often for energy. As promised, Cla'neen knew every path through the low dunes and every windbreak on the high. She taught Myka how to walk softly on the flatlands and how to tip her toes together when coming down a high

81

dune to keep from sliding uncontrollably. Tenk amazingly trotted along behind them and seemed none too worse for the wear by midday when the sun's heat became unbearable, and Cla'neen stopped suddenly, informing Myka that the midday hours were to be spent resting—a time known by the nomads as the *Ha'teem*. Pulling out a tarp and three sticks from her bag, she constructed a little makeshift lean-to on a small patch of flatland in between two dunes where the wind couldn't find them. Settling in, they drank water and ate dates while Myka rubbed her aching feet. She found it odd but noted that they didn't hurt as badly today as they had in the past few days—maybe even the past few years. Cla'neen quickly fell asleep, and Myka decided to lay down and rest by looking at her book.

Pulling it out, she flipped through until she came to the page with a drawing of a lovely forested glade. Just looking at it made her feel at once cooler and more relaxed. The scene was of an open, verdant meadow—replete with pine trees and berry bushes of some sort—and a lovely pond in the center. A tall water bird, perhaps a heron, was standing on one leg in the water. She closed her eyes and tried to imagine herself in the picture, smelling the green grass and hearing the birdsong. Breathing deeply and letting her muscles relax, she opened her eyes and scanned the page. Suddenly, there it was. Another word that she could read popped off the page at her. Blinking, she looked again. '*Lies*'. That was it. Standing alone amongst the other undecipherable words on the page, and right under the picture of the heron, was the single word, 'lies'. Had that word, like the others, been there before? Was she suddenly, for some inexplicable reason, able to read it only now? She didn't know. This book continued to be a complete mystery, but at least it hadn't *spoken* to her again as it had in Glanèt.

None the less, the word confused her. What on earth did it mean? That the book was full of lies? Or was it a warning of some sort? Suddenly feeling very unsettled, she sat up, giving up on rest. Flipping back in the book, she found the only other two words she had been able to read as well: *Palem* and *alone.*

Perhaps, then, the book had been written by a sensible person and not a superstitious sort. Maybe it was revealing that the myth of Palem was indeed a lie. Closing the book, she thought this a reasonable assumption. But if so, why did Bythim send his men to gather up the paintings she had made of its drawings? None of this made any sense. If the book was a refutation of a religious myth, then of what harm could it do to Bythim's rule?

She tucked the book back in her waist band and sat for the longest time just staring, mesmerized at the sand blowing and swirling outside the little lean-to. She didn't even realize she had fallen asleep until Cla'neen awakened her.

"Time to move on, friend." she said plainly. "The sun is beginning to set. It'll be cooler to walk now. Have some water and refresh yourself, and make sure to feed your pet."

Packing up the little tent and gathering their scant belongings, the two women resumed their journey south. The sky turned a bluish gray, and just as Cla'neen had foretold, the sun began to cast a golden glow over the dunes as evening approached.

Myka felt refreshed and somehow more hopeful than she had been in a few days. She also felt in good hands with Cla'neen; just being in her company lifted Myka's spirits. Tenk had all but stopped jumping into her arms, a fact for which she was grateful as well. The wind calmed down just as a few points of light tried to blink one by one through the slate blue twilight sky. And then, suddenly, the inky black of night quickly absorbed the blue, leaving only a soft hazy glow on the horizon. This lasted but a few minutes when, as if on cue, the entire sky burst to life with the most brilliant display of stars Myka had ever seen. They walked together under that sparkling sky as Cla'neen chatted on and on, telling Myka everything she knew about the desert.

With the cool night breeze on their faces, along with their happy banter, even traversing the highest dunes seemed a light burden. Myka listened as her new friend told her where the oases were (which Myka would never be able to remember), of the nomadic groups that were friendly and those who were not, (and how to identify them from a distance by their robes), of the friendly desert foxes who would chatter at night, but never harm you, and of the deadly sand tines that would. The tines burrowed into your skin—ultimately making way to your brain—causing first fever, then madness. Myka was most alarmed by that revelation and, upon being thus informed, felt every inch of her skin was itching. Cla'neen had laughed as she watched Myka scratching her arms for the better part of an hour before telling her that sand tines were only found in the deep desert, of which they had yet to encounter. She also reminded her never, ever to sleep directly on the sand, lest the tines find a way to one's skin.

After walking for about four hours, Myka was beginning to get tired. She was, after all, about three times the young woman's age. Noting her pace was slowing, Cla'neen suggested they stop for the remainder of the night until morning light, then travel until midday again.

Setting up the little lean-to, they both enjoyed a meal of dates and cool water, making sure Tenk had its fill as well. Cla'neen fell asleep quickly, having learned after years in the desert how to force rest upon her body when she knew it was needed. Myka, on the other hand, was bone-tired but not sleepy at all. As Tenk curled by her side, she thought to pull out the book and see if a new word could be deciphered this night.

She opened up to a page with a rendering of a man, no doubt a King, judging by the crown atop his head and the noble white steed upon which he sat. She had looked at this drawing only briefly before and had not thought to paint it. Her experience with Kings and Lords was not a pleasant one, after all. But tonight, under the blazing stars, he seemed a fitting subject to examine. The artwork, again, was exquisite—the man's face was kind, and he was smiling broadly. He wore shining silver armor, and his crown looked heavy and solid— encrusted with colored gemstones. She almost swore she could see them sparkling in the starlight. As with each of the illustrations in the book, this one, too, seemed alive with color and light. Scanning the page, no words of the ancient language were decipherable, but one word had a unique formation to it that drew her attention. It had round letters penned with flowing calligraphy that seemed to dance on the page. She felt certain that if she looked hard enough, she might be able to figure out what it meant. The characters seemed weighty, solid, and firm —like the image of the King himself. But stare as she might, there was no revelation to her mind. The word remained a beautiful, ornate, flowing thing, but she could not read it. Sighing, she closed the book on her chest, rested her eyes, and reached out to pet Tenk's head. His soft, contented 'tnk, tnk, tnk' wafted happily out on the desert breeze. That breeze, her physical exhaustion and Tenk's soft purring lulled her into an easy, sweet sleep, the kind where one's body relaxes entirely and one's mind slips off into a warm blackness. It was at the very precipice of this dropping off that she heard a voice.

A man's voice, warm and resonate, full of bass tones and treble splashes and infinite color. The voice said simply, *"Come"*. It was at once both inviting and irresistible. And somehow, at the mere sound of it, she fell into the deepest, most relaxed sleep she had ever known.

When she awakened, the first thing she noticed what that Cla'neen was already up and making a flatbread over a crackling fire. The smell was intoxicating, and Myka's stomach began to growl relentlessly. The next thing she noted was that she had slept with the book on her chest all night long, a thing that she had sworn not to do. It just seemed prudent to keep it hidden rather than in plain sight. Sitting up, she stretched and was amazed to note how good she felt. Her muscles didn't hurt, her back didn't ache, and her feet felt soft and supple. It was as though she had been somehow rejuvenated as she slept. As she mused upon these unusual changes in her body, she suddenly remembered the voice. That glorious sonorous voice she had heard as she was falling asleep last night. Was it a dream? She shook her head, picked up the book to stick it back in her waistband, but thought to look at the picture of that kind and handsome King once more. Opening to the page, her eyes fell once again to the word of which she had been so captivated last night, and her jaw fell open. For there, as clear as the sky above her head and as readable as her childhood primer was the word with the round, sturdy letters and flowing calligraphy:

'Come'.

The word from her dreams. The word spoken by the glorious Voice. Her heart nearly beating out of her chest, she shut the book, tucked it into her skirt, and went to break bread with Cla'neen. She felt at least ten years younger and inexplicably hopeful. Adding to her joy was the morning meal Cla'neen had prepared, a humble yet filling meal of warm flatbread, date paste, and cool water. They ate with abandon, chatting about the hike ahead as a happy Tenk gobbled up the leftovers. Afterwards, they wrapped Tenk's feet in the soft leathers for the journey and began to clean up their campsite. Myka was just pulling her shawl from the sand when a glint of light underneath her feet grabbed her attention. Reaching down, she pulled a shining crystal stone from the sand: a lovely clear thing rounded and smooth on one side chipped and faceted on the other, the sharp edges throwing sparkles in the sunlight. Smiling, she tossed it into her pocket with the others. These little stone talismans were becoming a welcome part of her journey; perhaps one day, she would do something artistic with them. That thought cheered her considerably, and she invited Tenk to her hip, wrapped her head and face against the elements, and followed Cla'neen up the next dune.

CHAPTER SEVEN:
The Deep Desert

The first thing Myka noticed about today's journey was the heat. It seemed the sun had redoubled its efforts to thwart their travel, and even the wind had stopped; its small help, cooling the sweat on their brow, was eliminated completely. It was just dead heat, heavy and oppressive. It was getting hard even to breathe, and at times Myka felt her lungs were being seared just by taking in air. By their second hour in the dunes, even Cla'neen had stopped her happy banter entirely, focused as she was on the work of simply walking in the burning sand. Making things worse, Tenk had given up walking on its own and was desperately clinging to Myka, its heat and weight making it almost unbearable for her to carry.

"Danger, Miss," it kept whispering in her ear. "Turn back now, Miss...*danger.*" Myka didn't need its warnings. She felt the danger in her body and all around her. It was at the third hour of their traveling that Cla'neen pulled up short, quickly set up their small lean-to, and declared it *Ha'teem.*

Huddled in the small comfort of shade, the two women drank what they felt they could. Their water pouches were nearing empty, as they had not filled them since their night at the oasis. Rationing was necessary. Neither of them felt hunger, but Cla'neen insisted they each eat a date. Myka found it hard to even swallow it, so dry was her throat. Tenk was her biggest concern. Having fur was detrimental in this heat, and the little glottin was so lethargic that Myka was having trouble getting it to even sip water. With glassy eyes, it kept looking up at her and whispering, '*danger*' over and over again.

Cla'neen spoke little, conserving her energy as best she could. "We are in the deep desert now...lay on your shawl and keep your clothing tight about your skin. We shall be out of it soon…an oasis is just over that next dune." With this, she closed her eyes. The thought of unlimited water and a date tree or two calmed Myka, and she found she was completely exhausted. She closed her eyes just to rest them for a moment.

It was about an hour later that Myka awoke, feeling uneasy and oddly uncomfortable. Her throat was dry, yes, but there was something else. She had not meant to fall asleep. Her blood turned to ice as she realized that she been sleeping directly on the sand. In her utter exhaustion, she had neglected wrapping herself tightly against the elements. Sitting up, she rubbed her legs and arms, only to notice that they were red and inflamed with tiny bumps that looked like a rash of some sort and burned like fire. Resisting the urge to scratch, she took a small sip of water and made Tenk do the same.

Cla'neen's eyes fluttered open, and she sat up as well, sipping water from her pouch. "Are you rested enough to travel one more dune? If we reach the water by nightfall, we will be fine, but we should try and get there as soon as possible. This heat isn't going anywhere soon."

Myka nodded as she absentmindedly scratched her elbow. Cla'neen, noting this, seemed to tense. "Myka, let me see your arm."

Myka pulled back her sleeve, revealing her reddened skin and rash. Cla'neen's face told Myka more than she wanted to know. Blanching, she bit her lip and spoke with an urgency Myka had not heard before.

"Get up. We must go. Now."

There was no need for her to say it. Myka already knew the cause of her itching. *Sand tines.*

Neither woman said a word after that but quickly packed up and headed up the next dune, hopeful of descending to the oasis before nightfall.

Myka had to carry Tenk again, and its weight was formidable against her exhaustion and the unbearable heat. To make matters worse, the rash on her skin was worsening and continued to burn relentlessly. Her inexplicable hope of the morning had soured into a resignation of hopelessness and fear by evening light as they descended the dune. Even the sight of the palm trees and the shimmer of water didn't help as they trudged towards the oasis, which was right where Cla'neen had said it would be.

Fairly collapsing on a grassy knoll next to the water and under the shade of a cluster of palms, Myka looked at her arms and legs. Blistered now, with several weeping wounds, she was fairly certain the fever that Cla'neen had told her accompanied the sand tines would happen soon. Tenk hobbled over to the water, drank deeply, and grabbed a date it found fallen beneath the tree, eating it greedily. It brought one back to Myka, looking at her imploring. Taking it, she chewed on the sweet date as Tenk curled by her side. "Go back, Miss. You will *die* here."

She felt the icy fear of its warning run through her body. Or was it the fever beginning? Cla'neen took Myka's pouch and filled it with cool water. "Here," she said, handing Myka the wet pouch, "Drink, please. You'll need it to fight the fever."

She left again, returning with a cloth and her oil pouch. Dabbing the cloth in oil, she gently soothed the rash and weeping wounds on Myka's arms and legs.

"Is there any hope for me?" Myka asked, wincing. It was a question she had avoided, for she assumed the worst.

Cla'neen dabbed at one more blister with the oil, then sat back on her haunches.

"There is always hope." She breathed deeply, then exhaled. "There have been rumors of a place, legends, if you will, of a lake…Lake V'esta…it is in a valley high in the K'olach Range. It is said that the waters from that lake heal the infection, kill the sand tines, and cure the mind and body of ill effect. I do not know the truth to these tales, but it is worth a try."

Myka swallowed hard. "How far?"

Shaking her head, Cla'neen sighed. "Far. Two days, at least. And you will be getting weaker each hour. Has the fever begun?" With this, she reached over and touched the back of her hand to Myka's forehead. "Not yet. You are fortunate. We may yet have time. This presents another problem, though. We will not have time to rest here for the night. To get you anywhere near Lake V'esta, we must leave immediately. Every minute brings you closer to fever and delirium. And the weakness will make it almost impossible for you to walk."

Myka felt all hope drain from her heart. Why hadn't she listened to Tenk? He warned her to turn back days ago. And now, she was to die in this desert, no doubt in a delirious state, weak and afraid, fever-ridden and burned by the sun. The terror of it all was too much. She began to weep.

Cla'neen reached over and gently stroked her shoulder.

"Others have made it to the Lake, Myka. So I have been told. We have water for our pouches, we have dates for our food. We can make it there, friend."

"But even so, there is no guarantee…"Myka said miserably.

Cla'neen shook her head. "No. But it is worthy of our best attempt, friend."

All Myka wanted to do was stay put in the shade of the palm trees and never move again. But something inside of her gave rise to a certain determination to keep going…to *live*. With this determination before her, she did what she needed to do to comfort herself: she began to sing. Just a humming of an old folk tune at first, but by the time she forced herself to her feet, she was given to full-throated song. Cla'neen stared at her, eyebrows raised, bemused. Smiling broadly, she helped Myka gather her things together and took Tenk upon her own hip to save Myka the trouble. "Perhaps the tines have already caused a certain degree of madness," she teased as Myka's voice rose loud and strong in the night air, the words of the old Drymacian folk tune lifting both their spirits.

Strong we shall be, when we be there again,

Dance in the streets, as wine and bread giv'n,

Hope flows as water, and love flows through air,

Endless our days, and our joy to be there.

The tune being simple enough, Cla'neen joined in after a few times hearing it and continued the song even as Myka's energy and then voice gave out. The heat was still dead and weighty, but mercifully the sun seemed to set early in the Deep Desert, and the night air was cool and invigorating. Myka didn't remember walking at all; by evening, the infection had taken her, and she had collapsed in the sand just as the night air made a meager attempt to cool her fevered skin. There was no way to get her out of the Prathian Desert now. The tenuous hope of Lake V'esta and its legendary healing waters had evaporated with the heat of the day. Cla'neen had made the lean-to, forced water into Myka's parched mouth, and cooled her with wet cloths until the sun rose.

She fed Myka's glottin and made sure it was hydrated, then fed herself and settled in next to the older woman to try and keep her cool with wet cloths throughout the night. The best she could do now was to help her through the madness that would inevitably come and then help her die. She fell asleep with one hand holding Myka's and the other holding a cool cloth to her head.

***

Myka's eyes flew open. She felt a sudden urgency to run. To flee. She bolted upright, knocking her head on the low canvas of the lean-to, and tried to get her bearings. Where was she? What was happening to her? Helplessly, she called out for Tenk, who was already at her side and terribly confused by her summoning. "Tenk here, Miss. Tenk here." It kept repeating in her ear, but it was as though she couldn't hear its voice at all.

"Tenk! Where am I? Tenk? Help me. *Tenk*!!!!"

Cla'neen was at her side in an instant, trying to calm her and get her to lay back down. It would have been futile had Myka not been so weakened by the fever.

"Shhhhh, lay back now, Myka. Tenk is here. I am here. You are safe here…all is well."

Cla'neen knew it was a lie but needed to calm the woman down.

Myka looked about wildly, shaking with both fright and fever. In her muddled mind, she was in her dwelling back in Cenecal, but nothing seemed right. Everything was distorted, and shadows danced across her mind. The terror she felt was palpable, and Tenk was nowhere to be found. She thought for a moment that she heard the marauders outside her door, and her heart nearly burst from fear. Clawing and swiping at invisible threats, Myka was completely given over to the devastation of the tine's poison.

93

Cla'neen, knowing the madness had begun, could do little but attempt to keep her still and from hurting herself. She had seen this before. It was a horrific thing to watch, but thankfully it would not last long. The victim of sand tine fever would usually perish within a day or two at most. The lingering was not long.

She continued to apply cool cloths to Myka's forehead and oil to her wounded arms and legs. There was not one inch of her now that was not covered in open sores and weeping wounds. Loosening Myka's garments, she removed the stones and book from her skirt, gently laying them on the sand. She would make sure her companion's treasures were buried with her in the sands when the time came.

At one point, Myka fell into a fitful sleep state, giving Cla'neen a chance to stand up and stretch outside the tent. It was early morning now, the sun just beginning its merciless stranglehold on the desert sands. The air was clear—little wind again today—and she stared out on her beloved desert with sadness. Usually, the blue sky and the white sands filled her heart with joy - but today, the weight of her new friend's suffering painted everything gray. How she wished she hadn't fallen asleep so quickly yesterday. That she had reminded Myka to wrap up against the sand tines. This was her fault, more than Myka's. She kicked at a pile of sand, sending the white crystals sparkling into the sunshine, and turned to go back and tend to Myka when she saw something on the horizon.

Squinting, she saw a form of some sort, about a hundred yards from her, behind a small dune. Large. Maybe a rock? No. It *moved*. Heart pounding, she picked up her robes and ran through the sand, stumbling as she did so until the figure came into view.

It was a horse. Tied pitifully to a stake in the middle of nowhere, a plain brown horse - thin but well-muscled with a long black mane. Seeing her approach, it whinnied and pawed the sand. Cla'neen approached it carefully, although when she reached it knew she was in no danger. She knew much of horses, having been raised with them in her father's stables. This horse was desperate for help and was showing no signs of aggression. She reached out, patted its velvet nose, and scratched under its mane. The horse nickered softly and buried its head in her chest. Its breathing was labored, and its nose was sunburnt. "Poor boy, you need water. Is your master about?" She gently untied the rope. "Come with me. Let's get you some help". She needn't have used the rope. The horse would have followed her anywhere, so desperate was it for food and water. Its master must have had succumbed to the desert—the sands taking him as they are known to do. But Cla'neen had no time to try and find his body amidst the blowing dunes. This horse needed help, and there was nothing she could do for its owner at this point. She led the horse to the lean-to, grabbed her water pouch, poured most of it into her hand, and offered it to the horse, who drank greedily. It wasn't going to be enough, Cla'neen knew this, but it was a start. She grabbed a few dates and fed those to the horse as well, all the while wishing for a bale of hay to offer the poor boy. Grabbing one of the extra pouches she had filled at the oasis last night, she offered the entire thing to the horse and noted its labored breathing seemed to ease a bit. She checked on Myka, finding her still in a fitful sleep, and suddenly realized she now had two problems, and they were conflicting. Myka couldn't be moved, and the horse had to be. She needed to get the animal to grazing grounds and more fresh water, and soon. Plopping down helplessly on the sand, she sighed. The horse had a better chance to live than Myka did, that was a fact. But to leave Myka alone here to die in the state she was in was unthinkable. Decision made, she rose up, took the halter and rope off the horse, slapped its hind end, and yelled, "Go on! Go! Find water! Get on, now!"

The horse startled, took a few trotting steps away from her, then turned around and came back, head hanging and eyes soft.

"Go, you stupid animal! I can't help you anymore!" She waved her arms about wildly, hoping to spook the poor boy, to no avail. The horse simply stood, mane hanging, feet not budging.

She threw up her hands. "Achhhhhh….you don't understand, do you? I have little water left and no hay for you, boy. I honestly cannot help you. Please. Go. Find water. Go!"

The horse had made up its mind, though. That was apparent. It stood fast, snorting softly. She patted it on the neck. "Well, then, if you're staying…."

She plopped down—using the horse's shade— to think about what to do next. Myka was beginning to dream again, apparent by her moaning and head jerking back and forth. It was horrible to watch. It was at that very moment that Cla'neen had an idea. It wasn't the best idea, but it offered her a way out of the impossible choice she had. If the horse was staying with them, then it could help get them all out of the desert. Myka couldn't ride, nor would it do to haul her up and lay her across the horse like a dead body (it was doubtful she could be lifted, and certain in her thrashing about that she would fall off), but she could make a sledge, a travois of sorts, and the horse could drag her. She had the lean-to poles (and thus the frame) and the canvas (and thus the sledge). Without missing a beat, she jumped to her feet and began disassembling the lean-to. "I'm sorry, Myka. You'll have to be in the sun for a bit," she whispered to her friend. Moving the horse over by Myka's side, the shade of the animal helped considerably, and Myka was in no shape to apprehend her situation, anyway.

Working quickly, she tied two pole ends together, wrapped the canvas in between them, and tied both sides well. She tore off a long chunk of her own robes in a thin strip and walked over to the horse. "Easy, boy…let's see how you do with this." Carefully and slowly, she wrapped the cloth around the horse's belly, tying it at the top. She then walked behind the horse and patted his round rump, up and down his back legs, and around his tail. Seeing no reaction, she affixed the poles to the belly strap, leaving the canvas sling laying on the ground. Putting the halter back on the horse, she led him a few feet to see if he would tolerate the unknown 'thing' dragging behind him. He seemed nonplussed and completely disinterested, moving forward with no spooking or startling. "Perhaps you once pulled a wagon or two in your day, after all, boy," she muttered, smiling.

Getting Myka on the canvas sling/sledge was harder than she had anticipated. Myka was writhing and lashing about, and Cla'neen didn't want to hurt her more than she had to. With great effort—the sweat dripping off her forehead—she dragged Myka over to the canvas and, with a final great heave, got her onto the sledge. Ripping yet another long piece of cloth from her robes, she used it to secure Myka to the makeshift sled by affixing the strip under her armpits, which would help her from sliding off.

After that, it was just a matter of picking up their meager possessions, their water pouches, and Tenk. She thought to toss Tenk atop the horse but then figured it not such a good idea. The horse had enough weight to pull, and besides, Tenk might frighten it. Instead, she hoisted Tenk onto her hip, grabbed the rope, and began to lead her little caravan out of the deep desert toward the K'olach Range and Lake V'esta.

It would take a miracle to get them there alive, but then hadn't finding the horse been a miracle?

CHAPTER EIGHT:

The K'olach Range

Myka was fighting demons. Huge things, with bat-like wings and jagged, razor-sharp teeth. They were swarming her, darting at her head and face. She was attempting to swat them away, but it did no good. For every one of which she managed to rid herself, two more would appear. Her screams fell silent, and her legs seemed frozen to the ground. She was trapped in a living nightmare with no way out. It was at the height of this certain and profound misery that the demons suddenly disappeared. A calm came over her, and she was able to catch her breath. She didn't see anyone, but there was a voice coming from somewhere not far away. She couldn't make out the words, but the voice was calm and solid. The words grew louder, as did a light that seemed to pulse with each syllable spoken. When at last she could hear the words, the light, too, had increased in intensity—becoming blinding, dazzling, overwhelming. She could hear the words clearly now.

"Come, Wounded One. You have never been alone."

She didn't remember anything else after that but fell into a deep and dreamless sleep.

Cla'neen had been walking alongside the makeshift travois for hours, keeping a watch over Myka as she thrashed and batted at invisible terrors. The good brown horse had plodded ever steadily toward the south, and it wasn't long before the sand had turned to soil and the dunes had leveled into flatlands. If she squinted, she could see vegetation on the horizon. They had made it out of the dunes and would be approaching the K'olach Range within the day. It was, indeed, a miracle.

Within an hour of their exiting the desert, Cla'neen found a small pond with sparse vegetation—bushes, reeds, and the such—but clean water and, most mercifully, a patch of grass for the horse and some scrub brush and early spring berries for Tenk.

The horse had perked up considerably as they approached and almost dove into the water the minute they reached it, drinking deeply before raising his dripping muzzle from the pond and starting in on the grass. Cla'neen untied the sledge from the horse and let Myka carefully down to the ground, noting she was either deep asleep or had passed out. It was impossible to tell which. It would be nightfall in an hour, and Cla'neen was hoping for a full night of sleep as well. She filled all the water pouches, then scrambled around the pond, grabbing what berries she could and scrounging for anything else to eat. As it was, the only thing she found were some frogs, and her hunger and need being what it was, she managed to catch three of the larger ones and, apologizing greatly (for she hated taking life, even that of a frog) dispatched them and prepared a fire.

Belly full of roasted frog legs and berries, sleep came upon her before she could really control it. The horse, too, after grazing and having several more drinks from the pond, cocked its hind leg and slept till morning light.

Cla'neen got her wish. She slept until mid-morning, awakening refreshed and hopeful. The first thing she did was check on Myka, who had mercifully and miraculously slept through the night as well. This doesn't happen with Tine Fever. No one avoids the terror and delusions with the sweet escape of sleep…ever. However, it wasn't her place to comprehend Myka's state or good fortune, but to simply appreciate and be grateful for it, then prepare for today's travels. Lake V'esta would be a days' journey from their current location if she remembered correctly. Brown Horse (she didn't want to name him— a nomadic superstition with 'found animals' that brought bad luck) was already grazing, and Tenk had busied itself with a berry bush by the pond. *"Good,"* she thought, *"everybody eat up."*

She took a water pouch over to Myka and, tipping it to her mouth, made sure a goodly amount got in. She gently stroked her throat to help her swallow and, in so doing, noted that her fever seemed to have broken. *Another miracle.* Her course of disease was not following the normal and expected pattern. Her wounds, however, continued to blister and bleed, so Cla'neen took the time to apply oil and soothe them again as best she could.

After this, she filled her food bag with berries, stuffing as much grass as she could into another bag for the horse, topped off the water pouches, and prepared to attach the travois.

The journey was an easy one. Brown Horse pulled Myka readily over the flat, dry ground, and the closer they got to the foothills of the K'olach Range, the more water and food-bearing plants became available. The spring was warm and productive on this side of the Prathian Desert, and Cla'neen was able to find sprouts, other early berries, and even some unripe but edible fruits. Additionally, there was plenty of grass for Brown Horse, and he seemed to gain energy as they traveled. Its labored breathing from the other day had all but disappeared, and he seemed to be thriving even though doing the work of pulling Myka behind him.

The going only became difficult as they entered the K'olach range proper, but Cla'neen knew of a pass through the steep and increasingly treacherous summit. The spring air cooled considerably as they climbed, and Brown Horse needed to stop more often not only for food and water but simply to rest. Cla'neen took off her outer robe and wrapped it around Myka at one point, so cold the air had become as they neared the summit. The season was early enough that there were still large glaciers all around them, and even with the strong spring sun, the snow, as well as the elevation, was causing the temperature to drop considerably. It was nearing nightfall by the time they crested the summit, Brown Horse snorting and covered with lather, Myka shivering on the travois, and Tenk clinging to Cla'neen's side for warmth. From there, she could see down into the Valley below, and even in the waning sunlight, she could see it was verdant and lush. And there, in the middle of that green, lush valley, was a lake. *Lake V'esta.* Shining like a blue diamond on the green velvet of surrounding grasslands, it was a most welcome sight.

They dropped down easily into the valley, and by nightfall, they had made it to the shores of the lake. Untying the travois from the horse, she let him go to graze in the deep grass and gently laid Myka on the ground. She then opened the food bag and let Tenk help itself to berries. Her next inclination was to go fill the water pouches and pour them over Myka, but all the legends said that a person must be immersed in the waters. It was the Lake itself, and not just its waters, that did the healing work.

Myka was still in some sort of deep sleep state, and there was nothing to be done but to drag her into the lake. Her dead weight was hard to handle, but Cla'neen managed to pull her over to the shore and, with Tenk's small help, dragged her into the icy waters.

Shivering, Cla'neen held Myka's head above water as she let her body float on the gentle waves.

Cla'neen watched carefully, awaiting the miracle. But there was no change in Myka's appearance. No awakening. No miraculous healing of her wounds. In fact, nothing at all happened. Cla'neen didn't know what to expect, but somehow she thought there would be a grand event of some sort. A flash of light, a swirl of water, a great sound from the heavens…*something*. But the moon simply shone cold and still upon the dark waters, the stars twinkled as they always did, and the lake lapped upon the shore quietly. After a few minutes, Cla'neen gave up, and pulled Myka's cold, wet body from the lake, wrapped her gently in her own robes again, and set about making a fire to warm her. It was the best she could do for her new friend, to keep her warm. Perhaps that was the best she could ever have done. It was, after all, only a legend that had brought them here. There had been no guarantees. Only stories. And a wild hope.

There was plenty of dry wood for kindling about the lake's edge, and a roaring fire was built within minutes. Tenk and Cla'neen huddled next to it, paws, hands, and feet extended towards the flames, drying fur and cloth. Myka was laying next to them, the firelight dancing across her face, peaceful in repose. Cla'neen looked around her at the high valley surrounding her. Even at night, this place was magical. Stars twinkling in the inky black sky, each point of light reflecting off the surface of the lake. The scents of high country heather and an undefined, yet palpable 'green-ness' of the place enchanted her. So different from her beloved desert. Very welcoming. She glanced over at Myka.

Cla'neen knew that her friend's death was imminent now. No one had lived more than two days after the fever began—and the shock of that cold water in the lake probably had done more harm than good. She took Tenk over and laid it down at Myka's side. "Stay with her. Keep her warm," she had instructed it. Tenk curled up in a ball next to its mistress, and Cla'neen noted it was whispering something in Myka's ear, but Cla'neen couldn't hear the words. She was just glad Myka's glottin could be at her side as she began this final journey from life.

Sometime during the night, Cla'neen had fallen asleep, the crackling fire and the warmth of it lulling her exhausted body into rest. Brown horse grazed contentedly nearby, and Tenk chattered on with its 'tnk, tnk, tnk' until it, too, fell fast asleep.

The morning sun filtered into the valley gently, slowly warming the lush greenery which was dripping with dew and condensation from the lake. Birds of every sort began their joyful song, awakening the valley with melody. Cla'neen's eyes fluttered open at the sound, and she smiled. For a desert girl, this was a lovely departure from the norm, and she had to admit the lush green and dewy grass all around her smelled sweet and refreshing. Sitting up and rubbing her eyes, she dared to glance over at Myka. Fully aware that her friend must have made her passage to the hereafter sometime during the night, she was almost afraid to look. The pallor of death was always hard—even shocking— to gaze upon. What she saw, however, was almost more shocking than the sight of death. The little sledge was laying where she had left it, but Myka wasn't there. Neither was Tenk. Brown horse was grazing on the other side of the lake, she could see him clearly, but Myka and Tenk were simply…gone. Mind racing, Cla'neen jumped to her feet and began running around the perimeter of the lake, looking for any sign of her friend. "Myka!" she called loudly, frantically, "Myka! Tenk!"

She had just rounded a little jetty, where some tall aspens grew in a lovely cluster, their tender spring leaves rustling lightly in the breeze when she saw them. Myka was seated by the edge of the lake on a large rock. Tenk was relentlessly trying to crawl on her lap, but Myka was shushing it away as she stared at something in her hands.

"Myka!" Cla'neen ran to her side and hugged her tightly before assailing her with a flurry of unformed questions. "What happened….how….when did…are you *well*?"

Myka looked up from the thing in her hands and smiled. She looked ten years younger, her face somehow softer—the harsh lines of age lessened by some unknown force.

"I don't know, Cla'neen. I only know I awoke this morning with the birds, and I *am* well. In fact, I'm better than well. I have never felt this good in my entire life! Did you put me in the lake?"

Cla'neen nodded excitedly. "I did, but nothing happened. Well, nothing that *I* saw."

Myka laughed. "Well, something happened. I am completely well…sound of both mind and body. And what on earth is all this energy I have? I feel as if I could run or jump or dance for days!" She tumbled the thing she had been looking at in her hands as she spoke, piquing Cla'neen's interest. "What's that, Myka?"

"Oh, just a stone. A most interesting one I found on here on the lakeshore this morning. I'm adding it to my collection. Here, look."

Handing it over, Cla'neen nodded in appreciation. It was one of the more unique rocks she had ever seen. Dark grey aggregate of some sort, but worn smooth by its years in the lake water. It was oval-shaped and impossibly shiny. The beauty of it, however, came from a blood-red streak running through its center, striking in its contrast to the grey stone surrounding it. It was as though nature had splashed the stone with color just for the glory of it.

"It's lovely," she mused, tossing the stone back to Myka, and plopping herself down beside her. She stared off into the distance, across the blue waters of Lake V'esta, and said nothing for the longest time.

"So the legend was true," Cla'neen said, at last, breaking the silence and putting words to the obvious.

"Apparently so," Myka responded, brushing Tenk off her lap again. "I feel completely whole. Better, even."

"Is it bothering you today…your pet?" Cla'neen beckoned the little glottin to her side and pet its head.

"I don't know what's wrong with me," Myka said bluntly. "I just know that when I awoke this morning, I found it hard to tolerate Tenk. Maybe I just want to be left alone." She shook her head. "No, there's more to it than that. Something about last night… I remember Tenk's voice. It was telling me there was no hope, that I was going to die. Yes, I *remember* that. It frightened me so badly. I just don't….I just don't want it around me today."

Cla'neen nodded. She remembered seeing Tenk whispering to its mistress last night as it curled up next to her. She didn't respond to Myka, but it made sense to her that the glottin would speak the truth to Myka in her final hour, even though its words might have been frightening. For, to anyone observing last night, Myka *was* going to die. She didn't fault Tenk for speaking what was most likely the truth.

Saying nothing, she simply nodded again and continued to pet Tenk, who was whimpering on her lap.

Myka stood up, brushing off her skirt as she added the grey and red stone to her collection and sighed.

"I almost wish my journey could end here, in this beautiful place."

Cla'neen smiled. "No reason it cannot, friend. There are fruit trees, clean water…you could build a shelter for the winter months and…"

"No," Myka interrupted her, "No. My journey is not yet done. I don't know how I know this, but I do. No, I am going on from here. I feel I need to head towards the west. I can't quite explain it, but every evening something deep inside tells me to head towards the setting sun." With this, she turned and faced her young friend, "Do you know what lays beyond the K'olachs?"

Cla'neen stood up, wrapping her robe around her head. "I do not." And then, after a long pause, she inhaled deeply and bit her lip before speaking again. "And Myka, my time with you has come to an end. I am of the desert, not this place, nor any that might come after. The summer solstice will happen soon, and there is no one in their right mind who would traverse the Deep Desert during the mercilessly hot days to come. I have to go back, Myka, and soon. Do you understand?"

Myka felt her heart sink. But she *did* understand. Cla'neen had been her guide through the Prathian and her help for healing. But this journey was Myka's alone. And she still had Tenk…

She looked over at it, still clinging to Cla'neen, looking pitiful and forlorn, confused at its mistresses' rejections this morning. Her heart softened, and she clapped her hands together, inviting it to her side. It fairly leapt into her arms and buried its snout in her chest.

"Tenk here, Miss. Tenk here."

Myka held her little glottin close but somehow felt as though a chasm of some sort had formed between them. It was inexplicable but palpable. Perhaps she should bring this up. Talk to Tenk about it. But then again, it had never steered her wrong in all the years they had been together. It had always been faithful to warn her of potential trouble, to keep her safe. She had never had anyone but Tenk to protect her from harm. And it had been good to her and truthful. Perhaps *too* truthful, like last night, but how could she fault the little creature for that? The thought of confronting her glottin quickly dissolved into forgiveness.

She hiked it up on her hip, deciding to sort out her feelings about this at a later time, and turned to Cla'neen, motioning with her head toward the brown horse grazing across the way.

"Do you want to tell me about *that*?" Myka smiled. "Or was the horse here at the Lake when we arrived?"

Cla'neen laughed. "Ah, Brown Horse. It was actually he, more than I, that saved your life. I'll tell you the story as we have our morning meal. The Lake wasn't our only miracle, that is certain."

The two women linked arms and walked over to the campsite together. Cla'neen fixed a breakfast of spring berries, chopped dates, and flatbread and began to tell Myka the story of her rescue from the Dunes: the finding of Brown Horse and the happenings of the previous night. They talked and laughed for hours, and it wasn't until midday when Cla'neen finally packed up her things, hugged Myka tightly, haltered up the horse, and said her final goodbyes. For she would be headed back to the desert, whereas Myka would be heading towards the unknown. Cla'neen started up the hillside out of the valley, Brown Horse walking behind her as she waved and yelled her goodbyes. "May we meet again! Travel well, Myka!" But then the oddest thing happened. Cla'neen hadn't gone but a few hundred yards before Brown Horse suddenly stopped up short and wouldn't budge another inch. Myka had just dropped Tenk down by the lakeside and was filling up her water pouches for the journey when she heard Cla'neen's 'goodbye's' turn into a more frustrated 'Come now, Brown boy…what IS the matter?' She was pulling on the rope with all her weight, but the horse simply wouldn't move. Like a stubborn donkey, it dug in its hooves and refused to go one step further with Cla'neen, yet kept looking back toward the lake and whinnying. Cla'neen, knowing horses, stopped trying to pull the beast and let the rope go limp. Once the pressure was off, Brown Horse simply turned around and started back toward the lake, dragging the rope behind him. Cla'neen stood, hands on hips, and laughed.

"I think you have inherited a traveling companion after all!" she yelled down at Myka. By now, the horse had taken up a trot, reaching the lake in a moment and grazing on the sweet green grass that grew around the shore.

"But I don't know anything about them…horses, I mean," Myka hollered back. "Please, come get it."

Cla'neen just shrugged.

"I haven't time to argue with him. He'll teach you all you need to know if he'll go with you, that is! Good travels, Myka! May we meet again one day!" And with that, she turned and began her ascent to the valley rim, leaving Myka alone but for a small glottin and a hungry horse.

CHAPTER NINE:

The Marshes of Nyster

Myka stood, staring into the horse's big brown eyes. It had stopped grazing and was standing, head down, eyes half closed in drowsy, full-bellied, sun-on-back comfort.

"Whatever am I to do with you?" she mused aloud as she patted the horse's neck.

Tenk was jumping up and down at her feet, full of protestations. "Warning, Miss…horse be dangerous…horse hurt Miss…*not safe*, Miss."

Myka felt the chasm between them grow wider with every warning it gave.

"Tenk. Stop it! This horse is no more dangerous than a tame dog. Look at him! He's calmer than you!"

Tenk whistled (an angry whistle) and slunk off to a rock near the lakeshore.

Myka finished filling her water pouches, gathered a bag full of berries, and checked on her four talismans. The stones were comforting to her somehow. Tangible. Solid. Beautiful. Each in its own way. She sat down on the large rock and pulled out the book to see if any new words would come to her today. Opening to a page she hadn't really looked at before, the picture drew her in immediately because it was of a horse. A stately white beast. Noble. It stood, head held high and proud on a cliffside: glossy white mane flying in the wind, one hoof raised as if almost pointing towards an unseen danger ahead. Its eyes were piercing and determined, and its nostrils flared. There was no fear in this noble beast. That was what she noticed about it most. Tracing it with her fingers gently, she looked over at Brown Horse, now sleeping in the sun, leg and hoof cocked, nose nearly touching the ground. She smiled. "Perhaps a distant ancestor of yours, Brown Horse….*very* distant." Scanning the page, she looked to see if the book would offer her a word today. After her ordeal with the sand tine fever…the demons she fought, the words she heard…perhaps the book would add to them today. Glancing at every letter, she waited to see if the magic of the book would reveal something. She found two words that interested her. The shapes of the letters were thick and solid, like her stones. She stared at them for the longest time, and then…suddenly, with no effort from herself, the letters began to move. They coalesced as she watched them re-formed into words she could read. And the two words were simply, '*No Fear*'.

She found the words caused her heart to leap and her breath to catch. "*No fear*". All she had *ever* known was fear. She couldn't imagine life without it, but somehow these words—be they an admonition or a promise—made her feel as though she could fly. As though a thousand tons of weight could be lifted from her heart. *Ten thousand tons.*

She closed the book, holding it close to her chest for a few moments before slipping it into her waistband, grabbing her food and water pouches, and turning to the horse.

"Well. I'm leaving now. If you're coming…come along. If not, then happy grazing here, and may your life be full."

Brown horse opened its eyes, lifted its head, and nudged her in the chest. Myka took its halter and rope off so that it could be free and patted its velvet nose.

"Off I go, then." She turned and called for her glottin, who was petulantly chattering away on a rock a few feet away. "Tenk. Let's go!"

Tenk gave one low whistle of disapproval, then bounded to her side, eyeballing the horse as it did so.

Myka began her journey toward the southwest, running her hands through her tangled hair once again to straighten it (as if that were possible), then wrapped her shawl about her shoulders and stepped out into the wet grass. She noted her step seemed lighter than when she began a week ago, and her body felt strong. The ache in her feet and back were almost unnoticeable, and she felt she was standing straighter than she had since she was a young woman of Cla'neen's age.

These feelings buoyed her, and even the steep incline she was attempting seemed a small thing. She had walked about five minutes when she glanced back and noticed that Brown Horse was following them, a few yards behind. She noted it, then simply continued on her journey. She knew nothing of horses, and if this one wished her company, then so be it.

The climb to the top of the valley wasn't as steep as it had been on the descent, although Myka knew nothing of that, delirious as she had been. The little band of travelers made it to the rim by mid-afternoon, and the spring sun at this altitude was warm and inviting. Taking off her shawl (having no need of it) she sat down next to a pine tree and had a long drink of her water, and ate a handful of berries. Brown

Horse, having kept pace with her, stopped to graze alongside, and Tenk begged for the one last date that it knew Myka still had in her pouch. Smiling, she tossed it to her greedy little friend and offered the horse some water cupped in her hand.

Its velvety lips tickled, and she was surprised to discover that the horse sucked up the water from her palm and didn't use its tongue like a dog or a cat, or even a glottin.

She patted the horse on the neck again, pursed her lips, and made a decision.

"I'm calling you Braydenthal. It means 'Desert One' in ancient Drymacian. That's where you were found. So, yes. Braydenthal. Bray for short. Does that suit you, boy?"

The horse made a soft nicker.

"Yes? Then Braydenthal it is."

She patted the horse again and then looked down onto the landscape below. It looked to be green. Very green. Bodies of water could be seen glistening every so often, but the water wasn't blue. Greenish-blue at best. It was impossible from this elevation to tell what exactly was down there, but at minimum, there would be water for them all and food for the horse.

Gathering up her things, she had a grand idea.

"Bray. How would it be if you carried our water and firewood?" Cla'neen had told her how the horse had pulled the makeshift travois all the way to Lake V'esta. These few bags would be nothing in comparison to that.

She tied both ends of her shawl, making large 'pockets' so that the water pouches and kindling could rest in either end, then gently lay the shawl over Bray's back. He neither flinched nor startled but simply continued grazing. She had brought the halter and rope with her—thinking they might come in handy at some point (horse or not) and now thought to put them on Bray so as not to lose him or their water bags. She managed to put on the halter (after a few missteps and a great deal of under-the-breath muttering), attached the rope, and gently gave the horse a tug. He immediately lifted his head and came along behind her. She felt it akin to leading a dog on a leash. A very large dog.

They began their descent to whatever land lay below in the heat of a springtime midday sun. Tenk was bounding alongside Myka, careful to stay clear of the horse's large hooves. She could hear it, every so often, muttering, "Horses be danger, Miss," but she ignored it. She realized she was beginning to tire of Tenk's incessant warnings. Especially on such a bright and sunny day as today. Besides, the words she had read, '*no fear,*' kept dancing before her eyes and lightened her heart.

It wasn't but an hour or two before they could see what the green water was. Before them, as far as the eye could see, were marshlands. As they reached the flat ground, the experience became challenging. Wet, black soil, dotted with marsh after marsh (some as large as small lakes), each encircled by cattails and covered with lily pads and green algae, were making it hard to walk. In fact, at times, it was impossible to tell where the ground ended, and the marsh began, so thick were the lily pads on the surface of the waters.

Bray's hooves sunk deep into the wet, mossy soil, sometimes covering his hooves entirely so that his feet made a sucking noise as he lifted them. Tenk practically threw himself at Myka, begging to be lifted to her hip, and she complied as she didn't want it sinking into a mud hole of some sort.

They slogged through the marshes slowly, Myka continually on the lookout for edible plants or berries. It was dusk when the heat of the day, colliding with the cool of the night amidst the marshes, caused a great fog to develop, billowing and swirling just above the ground, making it impossible to see where the land ended, and water began. It was at this point that Myka stopped and stood, ankle-deep in mud, looking for a place to spend the night. The fog was not only impossible to see through, but it was cold and wet, and within a few minutes, they were soaked to the bone. Starting a fire here at this muddy spot would be prohibitive, but the night had come on almost pitch black at this point, and she had no idea which way to go to find a bit of dry ground.

Tenk was at her ear again. "Miss. We freeze here."

Her blood suddenly felt icy cold from both the fog and the glottin's whisperings. This was not a place to camp. They'd all have heavy lungs by the morning, if not a good case of consumption.

It was at this very moment that she saw a bit of light flickering through the swirling fog. It was about fifty yards away from them, and she couldn't tell if it was coming from the water, or land, or a reflection from a star somewhere. But it was light, and they were in total darkness. And it was worth a shot.

Walking methodically, tapping the ground with her toes before stepping down to ensure the earth was solid beneath her, she pulled Bray's rope and headed toward the light.

The light became brighter even as the fog became denser and more enveloping. Myka squinted and waved the mist away to reveal the source. It was a lantern. Set atop a tree stump, which was covered in moss. Just a lantern. Burning brightly. No one around at all.

"Hello there?" Myka hollered into the mist. "Is anyone here? We are travelers from Lake V'esta. We don't know our way through these marshes….hello?"

There was no answer but the slight hissing of the lantern as its flame overcame the wet fog every now and again.

Feeling at once both calmed by the welcoming light of the lantern and apprehensive that no one accompanied it or why it was there, Myka pulled Tenk close to her side. It was helping to keep her warm, but continued to chatter on about danger and impending catastrophe if they stayed here any longer. It was probably right.

Seeing that there was no place to bed here for the night anyway (the ground too mossy and wet, the fog too bone-shiveringly cold), she decided to simply continue on through the marshes the best they could, one step at a time. She thought to take the lantern for light, but something told her not to.

For one, she didn't know who owned the lantern - whether they might be friend or foe. Secondly, she did not know why it had been placed there on that stump, to begin with. It was not hers to take. Sighing deeply and shivering from the cold, she pulled on Bray's rope, hugged Tenk a little tighter, and started away from the lantern. They had not taken but two steps when Bray suddenly reared up, snorting and pawing at the ground. It nearly jerked Myka off her feet and, having never been around horses, scared her badly. "Whoa, boy, easy, boy," she stammered, grabbing the rope from the mud where it had slipped from her hand.

Tenk was whistling now, almost shrieking, "Danger, Miss…it *comes…it is here!*"

If it hadn't been so dark or so foggy, Myka might have seen them before. But as it was, the figures that now surrounded them were very hard to see at all. They were dressed in what appeared to be dark robes, shredded and in rags, and their faces and skin were of a pale, sickly gray. It was almost impossible to see them against the night sky and mist. Myka swallowed hard. There was no way to escape, surrounded as they were, and nowhere to go, anyway.

"Greetings," she managed to say at last. "We are travelers, that is all. We mean you no harm."

The circle of black-robed creatures remained silent. Bray was still pawing at the ground, his nostrils flaring and his snorts coming every other second as he tried to calm himself. Tenk had become stiff with fright and completely silent, a fact for which Myka was actually grateful. She was frightened enough as it was.

"We just need to know the way out of these marshes, and we will leave you in peace. Could you be so kind as to point the way?"

For a moment, it looked as if the marsh creatures were just going to stand there and stare at them through what could only be described as yellowish slits in their gray faces, but then, just as silently as they had appeared, one moved from the circle, grabbed the lantern from the stump, and with a rather long, gray finger beckoned them to follow.

Myka suddenly felt every one of her fifty nine years. Her bones ached, her feet hurt, her back was screaming at her, and she had not felt this frightened since the last time the Marauders were outside her home in Cenecal.

Having few options (running in the opposite direction seemed futile), Myka nodded and pulled Bray along as they followed the Marsh dwellers along what seemed to be a solid path. At least her feet weren't ankle-deep in mud, and she could actually hear Bray's hooves clip-clopping on solid, rocky ground. Ahead, she could see the happy sight of a dwelling of some sort lit from within. The creatures walked before them, still silent, their black rags flowing in the foggy breeze. Upon reaching the dwelling, Myka could see it was more of a cave than a built structure: carved out of the side of a hill, with two windows of weathered glass and a door made of peat framed with wood. The door frame was covered in moss, and the windows with mildew and mold. Had they been in any other surroundings, the place would have held no appeal at all, but as it was, the warm light coming from within combined with the thought of being out of the icy fog made it seem almost welcoming.

One of the creatures took Bray's rope and tied him to a pole outside the dwelling, then motioned for Myka to enter through the mossy door.

The interior of the place was austere. Not a chair nor table in sight. Just a cold, stone floor, a roaring fire (for which Myka was grateful), and what appeared to be bedding against one wall, which looked as though it was made with either straw or fallen leaves or peat moss covered in the same black cloth the dwellers wore.

Myka edged herself close to the fire, sighing audibly as the warmth of it began to warm her bones, gratitude oozing from her every pore.

"Thank you for this kindness," she said quietly, breaking the awkward and off-putting silence. Tenk had jumped from her side and was curled up as close to the fire as it could get, still shaking from cold. The creatures paid no mind of the glottin but kept their yellow gaze solely upon Myka.

Still not one word they spoke.

Myka's eyes darted nervously about the room. The creatures that surrounded her seemed decidedly human, yet curiously not. Long, gray, or black hair hung from their heads, and all wore some type of crown on their foreheads. Not the festive, sparkling type of human royalty, but dull and dark, resembling intricate webs of some sort. Their gray skin was almost translucent, and Myka could see their veins, blue underneath the gray. Their faces were neither lovely nor ugly but nondescript—blank, utterly expressionless, and void of identifiable features.

It was minutes (although it seemed like hours) before one finally spoke.

"She is an ugly thing," said the one that had beckoned them to follow it earlier. Nods all around the room from the others. The creature's voice was raspy, like someone with a bad case of the croup or who had smoked a pipe for too many years.

"She is old, too," said another.

"It is unfortunate," said a third.

"Unfortunate, indeed," uttered a fourth.

Myka shifted her weight uncomfortably but didn't respond. What was there to say?

The creatures continued to make stark and rude comments about Myka. They seemed to be enjoying this activity, and it continued for quite a while. Observations were shared between them, such as,

"Her body has no form. She looks like a lump of coal." "Look at her skin. It is pink and wrinkled like a pig's." "Her hair is matted like a common dog's." "Her voice is grating. How can anyone listen to her?"

It was one of the most unsettling experiences Myka had ever had. As she listened to them, her initial thought was to argue and defend herself from this verbal onslaught, but as the taunts continued, she realized that nothing they said was untrue. She *was* old. She *was* uncomely. Her gray hair *was* knotted and tangled. None of this was new information to Myka, nor was it fallacy. These creatures, if nothing else, seemed to be truth-tellers. The question remained, what were they going to do with her?

After quite a while of this conversation, the creatures fell silent once again, staring at Myka as she stood by the fire, rather deflated after such a verbal upbraiding.

At last, she mustered a bit of courage and spoke.

"May I ask who you are…and where I am?"

The leader spoke first again.

" We are the Keepers of the Marshes. And these are the Marshes of Nyster. Have you no knowledge of geography?"

This last comment elicited the first laughter of the night, or at least what Myka assumed was laughter. It sounded more like the squawking of geese than anything else.

"I'm…I'm from Drymac…far to the north and east of here. And I do apologize for not knowing of your home. I mean no offense by my ignorance."

"Ignorance, yes..yes…ignorant as well, she is," laughed the chorus.

"Ignorant as she is ugly," remarked a rather loud one, her voice supplanting the others. "As are you, Thaylem," responded a younger-looking creature, directing its words to the loud one. This brought an even greater raucous round of squawking and guffawing from the crowd, with each of them punctuating either the word 'ugly' or 'ignorant' over and over again as they began to point at one another rather than Myka.

At this point, Myka had all but given up civility with these obnoxious creatures and, risking any harm they might bestow upon her, stamped her foot loudly on the floor to get their attention while simultaneously yelling, "Enough! Show us the way out of your marshes, and we shall gladly leave you be."

They stopped, as in unison, with this admonition, startled as they were with her outcry.

The leader, first always, spoke again. "The way out. Yes, you should go out. And away. Take your ugly pig skin and saggy flesh and leave our sacred marshes. Yes. This is best."

Myka breathed a sigh of relief. Rude, they might be, and miserable, but apparently not dangerous.

The leader pulled her hood up over her long gray hair, grabbed the lantern, and pushed past the others.

"Follow me, then," she grunted, "We are glad to be rid of you. It is hard to gaze upon your ugliness."

"As it is to gaze upon yours, Quaynsike," retorted a large creature to the leader, eliciting another round of squawking and talon pointing.

Myka beckoned Tenk to her side (reluctant as it was to leave the warmth of the fire) and walked out the door with the lead Keeper. She grabbed Bray's lead rope and, with no more discussion, followed the creature down the stony path for about three miles until suddenly, the Keeper swept away in the darkness, as quietly and silently as upon their first encounter, and was gone.

Most interestingly, she left behind the lantern. Myka thought it perhaps a final gesture of something akin to kindness, or more likely, it was motivated by the creature's desire to rid the Marshland of the visitors. Either way, Myka was grateful for the light and the fact that no bodily harm had come upon them at the hands of the Keepers. They headed toward the moon for the next few miles until they were completely out of the fog and onto dry ground. Myka found a grove of trees, with an inviting under-bed of needles and leaves left behind from last winter, and they made camp for the night. Lighting a fire was an easy task with both available kindling and the lantern's flame, and she and Tenk were sound asleep within minutes. Bray had found some grass to graze upon and made himself busy with feeding until morning light.

When she at last awakened, Myka breathed deeply of the fresh morning air to find it tinged with the scent of pine and the uniquely greenish smell that only spring brings along. They were in a forest, or at least the beginning of one. The soil was soft and brown, with sweet grass growing abundantly. The evergreens were pine and cedar, with a variety of newly budding deciduous trees growing in and amongst the evergreens. They were currently in the middle of a meadow under a small grove of poplars. The meadow was sprinkled here and there with spring blossoms: snow lilies, hyacinth, and an abundance of early blooming colorful primrose. Braydenthall was grazing on the sweet spring grass, and Tenk was bounding about eating petals from the primroses, a fact that surprised Myka greatly.

"So, you eat flowers now, do you?" she called to her glottin, shaking her head. Tenk just chattered happily and bounded to another flower.

She opened her food pouch, finding a few berries from Lake V'esta still in it, as well as one date that somehow she had missed. She picked it up, thinking of Cla'neen and missing her mightily. Such good fortune to have had her help…she would have perished in the desert sands had it not been for her care and loyal friendship, temporary though it was.

She sat up, leaned against one of the trees that made up the canopy under which she had slept and chewed on the sweet date. As she did so, something caught her eye by an exposed root of the tree. It was black and perfectly round. It looked like a gaming piece used for gambling in the pubs of Cenecal. She picked it up and rolled it about in her fingers. It was satisfyingly smooth and surprisingly heavy. But this was no gaming piece. It was simply a rock, smoothed by the elements, and of a strange glossy black stone. Smiling, she tossed it up and down a few times in the air happily. *Another talisman for me.* She plopped it in with her others and gathered up her things. The forest was, in fact, far more welcoming than the marshes had been, and she was excited for the journey today. A thought had occurred to her last night as she trudged through the wet mud of Nyster. Would Bray let her *ride* him? And, of more importance, would she be *able* to? She had never ridden a horse before, although she had seen Lord Bythim's men and their courtiers often ride on their fancy steeds through the streets of Cenecal. Of course, they had bejeweled saddles and fancy headpieces on their horses. She glanced over at Braydenthall and bit her lip. There was a sad halter and a tattered rope. But his back looked strong and smooth. It could be worse. Yes. She would try riding him today. How hard could it be?

Calling to Tenk, she breathed deeply of the forested air, wrapped her shawl about her shoulders, and walked over to the grazing horse.

CHAPTER TEN:

The Forest of Landor

As it happened, riding a horse was harder than she had anticipated. Of course, not having a saddle put her at a great disadvantage: no stirrups to help balance, no leather to help her hold her seat. But Braydenthall had been willing enough, she had seen to that before mounting. She had laid herself across his back several times to see if he would buck or start, but he had seemed calm enough. She had then led him to a large fallen log which she climbed upon and mounted from there, as her old body couldn't make the jump from the ground to the horse's back without stirrups. Once seated, she made a clicking noise with her tongue (she had heard people do this) and Bray had happily complied by moving forward. Unhappily, Myka had no idea how to balance on a moving horse and had slipped, unceremoniously, right off his back before they had gone even ten steps. Embarrassed (and later to find herself bruised) she attempted this over and over again until she figured out how to hang onto Bray's mane whilst simultaneously tightening her stomach muscles and thighs—using them to hang on. This seemed to work well, and as long as Bray stayed at a walk, Myka was staying on, and learning more with each mile. She learned that if she relaxed her body like a sack of flour, that her balance increased and she stayed seated well. She learned the hard way that if she pressed her heels into his belly, Bray would increase speed. The first time she did this, Bray broke into a trot, sending Myka flying off once again. It seemed that whenever the horse went up, Myka was going down, and vice versa. It took about five times of attempting a trot before her body figured out how to rise and fall *with* the horse. Tenk was happy as a glottin could be, as Myka had invited it to sit in front of her on Bray and, to her surprise, finding that it had no trouble at all staying on, no matter what speed or gait the horse employed.

Once she figured out the riding part, the journey was a lovely one, indeed. The forest was verdant and full of streams and meadows. Wherever she looked, there were birds and wildlife of every sort, and the sun shining through the canopy of trees was warm and nurturing. The forest was alive in the truest sense of the word. Every few hours, Myka would find a stream and slip off Bray, leaving him to graze while she and Tenk would forage for some food as well. Myka knew how to find edible mushrooms and, having long loved them, was finding that they, combined with some sweet berries she had brought along were all the refreshment she needed. The streams in this part of the land were cold and bubbling, and she made certain the water pouches were always full before mounting again and resuming the journey.

It was at about midday, on the second day of this rather idyllic and uneventful part of their travels, that Myka saw some smoke rising above the treetops. Curious and in need of some new staple food, she turned Bray toward the smoke and hoped for the best.

The little village they entered was welcoming from the start. From the very entrance of it (a beautiful wooden arched gate carved with forest scenes and adorned with pine greens), the well-kept dirt road wound through a collection of meticulously maintained wooden homes: small, but ornate of woodwork on both doors and windowsills. Master craftsman had obviously worked on these homes, and it showed. Robins flittered here and there amongst the houses, and a stray cat or dog could be seen on the doorsteps, bathing in the spring sun.

Bray clip-clopped through the main road of the place, and Myka wondered where all the inhabitants might be. For not one soul had they yet to see anywhere in the village. The further they walked into the place, the stranger it became. Upon arriving at the town well, Myka dismounted, pulled up a bucket of water from which Bray and Tenk could drink (hoping that no one would mind.) She twirled around, looking from house to house. Other than the birds, an occasional squirrel and a dog or two, there was no movement or sign of life in this quaint village at all.

"Perhaps it is a hunting day...or a festival of some sort," she thought to herself, *"and the entire village has gone out for it."* This seemed a stretch, as what of the elderly or infirm, and the mothers with infants who couldn't participate in something like a hunt? Having no real inkling of where the townspeople might be gathered, she walked up and down the streets looking for a marketplace or mercantile of some sort from which to gather information and perhaps some food.

But house after house, building after building was empty, and with no sign that anyone had been here for quite some time. In fact, the closer she looked, the more clues pointed to this very fact. The dogs and cats, upon close inspection, were thin: ribs showing. The hay bins for livestock were full but covered with a layer of fallen pine needles that obviously hadn't been disturbed in a few weeks. The porches of the quaint wooden houses were covered with yellow spring pollen, not swept clean nor disturbed by footprints. The smoke she had seen from a distance turned out to be a deep fire pit near the center of town, one that looked as though it had been burning for days, and was still smoking from embers long since deprived of fuel.

Myka felt her chest squeeze with anxiety. Something was very wrong in this village. Something had *happened.*

She walked back to the well, bid Tenk onto her hip, grabbed Bray's rope and turned back toward the town gate. Whatever had happened here would remain a mystery, one Myka was not sure she wanted solved.

They left by the same pine festooned gate they had entered, walking slowly, cautiously. Once back into the woods, Myka finally exhaled and found a log suitable to use as a mounting bench. Bray nickered softly as she turned his head back toward the deep forest and pressed her heels into his side, asking a trot.

Tenk, not to withhold his warnings, managed yet another before they had gone but a mile.

"Me smell death, Miss. Death. Turn around, Miss."

Myka rolled her eyes. She had, during this journey, grown weary of her glottin's constant fear mongering, and her trust in its prognostications had grown less certain as well. "We are fine, Tenk. There is nothing to smell but the pine and the warm soil."

Tenk squeezed up tighter to her on the horse.

"Death, Miss....*death.*"

As was always the case, her heart squeezed a bit as its warnings continued, and her blood turned cold with Tenk's words. Weary as she was with its warnings, she knew to listen to them. She slowed Bray down to a walk, and that was exactly the moment she saw an encampment before her, about a hundred yards away, in a clearing by a stream.

A group of rag-tag tents and make-shift huts were scattered about beside the little brook, and a fire was billowing black, solemn-looking smoke from the center of the camp. It wasn't but a moment later when a man jumped out at them from behind a tree, making Myka shriek and Bray spook and jump sideways, almost dumping her on the forest floor.

"Be gone!" The man rasped. "Unclean, *unclean*…be gone from here!"

He was dressed in tattered rags, his face and arms covered with red marks that looked like burns, his expression that of angst and pain.

He looked at Myka and spoke again, this time in a calmer voice, "Please. *Please* leave this place. I implore you. Now."

Myka looked up at the camp and began to intuit what had happened to the village. Person after person began to emerge from the ragged tents, each with the same red markings and haggard, sullen appearance. Men, women, children and infants crying in their mother's arms. They were all afflicted with something…of that she was certain. She stopped Bray and inquired of the man, who was still begging them to leave.

"What has happened here?" she asked quietly.

"A plague, Ma'am. It came suddenly. Those of us afflicted came here, away from our village, to keep the others safe. It did no good. One by one, all of us, every single person, has been struck down by it. Most have died. There are only a few of us left. Now, please….you must leave. Even this short time with me may be the death of you. I implore you."

Tenk whispered again to Myka. "Death, Miss, death."

Myka found herself backing Bray away from the man and holding her breath instinctively. The sounds of muffled coughing and moaning came from the tents, how had she not heard them before?

She looked at the man, her eyes filling with tears.

"Is there anything I can do? Is there…"

The man waved her off, interrupting her.

"No. No one has found a cure. No one has found a way. Now, please…you must go. Already, it may be too late."

Myka felt her pulse begin to race. She had feared the plague since her childhood. Her parents had been taken by it, and she remembered well their suffering. Stifling the impulse to sob, she instead turned Bray, kicked him hard in the ribs, and let him fly. She had not ridden a gallop before and almost fell off at the very start, but grabbed a handful of Bray's mane, leaned forward and held on for dear life. Tenk was hanging on to her and whistling. Myka didn't let the horse stop until Bray began to slow on his own, winded and lathered in sweat. Myka was panting hard as well, both from the work of staying on the horse and her own fear.

She dismounted and squatted down by a tree, wrapped her arms around herself and sobbed. Had she breathed in the plague? Was her lot to be that of her parents, suffering and languishing in pain with no tinctures, no help? Was this forest to be her place of death—alone and forsaken of human touch and care?

The thoughts were coming fast and hard now, and she couldn't stop the panic in her old body. She leaned against the tree and cried until she could cry no more. She must have fallen asleep, for the next thing she knew, she was sitting up and trying to remember what had happened. The icy terror struck her with the first remembrance. *Plague*. She might be infected. Madly, she pulled back her sleeves and looked. No red markings had yet appeared. She took in a deep breath. Her lungs were clear. But for how long? Trying to calm herself, she took several more deep breaths. She was alright. For the moment, at least. She thought of the words the book had bid her read but two days before. *"No fear"*. The words fell short and weak today. What else was there *but* fear? Biting her lip, she stood up, brushed off the dust and pine needles from her skirt, and walked over to Bray, who was grazing on sweet grass, blissfully unaware of the danger his human was in. She threw her arms around his strong neck and felt the steadiness of the horse. He lifted his head and nickered softly. Somehow, this animal helped her in a way no other could. Scratching him under his mane, she looked around to assess their situation. It was almost evening, and there were gray clouds gathering on the horizon. Here, there was a good canopy above them in case of rain and plenty of kindling on the ground with which to make a fire; it would do well to camp here for the night. If she had contracted the plague, it would do no good to worry about it now. There was nothing she could do. Absolutely nothing. *'No fear'*, she said under her breath as she tried desperately to hold the words in her heart. She gathered up a good amount of kindling and small fallen logs and used her flint and stone to make a fire. She found she wasn't hungry (fright always pushed away her appetite) but forced herself to drink some water and made Tenk do the same. Every few minutes, she would lift her sleeves or her skirt and check her arms and legs for the telltale red markings that might seal her fate. Once darkness fell, and it was too hard to see, she simply quit looking, realizing it did nothing whatsoever to control or change whatever might occur anyway. She would sleep. And if she awoke with the markings, then she would know. Curling up by the truck of a large oak tree, she was asleep before she knew it, drained as she was by her anxious heart.

The wind picked up, lightning began to flash over the forest, and within minutes the rain began to pour down, thankfully filtered by the thick canopy of trees so that only a few drops actually ever hit the sleeping travelers. Tenk continued to chatter throughout the night, whispering in Myka's ear all the warnings of things it knew to be possibilities. She slept uneasily, waking every now and again to ponder the terrors of which Tenk so readily conveyed, and with every awakening, she felt the corresponding ice of panic in her veins. She finally gave up and arose, sometime before dawn, while it was still dark. Throwing another few logs on the dwindling fire, she sat down next to it to think. Unable to resist the urge, she pulled up her sleeves and checked for any skin changes in the light of the fire and, seeing none, exhaled gratefully. In an attempt to get her mind off the plague, she turned her thoughts to the journey thus far. She took time to ponder each event—meeting Marinda and Petrul, finding the book, escaping Cenecal, the good people of Glanét, the sweet friendship of Cla'neen, the nightmare of the Sand Tine fever, the refreshing healing waters of Lake V'esta, the keepers of the Marshes. In reflection, she found herself most focused on and drawn to the words from the book that had been given to her. *Given her.*

She was suddenly aware that she had never once considered from where the book's revelations had come. Until this very moment, she had considered it either fate, or destiny, magic or even perhaps her own imagination. But the words seemed to have been revealed to her in a very specific manner, methodically, intentionally. The book revealed things she wouldn't have, *couldn't* have designed, or known. She pulled it out of her waistband, opened the cover almost ceremoniously, and found the words—the words *given* her. She read them each slowly. Carefully, slowly. One by one, she gently turned the pages, ingesting each word by the flickering firelight.

Palem. Alone. Lies. Come. No fear. As she looked upon these potent words, she remembered each of her emotions when first reading them. The disbelief of *Palem*. The grief and sorrow of *Alone,* and how that word had seemed to read her, not she the word. The confusion of *Lies (what was the truth about all this, anyway?)* the warm invitation of *Come,* and the solid, desperate longing for *No Fear*.

She then considered the word the book had spoken to her aloud: *Wounded*. It resonated with her. It revealed something about her she had been too proud to see. She wasn't strong nor resilient as she had always imagined herself. No. She was *wounded*. Through and through. Wounded from the loss of her parents. Wounded by her own self-reliance. Wounded from being alone. How could the book know things about her that she, herself, did not? It made her wonder. What if there is a power beyond fate? A presence beyond destiny? A *person* beyond her own imaginings?

The thought was so new, invigorating, and somehow wildly hopeful. It was also highly superstitious and sounded much like the dinner musings of Petrul and Marinda's, a conversation which, at the time, she had found off-putting, pedestrian, and wholly insulting. That dinner seemed like a lifetime ago. She smiled sadly. She would not have left so quickly had she met that sweet elderly couple today.

Glancing up from the book, she noticed that the sky was beginning to lighten in the east, and the clouds from the night had dispersed, promising a clear sunny sky for the day. That, combined with the new idea of a…a…*something* outside of her, something that knew her better than she knew herself, was giving her a momentary respite from her fear about the plague. In fact, it enabled her to get up from the fire, splash some icy water from a nearby brook on her face, and attempt, once again, to run her fingers through her tangled mess of hair and wind it into a manageable braid. She would meet the day with as much courage as she could muster. Tenk, awakened by her movements, bounded over to her. "Check again, Miss. See if sick. Check, miss, look." His words completely punctured her courageous intentions, and the fear came whistling through her body and mind once again. She quickly pulled up one sleeve and then the other and sighed in relief. No red rash or welts. Perhaps she *had* escaped this terror. "Thank you, Tenk. You always know how to help me. You are right…you are always right, dear friend. You always know what I should do." She hugged her little glottin close and opened the food pouch. The sun was just beginning to shine, and she was beginning to feel the hunger of having not eaten last night. There were a handful of berries left, but that was all. Time for mushroom foraging, indeed. Besides, it would occupy her mind.

Checking on Bray (who was happily grazing near the brook), she motioned Tenk to her hip and started out towards a meadow she could see not far away between the trees. Upon arriving, Tenk popped off her hip and began to find and nibble on the myriad of primroses that grew there, leaving Myka's hands free to dig in the soft, brown earth. The base of the trees was the best foraging place, and there were many trees dotting the perimeter of the meadow. Mushrooms were plentiful here, and last night's rain had seemed to conjure them up from the earth like magic. She gathered up a great many of them and was about to head back to her camp when she saw a gigantic cedar at the edge of the meadow. Even from here, she could see huge, meaty mushrooms near the base of its ancient trunk, and the look of them made her mouth water in anticipation. She headed toward it, only to find its massive branches formed a kind of natural cove, a living sanctuary of sorts with the sunlight streaming through the branches like stained glass. Here, on the floor of this little sanctuary—as well as on the bark of the giant tree—were an abundance of mushrooms peeking up from the still decomposing leaves that had gathered there last fall and winter, generously giving birth to the tender mushrooms today.

As she knelt down and began to gather up what she could carry, she heard a rustling in the leaves behind her. Heart pounding, she whipped around—certain to see another plague victim or a wild animal ready to attack. Instead, she saw a woman. The shock of it knocked her backwards, and she fell into the soft, damp leaves, sprawled out like a toddler playing in the dirt. Her first thought was that she had just run into an infected villager, and she instinctively held her breath. But the woman had no tell-tale red marks on her skin, and she was smiling, the warmest, most inviting smile Myka had ever seen. Immediately she was put at ease and exhaled. The woman was younger than she (or so it seemed, it was hard to tell), but one thing was obvious, she was the most beautiful thing Myka had ever seen. Dressed in a gentle flowing brown velvet gown, with an empress bodice and tiny pearl beads about the neckline, she looked for all the world like a woodland goddess—the sort you might see in a fairy tale. On her head of long brown hair sat a delicate silver crown made of intricately woven sparkling vines and flowers. It reminded Myka immediately of the crown she had seen on the drawing of the tiny doe in the book.

"Welcome," said the Lady.

"I, uh…I …:" stammered Myka, finding herself quite unable to speak.

"I am the Lady of these woodlands. Welcome, Myka, to the Forest of Landor."

"How do you know my name?" Myka asked breathlessly. "How could you possibly…"

"I know all about you, daughter," the Lady spoke quietly. "And I have been expecting you."

Myka had nothing to say. How could anyone know of her journey to this place when she had no idea of it herself? And why was this woman calling her 'daughter' when she was obviously younger than she? Myka shut her mouth and said nothing more.

"You have much further to go, daughter," the woman continued, "although I wish you could stay here a bit longer with me. But a plague has come to my forest, and you must go quickly from this place."

Myka swallowed hard. In this strange moment, she had completely forgotten about the illness. She felt the fear again enter her bones. "I met the villagers yesterday," she said weakly. "They are not well, my lady."

The Lady hung her head. "I know this, child. I am on my way to them now. I was hindered in my arrival, but that is not your concern.

I can bring healing to some; for others, it is too late. For you, I have come in time."

With this, she looked with a compassionate gaze at Myka, nodding at her arm. Looking down, Myka gasped. It was covered in red welts. It had begun.

Myka looked up at the Lady with tears in her eyes. "You have come in time? Can you help me, then?"

The woman nodded and laughed gently, tossing her head back, her long brown hair sparkling in the sunlight. "Come, daughter. I can do nothing but."

Myka rose up slowly and moved toward the woman. What happened next was the most unexpected thing. Instead of tending to her arm, the woman reached out and took Myka's hair, undoing the messy braid she had attempted that very morning, letting the tangled mass fall to her shoulders.

"Sit, daughter, here," said the woman, pointing to a moss-covered tree stump. Myka obeyed, confused and bewildered by the woman's actions.

Taking her delicate fingers, the woman began to pull at the knots in Myka's hair. She worked methodically, slowly and gently. Strand by strand, she untangled the long gray beauty of Myka's hair until at last, it was flowing soft and long about her shoulders, almost as long as the Lady's. Reaching up and touching it, Myka began to cry. Her hair had not been tended to by anyone since her mother had brushed it when she was but a child of five. She, herself had found it utterly impossible to undo the tangles forged by the years of neglect. She looked at the lady and could barely speak.

"Thank you," she managed to squeak out.

The woman smiled. "Here, let me do one more thing." With this, she pulled out a lovely golden hairpin from her hair—one with a design on it that Myka couldn't quite make out—then wrapped Myka's hair into a soft bun and affixed it with the pin. Myka was suddenly overwhelmed with a sense of true, pure humility. A clean, lovely feeling that was accompanied by an undeniable sense of worth. Not having a mirror, Myka couldn't see herself, but she felt…beautiful. A feeling she had never, not once in her life, experienced.

She looked down at her arms, and still, the red marks remained. But this time, instead of fear, she just felt gratitude tinged with sadness.

The Lady moved back from Myka a few steps and smiled again. "You see, daughter. There are some things more needed than others. The first was more important than the last. I must go now to help the others, but I leave you with this, Myka. Find the King. Whatever you do, do not stop until you find him."

With this, the woman was gone. Simply vanished, leaving nothing behind but a sparkling golden light that flickered for a long moment in the tree branches of the natural grotto.

Myka sighed. Somehow, it didn't feel terrifying to face the plague anymore. Indeed, her heart felt healed and whole in such an extravagant manner that it completely overshadowed even the painful welts on her flesh. She sat for a long time, letting her heart marinate in the experience with the Lady. Had it not been for Tenk, she might have stayed there in that cove all day. But she realized after a bit that Tenk was nowhere to be found. In fact, it had not come anywhere near while the Lady had been there. She gathered up her mushrooms, stood and brushed herself off. She had to find Tenk.

Calling out, she left the tree canopy to the meadow proper and looked everywhere for her friend. Fully expecting to see it come bounding over with a snoot full of primroses, she was confused when it didn't appear.

'*It must have gone back to Bray,*' she thought as she wandered back toward her little encampment. Upon returning, she indeed found Tenk curled up by the fire and Bray resting contentedly nearby. "Tenk, you left me," Myka scolded. Tenk said nothing in response. In fact, it appeared as though it was pretending to be asleep. Shaking her head at its petulance, she ignored the odd behavior and set about making a breakfast of mushrooms, all the while feeling more lovely than she had ever felt in her life.

It was midmorning by the time she gathered her things and readied Bray for the journey. A journey that at last had a direction to it. A journey she hoped she could complete before the plague took her. *Find the King.* The lady's mysterious words echoed in her head. Words that felt at once both important and inviting. She was just putting her water pouches (full from the brook) up on Bray's back when her sleeves slipped down, revealing her arms. She froze. The red rash and marks were gone. Her skin was completely clear, not a mark on it. She grabbed at her skirt and looked at her legs. Pink and healthy. Whipping around, she looked toward the meadow and the giant cedar tree beyond it. What had the Lady said? "*There were some things more important than others.*" Her loving touch had unknotted Myka's hair and something in her heart. That was the thing of most importance. But the other had been attended to as well! She was healed! Unable to contain herself, she began to dance a little jig…something she hadn't done in decades. Bray startled, throwing his head up and stepping sideways at the odd behavior, and Tenk whistled in disapproval. Lifting her skirt up about her ankles, Myka danced for the longest time, prancing about in the soft soil until she had flattened it with her joy, creating a makeshift dance floor in the middle of the Forest of Landor. After one particularly wild twirl, the little golden hairpin fell right out of her hair and bounced on the ground, letting her long gray glory fly through the air like a little girl's, falling soft upon her shoulders as she stopped to retrieve the pin. Looking at it, she could now clearly see the design. There, etched in the gold, was a butterfly, flying free, its wings unfurled in delicate glory. She wrapped her hair into a soft bun, affixed it with the pin and caught her breath from the dance. Something inside her had changed. She couldn't explain it. But life was never going to be the same, and she knew it. As she looked for a good place to mount Bray, her attention was drawn to yet another thing…something standing out upon the dirt floor of the forest. This caught her eye because it was pure white (at first, she thought it was a mushroom), but she soon saw that it was a rock. Half expecting to find a stone of some sort anyway, she wasn't surprised to find this one. Scooping it up, she admired it. It was light, feeling more like volcanic stone than anything else. But it was as white as the freshest snow and as smooth as anything you would find at a lakeshore. She tossed it into her pocket, feeling as light as the stone itself.

She found a good boulder to use as a mounting stone, popped onto Bray and kicked him straightaway into a gallop.

It wasn't until they had reached the edge of the meadow that she realized she had forgotten Tenk. She pulled Bray up, circled back and found it sulking by the small brook, whistling angrily. She could do nothing but laugh and beckoned it up on the horse with her, continuing the journey west.

CHAPTER ELEVEN:
The In Between Land

The day was bright and sunny, and the forest continued to offer water, berries, mushrooms and shade. It was a glorious day of travel. But sometime after noon, the forest began to blend over time into a more sparse land, resembling perhaps a prairie or even a tundra, had it been colder and snow-covered. The deciduous trees began to be seen with less and less frequency, and the evergreens had become squat and windblown—some of them actually bent sideways from years of survival in this place. The wind here was indeed notable: strong and getting increasingly gusty with wheezes and whistles and whines, picking up dirt and swirling it around Myka's face. She wished she had not used her shawl for the makeshift saddle bag. As in the desert, it would have been good protection from this wind. Tenk sat in front of her on Bray, burying its head in the horse's mane to get out of the swirling dirt, and Bray's head was down, plowing through the headwinds like a good boy. As stark as this place was turning out to be, Myka's heart was still singing. She had wisely pulled out her lovely golden hairpin and stuck it in with her stones, afraid to lose it in this squall. Her hair, free knotted tangles, blew behind her like a sail, and it felt good. She felt so…young. Maybe it was from riding the horse, but the muscles in her legs and arms felt strong, stronger than they had ever been. She noted sometime ago that she had lost the softness she had carried for years about her midsection. In fact, she had been amazed to find the other day that she had a waist again! It made sense. For her entire life, she had only worked in the market, selling her artwork. None of it took much physical exertion outside of walking to and from the market with bare feet (having no coin for shoes) and standing on those bone-tired feet for hours. The callouses on her hands had come from stacking and gathering firewood daily but never had her muscles been worked as they had been on this journey. She felt better than she had when she was in her third decade, which was the last time she remembered feeling good at all.

The wind was now howling all around them, and it was getting very hard to see through the swirling dirt and tumbleweeds that blew past at regular intervals. She saw a ridge of a cliffside not far from them and turned Bray in that direction. Perhaps there was a cave or a gulley within which to take refuge.

The cliff turned out to be part of a larger plateau, one that looked as though it ran for miles throughout this prairie. They were at the base of it. Perhaps this place had once been a river, and the cliffside the remaining carved walls. In any case, there were indentations and caves aplenty throughout the soft stone cliff wall, and they found a suitable one that fit both horse and human within which to ride out the storm.

The cave was dark, but quiet and protected from the screaming winds. Myka pulled Bray inside (he was reluctant at first) and quickly made a fire from kindling she had carried from the forest. Once the cave was lit, it warmed immediately, and in the flickering shadows of the firelight felt almost cozy. Tenk curled up by the fire, but not before pointing to its mouth and saying, "Food, miss. Hungry Tenk." She gave it plenty of mushrooms and had some herself. Feeding Bray was going to be a different story; she even tried giving him a mushroom, which he tried, but spat back out. She knew, however, that he had eaten well in the past few days, so offered him some water, cupped in her hand, and hoped the winds would die down before morning. They would find something to graze upon then.

She took advantage of the calm and quiet to pull out her stones and the book. Leaning against the smooth wall of the cave, she lay the rocks down in the soft dirt in front of her. Each was lovely in its own way, each meaningful to her heart. The lovely blue gem, the smooth red stone, the crystal with the one smooth and one faceted edge, the aggregate gray splashed with red, the smooth black stone that shined like a mirror, and the new snow white, light as air stone she had just found in the Forest of Landor. She tried arranging them in different ways, just for the fun of it, and finally, tired of that, stuck them back in her pocket. She gently touched the book, wondering what words it might hold for her today if any. Suddenly, it occurred to her that perhaps she might *ask* for a word to become legible today. Ask the…something or someone that might be out there for revelation. This was such a new thing, a never-before-considered thing up until yesterday. But tonight, here in this warm cave in the middle of nowhere, it seemed right.

Not knowing how to begin, she simply closed her eyes and said aloud, "Please. Whoever or whatever you are. Please. Give me the ability to read another word tonight. As I have the others. They mean so much to me."

She opened her eyes, realizing she had just uttered what could be considered nothing less than her first prayer. She had no idea to whom or what she had just prayed, but there it was. Her first venture outside of her own self and her own imaginings.

She opened the book slowly and flipped through the waxy pages. Landing on a page she had not really considered before, as the drawing on it did not interest her (it was of a tree, ragged and bare of leaves, stark against a dark background of a moonless and starless night) she looked at the letters on the page, hoping for the best. Nothing happened, and after many long minutes of staring at the undecipherable characters, her eyes wandered back to the image of the tree. It wasn't particularly well drawn nor engaging. *Perhaps the original illustrator had not been available for this drawing*, she thought. And the subject matter was…depressing and forlorn. It made her heart ache in an odd, lonesome way. Yet, the longer she looked at that tree, the more she was drawn to it. A little longer, and suddenly she became overcome with sorrow. An inexplicable sadness. So deep, it was impossible to cry. Just a paralyzing sorrow for which there was nothing to be done. Uncomfortable, she wanted to shut the book and rid herself of the image of that tree but was unable. It was at that very moment that a word curiously sprung from the page as though it had been legible the entire time. The word was '*love*'.

It was then that her tears began to flow. She didn't understand it, but that tree, forlorn and lifeless…it represented love. A love she had never known, not even from her parents. A love mysterious and almost disagreeable in its complexity. Nothing about this page made sense. She only knew it made her feel sadness and gratitude. And it made her feel loved.

She shut the book, wiping away the tears with her sleeve. Tenk had fallen asleep by the fire, and Bray was resting as well, hip and foot cocked, head low to the ground. The wind continued to howl and shriek outside their cave, yet she had never felt such peace in the midst of a storm.

She fell asleep easily, listening to that wind. And for the first time in her life that she could remember, sleep came with not even a hint of fear accompanying it.

***

The wind had stopped. Myka and her traveling companions had awakened inside a dark cave to a soft and remarkably still morning. Tenk had gotten ahold of the food pouch and was helping itself to some tender mushrooms, and Braydenthall was staring out of the cave and flicking his ears, no doubt thinking of some green grass he might find.

Myka got up, stretched, and patted Bray on the rump. "We'll find you some food today, boy," she said encouragingly. She thought to build a fire but then decided against it. It would be better to get on the road than to dally here in this cave. She checked her pocket for the stones, realizing it was fast becoming full. *"I'll have to start using a food pouch if I find any more of these,"* she mused. Sticking the book in her waistband (which she noted happily she was having to tighten almost every day) and patting it for safe keeping, she slipped Bray's halter on, gathered up her near-empty food and water pouches, and lifted them onto his back. Allowing Tenk to finish its last mushroom, she then hoisted it up onto Bray's back and led them both out into the light of day.

With the wind calm, and no dirt obscuring their view, the prairie was quite interesting, if not beautiful. Plenty of windblown scrub pines still dotted the landscape, but there were other interesting and diverse vegetation as well. Yucca, small cacti, sagebrush, tumbleweeds, and some type of short hardy deciduous tree grew in abundance everywhere one looked. The most interesting and

146

captivating component of the place were the many and varied remarkable rock formations. Made of tan and red stone, there were arches, buttes, and gigantic boulders of every size and configuration—some the size of small houses—that had calved off the cliffsides and fallen to the flat lands below. It looked for all the world like a giant's chess set, with pieces scattered about a huge board. To Bray's delight and Myka's relief, there was also an abundance of fresh grass growing on the floor of the canyon. Not exactly the sweet, tender green grass of the forest, but the hearty, thick-bladed, and tough grass of the tundra. Bray immediately found a place to graze, leaving Myka to scout for a water source. Tenk jumped off Bray and scurried about, looking for edible flowers or berries. "It will be too early in the season for berries here, Tenk," Myka yelled after it. Truer words could not be spoken. The temperature here was a good twenty degrees cooler than in the forest, even with the sun shining. She doubted edible berries would be available in this climate until mid-summer, maybe even fall. Tenk, however, had already found some tender cactus to chew on, carefully avoiding the needles as it ate. It didn't take but a few minutes to Myka to find a river (she stood on one of the boulders to scout). It was only a few miles off, if that, and in a westerly direction, which was just what Myka had been hoping. A meandering thing—old and slow— not the fresh, bubbling brooks of the forest, but water, nonetheless. She didn't feel hungry this morning, and so, after a few minutes of letting Bray graze, she called to Tenk, and they resumed their journey West toward the river.

Myka let her hair down today after running her hands through it to rid herself of any tangles accrued from the night's sleep. Careful to put her golden hairpin into her pocket, she trotted along on Bray, her hair blowing in the wind. She had never felt so peaceful, lovely, or free. She was indeed the butterfly on her hairpin.

They reached the river in no time, and Myka dismounted to fill the water pouches. Bray drank deeply from the slow moving river, wading in up to his knees and letting the current flow around his legs. The water, though slow moving, was cold as ice, and Bray made his way to the shore after only a few minutes. While filling the water pouches, Myka noted an abundance of fish darting here and there amongst the colorful river rocks, and her stomach began to growl. The thought of fresh fish for a midday meal was a giddy one, having lived on fruits and mushrooms for the past few days. She had seen the men outside of Cenecal, at the Crasten River, catch fish with sharp sticks, which they plunged in the water. It seemed a skill she perhaps could not navigate, but the idea of fish cooking over a hot fire made her almost crazy with hunger, and she thought to give it a try. She found a tree, plucked off a few long, hardy branches, and set about trying to sharpen one end. It was futile. Without a blade of some sort, the best she could do was to strip the bark from the branch at the tip. Sighing, she had just about given up when Tenk popped over to her side and grabbed a branch from her hands. "Give to Tenk, Miss."

"You can't eat a tree branch, you silly glottin," she remarked, pulling the branch from its hands. This only seemed to motivate the little glottin even more, and it made a dart at the branch, grabbed it, and ran off to the streams edge. It began gnawing on the end, using its sharp little teeth as fast as it could. In a matter of moments, Tenk presented the branch to Myka. Gnawed to a perfect sharp tip, like a dart, the branch was perfect. She patted Tenk on the head, thanking it profusely, and set about trying to catch some fish.

Her first few attempts were, as anticipated, abysmal, and she almost lost the makeshift spear several times in the water. But the tenth time, she somehow managed to spear a large brown trout and, squealing with delight, pulled it ashore.

Never had a woman had such a meal. She had skewered the trout with the spear and placed it on top of a fire she had made near the river's edge. The smell of it cooking was in and of itself intoxicating, but that first bite! She hadn't realized how hungry she was, nor how much she had missed real food. Sharing it with Tenk (and tremendously glad Bray didn't eat fish) she devoured it in less than five minutes, then sat back on her haunches to let it digest.

The sun was up full now, and the temperature had risen to a comfortable level for traveling. She thought about trying to catch another fish and pack it along for the trip but then realized there was no way to keep it from spoiling. Besides, she could follow the river west, as it seemed to meander as far as her eyes could see. Perhaps there would be fresh trout for dinner as well!

As the day went on, their journey in these flatlands was proving to be somewhat monotonous. Outside of the interesting rock formations —of which there were less and less—there was little else to see: a tumbleweed here, a cactus there, some scrub grass for Bray to graze upon every so often. The entire tone of the place was somber—giving rise to almost no emotion at all. No flowers to elicit joy, no animals to scamper by and amuse. *An in-between kind of place,* Myka thought to herself as she patted Bray on the neck to encourage him. As dusk came on, Myka scoured the landscape for the best place to make camp, but as they had long left the cliffside, there were no caves in which to take refuge tonight. There had mercifully been no wind today, but the bent trees reminded her that wind was ubiquitous here, and today's calm had, no doubt, been a fluke. They would need shelter of some sort for the night.

By the time the first stars began to twinkle in the ever darkening sky, she became anxious. A slight breeze had also begun—the harbinger of a night squall. A few tumbleweeds crossed in front of them, and Tenk was already pulling at Myka's sleeve, letting her know what she already knew.

"Wind, Miss. We take cover? Find place, Miss?"

"I've been looking, Tenk. I just can't see anything but this flat land…anywhere."

The wind continued to pick up, as did Bray his pace. He was tossing his head in the wind, as horses do—and Myka was feeling more and more anxious. The moon had just come up full, and in its light, Myka saw something in the distance. It was a nondescript something but definitely stood out against the flat nothingness of the tundra. Turning Bray toward it, she spoke once again to the Other that might be there.

"If you are there, whatever, or whoever you are, could you help us find shelter tonight?"

It was her second prayer, the first having borne the fruit of *Love* from the book last night. It seemed reasonable that whatever force was helping her would help her again. And so it was, for no sooner had she uttered this prayer when they came upon the structure she had seen from a distance. It was a wooden cabin. Small, weather-beaten, and standing like an inviting beacon against the wind. She dismounted, took her makeshift saddle bags and halter off of Bray, and patted his hind end. Not minding the wind at all, he tossed his mane and galloped off to find some hardy grass to graze upon, and Myka smiled. *Such a good boy*, she thought, as she opened the door to the small cabin and fairly pushed Tenk inside. The little structure reminded her much of her home in Cenecal. A small, humble room, with a fireplace against one wall (complete with a few chopped logs left behind by some kind soul) and an animal skin of some sort, tacked against another. A hunting cabin. Of course. In the middle of nowhere, well made and weather-worn. Glad of its existence and thrilled to find a fireplace, she ran outside to grab up an armful of kindling and, within minutes, had a roaring fire going. Feeling her stomach grumble, she suddenly wished she had the skills of the hunters who previously used this place, for there was nothing left in her food pouches at all, save some mushroom stems that she handed over to Tenk. Thankful for the shelter and the fish with which she had filled her belly at midday meal, she decided rather than sulk about what she didn't have, she would be content with what she did: warm shelter against the ever-increasing wind, a faithful glottin, a steadfast horse and the book. Her stomach could wait for another day.

She found a comfortable place by the fire and pulled the book out to see what she might be able to read today. It had become the most exciting and anticipated part of her day to open it and wait for a new word to be revealed. With that very anticipation, she slowly (and almost reverently) opened the book. Today her interest was held by the tenth page. It was an illustration of a sunrise over some mountains. As always (with the exception of the drawing of the tree) the artwork was exquisite. The mountain looked as though she could reach out and touch it: the sun as though she could feel the very life and warmth and promise of a new day. She inhaled slowly and took the scene in for a very long time, not even bothering to look at the characters below.

When at last she did, it wasn't but a second before her eyes could read an entire portion of the page! The words once again fairly leapt out at her, and while some of them were familiar, several were new, but this time she found them not comforting at all. These words were completely off-putting. The phrase read:

"Come, Afflicted One, and put that which you have chosen behind you. Put the King ever before you, for he desires your beauty and he will protect you."

She felt her heart draw back from the words, instinctively, almost angrily. *Beauty? Someone desiring her? Protection from a King?* These words were absurd, nonsensical. Meant for someone other than her. For some reason, she felt betrayed by the words. They made her furious. She slammed the book down on the wooden floor and sat for a minute in the stillness. It was a full five minutes before she realized her fists were clenched, and her breath was coming in angry gulps. Tenk had been at her side within moments, comforting her and trying to calm her.

"Miss sad? Miss upset? Tenk, take book away, Miss."

And before she knew it, Tenk had grabbed the book off the floor where it had landed and had tossed it into the roaring fire. It took Myka another moment to realize what it had done, and screamed, "No, Tenk...*bad* Tenk!" as she scrambled to retrieve it from the flames. The waxy leather cover was smoking by the time she tossed it onto the floor and smothered the flames with her skirt. Upon a quick inspection, she noted that only the cover (that Tenk had gnawed on previously) had been damaged, and it, only slightly. She turned her attention to Tenk, who was shaking in the corner of the cabin.

"I told you this book is *mine*!" She yelled at the little glottin. "What were you thinking?"

Tenk was whistling quietly, an angry whistle, which surprised her.

'Book upset Miss. Miss needs Tenk's help," was all it said, but she noted its teeth were bared.

"I don't need your help tonight, Tenk. I really don't. Not tonight, Tenk. I'm too angry with you."

Tenk then did something it had never done before. It got up, ran to the door of the cabin and opened it, darting out and disappearing into the darkness.

Suddenly panicked, Myka ran to the open door, which was swinging wildly in the wind, and screamed out into the night.

"Tenk! Tenk, come *back* here! Teeeenk!"

The little glottin was gone. She pulled the door shut against the howling wind, making sure not to lock it so Tenk could get back in. It had never left her like this. Ever. Her heart was pounding, and she began to cry helplessly.

First, the stupid and insulting words from the book, and now her only, best help and friend in the world had left her. For all she knew, she had hurt its feelings too badly and it would leave her forever. She could only hope not. She thought for a minute to toss the book back into the fire and let it burn, but something stopped her from doing that. She left it on the floor, kicking it to the side, and curled up in a ball next to the fire.

She had not been alone like this ever in her life. Tenk had been there since her parents had been taken by the plague. Her only source of safety and comfort. Her only warning from danger. She was completely lost without it.

In her desperation, she thought to try praying again. Cautiously, she formed the words she thought the Other might hear. "Please, please bring back my Tenk. If you are there, please…." Sobbing, she fell asleep next to the fire, almost wishing she could die.

The cold of the cabin awakened her at dawn. The fire had long gone out, not even an ember remained, and her worst fear was realized as her eyes fluttered open and consciousness came sweeping back. Tenk was nowhere. It had not returned during the night. Shaking and quite unable to calm herself, she thought suddenly of Braydenthall. He had not left her as well, had he?

She bounded to open the door, only to sigh in relief. Bray was standing outside the cabin, nibbling on a small patch of grass he had found, his head snapping up as the door opened. He nickered happily at Myka, and she literally flew to him and wrapped her arms around his strong neck. Her tears flowed freely, and the surprised horse simply nibbled her arm gently, then returned to grazing.

Drying her eyes on her sleeve, she looked around the outside of the cabin for Tenk. It was nowhere to be seen. Her heart sank, and she had never felt so abandoned in her entire life. Not even after her parent's death, for they, after all, didn't leave her volitionally. She was so angry at herself for yelling at Tenk. She had hurt its feelings. She had rejected it. No wonder it had left her. Furious with herself for losing her temper so, she realized there was nothing she could do. Glottins were, if nothing else, fiercely independent and clever. It would do fine on its own. It was she who would suffer the loss of her friend.

She checked the sky. A clear day, and, once again, the wind had abated during the night. She and Bray would make good time, although as to their destination, she still didn't know. The Lady of Lanthor had told her to *'find the King'*. Not only did she not know what that meant, as to who or where the king might be, but she had no idea in which direction to travel. She just felt a strong urging to go west. It was as she remembered the Lady's words that the text she read last night came bounding back into her head. What was it? Something about *'putting the King ever before her, and he would protect her?'* There was something else about *'him desiring her beauty'*, but she knew that wasn't for —*couldn't be*—for her. Why the book had let her read those insulting words was, to her, an angry mystery.

So. Both the Lady and the book had told her to find the King. But the King of where? What land? With nothing else to go on but those vague and cryptic directions, she thought it best to start her journey straightaway today and see how far they might get. Packing up her scant belongings, she double checked the fireplace to make sure there wasn't a hidden ember that might still be alive (she didn't want to burn the little structure to the ground) shut the door and secured it tightly, and found a good rock to use for hopping onto Bray.

They quickly made their way from the hunting cabin back to the westward flowing river and followed it till midday. The absence of Tenk riding in front of her, warm against her chest, was both sorrowful and lonesome. It seemed as though she was somehow profoundly untethered and completely unprotected. Had it not been for Braydenthall, she felt as though she might have curled up into a ball like last night and wished for death again. But the warm back of the horse and his rhythmic clip clopping felt sturdy and strong, and she was grateful for his companionship.

The landscape continued to be notably dull, engendering the feeling, once again, that she was in an in-between place. Her thoughts wandered as she rode along, with nothing particularly interesting to distract her. This king. Who was he, and where might he be? The Lady was firm in her instruction, but she had given no direction to it. Myka only knew she felt under a compunction to continue westward, a feeling she had had since beginning the journey from Lake V'esta. She would continue in this direction until or if something or someone told her otherwise.

By midday, the sun was actually warm, and Myka thought to stop by the river and cool off in the water. Her thoughts of catching another fish had long since faded. Without Tenk to help fashion a spear, in fact, without Tenk at *all,* she found she wasn't even hungry. But Bray needed to eat, and she needed water.

Sliding off his silky back, she grabbed her water pouches, took off the halter and patted him off to graze. She knelt down at the river bank to fill her pouches when she saw something move out of the corner of her eye. Startled, she jumped up, almost falling into the river as she did, only to find herself face to snout with Tenk! Muddy, and covered with tumbleweed dust, it was standing in the water next to her, making its telltale chattering sound. Never in her life had she been so glad of seeing someone!

"Tenk! Oh, dear Tenk! You've come *back* to me!" She reached out and pulled the muddy little glottin to her chest. It buried its nose in her bosom and practically purred.

"I'm so sorry I yelled at you, friend," she muttered as she wept in joy. "I'm so sorry. I was just so very angry. And you were only trying to help me. I see that now. Will you ever forgive me? Please stay with me, dear Tenk. Don't leave me again, please."

Tenk stopped its chatter and looked her square in the eye as if deciding whether to stay or go.

"Tenk stay. No send Tenk away again, Miss."

Her heart leapt for joy. "I won't. I won't, dear Tenk. Thank you. *Thank* you," and with this, she hugged the little beast tighter than she had ever hugged it in her entire life.

Immediately (but not surprisingly) her appetite came roaring back within seconds of finding her dear glottin, and Tenk, seemingly intuiting her needs, ran off quickly and came back with a stick, already sharpened by its little sharp teeth. She used it again to catch a fish (this time a small, brightly colored one that only took her six tries to spear) and shared it with Tenk happily as they lounged on the riverbank in the warm noonday sun.

Wanting desperately to sneak a peek at the book, she thought it best not to today, as this was at the heart of their disagreement last night. Best to let sleeping dogs and glottins lie.

Instead, she thought to search the river bed for another stone to add to her collection. It was true that until now, the rocks had just 'presented' themselves to her, but this riverbed was so full of beautiful stones she thought that perhaps she could just find one herself today. She walked up and down the riverbank, never really finding anything remarkable, but picked up a rather interesting-looking yellow-ish rock from beneath the waters and tossed it into her pocket anyway. If nothing else, it would remind her of the happy reunion with dear Tenk.

The three were back on the road—stomachs full and spirits high—as they followed the river westward until early evening, when suddenly, coming around a bend, the river took a sharp turn in the other direction leaving Myka to decide what to do. She could continue west into the unknown, which was her instinct, or follow the river east, assuring them water and food for their travels. The allure of the latter almost convinced her, but still following her odd compunction, she turned Bray away from their meandering old friend and toward the setting sun. Tenk had made some noises about this decision, whistling a low warning, but in the end, had settled against her chest and fallen asleep with the rhythmic movement of the horse. By the time the moon rose, they had still to see any notable change in the landscape—just more flat land, small succulents, and scattered boulders—Myka decided to make camp next to one of the larger of these, hoping it would act as a windbreak in case of another night squall.

As the wind had come from the east the past few days in this land, she made a fire on the west side of the boulder, hoping for the best. In the light of the crackling fire, she waited for Tenk to fall asleep, hoping to be able to read a bit from the book before nodding off herself.

Double checking that it was indeed sleeping, Myka quietly cracked open the book, which still smelled strongly of smoke from its near demise. She opened to a page that curiously had no drawings nor illustrations on it at all, outside of an ornate character that began the page—like the initial illuminated letters in her primers. No words sprang to life from the page, however, no matter how long she stared at it. She thought to find another page but couldn't take her eyes off that decorative first letter. As she stared at it, it suddenly seemed to come alive - swirling and twisting before her eyes, and she actually had to blink to keep from falling over dizzy. Squinting, she looked at it again, and this time she felt something. She didn't read it. She *felt* it. Amidst the swirling and confusion she was currently experiencing, she felt something akin to fear—no, not fear—it was a *warning*. Yes, the swirling letter was warning her of something. She quickly shut the book, letting her dizziness settle as she stared at the fire. Glancing over at Tenk, she made certain it wasn't the glottin that was chattering a warning in her ear. No, it was still sleeping soundly. Truthfully, she already knew that. For the warning she felt from the book felt deeper and more profound than any she had ever heard from her faithful Tenk. Tenk's warnings were about marauders or food deprivation, or possible sickness; this warning was about annihilation. Her very *existence* hung in the balance somehow if this warning wasn't properly heeded.

Her skin crawled. What was the warning trying to tell her? Was she to stop her journey? Was she to find another place to camp for the night? Was she to *not* listen to the Lady's directive? *What was it?* Mind racing, she tried to lay down and close her eyes against her raging thoughts and sleep, but it was of no use. She even tried singing to calm down but couldn't seem to force a single note from her tight, dry throat. All she could think about was the warning from the book. A warning… but of what, she did not know.

She didn't fall asleep until it was almost dawn. Mercifully, the wind never blew on the tundra that night, but billowing, black clouds had gathered, unseen by a sleeping Myka. She awakened from her short rest just as the first pelting drops of cold rain hit her face.

CHAPTER TWELVE:
The Great Abyss

By the time Myka had gathered up her things and climbed onto Bray, the rain was pouring. And pouring in a way she had never experienced in Drymac. It was coming down in great sheets and the wind-hardened prairie soil was unable to absorb it, causing quick-moving waters to swirl around the rocks and Bray's hooves, threatening to whisk them away. Tenk was buried in her chest, shaking, muttering about 'death by drowning', and Bray was equally uneasy—each step being uncertain, his fight against the currents fast becoming more and more difficult a task.

Myka saw a small hillock ahead and urged him up to higher ground. Once safely there, she dismounted and watched helplessly as the prairie floor simply filled up like a water basin. For about ten minutes, everything was a swirling, splashing mess of mud and water when suddenly the rain stopped almost as quickly as it had begun, the sun pushing away the black clouds, and the flood waters beginning to recede almost immediately thereafter. Grateful for this, Myka found the next problem almost as insurmountable as the first. For the flash flood had left the prairie floor swamped in mud and rock and piles of tumbleweeds as far as the eye could see. It had become utterly impassable. She looked around at their options. The little hill they were standing on was connected by rocks and terraces to a higher grouping of hills. Once past these, a tall cliffside (like that of the kind they took shelter in the first night) rose like a sentinel, dark and foreboding, casting shadows onto the floodwaters below. It, too, looked impassable.

Bray had found a patch of green grass on which to graze and was busy with that task while Myka slumped down on a rock to think. The sun came back hot, leaving the ground steaming from the sudden temperature change and filling the valley floor with a thick fog. There was no going any further that way. The only way out of this land was up and over the cliffside behind her. And that prospect looked just as improbable. Sighing, she got up, wrung the water from her skirt and hair, then grabbed Bray's rope. It was either wait until the mud hardened on the valley floor or attempt to navigate the cliffside behind them. Having neither food nor water enough for the first option, she swung Bray around on foot, and they started for the sandstone terraces that marked the base of the cliff. At first, the going was fairly easy— in fact, Bray was remarkably sure-footed and without Myka's weight on his back, he was doing well following her on narrow little deer trails that kept presenting themselves as they walked. The higher they climbed, however, the more rocky it became, and the deer trails soon disappeared. They found themselves looking up at an impossibly steep cliffside with no observable way over. Myka stopped. Turning around, she could see they were far above the muddy tundra floor, and there was no sense going back that way. From this vantage point, it was quite apparent. The entire valley was still knee-deep in mud and tangled vegetation, with little to no dry land exposed at all. It was up that cliffside or wait a few days for the mud to dry.

She turned around and scanned the cliff before her. And that is when she saw it. An indentation, about a stone's throw from them. Perhaps a cave, the sort of which they had spent their first night upon arriving here. It was worth a try. She pulled Bray along a small, rocky ledge towards the feature. Stones clattered from the narrow ledge to the valley below as they walked, making Myka nervous but even more determined. Reaching the indentation, she breathed a sigh of relief to find it was, indeed, a cave. Entering cautiously, Myka was surprised at the size of the thing. It was huge, more a cavern than a cave; she couldn't even see the back wall. The most interesting fact, however, was that there was a warm yet fresh breeze coming from the far side of the cave. Her heart leapt at the thought: there *was* no back wall! This was a passageway *through* the cliff! Aware of the potential that the breeze was making its way through an impossibly small opening (perhaps too small for a human, let alone a horse) it was, nevertheless, worth a try. They would need light. She took a thick piece of kindling and her flint from the makeshift saddlebag, grabbed the water pouches, then said goodbye to her shawl. Wrapping it tightly around one end of the wood, she made a torch and lit it (easier said than done as her attempts with flint to keep a flame going repeatedly being quelled by the constant breeze in the cave.) The shawl wouldn't burn for long, so they immediately started into the cavern, using the fresh breeze as a guide whenever there was a junction of any kind. Tenk was beside itself with fear and kept reminding Myka how dangerous this endeavor was and how uncertain their hope of coming to an exit might ever be.

However terrifying Tenk's warnings, the torch managed to stay lit, and it wasn't long before Myka was certain she could see light far up ahead. Bray seemed to see it, too, for he picked up his pace and was walking beside Myka now instead of following reluctantly behind her. Within minutes, the cavern opened up; the sunlight flooded in, and they found themselves simply walking out of the cavern into a lovely green meadow, wholly unlike the tundra-prairie land they had been in just a few minutes before. Braydenthall, for the first time since he had been with her, pulled the rope out of Myka's hand and galloped full speed ahead of her into the field, tossing his head and bucking like a colt. Myka laughed out loud and yelled after him, "Didn't like that cave, eh?" Truthfully, she would have tossed her mane and bucked too if she could have. The entire cavern was everything she hated: dark, dank, enclosed, and dreadfully lifeless. She stood for a moment, just letting the warm sun wash over her face as she watched Tenk run off in search of something edible. Myka took advantage of this moment to say thank you to whatever was out there watching over them. For, in that moment, she was as certain as she had ever been that someone or something *was*. To find a cavern—a passageway—through that cliffside was nothing short of miraculous. Luck and destiny be damned. *Someone* was helping her, just as had the Lady of Lanthor. She gently touched her hair and smiled. Yes, someone was helping her.

While Bray and Tenk foraged and played in the green meadow, Myka sat down by a tree and opened the book. She hadn't but opened it when a word jumped off the first page her eyes fell upon. The word was "*Believe*".

It felt like a proper word for the moment. Hadn't she just been thinking that someone must be helping her? And wouldn't that require belief of some sort? Yes. The word was perfect. She would believe. She shut the book and, feeling quite comfortable with her new belief, got up to scout out a stream or brook. They would need water and food as they continued the journey, no matter how much belief she put in anything.

Bray had already found a small brook and was drinking from it when Myka caught up to him. This climate was much warmer than the prairie from which they had come, and she found a multitude of fresh berries already mature and ready to eat by the brook's happy waters. She filled an entire food pouch with them and her water bags as well.

Tenk had already found the berries and had red juice dripping from its snout and paws when Myka called it to join her on Bray. She had already decided: they would continue to head west until evening and would make camp early before the sunset.

The lovely meadow seemed to go on forever. In fact, the further west they traveled, the more beautiful it became. Dotted with deciduous trees and replete with tall green grasses and wildflowers, it reminded Myka of the lofty alpine meadows she had visited as a little girl outside of Cenecal, high in the Circacian Range. Every so often, a deer or two would dart out of the trees and trot by Bray, who spooked not only at them, but at several large rabbits that had popped out of nowhere and bounded past. Everything about this place was magical and inviting. Myka was again certain she was headed in the right direction, and this lovely meadow simply confirmed her intuition.

They stopped midday at a small bubbling brook to eat and rest, and Myka shooed Tenk off to find berries so she could read a bit. Opening the book, she found that today all she really wanted to do was to look at the illustrations again, turning each page and absorbing the lovely drawings. She missed drawing—painting on cloths and selling them at the market. Maybe one day, she would settle in a place where she could do that again. Sitting on the ground next to that brook, thinking of her past life, she was suddenly aware of how fit and strong she felt. Her back hadn't ached in the longest time, and her arms and legs, strengthened from riding and walking for miles at a time, were taut and limber. The midlife paunchiness she acquired had continued to melt away, making every movement easier, and even daily aches and pains had seemed to disappear with every new cinch of her waistband.

She smiled, let down her hair, and braided it easily. Ever since the Lady had visited her, she had begun to feel her own worth and a certain unique loveliness. It was such a new and unexpected thing. A beauty she may never be, but strong and healthy was within her grasp. She glanced back at the book on her lap. The pictures were so lovely. Yes. She would paint again one day, and these illustrations would inspire her. She tucked the book away and stood to gather some berries from a bush nearby. As she stood up, she saw something out of the corner of her eye. Could it be another rock for her collection? Excitedly, she bent down and pulled the tiny little thing from the soil. It was like nothing she had ever seen. It was indeed a stone. It was multi-colored, yet crystalline, and when she held it up to the sun, it literally tossed out a rainbow of light like a prism. It was very small, about the size of a coin, but seemed, in comparison, more powerful than any stone in her collection. She played with it in the sun for a few minutes before slipping it into her pocket with the others and grabbing a handful of berries from the bush. The day didn't seem as though it could contain any more glory.

After a good rest and a belly full of berries, Myka thought to try something new as she was feeling so nimble and youthful. She tossed Tenk up on Bray's back, then grabbed his mane and swung her body up and onto the horse from the ground. She laughed out loud once seated at the sheer joy of it. No more searching for boulders or fallen logs! Pulling her butterfly hairpin out from her pocket, she wrapped her braided hair into a bun and secured it well. Urging Bray into a gallop, she closed her eyes, let go of the mane and spread her arms out like a bird. She was flying. Flying free on the back of her horse, like the butterfly in her hair.

Braydenthal slowed to a trot after a few minutes, then to a jog, and then, finally, to a walk as they traversed the glorious meadowland that seemed to stretch on forever. It wasn't until about dusk, when the air cooled and the sun's rays said their last goodbyes, that the landscape began to change as well. The meadow went from producing lush grasses to offering up a rocky, sandy soil, and the trees were noticeably absent as well. Bray walked along, his hooves now making a lovely clatter on the stony ground. This was the time of evening Myka had planned on making camp, but there wasn't even a small grove of trees within which to build a fire. Shrugging it off, she decided they would simply stop where they were and hope for no wind or rain this night. The meadowlands showed no signs of having harsh weather or winds, and her heart was still singing from the glory of the day. No negative thought was going to ruin it. Tenk, of course, had other ideas and kept bouncing up and down on the rocky ground, chattering on about 'having no berries', and 'the storm that might come.' Myka inhaled deeply and ignored it. Not tonight. Wasn't the book's very message to her today that of 'belief'? Well, then. She would believe in a calm, warm night.

As it happened, she was right, and the three of them slept soundly with no incident and awoke to the sunny sky once again. They ate the remaining berries and emptied one of their water bags before continuing on. It was a bright, warm morning but the joyful, lush green of the meadowlands was sorely missed by all of them. Bray was finding this part of the journey difficult, as there was not one blade of grass the further they traveled. Tenk was whimpering to Myka about having no food again, and she bit her lip as she listened. If this terrain lasted much longer, they would have to make a decision. The memory of the meadow, however, continued to calm her nerves. They could always go back if they must. She took her hair down, slipped the golden pin into her pocket, and urged Bray to a trot.

His hooves clip-clopped along on the rocky ground as the place became more and more sparse. It was now just stoney, sandy soil as far as the eye could see, ending abruptly at the horizon, with no change in scenery at all. No lake, no mountains, no cliffs at the horizon's summation. Just an abrupt end to the stony soil. It made no sense. Myka again urged Bray to a trot so she could see more clearly, and they soon realized the horizon was not a horizon at all. The land simply stopped. She got off Bray and looked down. She was staring into the mouth of an abyss, so deep she could not see the bottom, and the other side of it so far away it was barely visible. She looked to the right and to the left, but the chasm seemed endless in both directions. It was as though the earth had simply split in two at this place, with no way over, through, or around.

The joy she had been feeling just moments before quickly evaporated. She knew they could turn around and go back to the meadowlands, but what of her journey? What of the Lady's instructions? What of the compelling urge in her heart to continue west? What of this king? Were all the changes that had occurred in her and all the travels thus far to end here at this great chasm?

She hung her head and patted Bray's withers as he moved some rocks around on the ground with his soft lips, looking for anything to graze upon.

"There's nothing there, boy," she sighed. Tenk was clinging to her side and extremely quiet. She pet it gently. "No words from you, my friend?" Tenk buried its head in her chest in response but said nothing. That scared her more than anything.

She sat down on her haunches and looked over the abyss to the other side. It must have been a mile across, if not more. There was no bridge that could possibly be made that could traverse that span. There was no sense riding parallel to the chasm to find one. And it was bottomless, as far as she was concerned. Too deep to even attempt a descent and too steep to ascend the other side, even if a descent could be managed. Her stomach growled. They were going to have to go back to the meadow. There was no other choice. And from there, back through the cavern, and hope that the tundra was now passable. There might be another way west. But this path, this journey ended here.

It wasn't a minute after this decision that she remembered again the word from the book today. *"Believe"*. The word seemed to get louder and louder in her head and she couldn't push it away. *"Believe!"* It rang clear and strong like a clanging bell and became less of a comfortable thought (as it had been this morning) and more of a *challenge*. She stood up, shaking the word from her head, and tried to think. Believe what? That they could somehow cross that great chasm? That was impossible. What was the book trying to tell her to do?

Surrendering to her back-up plan, she grabbed Bray's rope and told Tenk to hop on. "We're going back to the meadow," she said plainly, turning around taking about fifteen steps in the direction of the meadow before stopping quickly in her tracks. Something was…behind her. Turning around slowly, she jumped back in terror. For there, standing about four feet away from her, was a man. Tall but thin, robed in brown, with a cord about his waist as a belt, leather pants, and a staff in his hand. He was bearded, but barely, like a man who hadn't shaved in a few days. He had the most brilliant grey eyes

Myka had ever seen. His hair also was grey, peppered with the remaining black of his youth, and he was smiling.

Her heart pounded, and she instinctively stepped away from the man. A meeting like this in Cenecal would never have ended well.

"Where did you come from?" she managed to ask, her voice breathless. "Who are you?"

He took a step back, relieving her tension. "I am Azar, and I was sent by the King to help you."

Her mind was spinning. Up until this point, the vague thought of finding this king was only that: a thought—an idea. Here was a flesh and blood man sent *by* the King. It seemed too much to absorb.

She straightened her skirt and hair, wondering if she should curtsey or something. Instead, she just stood there, rather clumsily shifting her weight from one foot to the other, finally reaching out to steady herself by leaning on Bray.

Azar smiled. "A fine horse you have there, Myka."

Her mouth dropped open. "You know my name?"

Azar tossed back his head and laughed joyfully. "The King knows your name, yes. And, as I said, if you were able to hear, I have been sent by him to help you."

For some reason, this last news sent a wave of emotion through Myka. She felt as though someone had just hit her in the stomach. How could anyone of import, let alone a King, know her, let alone her name? Even as a child, no one knew her name. She let herself be called Mikala, Madistra, Mira…anything would do. She never corrected anyone. She had no right to a name, no right to an identity outside of that of Orphan. The Lady of Lanthor had known her name, and that was overwhelming enough. But a King? It was inconceivable.

She leaned back on Bray, feeling his solid warmth, and tried to absorb this information. Azar looked over his shoulder at the abyss, then back at Myka. "We should get going if we are to make any headway at all today."

Myka raised her eyebrows. "Headway? Forgive me, but I see no way down into or across that chasm. You are jesting, aren't you?"

Azar picked up his staff and clacked it on some stones a few times. "The King has sent me to help you. That is all you need concern yourself with, Myka. Besides, what plan did you have for today's journey?"

"We are going back to the meadowlands. There is food and water, and I'll figure it out from there," Myka said, her jaw jutting out, not masking her defensiveness well.

"Back, you say?" Azar nodded, pursing his lips. "Back. Hmmm. Well, I guess that *is* an option. But does it accomplish your goal?"

Myka bit her lip. Truth be told, she didn't know what her goal was. This entire journey started against her will and had continued by force of sheer curiosity and an odd compunction to keep heading west. That's all she had. Never had she thought of having a goal. Outside of The Lady's directive to 'find the king', she had no end in mind at all.

"Well. I don't know as if I actually have a goal," she finally answered, "But I do know that I see no way across that abyss. The journey, as you say, seems to end here, sir."

"Call me Azar," he said, laughing again. "And pardon me for saying this, but what you know is very little." He looked at her—his eyes dancing with life. She didn't feel at all demeaned by his light chastising. He was still smiling as he tapped his staff on the ground again, moved towards her, and looked even deeper into her eyes. "N'er the less, be it as you wish. If you want to go back, go. But if you wish to go on, if you wish to meet the King, then follow me."

Tenk was pulling at her skirt, and she pulled it up on her hip as it whispered in her ear, "Go back, Miss. Miss not know strange man. Abyss be dangerous, Miss."

Azar's face grew stern. "The glottin is right, Myka. You do not know me. And that abyss is dangerous. Nothing it says is untrue. The question is, who do you want to listen to right now? What is your heart telling you?"

Myka wished for all the world that Azar would go back to from whence he came. Her glottin had been her friend for decades. Who was this man telling her to choose between him—a complete stranger—and her faithful ally for over fifty years? She felt the same alienating, defensive anger she had felt when Marinda had told her she wouldn't feed her little glottin. And again, in the village of Glanét, when Naruk had told her Tenk was not welcome with them there and then had stolen it from her. It made her heart ache and her head spin. Did these people not know that Tenk was all she had? All she had ever had? The only friend that helped save her from the gods-only-know-what perils? That it had been faithful when absolutely no one else had? What did her heart feel? Her heart felt…her heart felt…torn in two.

For something about what Azar seemed to be offering filled her with inexpressible joy and hope, a new thing…a new life. A hitherto unimaginable sort of life with Kings that knew her name and Ladies that took the time to attend to her knotted and tangled hair and heart. But with Tenk her life had been just fine. They had lived in relative safety in Cenecal (they were the lucky ones, after all) and besides, it was all she had ever known.

Azar stood still, his look now more of compassion than anything else, but said not one word.

Myka closed her eyes and thought of her travels thus far: the discovery of the book, the way the words had come to her revealed things about herself, the journey of becoming stronger and in less pain with every step. Of meeting the Lady of Lanthor, and the wild, inexplicable healing of something deep inside of her, of this news that a King knew her name.

It was as she was musing over all this that the word again struck her heart, *"Believe."*

Believe what? That all this could be real? That the King really sent Azar to help her? That listening to her deepest longings might be better than settling for the safety of the known?

She opened her eyes.

"No. I mean, yes. Yes, I want to go on, not back, Azar. Take me forward, even though I don't see a way. I choose to *believe*."

Azar clapped his hands together joyfully. Tenk gave a low whistle of warning but stopped as soon as the man looked at it sternly.

"Let's go, Myka. You will need to lead the horse…what is his name, then?"

"Braydenthall. I call him Bray…" Azar interrupted her, "Desert One? Good name for a horse."

Myka nodded, wondering how on earth Azar knew ancient Drymacian, then responded. "I found him…er…a friend of mine found him in the Dunes of Martauk. It's a long story."

"I imagine it is," Azar remarked, "and one I would like to hear one day. Now, put the glottin on Bray if you must, and follow me."

Azar turned and began to walk along the rim of the chasm, turning every now and again to ensure Myka and Bray were following well. They hadn't gone but about a mile when Azar stopped abruptly and planted his staff in the ground.

"Here," he said loudly, obviously a proclamation of some sort. "Here is where we shall begin."

Myka looked over the ridge and swallowed hard. The cliff's edge was sharp and went straight down. No path or trail could be seen, nor could she imagine one could even be carved into the steep rocky walls of the cliffside. "Begin? I don't mean to be difficult, Azar, but I see no way to cross over or climb down." It was at that minute that she thought she might have made a terrible mistake following this stranger. After all, she didn't know anything about him, and just because he somehow knew her name didn't make him trustworthy. She looked again over the edge of the cliff and backed away from it slowly.

Azar smiled again. "Myka. This is where you have to decide. This is the time. And this is the place. You said earlier you wanted to move forward. This is the way. There is no other."

"But I don't see how Azar. This makes no sense. Are you trying to get me to trust you? I have no reason to. And I know what will happen if I try to somehow get across that ravine."

He smiled again. "Do you?"

She shook her head in frustration. "Is this your way, Azar? To aggravate and use cryptic language and question someone to death? Is this what you do? Is this a test of some sort? If so, I don't like it. And I don't like being toyed with."

"I am not toying with you, I assure you," he said calmly. "But this (and here he pointed his staff to the chasm) is the way to the King's land. There is no other."

The wind had picked up a bit and was whipping through Azar's grey hair. He looked for all the world like a soldier headed into battle as he stood on the ridge, staff in hand, eyes steely and determined. Tenk was screaming in Myka's ear by this time, becoming harder and harder to ignore. It, too, saw no way down or across the chasm and wasn't about to fall to its death without a fight.

Myka's mind was racing. This man, this stranger from out of nowhere, was offering her the unknown. A way forward to a possible land and a potential future. There were no guarantees. She reached over and scratched Bray under his mane. "What do you think, boy? What should we do?"

Bray nickered softly and pushed her with his soft, velvet nose. *Such trust*, she thought. *He would follow me anywhere.*

Inhaling deeply, she turned to face Azar.

"What must I do?"

"You jump," he said softly.

"I what?"

"You jump. And you believe. There is no other way."

"But Tenk and Bray. What of them?"

"I will take care of them," Azar replied. "You need only to do what I say. And believe."

She looked down into the ravine again and stepped back, dizzy. Turning around to Azar, she said, "I cannot…it is too…"

But he was gone, as were Bray and Tenk. She was alone at the precipice of an abyss, with only an insane directive to jump into it.

She stood for about a minute, the wind blowing in her hair as she stared across the great chasm. Instantly the feeling from the book the other night roared back into her heart. That feeling of great warning. An existential warning. A life or death warning. *This* decision was what the book had been warning her of. *This very moment*. She pulled out the book and opened to the page with the word 'believe' on it, looking at it long and hard. Too much had happened to turn back. Maybe there wasn't enough evidence for her to believe. But one thing was certain: too much had happened for her *not* to. None of this journey made sense, but every step had been good for her. And what was there to go back to in Cenecal? She lived alone, in terror, in a horrid town with one friend that wasn't even human. She had lived in pain and sorrow—of both body and mind—for fifty nine years. It was time to believe in something beyond her own imaginings and Tenk's warnings.

Besides, Someone out there knew her name.

She walked to the cliffside, toes balancing over the edge, closed her eyes, and let go.

CHAPTER THIRTEEN:

The Beach of D'ecora

When she opened her eyes, she realized she had fallen; she remembered that— but had no memory of hitting the ground. She was lying in the sand, but not the kind she and Cla'neen had been in during their time in the Prathian. This was wet sand—cool and soft. Sitting up, she saw that she was on a beach. As far as she could see, white sands ran up and down a coastland, blue waters lolling up against it in soft waves.

Scanning the horizon, she saw no one or nothing else. She was alone here, but she was uninjured. Standing up slowly, she wiped the sand off her skirt after first checking for her stones and the book. All was in place, save for the flint that Cla'neen had given her, but somehow she felt she wouldn't need it here. To her joy, even the golden hairpin was still in her pocket; that one detail making her happier than anything else.

She took off her shoes and walked barefoot along the water's edge, watching her footprints disappear with each wave's retreat. She had never seen an ocean before and truthfully didn't know if she was seeing one now. This could be a great lake of some sort. She reached down and touched the water, lifting her fingers to her lips. Salt. Her first ocean!

The sun was bright and warm, and she was dry within minutes. While watching her footprints melt away with the waves, a little stone, or maybe a shell shining in the sand, caught her eye, and she knelt down to pick it up. It was a light, crystalline blue like the ocean and shaped almost like a star, with jagged edges. She smiled broadly. It was fitting she would find a stone here, and she tossed it in her pocket with the rest.

After a while, she began to wonder what to do next. Azar had not told her what to expect after she had jumped into the abyss. Was she to walk along the beach? Stay put and wait for help? Call out to someone? There were no answers, but the sun felt good, as did the sand between her toes, so she just kept walking. Probably an hour had passed before she saw anything of note along the beach. It was at that time that she saw a figure coming towards her. She assumed it to be Azar, but as the person approached, she saw the obvious outline of a woman. The figure drew near, and —it couldn't be! The Lady of Lanthor! Within a second, Myka had run to her and fallen down at her feet.

The Lady gently touched her shoulder. "No, Child. Rise up. I am here to walk with you, not to have you kneel at my feet."

"My Lady. I thought you were of the Forest only," Myka said breathlessly.

The Lady smiled, "I am the queen of many lands, sweet child. And this…(she motioned here at the white sands) this is the Beach of D'ecora.

It was only at that moment that Myka noted that the brown velvet gown the Lady had worn in the forest had been replaced by a light satin one—blue, the color of the waves and the sky. Its soft folds and drapes fluttered easily in the breeze, and to Myka, the Lady looked as frothy and lovely as the ocean itself. Her crown today was a circlet made of gold, with delicate seashells and ocean waves carved into it;

the sunlight catching and throwing rays of light from it onto the beach as they walked.

They walked in silence together, side by side, for a good while. Myka noticed that the Lady was barefoot as well, a fact that somehow delighted her all the more.

Upon reaching a small grove of palm trees, the Lady beckoned Myka to sit, and they settled in the shade together.

"Do you still have the pin I gave you?" the Lady asked.

Myka reached into her pocket and pulled it out.

"I wouldn't lose it. It means the world to me."

The Lady smiled. "Here, turn around. Let me attend to your hair again. You are to meet the King soon. Let's ensure you are at your best."

Myka's heart nearly skipped a beat. Meet the King? She had never met so much as a courtier or a Lord, let alone a King.

The Lady worked Myka's hair gently. "You have managed to get a few more knots in this since I've seen you last," she laughed, "let me help you."

Myka sat still, letting the woman first untangle, then arrange her hair. This time, rather than a soft bun, the Lady braided it in several braids, then using the pin she had given her, worked them into an intricate design atop her head and fastened it.

"There," said the Lady, smiling. "You look lovely."

Myka bit her lip and turned her head away.

"What?" asked the Lady. "Why do you resist my words?"

"It's just that…that…I wouldn't think you one to lie, my Lady. It bothers me when I hear such things."

"Ah," said the woman, "I see. And how is it that you think I am deceiving you?"

Myka sighed. "I have never, once in my life, been *lovely*. I have been smart, I have been clever, I have been a survivor. But lovely? Please, it hurts me when you use such words. It is as though you are almost mocking me."

The Lady nodded in understanding. "Myka. I would never mock you, nor can I lie. Therefore, my words must be taken as truth. For what else is there?"

Confused by this, Myka felt her eyes fill with tears. "But, I have *lived* this life. For fifty nine years, I have lived it. I have been called ugly. I have been mocked, and, at best, I have been utterly ignored by people. I have seen *true* beauty in the courtiers of Lord Bythim's court, and I have then looked in mirrors at my own image. How can you contest this?"

The Lady reached inside her robe and pulled out a small golden object.

"You say you have looked in mirrors? Have you really?" With this, she handed Myka the little golden thing. It was a palm-sized locket, a compact of some sort, with a hinge on one side and intricate carvings on both sides of the golden exterior.

"Go ahead," urged the Lady. "Open it. Look".

Myka opened the locket to see herself reflected in the mirror therein.

She looked at her image, then back at the Lady in disbelief.

"What kind of magic is this?" she whispered softly. For the image she was looking at was hers, to be sure, but the woman looking back at her - *this* Myka - was absolutely beautiful.

"No magic, child," said the Lady. "That *is* you. It always has been you. It is *how* you see that is changed. You are seeing now through eyes of truth, not marred by what was spoken over you, nor to you, nor even what you came to believe and say about yourself." She paused for a moment, then continued. "Do you remember in the village of Glanèt, when you heard the word 'wounded' spoken to you as you held the book?" Myka nodded, remembering her fear of insanity that night. The Lady smiled. "That was my voice. Speaking truth to you. Whispering to you your brokenness and inability to see aright". Myka swallowed hard. The Lady pressed on. "And do you remember when you traveled through the Marshes of Nyster and met the keepers that live therein?"

Myka nodded. How could she forget those insulting creatures?

"And you thought they spoke truth to you, did you not?" asked the Lady.

"Nothing they said was untrue," agreed Myka.

The Lady shook her head. "The hags can speak only what a person feels about themselves. They are simply reflections of how you see yourself. A warped mirror, if you will." The Lady continued, "It is not your fault, Myka. You couldn't see yourself properly before because you couldn't *see properly at all*. And, as it was with your hair, the lies in your heart had to be untangled as well. This had to happen before you could find the truth about anything."

Myka gently closed and handed the little mirror back to the Lady, still uncertain of what she was hearing.

The Lady pushed it away gently. "No, no…keep it. Your loveliness is now yours to own, as is the mirror," said the Lady smiling.

"And now, ready yourself, for soon we shall meet the King."

With that, she stood up, extended her hand to Myka, and pulled her up from the sand.

They walked inland toward a series of rugged stone steps, hoary with age and scarred by the wind and sand. They led away from the beach upwards to whatever land lay above D'ecora. As they walked, Myka inquired of Bray and Tenk. The Lady assured her that they were well, that Azar had taken care of them, and that she would see them both soon.

They climbed the stone steps, which, at the top, opened up to a lovely meadow—not unlike the one in which they had traveled before the Great Abyss. Myka and the Lady walked through the soft green grass and colorful wildflowers and were greeted with birdsong and a variety of other animals. They would dart up and then dart off as though they were checking in. Dogs, cats, squirrels, and quite a few deer all made their way over and nosed them—then ran, trotted or bounced off happily. A small herd of horses greeted them as well, trotting up and nickering their welcome. They stopped and rested their heads against the women's chests for a moment before galloping off toward a waterfall in the distance. Myka felt it was the nicest, most unique, and warm reception she had ever received.

The meadow gave way after a few minutes to a pathway, but unlike any Myka had ever seen and completely unlike the stone steps which had risen from the beach. The stones of this path were of the whitest marble, inlaid with what appeared to be streaks and swirls of gold. Sparkling in the bright sun, it almost felt as though she was stepping on pure light. They walked together in silence, for that was what Myka felt was right. Words would sully this place somehow.

Upon turning a bend, Myka looked up and gasped. There, on a hill not far from them, was what could only be described as a palace. Shining with the same marble flecked with gold it stood, its alabaster stones at once both inviting and breathtaking. A large gate stood between them and the beautiful edifice, and as they walked toward it, the great gates swung open gracefully, and Myka saw two guards dressed in shining silver armor at either side of the gate snap to attention as they walked through. Once past those, the marble walkway became part of a greater garden—with roses and lavenders and a myriad of beautiful fountains sprinkled here and there on the grounds. It was beautiful beyond Myka's wildest dreams and certainly more inviting than anything anyone had ever seen in all of Drymac. Everything in this place begged a person to stay, and wrapped a person in welcome.

It was by one of the sparkling fountains that the Lady again spoke, asking Myka to sit down on a bench and wait. She then disappeared around a large pale yellow rose bush, a few petals falling in her wake like blush-colored snow.

Myka sat on the bench, swinging her legs like a child in the sunshine, when suddenly there appeared two women, both wearing gowns of the same lovely light blue the Lady had worn, walking toward her. Upon arriving, they greeted her with a bow, then said softly,

Welcome! We are here to take you to the Room of Preparation. Follow us."

With no other ceremony or words (and Myka confounded by the fact that they bowed at her) she got up and trailed behind the two women in their diaphanous gowns. They walked to the side of the main building, to what looked like a small guest quarters, and opened the door for her. Upon entering, she found the place quite sparse: with one chair, a dressing table, and a large armoire made of a very dark, very exotic-looking hardwood with vaguely familiar carvings all about. She walked up, and upon close inspection, she remembered! The carvings were of Solemn Memories she had seen at Petrul's house and on his cane! Her eyes grew wide, and, whipping around to the attendants who were standing by the door, she asked, "What is this place? I mean, what is the name of this land?"

"This?" the shorter one asked. "Why, this is Palem, Land of the High King."

Myka felt her legs go weak, and she slumped into the chair slowly.

Palem was a myth. Palem was a superstitious place longed for by the weak and dying or daft old women. There *was* no such place. Of course, all this was moot now, and either the two attendants were lying to her, or she was imagining all of this, or…or it was all true.

The latter was the hardest to believe.

"There is appropriate attire in the closet," said the short one, pointing to the armoire. "Choose what you will." The taller one stepped over and inspected Myka's hair. "This is exquisite work. There is no need to do anything further, except perhaps…" She reached into her pocket and pulled out a beautiful golden hairpin. It exactly matched the one the Lady had given Myka in the woods. "Here. One on each side." She smiled as she placed it into Myka's hair and patted it gently. "There, that's better."

With that, the two women swept out of the room, leaving Myka to herself and her thoughts. She exhaled through her mouth slowly and bowed her head. This was all too much. Every word the book had let her read - every single word now came screaming into her head with complete clarity. *Palem. Alone. Lies.Wounded. Come. No fear. Believe.* She had, in her life in Cenecal, no idea how alone and wounded she was. She had no ability to even consider the reality of this place, Palem. When Petrul and Miranda had spoken of it, she had literally dismissed them as old fools. She had been told lies her entire life - about herself, reality, and the existence of something —*someone* outside of herself that could lead her to peace. To freedom. She inhaled deeply and let this moment sink in. She was in Palem. The myth was true.

There was still one part of the book that still confused her. Pulling it out of her waistband, she opened to the page where the entire phrase was legible and looked at it again.

"Come, Afflicted One, and put that which you have chosen behind you. Put the King ever before you, for he desires your beauty and he will protect you."

Although still confounding, she found the words didn't sting as badly today. Somehow she could read about 'her beauty' without having to react defensively and the anger that it brought. But the rest of it. What was she to put behind her? Her life in Cenecal? The hopelessness she had experienced for decades? Maybe all of it? She shut the book gently and set it on the dressing table, then walked over to the armoire and opened it.

Gasping, she took a step backwards. There, in this lovely closet, were three of the most remarkable and beautiful dresses she had ever seen in her life. Suddenly and acutely aware of her own tattered, filthy state, she looked around for the attendants. Not seeing them outside her room, she thought to choose a dress and worry about a bath later.

She picked out a simple dress, the plainest of the three, which, in her economy, was still the most beautiful thing she had ever laid eyes on. The material was like nothing she had ever seen, like nothing in Cenecal. Never had she painted on cloth such as this, let alone seen it at Market. Silky and shimmering, yet with a certain weight to it that held its shape and color that was indescribable. It sometimes shimmered an earthy brown, sometimes an opalescent cream, depending on which way the light hit it. Clean lines, and an elegant draping shape, with a thin and delicate golden belt, she felt it most like the plain blouses and skirts which she had worn for her entire life. It felt like home, but a sparkling new home.

She pulled it out of the closet, laid it over the back of the chair, and sat down again. There was to be no trying it on until she had bathed, that was for certain. She would wait for the attendants to return and inquire about that. She took a moment to pull the rocks out of her skirt pocket and set them on the dressing table. They made a lovely clinking noise as she moved them about the marble-topped table, and she arranged them over and over again, remembering each place they represented fondly. Her reverie was interrupted suddenly by the two attendants who opened the door and walked in quietly behind her.

"You have chosen," said the tallest of the two, smiling as she noted the gown laid out on the chair. "Excellent. It is time for your bath now."

Myka sighed, looking down at her filthy clothing and dirty feet. Since she had entered Palem she had felt the weight of her unworthiness. It seemed a lifetime of walking the earth had stained not only her feet, but her soul. She also felt there was absolutely nothing she could do about it. Accepting the bath felt right. Necessary. She smiled back at the two attendants. "That sounds perfect, thank you."

The two women practically glowed as they opened the door, showing Myka out. She followed them again, this time to a small side building shaped like a circle with a glass dome atop. Never in her life had Myka seen such a structure. Upon opening the doors, she was amazed even further to find a large pool of water, larger than her entire dwelling back in Cenecal, filled to the brim and steaming.

Her mouth open, she looked at the two attendants in disbelief.

"This? This is a...a bath? I've never so much as bathed in anything but a watering trough and never with water as hot as this. Are you sure this is for me?"

At this, the two women began to laugh again, and nodding her head, the shorter one replied happily, "Yes, Myka. This is for you. It is for all those who come to the King, made ready for you by his hand in preparation for you to meet him. Now, lay your dirty clothes over there, and you'll find dry towels over here. And there is soap on those floating platters in the bath. A variety. Choose whichever you like." They bowed again and left Myka alone in the bathhouse.

The luxury of that bath was one she hoped never to forget. The soft, hot water, the pure white alabaster marble of the bath walls, and the soaps smelling like lavender, cinnamon and rosemary (she used them all). By the time the attendants returned, she was sitting, wrapped in a ridiculously soft towel, feet dangling in the water and grinning ear to ear. She felt like a child. A brand new baby. She felt…new.

The attendants looked at each other and smiled.

"Come. Let us get you dressed and ready."

Myka followed them back to the guest house, fairly floating - feeling as though her feet never even touched the marble walkway streaked with gold.

CHAPTER FOURTEEN:

The King of Palem

She stood, looking at her reflection in the mirror. Who was this? Tall, fit, with beautiful hair, braided and arranged ever so, clear eyes, a lovely smile, and a dress so beautiful in its shimmering simplicity that it fairly took her breath away. She tightened the little golden belt and stepped back from the mirror, looking again at her image.

This is not the same woman that unwillingly started a journey but a short while ago. This is not the ugly old woman with the bent back and calloused feet, who day by day sold her wares for coin hardly enough to live on in the Marketplace, and who, night by night, shook in terror under her rough, muslin blanket. Who is this woman? And why has she been brought here?

There was a knock at her door, and she spun around. It was Azar! He was standing in the doorway of the guesthouse, and he was smiling at her like no one had ever smiled at her before. It made her feel a bit uneasy. Like she was being seen for the first time.

"I see you believed," he said quietly, his eyes sparkling with joy.

"Azar. It is good to see you. And yes, with your encouragement, I somehow found the courage."

"That is good," he said earnestly. "Not all do. Now. Come, if you are ready, the King is receiving."

Drawing a deep breath, Myka stepped out into the sunshine of Palem, walking beside Azar, her bare feet feeling the warmth of the marble walkway. She noted that, for all the beauty of her gown, the attendants had not brought her shoes. She had noted this but not thought much of it until now, for Azar, too, was barefoot as he walked beside her.

"Does no one wear shoes here in Palem?" she asked with a smile.

Azar chuckled but said nothing. Myka shrugged. It was of no matter to her, for as it was, the warm stone felt good under her feet.

As they reached the outer portico of the palace, Azar bade her sit down on a bench near the entrance. Disappearing for a few moments, he returned, leading a brown horse. It looked for all the world like Braydenthall, but it couldn't be him. For this horse was magnificent: shining coat, long black mane braided with silver ribbons, head held high, adorned in the finest breast collar and bridle, both inlaid with some sort of shining metal that winked and flashed in the sun. Next to him was a small, furry creature slinking along beside the horse. It looked forlorn and kept nipping at Azar's hand with its sharp teeth.

"Here you go," Azar said, presenting the pair to Myka. "I told you I would take care of them for you."

She looked at the horse and the creature and blinked. "Bray? *Tenk*…is that you?"

The little glottin, seeing its mistress, broke free from Azar's grip and fairly flew into Myka's arms, chattering and nestling in her chest. Bray, on the other hand, simply arched his magnificent neck, stepped forward, and bowed down before Myka.

She looked at Azar in amazement. "What did you do to these two?"

"I did nothing, friend. Outside of putting the lovely tack on your horse, this is what Braydenthall and Tenk are actually like. Here, in Palem, even the creatures become their true selves."

Tenk was chattering still, purring its 'tnk, tnk, tnk' in Myka's ear. It was at this moment that it also hissed in her ear a warning. "Do not go in palace, Miss. They lie to you, Miss."

She swallowed hard and set the glottin down on the marble walkway. There, on the shining white and gold of the path, the little glottin's fur looked dirty and scruffy in comparison. It was looking up at her imploringly. "Do not go in, Miss," it said one more time, loud enough for Azar to hear.

"You've listened to it for a long time, Myka," he said, nodding at Tenk. "Will you listen still?"

For a moment, Myka felt terribly confused. Tenk had never steered her wrong. But this place. This place was different. This place wasn't even supposed to exist, yet here she was. She looked at Tenk and felt her eyes fill with tears.

"I have to go," she said at last. "This is why I have come on this journey. This is the reason. I just *know* it. I'm to meet this King. Stay here if you want, little one, but I'm going in."

Tenk whistled a warning but said nothing more. Myka turned to Azar. "I'm ready, friend."

He smiled jubilantly and took her hand.

"The King will be pleased," was all he said.

The great golden doors of the palace suddenly swung open wide, and they crossed the breezeway of the portico and entered in. The first thing Myka felt as she entered the Great Hall of Palem was a sense of wonder. The next thing she felt was a sense of peace. Like nothing she had ever experienced in her life. The Great Hall was several stories high, made of the same alabaster stone and gold as the pathways, giving an open, clean, and inviting warmth to the room. There were huge stained glass windows that went from floor to ceiling on every wall, each with images of the sort that were in the book, throwing beautiful colors into the hall as the sun shone through them. In fact, she was certain the doe with the tiny silver crown, and the living waterfall from the pages of the book were two of the exact images she was seeing in stained glass before her now. There were also many flags and banners adorning the room, some on the walls and some draped like garlands from side to side. At the far end of the hall, there was a throne, but not an obvious one. Looking more like a humble wooden chair one might have in a library or perhaps in a living room next to a fire, it stood alone on a platform with three steps leading up to it. It was empty, save for a red banner casually slung across the back and a red pillow on the seat. Fully expecting a full entourage to be present, Myka was surprised to find no one was in the hall at all, save for her and Azar. Their footfall was almost as silent as the room, their bare feet making no sound as they walked the length of the hall toward the throne.

They stood at the bottom of the three steps and waited. Azar let go Myka's hand, bowed to her, and walked to the side of the room. Myka felt as exposed as she ever had in her life, yet also somehow welcomed and wanted. She stood, shaking, as a door in the side of the hall opened. She almost cried for joy as the Lady of Lanthor walked out into the room, her silken blue gown fluttering in the breeze of the place and smiling at Myka. The Lady came to her side, grasped her hand tightly, and said, "Welcome, Child. Let me introduce you to the King."

It was at that instant that a door behind the throne (one Myka had not noticed before) opened, and a man walked out and stood before them. She would have recognized him anywhere, for he was the King from the pages of the book. The one who had been on the noble steed, with the weighty golden crown encrusted with stones. But he was not in armor now, nor was he wearing a crown. In fact, there was no demarcation of worldly kingship on his person. He was wearing a brown leather shirt, and soft black pants, much like a hunter might wear. His robe was of a coarse material perhaps goat hair—and his shoes were simple with no adornment. His black hair was neither long nor short, cut, yes, but not in the fancy and ostentatious styles the likes of Lord Bythim would sport. This man had the look more of a humble farmer, a man who worked with his hands more than a King. He walked not to his throne but directly down the three steps towards Myka and the Lady, but his eyes were on Myka alone.

He stood before her, and she realized she was shaking uncontrollably and couldn't seem to breathe.

He reached out and took her hand from the Lady and held it tightly. Smiling, his eyes filled with tears.

"Lanthrea," he said, "Welcome home, child. I have waited for so long to you to come."

Myka blinked a few times and pulled back from him, feeling as though she'd been punched in the heart. He didn't know her name *at all*. He had the wrong person standing before him. There had been a terrible mistake! Suddenly ashamed and embarrassed beyond her ability to bear, she averted her eyes and pulled her hand from his.

"Sir. I am sorry. I did not mean to mislead you. I mean, I don't know what they told you. But I am not this person you just greeted. My name is Myka. I have traveled here from Cenecal, and I…"

He bowed his head for a long moment. When he looked up again, she was certain she would see disappointment and perhaps even anger in his face at having been presented with the wrong woman. Instead, his eyes were shining with tears, and in them all she could discern was some wild kind of acceptance.

"Myka. I know your name. I know who you are. I know everything about you. It is I, after all, who have called you here. It is I who had Petrul meet you that day. It is I who placed the book in that house in Old Town and spoke to you through its words. It is I who called you to come on this journey. And Myka, your real name…the name I have given you since before the dawn of time….your *true* name… is Lanthrea."

Her mind was having trouble absorbing this information. She said nothing but looked rather helplessly over at the Lady, who was still standing by her side.

Smiling, the Lady in blue simply nodded in silent agreement and said, "Welcome home, Lanthrea."

The King then let go of Myka's hand and reached under his robe, pulling out a delicate, lacy silver crown. Placing it gently on her head, he smiled again before saying, "By creation, you are my daughter, by answering my call, you are my friend, by the cleansing of my waters, you are made new, and by the spilling of blood not your own, you are royalty in this court." He then turned to ascend the three steps to his throne. Sitting down, he clapped his hands together and announced in a loud, booming, joyful voice, "Let the celebration begin, for our daughter Lanthrea has come home!"

Within seconds, four massive doors, each under one of the stained glass windows on the four walls of the hall, opened, and a veritable flood of people and animals of every sort (some sort Myka had never seen before) came pouring into the hall. Within a few minutes, tables had been moved in, food was arriving in great quantities and varieties, and a group of musicians was setting up and tuning their instruments at the far end of the hall. Her head was still spinning; the words the King had spoken to her still whirling about in her mind like a dream. The Lady led her to a large table festooned with garlands of greenery and lavender and bade her sit. The rest of the night was a seemingly never-ending parade of the finest foods, the best music, the merriest dancing, and the happiest faces Myka had ever seen. Even the animals joined in the merriment, with small animals scampering about table to table begging for food, the larger ones bobbing along with the music. Bray was prancing around by the far door, tossing his mane and whinnying every now and again in glee. She looked, but Myka couldn't see Tenk anywhere in the crowd. However, there was so much going on that she had stopped looking for it after a few minutes. Person after person would approach Myka and hug her or congratulate her, or just give a small smile of encouragement. She had never before felt such acceptance. She had never before been part of such a *family*. It was, in a word, overwhelming, and by the time the musicians had packed up to go, Myka was exhausted and could hardly wait to find a place to sleep for the night. As it was, she had no need of finding a place, for the Lady of Lanthor, seeing her exhaustion, had called for the two women in blue, who had come to Myka's side and helped her from the Great Hall.

Once outside, in the calm and quiet of the soft night, Myka walked in complete silence with her two attendants. Sensing her need for contemplation, they said not one word but simply led her to a little cottage, opened the door, and let her in.

If one more thing could have taken her breath away this day, it would have been this little house. For, being no bigger than her dwelling in Cenecal, it was the exact opposite *of* it. Where hers had been dark, dreary, and harsh, this was light, bright, and welcoming. A small bed, replete with a goose down comforter and soft pillows—the type of which she had always imagined the Courtiers of Lord Bythim's court slept upon —were piled high. A nightstand with a jug of cool, fresh water awaited her on one side of the bed, and a nightstand with a vase of lovely flowers from the palace gardens adorned the other. A fire was crackling cheerfully against the far wall, with an entire pile of chopped wood next to it. A lovely carved rocking chair was set in front of the fire, with a soft woven blanket neatly folded upon the seat. The windows (there were four of them!) were fixed with colorful curtains, but not the gaudy, flowery type an old, stodgy woman might have. Everything about the cottage was warm and bright and overwhelmingly perfect. It was as if someone knew her.

That thought, and no other, informed her dreams this night as she literally fell into the soft bed and into the calmest sleep she had ever experienced. Someone *knows* me. Someone knows *me*. *Someone* knows me.

CHAPTER FIFTEEN:
The Telling of Things

Her eyes fluttered open with the birdsong. She sat up slowly, relishing the soft comforter and not wanting to budge from the bed. The events of the last night came spinning back into her mind like the ladies who had danced and twirled upon the marble floor with the handsome men of Palem.

None of this made sense. Somehow, she had appropriated and absorbed it yesterday, but today, after a refreshing sleep, she was having trouble. She, an orphan from Cenecal, old and unwanted for a lifetime…she was…royalty? A daughter of a King? She looked over at the nightstand with the flowers on it. There, sparkling in the morning sunlight, was the delicate silver crown the King had affixed upon her head last night. Next to it, someone had put her stones and the book, along with her old clothes, which had been folded neatly after been obviously washed.

Her old self and her new self. Right there on the nightstand for her to see. A crown and some tattered clothing.

None of this made sense.

She got up, washed her face with water from the jug, and slipped into her clothing. The lovely gown from last night was laying on the chair by the fireplace. She hardly remembered taking it off, so exhausted and overwhelmed was she. She thought to put it on again, but it just didn't feel right today.

Opening the door to the cottage, she stepped out into the bright sunlight and ran headlong into Bray, who was grazing on the green lawn. His head popped up, and he walked over and stuck his big nose in her chest. She scratched between his ears and almost cried for joy.

Who knew you were such a handsome fellow, eh?" she cooed at him as he lipped at her arm. Looking around, she called for Tenk. She hadn't seen it since yesterday afternoon with Azar, before the celebration. She called out to it, clapping her hands as was her custom to get its attention.

Seeing some rustling in a rose bush nearby, she walked over only to find a tiny snout emerge.

'Tenk, come out now. Where have you been all this time?"

Tenk came crawling out from the rose bush, and Myka was immediately struck by its size. For it appeared even smaller than it had yesterday, and its fur was even more patchy and dull. She picked it up and petted it softly. "Tenk, what is wrong with you? Are you sick, dear Tenk? I shall take you to someone for help. You will be alright, little one."

It clung to her side and stuck its snout under her arm. Worried about her friend, she picked up the pace and headed towards the palace, although she had no idea where to go. She went by the Great Hall, but it was empty, with no sign of life. Continuing along the marble path, she heard some voices and followed in that direction. Rounding a corner, she came upon a grand open pavilion, and there, in the center of it, was the King, laughing merrily amongst a group of people that Myka didn't remember seeing last night. Upon her arrival, they stopped, and the King smiled at her, waving her come.

"Lanthrea! Welcome! Come, have morning meal with us."

Clutching Tenk close to her side, she walked over and sat down at a large table with several others. They each greeted her, shaking her hand and giving their names. She, in turn, introduced herself as well.

It was as she was doing this that the King walked over and put his hand on her shoulder.

"It is good that you all get to know one another," he said, "but I'm afraid Myka is still offering you her old name, not her new one." With this, he turned and, in his booming, genial voice, said, "Ladies and Gentlemen, this is Lanthrea, daughter of the King and sister to you all here today!"

They exploded in applause, each of them greeting her by her new name. Myka found it completely unnerving, but who was she to argue with the King?

After a satisfying meal of hot oats and honey, the people of the pavilion all sat back and relaxed on the grass. The King sat in the middle of them and asked them each to tell of their journey to Palem. Myka listened, fascinated. For each person, there had a completely unique and wonderful tale of how the King had called them to Palem. One, named Fralen, had been a thief, in fact, a member of the Sarastans; it was some of his kind that had robbed Myka of her coin in the Prathian Desert. He lived his life marauding and killing for his own gain with no thought of it. One day he robbed an old man and beat him badly, leaving him to die on the side of the road. One of the items he had taken had been a drawing the old man had in his pocket. Thinking it worthless, Fralen had looked at it quickly, then tossed it away, but the image kept bothering him until he had actually gone back to find it in the desert sands. The image was that of a tree, broken and barren, devoid of life. The picture had made him angry, then sad. After the sadness had come guilt—a guilt so great he hardly had the courage to face it, but once he did, he had become despondent, to such a degree that he no longer wanted to live. He had met a man in a pub one night who told him of a place called Palem and the King, who he was told would be 'the only way forward'. So desperate was he to rid himself of the pain that he had traveled westward alone, finding himself eventually at the Great Abyss, where Azar had met him, and the rest was history. One woman named Brillanne told her story of her journey west. Born to a noble family in a land far to the east of Drymac called Br'nai, she was both beautiful and wealthy. Her position in the court, however, never satisfied her heart; no gold could cheer her, and no purchase brought her joy. After a myriad of attempts at self-satisfaction by way of an endless stream of banquets, travels, and the acquisition of the best and most beautiful things, she fell into despair. One day, her most faithful servant (a girl of great constancy and good spirit named Janue) was attending to her when Brillanne had become enraged. The mere fact that the girl was so kind and so at peace while simultaneously having nothing at all in terms of worldly gain or status was completely maddening. She had struck Janue that day for no reason other than that she had dropped a hairbrush, and she'd had her cast her out onto the streets. The next day, overwhelmed by guilt over what she had done, Brillanne found the girl and, letting down her pride, asked her how she could be so hopeful in spite of her low station and circumstance. The girl had told her of Palem and a King who didn't need to acquire things nor lord over others. A king who cared more for his servants than he did for himself, and a kingdom where wealth didn't matter at all. Intrigued by this story, she had begun the journey west (she told herself) simply to meet such a king, but in truth, the thought of finding joy was her real motivation.

The stories went on and on, each person's story different, each journey to Palem unique. It came time for Myka to tell hers when the King stood up, took a deep breath of the morning air, and said, "Thank you all. It is my joy to share in yours." Feeling suddenly quite dismissed by him, Myka hugged Tenk a bit tighter and wondered why she wasn't invited to tell her story. She hadn't much time to think about this, however, for the King motioned for her to come to his side as the others dispersed.

She stood up, still clutching Tenk, and followed him as he led her down the stone path into a quiet garden in front of a forested area. There, he sat down and asked Myka to join him.

Gesturing toward Tenk, he said quietly, "Your glottin, it doesn't seem well."

She exhaled a bit and held it close. "No. I was…I was going to ask someone for help. It seems sick, and I don't know what to do for it. I don't think it has eaten since we got here, and if you knew my Tenk, you'd know that wasn't normal." She looked up at the King imploringly. "Do you know what is wrong with it? Can you help it?"

The King smiled sadly and took another deep breath.

"Lanthrea, did you notice I stopped our discussion before you could tell your story?"

Glad he addressed that but confused as to why he ignored her plea for help with Tenk, she simply nodded, not knowing how far she could rightfully go in pressing upon the King with her questions.

"I didn't let you tell your tale because your journey here is not yet complete." He nodded at the glottin. "You ask why your glottin is not well, and you ask for my help to heal it. I can answer your question, but I will not help it—at least not in the way you think."

Myka was completely confused and once again feeling the anger and defensiveness that she had felt with all the others on this journey who had taken issue with Tenk: Petrul, Miranda, Neruk, and Azar. She pulled the glottin closer to her, feeling the tears begin to well, and her cheeks begin to flush. The King said nothing for a long time, and then, softly, he began to speak.

"Come, Afflicted One, and put that which you have chosen behind you. Put the King ever before you, for he desires your beauty and he will protect you." Looking at her intently, he asked, "Do you remember these words?"

Myka flinched. That was the passage from the book that had angered and confused her so. She nodded but said nothing.

"Do you know what they mean?" The King asked quietly.

Unable to speak, for fear she would cry, she simply shook her head.

The King continued. "Long ago, when your parents died, you were left alone. And with no one to tell you about me and my great love for you or how to find me, you had no choice but to care for yourself. Myka (here he called her by her old name) you did *such* a good job. And you found the glottin, and you invited it in, and you thought it helped you. But, Daughter. It was never to have been your job to care for yourself. And that (nodding at Tenk) well…you don't need it any longer. It is not what you think it is."

She looked up at him, heart pounding. "What do you mean?" she asked, completely confused and not a small bit threatened by his words.

"Your glottin, has it ever once offered you words of hope or encouragement?"

Myka's first inclination was to respond with a resounding 'yes', but something held her back. She thought about it, pouring over her life. She thought about the journey here and how she had, indeed, felt a chasm growing between her and Tenk. Its words had, in fact, never been encouraging nor hopeful but instead had always been warnings: of death, disease, and danger. But those warnings had always saved her, hadn't they? Hadn't she had learned to rely on them to stay alive in a dangerous world?

Not knowing how to answer the King, she simply said, "It has been my only help, sir."

He looked at her with great compassion. "It need be no longer, Myka. You have come this far. You are safe with me now. I will protect you….I promise."

Tenk, although weak, was whistling a warning as best it could. Myka held it close.

"But sir, I hardly know you. How can I trust you? And, if I may, you have not been there for me for fifty nine long years; Tenk *has* been." She bit her lip at her petulance, hoping he wouldn't become too angry.

He only nodded, no anger in his eyes at all.

"I have been there for you, Myka, but you would not have me. You could not see me for you had chosen the glottin, and until you let it go, I cannot do much at all. Will you let it go?"

She squeezed Tenk all the more.

"But, sir…I have no one else."

"You have me."

"But you were never there for me before. I had no one…"

"I was always there. Tenk's protection of you was weak, inadequate, and, if I may, often sheer coincidence. It has no real power to protect you. Its warnings only served to frighten you, restrict you, and keep you from living fully. You are alive today and here in this place, not because of the glottin, but because of me. I have always been watching over you, daughter."

She was certain that he meant to comfort her, but instead, she found herself enraged. Risking his wrath, she fairly spit out her next words.

"You have *not*, sir. Never once have I been protected by anyone, nor watched over. I have been invisible to most and have had to rely on myself and dear Tenk just to *survive*. I have been alone my entire life. So alone…and so afraid." And here she started to cry, great sobs between gulps of air, and she couldn't stop. Feeling like a three-year-old child, she pulled Tenk even closer and turned her back to the King.

She felt his hand on her shoulder, and certain he was going to punish her somehow for her impertinence, she pulled away.

"Do you have the mirror the Lady gave you?" Was all he said.

She sniffed and turned to face him, wondering what kind of question this was. His expression, not of anger, but still full of compassion, surprised her. "Mirror..I…I…yes, I have it here." Pulling it out of her pocket, the King took it from her hand and opened it.

"Daughter, look."

She looked at herself in the reflection, surprised once again at her image.

"Do you remember what the Lady said to you? You have always been this lovely, daughter. You just had no eyes with which to see. You were wrongly disposed to see the truth about yourself. Do you remember?"

She nodded, remembering.

He gently closed the golden compact and handed it back to her.

"So it has been with your ability to know my presence and involvement in your life. You had chosen your glottin and your own self-reliance to survive, knowing no other way. Those choices warped your perception. But Myka, I am now offering you another way."

She inhaled and tried to calm her crying, her breath coming in short little gulps like a child.

Looking at him now, his eyes were still full of compassion and love and acceptance. Maybe she could believe him. Maybe he *had* seen her, known her, and watched over her for her entire life. Dare she believe this?

"I don't know how to accept your offer," she finally said helplessly.

He threw back his head in relief and grasped both her shoulders with his strong hands.

"That is an excellent response, daughter. Let me help you." He nodded at Tenk. "Put the glottin down," he said softly "you cannot keep both fear and faith in your hands. The glottin offers nothing but fear. Myka…*Lanthrea*, I am offering you faith. A new name. A new identity. New relationships. Put the glottin behind you. It is time. I cannot be what you need me to be until you choose me over *it*."

She looked down at Tenk. It was still clinging to her but was so shrunken and thin and weak now that she could barely hear its whistling.

The King spoke again. "Know this. Its help was never for your good. You know why they are called glottins, don't you? Because they are gluttonous creatures with voracious appetites. They feed off your fear, and they offer you nothing in return but terror. They do not keep you safe, woman; they keep you from life and chained to terror. Their friendship is a pretense, they have but one goal, once let into a person's life. To utterly destroy you. Here now—think back on the day Tenk chewed the book back in Cenecal? And then threw it into the fire at the hunting cabin? Daughter, it would have done anything to keep you from reading the words of life and hope found in those pages." She thought back, remembering how Tenk had taken the book, half eaten the cover, then hid it in the firewood. And then lied - pretending hunger had motivated the entire episode. She looked at the king helplessly, her eyes wide in disbelief.

He sighed deeply. "It has never once been for you. Put it behind you, Lanthrea, and let me protect you."

She looked down again. Tenk was the size of a small rat now, with hardly any fur left, looking quite pitiful. It looked up at her as it had for so many years, yet this time, her eyes seemed to be opened —for she saw Tenk through the lens of truth. What she saw made her draw back in horror. For as it looked at her now, she could see its true self. Its once soft eyes now held instead a certain evil, and its silly snout was lined with terrible sharp teeth, which it was now baring at her as it snarled and thrashed about. Its entire countenance was that of darkness; a ravenous predation she had never been able to see before.

Shocked (and not a small bit uneasy), she looked at the King, picked Tenk up from her lap, being careful of its teeth, and looked at it sadly. She then took a deep breath and handed it over. The King took it from her carefully (thrashing about though it was) then turned and walked away from her toward a forested area not far from them. She could hear Tenk's furious whistling trailing away from her as the King entered the woods.

For a moment, she felt as though she was falling off a cliff, like the moment as she fell into the Great Chasm. But then, almost instantly, she felt a fierce peace come over her. An unusual peace, an active peace. It was like nothing she had ever experienced before. The next thing she felt was relief. She had been protecting herself for almost sixty years, and she was exhausted, completely and utterly so. She felt as though a weight of inestimable measure had been lifted from her heart.

Sitting in the wake of this relief, she saw the King returning from the forest, hands empty. Tenk was nowhere to be seen.

"Did you….did you kill it?" she asked sadly.

The King smiled, "I didn't have to. Once in my hands, it simply disappeared. Glottins cannot live in my presence. That is why it was getting smaller and weaker once you arrived here. Fear has no purchase in the presence of Love. But look! I have brought you another companion, a faithful and true friend. Behold!"

Out from the forest, Braydenthal himself came galloping towards her, head held high, nostrils flared, mane flying in the wind. He pulled up short next to her, bent his neck down, and touched her with his velvet nose.

She laughed in delight. "Bray! Sweet Bray," she exclaimed, rubbing his forehead and scratching under his mane.

Looking up at the King, she smiled. "But this is not a new friend. He has been with me since Lake V'esta, Sir."

"Yes, and even before that," the king replied. "It was I who tied him in the desert for Cla'neen to find. He has been helping and watching over you ever since. You thought him simply a stray horse, but he was a gift from my hand. And, as your real name is Lanthrea, let me tell you his." He lay his hand upon the horse's neck.

"Lanthrea, meet Elpinhoeve. His name means 'hope on hooves' in the ancient tongue."

Elpinhoeve arched his neck and bowed before her as he had yesterday when she had first seen him with Azar. She found herself giggling like a schoolgirl and stood, then curtsied back.

The King looked at her and raised an eyebrow. 'Well, then. Aren't you going to go for a ride?"

She took one look at the King, laughed out loud, then swung herself onto Elpinhoeve's back, kicked him into a gallop, and rode like the wind on the back of Hope into the inviting forest of Palem.

CHAPTER SIXTEEN:
The Returning

The next few weeks seemed as though they were a dream. Between sitting at the King's feet and learning from him, then exploring the land on Elpinhoeve's strong back, Lanthrea was happier than she had ever been. Never having known freedom from Tenk's constant fear-mongering and the terror it brought, she felt as though her heart had been set free, and, in truth, it had.

In her short time so far in Palem, she had met so many incredible creatures and people. She had seen so many wonders. She had even met a relative (many generations past) of the little doe from the book, the one with the tiny silver crown. It turned out that it was one of the few remaining talking animals that had long ago made their escape from other lands and came here to avoid being hunted. She discovered that all the talking animals here wore silver crowns to ensure everyone knew who they were. Her most wonderful experience, however, had been her opportunity to see and even swim in the pool beneath the great living waterfall— the drawing of which she had been so intrigued.

She learned that her old, weak voice was a delight to the King, and others seemed to enjoy it when she sang Drymacian folk songs in the Great Hall now and again. Everything about her seemed redeemed in some manner or fashion—each thing surprising her more than the last.

It was about the sixth week of her stay in Palem when her heart began to feel a stirring. She couldn't explain it nor identify it, but it was like a whisper she couldn't ignore. One day, while sitting in a shaded glen in the forest with the Lady, she brought the subject up.

"Lady, I have something to ask you."

"Ask away," the Lady smiled as she plucked a wild rose from a nearby bush and inhaled its fragrance.

"I have begun to feel…unsettled. Like…rather like the anxiousness I used to feel in Drymac, but not as fearsome. Like a happy anxiousness. Does that make any sense?"

The Lady laughed. "It does, child. It happens to all who come here at one time or another."

Lanthrea (she had taken her new name by now) looked at her questioningly.

"It is the Call to Return, child, clarified the Lady. "Did you think the King brought you here to stay forever?"

Lanthrea had never thought about it. This place seemed like the Forever Land some people still spoke of, even in Drymac. Could anything, after all, be better than this?

The Lady, intuiting her thought, said, "No…this is not the Forever Place…the only passage to that Land is through death. This is Palem, the place of peace, the land of the King. This is where you learn and are changed forever. This is where you are given a new name. And it is from here that you return."

Lanthrea sat up straight, uncomfortable with the lady's words. "Return?" she asked, "return to where?"

"From whence you came, child. Back to Drymac in your case. To love others with the love you have received, and to tell anyone who will listen of this place."

Instantly she thought of Petrul and Miranda. "Ohhhh...." She exclaimed, her mouth dropping open. "Oh, my Lady, did you ever meet a lovely couple named Petrul and Miranda? Had they ever *been* here?"

The Lady laughed again. "Of course, child. They were here when they were first married. Their old names were Mactoff and Nara. They were brought here by the death of their first child. So full of grief were they that they had given up on life itself. Taken to drink and self-loathing and blame of each other for their loss. So paralyzed were they by their sorrow that we had to send Azar *to t*hem in Cenecal to lead them here. Of course, this was long ago, when believers in El-Gudan and the King were plenty, and Azar could enter the town without restriction."

"El-Gudan, yes. The King has spoken of him. Can you tell me more about him?"

"He is the High Lord of All, child. No one has ever seen him, but from him, all exist. The King will tell you of him in good time."

Lanthrea fell silent. "Petrul and Miranda…they tried to tell me of Palem. But I was so offended. I was so…afraid."

The Lady smiled. "All are, child. If El-Gudan's hand had not softened your heart, even you would have been unable and unwilling to follow it west."

It was all a bit much for Lanthrea, and she fell silent once again.

"Lady," she finally spoke. "When do I return? And what is to be my mission there?"

"Questions best left for the King," she answered kindly. "But if you are already feeling the Call to Return, then it is time to ask the questions."

They left the forest that day, with Lanthrea still feeling the anxious excitement and ready to inquire of the King in the morning.

***

Slipping into her new clothes and gently affixing her silver crown to her long gray hair, Lanthrea left her cottage for the last time. She fluffed the pillows just so and smoothed the comforter on the bed. Elpinhoeve was waiting for her outside the cottage, wearing the saddle and bridle of a simple horse, not the silver breast collar and sparkling bridle of Palem. She mounted easily, feeling the youth of her sixty years - as odd as that seemed. For her day of birth had come while she was here, and a new decade had begun for her. She was aware that she was closer now to the Forever Land, but she didn't feel it this morning. Today she felt young. Her back and muscles strong, her hair thick, shining and flowing underneath her crown, and her face alive with a broad smile. Her blue eyes shining, she rode slowly toward the Pavilion.

As promised, the King was there to meet her. He, and he alone. He walked to Elpin, grabbing his bridle.

"Are you ready, then?" he asked, smiling.

She nodded. "I am, my lord." She stopped and looked at him sideways, "And you will be with me all the way?"

He threw his head back in his joyful manner she had come to love and laughed. "Forever and always, Lanthrea. Now, let me do a few last things for you before you go. First, give me your crown."

She felt as though a dagger had just gone through her heart. For the little silver crown reminded her daily of her status as his daughter. To give it up filled her with great sorrow. Nevertheless, learning to trust him as she had, she took it off and handed it over. Taking it in his hands, he turned around from her and spoke some words she couldn't quite hear. When he again faced her, the crown was no longer in his hands but instead was a small silver ring.

"Here. It would do no good for you to return to Cenecal with a crown on your head. Wear this instead to remind you of your place in my court."

She slipped it on her finger and smiled. It was perfect, just like everything the King did.

"Now, for the last thing," he said, his eyes sparkling. "Hand me your stones, the ones you gathered on your way here."

She handed them over hesitantly, wondering what on earth he wanted with a handful of rocks, but pulled them out of her saddlebag (a real, leather one for this journey!) and plopped them into his hand.

He took them, and drew a small circle in the soft dirt below him, then placed them inside.

Looking at them, he quickly plucked out the yellow one she had picked up by the river before the flood and tossed it aside. He then knelt down and began moving the stones into a pattern, arranging them very specifically until a lovely mosaic appeared. Speaking again over the stones, but in a language she couldn't understand, he then picked them up, as they were now somehow cemented together in a kind of flat, round shape—like a small plate.

"This is your crest, Lanthrea. The story of your journey here, set in order by my hand."

She pursed her lips. "But why did you throw away the yellow river rock, my lord? I rather liked that stone. That's why I picked it up."

"Indeed, but it was not from my hand, child. It is I who sent you the others. You found that one on your own. You say you rather liked it, but it did not capture your heart. Your stones, as your story, cannot be arranged by your own hand." With this, he handed her the little mosaic, with all her lovely stones set therein, looking somewhat like a small shield. She slipped it into her saddle bag and thanked him.

He then looked deep into her eyes and gave her what could be thought of as nothing other than a benediction.

"Go now and pour yourself out for others. Love well and love all. And tell them, any who will listen, of this place. I will be with you in the joy and in the danger - for there will be both. Find those who are hurting, in despair and terror like you were. Let them know there is another way. Let them know that life without fear and life with great love awaits them."

Her eyes welling with tears, she nodded as she placed her hand over her heart. His words would live there now. She bowed before the King, then climbed onto Elpin's strong back, clucked her tongue and kicked him into a gallop.

CHAPTER SEVENTEEN:
The Valley of Sorrow

Elpin was struggling—his hooves slipping on the rocky path as he continued to painstakingly pick his way down the steep switchbacks. Lanthrea (glad of a saddle) used the stirrups for balance, leaning back as far as she could to help better distribute her weight on the horse's back. She thought more than once of dismounting, but looking down at the steep, narrow pathway they were on, she had ultimately decided to let the horse carry her. His four feet would do better than her two.

She had been given very specific directions from the King on how to return to Drymac, and she had assumed the trip would be an easy one. How wrong that assumption. It had been almost three days now, and the roads had been rough, full of high mountain passes and deep ravines—the weather formidable, with wind and rain almost every day. Food of any sort had been sparse as well and had she not a full saddle bag with dried meats, berries, and cheese, she could not have had eaten much, if anything, since she'd left Palem. Mercifully, there had been good grazing for Elpinhoeve and brooks aplenty, providing water for them both.

Elpin skidded down another few feet on the path, rocks clattering over the drop-off and falling to the valley floor below. Lanthrea closed her eyes and didn't look down. She would have to trust her horse's footing and instincts to get them to the bottom. If this afternoon had been rainy, it was a foregone conclusion that they wouldn't have made it even this far; the rocky trail would have been too slick for a horse, perhaps even a mountain goat! As it was, the mid-summer sun was shining brightly and getting warmer with each foot they descended. Taking a deep breath and exhaling slowly to calm her nerves, Lanthrea tried to relax in the saddle. If the King had sent her this way, she would have to trust his directions. But it was getting more difficult each day. It was so much easier to trust him in Palem, where she slept in her quaint cottage, ate good foods with her friends in the Great Hall and at the airy pavilion, and wanted for nothing. She, in three short months, had forgotten how hard life was outside of Palem.

Although it seemed to take forever, it was only a matter of minutes before Elpin made his final slide and skidded safely to the bottom of the trail. He stood with his muscles shaking for a few minutes, chest heaving and lathered in sweat. Although he had been moving slowly, he had exerted tremendous energy descending the precipitous switchbacks and was exhausted. Lanthrea slipped out of the saddle immediately, quickly surveyed the valley floor, and walked him over to a large grove of trees with a small stream babbling happily nearby. Pulling off the saddle and bridle, she patted Elpin's hind end as he trotted over to drink and graze. She found a stump on which to toss the saddle and bridle, then stretched her muscles for a bit. The sun was hot down on the valley floor, and the shade of the trees felt good. She wandered over by Elpin, grazing by the stream side, and filled her water pouches before flopping down against the trunk of a tree to drink.

Reaching into her pocket, she pulled out the small paper folded therein. Opening it, she looked again at the map the King had given her. The trail they had just descended opened up into this green valley, in which they were to continue east for about a day before heading due north and running into their next obstacle: ascending the Cliffs of

Abalor. She folded up the map and sighed. It was hard enough getting *down* from this last incline, which was seemingly incidental enough to not even be mentioned on the map. The thought of scaling some cliffs formidable enough to be drawn and named on a map was daunting, so she dismissed it quickly and thought to have a bite to eat rather than worry unnecessarily. One thing the King had taught her during her time with him was how to not imagine a terror but to wait and see what was real. Tenk had always scared her badly with its imaginings and continual warnings. She never had any agency to refute Tenk or the terrors it foretold and the horrors she imagined. Until now.

She got up and walked to the old stump on which sat the saddle, pulled some cheese from a saddle pack, and decided to walk about and explore a bit while eating. The valley was really quite lovely. Full of deciduous trees and berry bushes, the continual rain as of late had made the entire place green and lush. It was as she was following the little brook that she heard a rustling in the bushes in front of her. She stopped, waiting to see what might be the cause, only to see a pair of golden eyes staring at her from behind a particularly large blackberry bush. She froze, then began to back away slowly. Not knowing any creature with golden eyes outside of wild cats and having some small experience with mountain lions in the foothills of the Ciracs outside of Cenecal, she knew better than to run. She continued to back away slowly, raising her arms above her head to appear large. If it were defending young or even simply guarding its territory, it might be apt to attack. She also thought to back away from the brook, away from Elpinhoeve, as she had also seen what a mountain cat could do to the hindquarters of a horse —raking their flanks with sharp claws as they brought them down for a kill. The thought made her shudder.

Within a second, and before she could prepare for it, an absolutely enormous mountain cat leapt from the bush and charged her. She screamed, stumbling backwards over a rock, only to find herself helplessly scrambling to get up as the great cat pinned her to the ground. Closing her eyes, she turned her head and waited for the inevitable bite to the throat. It was in that frenzied moment that she saw Elpin charging through the brush, shrieking and striking at the great cat. The cat turned, growling, and charged at the horse, allowing Lanthrea a moment in which to roll quickly away and scramble behind a tree. Between the horse screaming and the great cat growling, the dust of the hooves, and the white of bared teeth and claws, Lanthrea was having trouble knowing what was happening as she stood, shaking behind the tree trunk. At one point, she heard what sounded like bones breaking and a great squeal followed by a thud. Afraid to look, she waited until all was quiet and then slowly looked around the tree. The cat was lying, its back broken by the look of it, on the ground, covered in dust and blood. Elpinhoeve was standing over its dead body, chest heaving, covered in sweat, with a huge gaping wound on his withers, flesh literally hanging off as though it had been flayed. Lanthrea gasped and ran to him, trying to assess the damage.

Elpin was bleeding badly, and she knew she needed to make some sort of a salve or compress. Running to the brook, she grabbed a handful of mud from the bank and ran back to Elpin, gently applying it to the wound. It was hardly enough to stop the bleeding, even after three applications, but it would help. It seemed to ease his pain somewhat as well, but he was limping badly as he followed her slowly back to their small campsite. She dug in the saddle bag and found nothing to help outside of a small bottle of ligament oil she used for her knees every now and again. It would do once the wound began to heal, to soften the scab, but would offer nothing of any benefit now. She slumped down on the ground and began to cry, helpless as she was to assist Elpin in any appreciable way.

Elpin limped slowly over to the brook and had a good long drink, then went about grazing, his breathing slowing and the whites of his eyes calming. Lanthrea watched him, blinking away her tears. Maybe he would be alright. She really knew nothing of horses and how they might heal from a wound such as this. The biggest problem, she assumed, would be wound fever, and all she could do was hope for the best. One thing was certain. She would not be riding him out of this valley. At least not now. She slumped against the tree stump and took mental inventory of their situation. The valley was lush and would no doubt provide food and water for weeks if needed. She had, before leaving Palem, packed poles and a tarp to make a lean-to, the type of which Cla'neen had made, having found it so helpful in the Prathian Desert. The canopy here was thick, with high oak and poplar trees aplenty to fend off wind and rain and the worst of the elements, and the summer weather would last at least two more months before autumn came knocking. Her main concern was that of the wildlife that obviously dwelt here in this lush land, but there was nothing she could do about that except keep her food packed away and her eyes and ears open. She decided, once again, to eat, as she had dropped the hunk of cheese when the great cat had charged her. She pulled a piece of dried meat from her bag and chewed it slowly. She must have been exhausted, for she was asleep before she knew it, with the saddle as her pillow and her wounded friend still grazing by the brook.

Elpin's soft nose awakened her. He was nudging her and nickering softly. Shaking off the sleep, she jumped up and looked at his wound. The mud had slipped off, but the bleeding had lessened considerably.

"Let's get that wound cleaned now, shall we?" She spoke softly to him as she grabbed his mane and walked him over to the stream. He followed willingly, head down, and a slowness to his movement that let her know he was in considerable pain. She took the cool water and splashed it on the wound, over and over, until all the mud was gone, and the flesh was exposed and raw. It didn't look as bad as she thought it would. The main problem was, again, wound fever. She felt his withers all around, and he did feel quite warm to the touch. She bit her lip, trying to think of what to do. The flap of skin needed to be sewn back on as well or cut off completely. She decided it best to leave the wound open to the air and let the skin fall off on its own. She took a deep breath. At Drymac, in the woods of the Circacians, there was a plant that grew… she racked her brain. What was that plant? It was said to have healing properties and could make a good poultice on open wounds. All she remembered about it was that it was a deep green low growing shrub with leaves that had three (or was it four?) spiky prongs. She had seen it only a few times, but that was back before her mother had died, and she was only five years old. Her memory of it was more an amalgam of ideas than a real memory. It couldn't hurt to try, though.

She patted Elpin and started walking, wary of any movement at all in the bushes. A bird or two fluttered out of some salmon berry bushes, and she about jumped out of her skin but calmed herself and continued to search for any low-growing dark green plants. She found one, but its leaves were rounded, and it had a white flower that she didn't remember seeing as a child. The next one she found was a good candidate. Low-growing, deep green leaves with three spikes on each. It was worth a try.

She plucked a great many of the leaves, noting that the sap poured out white and smelly, and she hoped it didn't hurt her hands. Taking the leaves back to her little camp, she dug in her bags for her bowl (a small wooden thing that she had taken from the Great Hall with the permission of Mintra, a lovely woman who helped with service there). She found a good, palm-sized stone and used it and the bowl as a mortar and pestle, crushing the leaves into a poultice. It smelled badly, and she had to hold her breath to get through the task.

Elpin was grazing again but seemed listless, nibbling at the grass but not tearing at it hungrily like he usually did.

"Here, boy, let's try this, shall we?" She ran her hand down his neck to his wither, noting that he flinched when she got within a few inches of the wound. "I fear this is going to hurt, boy. Hold still now…ho..ho…easy." She continued talking to him gently as she applied the smelly mash on the wound. He pulled away from her at first, but she noticed that by the last application, he had relaxed considerably. She took a tiny bit of the paste and stuck it on her tongue. It went numb immediately! That, if nothing else, encouraged her, and she said a little prayer that it would help heal Elpin as well as relieve his pain.

She spent the rest of the day and early evening making a proper camp and then lay down in her makeshift tent to read from the book. She had learned how to read the ancient language during her time in Palem and no longer needed the assistance of the King's magic to do so. The words were just as revelatory, but it was a joy to be able to open to any page and read. She learned that the book contained the words of El-Gudan, the High Lord of All, and had been written to instruct and encourage His followers and those who had followed the call westward to the King. There were very few copies of it left, and in places like Drymac, there were only a handful. Lord Bythim had seen to it that the lion's share of them were destroyed when he had taken control of the kingdom.

He had learned the danger of the thing: that people who read it were inexplicably *un*afraid of him and, while remaining compliant to the general rule of law, were unwilling to entirely submit to all of his edicts. Robbing others to line the court's coffers for instance, was a popular civic requirement. Known as the 'Duty to the Treasury' it offered a small portion of the spoils gained to the thief himself. It was to edicts such as this which the followers of the king would not submit. This active resistance infuriated Bythim. To this end, he had had the books rounded up and burned, and their owners either imprisoned or executed, depending on their level of non-compliance.

Lanthrea remembered how Maruk had reacted when he had seen her with it at the Market that day. She now understood. Wondering how her old friend was and excited to see him again soon, she settled in and opened the book to the chapter with the illustration of the winged horse. It had always captivated her, and now, having actually met one in Palem, it had become her favorite chapter of the book. She traced the figure of the winged creature lovingly, remembering the first time she met Garanthor only a few weeks ago.

She and Elpin had been out for a ride in the Forest of Palem, and the trees had just opened up onto a large, sunny meadow, Elpinhoeve's favorite place to gallop. They were just picking up speed when, far above them, they saw what Lanthrea assumed was a giant hawk or an eagle circling slowly, getting lower with each pass.

By the time she had realized it wasn't a hawk at all but some kind of winged horse, Elpin had realized it too, rearing up terrified and dumping Lanthrea onto the soft ground. Elpin ran like the wind for the trees, but Lanthrea had stayed put as the beast landed, rather helpless to outrun it as it snorted and pawed the ground. It was at least two times the size of Elpinhoeve, and its wingspan was that of a small building. Its coat was of a glistening grey, with a magnificent black mane and tail, both of which hung nearly to the ground. She stood slowly, noticing the silver crown on its head, and exhaled happily. The talking animals were firmly devoted to the King, and if nothing else, she could trust its goodwill.

He had folded his enormous grey wings gracefully over his back and approached Lanthrea, bowing low before her before saying (in the lowest voice she had ever heard),

"Greetings, O favored of the King. My name is Garanthor of Eldenhall, from the clan of Mygrathia. May I inquire of yours and of my cousin, the horse?"

Lanthrea's heart was pounding, but she stood her ground and bowed back at the giant beast.

"My name is Lanthrea, from Cenecal in the kingdom of Drymac. My horse is named Elpinhoeve, and I'm afraid he is…well, a bit timid today."

Garanthor looked over at Elpin (still peering out at them from behind a tall elm tree) and began to whinny and nicker simultaneously, something Lanthrea assumed akin to laughter, and responded (between whinnies,) "I see that, human…I see that. He glanced again at the horse who was watching them, quite wide eyed, from behind the tree. "Do you think he might *ever* come out?" And then he nickered and whinnied again for quite a while.

It took some time, but eventually, Elpin came out and met his huge cousin, looking almost like a toy next to him. He took to grazing in the green meadow as Garanthor had spoken to Lanthrea about his kind's interesting and sad history. He told her that he and his brethren were once everywhere, flying wild and free in the skies of all the kingdoms. But now they were rare, even here in Palem. Most had been hunted by merciless men in other lands who either wanted their wings on their walls as trophies or their mighty strength for use in their wars. Either way, it meant the death of most of them, and Lanthrea was saddened by the conversation. Garanthor had been brought to Palem as a colt by a kind man who found him wounded in the Forest of Landor. He had been here ever since, rarely leaving Palem. He then had invited Lanthrea for a ride, but she had declined, feeling bad for Elpin (not wanting to make him jealous) and also uncertain of her ability to stay on such a beast during the flight. Garanthor had nodded, bowed his long neck in farewell, then took back to the sky, a mighty whinny as he went.

She closed her eyes and remembered him now, smiling, grateful for the chance to meet him.

Turning the page, she began her reading for today.

Call to the King, and he will give you courage.

A fitting passage for today's meditation. For she needed courage if she were to stay in this valley, with who-know-what other predators and a lame horse to protect. She was feeling less than courageous today and also not a small bit irritated. This setback would cost them dearly, and if Elpin didn't recover from his wound….her heart broke at the thought of it. She reminded herself not to imagine the worst and used the passage she was reading for direction.

"Lord of Palem, my king, I call to you from this valley. I am afraid. For myself, for Elpin, for the journey. Please give me courage."

It was a simple request, the kind the King himself had taught her. She immediately felt peace come over her, the quiet peace of giving a hard situation over to someone greater than yourself, a *settled* peace, not the more fleeting kind—where you are certain of a given outcome but only for the moment.

It was an honest, clean feeling—full of hope and trust—like her prayer.

She closed the book, realizing that it was too dark to read without a fire, and having not yet started one, decided it time.

The summer heat really didn't call for a campfire, but the flames and smoke might keep the beasts and insects away and would allow her to see during the night.

She built one quickly, laying stones from the stream around it to keep it contained (the valley was lush and green, but one could not be too careful). Glancing over at Elpin, who was sleeping, head low, hip cocked next to her, she lay down on the soft dirt in her lean-to and closed her eyes. Hearing no rustling, no growls, no movement of any kind, she fell quickly into a dreamless sleep.

The sunlight filtered through the high canopy of oak trees, and Lanthrea felt its warmth even through her canvas lean-to. Yawning, she sat up and blinked against the light, then scooted out of the lean-to and stood to go and check on Elpin. She needn't have looked far, for he was right where she had left him last night, standing by the tent, grazing quietly. Walking over, she checked his wound and felt the skin around it. It was cool to the touch this morning—a good sign! She peeled the poultice she had made off and looked. The skin was beginning to scab, and there was no pus or oozing to be seen. Her heart rejoiced, and she patted him on the forehead, kissing his nose.

"You're gonna be fine, good boy," she said softly. "I'm going to make you another poultice. You stay here."

With that, she took the remaining leaves and pounded them into a mash, then applied them again to his withers. He didn't even flinch this time, and she was grateful beyond her ability to express. "Good king, I thank you for answering me. Thank you for helping my horse, and continue to give me courage on the journey home."

Suddenly realizing her hunger, she decided rather than use up some of her supply of dried meats and cheese, she would forage a bit instead. The valley obviously offered a fine variety of berries. Perhaps there were other delicacies as well.

Wishing she had a weapon of some sort beyond the small hunting knife the King had given her, she grabbed a large stick with which she figured she could at least scare off a predator, sharpened the tip, and headed into the brush beyond the little stream. She had a cloth gathering sack tied to her belt and hoped to fill it with fresh berries or mushrooms before returning to camp. As it so happened, her foraging proved more than fruitful, as she found a multitude of berries: black, salmon, and raspberry bushes grew in abundance in this rich, black soil. Additionally, she found wild apple trees—with a few almost ripe mid-summer fruit—and a goodly amount of mushrooms poking up from the pine needles left behind last fall. No predators were seen or heard, and she began to wonder if the great cat was perhaps out of its normal territory and was an aberration for this part of the valley.

With that as a hope, she took her bounty back to the camp and prepared a feast of sweet berries, sliced apples, and mushrooms (even breaking out one small bite of cheese from her saddlebags to round out the meal.)

Elpinhoeve continued to graze and rest by her side, and she noted his walking was less labored, and the limp was decreasing as well, as long as he was on flat ground. She assumed he would be unfit to ride for at least a week or two, but was beginning to think that their stay here might be far less than she had originally thought. He could, at least, be walked through the valley with her leading him on foot. They would have to decide what to do once they hit the Cliffs anyway, as there was no guarantee whatsoever that a horse could be ridden up them.

She thought today to try and secure a perimeter for her little camp, at least with some noise makers to warn her of any animals that might try to come near. To this end, she gathered up armful after poking armful of blackberry bushes (cutting them with the hunting knife) and laid the spiky bushes around the camp. They might deter smaller animals, maybe even larger ones, and they most certainly would rustle her awake if anything tried to cross over.

That task done, she sat down to look at the map once again. The valley they were in looked to be about a day's ride wide and two long. The cliffs were at the north end, meaning they would need to travel through the entire valley to reach them. She knew this already but was looking for a shortcut, if possible, for Elpin's sake. There didn't seem to be any quicker way out of the valley except to go through it.

Sighing, she folded up the map and closed her eyes to think. If Elpin were even better tomorrow, they could start the journey north, with her leading him. She would have to put the saddle on him, however, as she couldn't carry it any worthwhile distance. Worried that the tack might pull on his withers, she wondered if it was even worth a try. Groaning in frustration, she decided to see what she could see tomorrow. Tomorrow. Today, she could do some more exploring.

Armed with her (now sharpened) long stick, she tied her gathering bag around her waist and patted Elpin on the back. "Stay here, boy. I'm going to go look about a bit." Elpin barely looked up from his grazing, then was back to it. She smiled and patted him again, then took off into the woods, the same direction she had gone before when the great cat had attacked. Curious about the area and wondering if the cat had unfortunately left some kittens about in the undergrowth, she headed back towards the trees. Passing the cat's carcass was uncomfortable, and the rotting body was already putting up a great stink. Pushing past, she found a deer trail that led around the gigantic blackberry bush from which the cat had attacked. Hearing and seeing nothing of note in the bushes or dense undergrowth, she assumed the cat must have been a loner, perhaps out hunting. The deer trail she was on continued into a heavily forested part of the valley, and Lanthrea found it beautiful. The only animals she encountered on the trail were some rabbits, an occasional deer, and a plenitude of brown squirrels. She did, however, see the tracks from what looked like perhaps a fox or coyote and multiple cat tracks of various sizes that proved her attacker was not the only predator in these woods.

That fact made her quite uncomfortable. She was about to turn around and head back to camp when she saw smoke. Not the fast-moving, dark black smoke of a wildfire, but the white and gray stationary smoke of a campfire or a chimney! Blinking in disbelief (the map said nothing of inhabitants here) she walked towards the smoke, until turning a corner when a small dwelling came suddenly into view. A single little cabin made of rough-hewn logs, stacked and held together by some sort of clay, with a roof made of mud and pine branches and no windows whatsoever. The chimney was made of river rocks and was, indeed, spewing out smoke. Someone lived here!

A tightness in her chest informed her of her apprehension in approaching the little cabin, but it seemed impossible not to check it out. Perhaps whoever lived here could help with Elpin's wound or at least tell her of a quick way to the Cliffs of Abalor. And curiosity did the rest. Resisting the urge to turn around for fear of trouble, she walked up, stepped onto the porch of the place, and knocked on the door. For a second, nothing happened, but then she heard, from inside, a distinct rustling and then footfall. A moment later, the door swung open, and Lanthrea found herself face to face with a very old, very small woman. The woman had been crying—her eyes red, a used handkerchief in her hand. Her eyes widened in surprise upon seeing her guest, and she dabbed at her eyes, blinking from the sunlight.

"Greetings," Lanthrea said softly. "I, uh…I am traveling through your valley and saw your smoke. My name is Lanthrea."

The little woman cleared her throat, and when she spoke, it was as if she hadn't used her voice or even thought about speaking in the longest time.

"Er…um…My name…my name is…" her voice was hoarse, and she was having trouble finding words, "My name is…is…Mairen. Um…do, do…come in, if you must." She opened the door wide, and Lanthrea stepped inside. Once the door shut behind her, the place was completely dark, save for the light from the fireplace and one small lantern burning by a chair in the corner of the room. Letting her eyes adjust, Lanthrea stayed standing as the old woman tottered over to the chair and plopped down in it.

She didn't speak a word after this, and Lanthrea cleared her throat, wondering what to do or say.

"I uh…you uh…have a lovely home here," she stuttered, breaking the awkward silence.

Nothing from the old woman in the chair.

"I am traveling through the valley on my way to the Cliffs of Abalor. On my way to Drymac, to the north and east. Do you know of it?"

Silence from the old woman, who simply sighed deeply and continued to stare into the fire.

Lanthrea walked over by the chair, hoping to catch the woman's attention. "Have you lived in the valley for long? It is a lovely place."

The woman grunted and dabbed at another tear.

"Are you alright?" Lanthrea was getting quite concerned at this point. "Can I help you with anything?"

The woman said nothing but sighed a huge sigh, sounding for all the world like a bellows deflating.

Confused at this point and concerned as well, Lanthrea went over and knelt in front of the old woman.

"Mairen," she said softly, "Are you alone here? Is there anything I can do for you?"

The old woman dabbed at her eyes again and slowly turned to face Lanthrea.

"There is nothing that can be done," she said softly, her voice cracking from lack of use.

"About what?" Lanthrea pressed. "What needs to be done, Mairen?"

The old woman waved her hand at the cabin. "This. All this. There is nothing….." Her voice trailed off, and she began to sniffle and dab her eyes again.

Lanthrea was silent for a moment before having an idea that might soften her host's sensibilities. "Mairen, do you have any tea? And a pot?" The old woman nodded, pointing to a table in the corner. Lanthrea got up and grabbed a copper pot (which she noted was dented and unpolished, green with patina) and found a box of tea with but a few scant leaves therein.

She found a jug of water on the table as well, and filled the pot, then set it in the fire outright as there was no pot crane nor hook. She rustled about in the one cupboard she found (hard to see, for it was far from the lantern) and found one cup. It, too, showed the ravages of time and use but seemed clean and uncracked. It would do.

She put a small scoop of the tea leaves in the cup, then added the boiling water. Once ready, she then carefully picked out the leaves with her fingers (finding no utensil anywhere) and handed the cup over to Mairen.

"Here. Drink this. Tell me of your troubles, if you will."

Mairen took the cup, eyes wide with astonishment at the small kindness before filling once again with tears. But this time, the tears came like a waterfall, flowing down her cheeks and falling onto her rough cotton blouse. She cried for a few minutes before even taking a sip of the tea.

"I came here long ago, decades now, I'd guess," she finally said. "I, too, was on my way through this valley, on my way home from Palem, as I'm certain you are." She held the cup in her hands, warming them, and nodded at Lanthrea. "This is true, no? You are traveling through from Palem?"

Lanthrea felt like she'd been hit with a brick. "Yes, why…yes. I am. Mairen, you were at Palem? You know of the King?" Her excitement was growing by the second.

Mairen nodded, then took a small sip. "I was. And I do. For all the good it did me."

And here she set the tea down on the floor by her chair and stared again, blankly into the fire. "You asked if I was alone here. I am, but that was not always the case. I came here with my husband. We had journeyed to Palem together. He and I were heading home, so happy to start a new life together there. The King promised he would be with us, and we had been dense and naïve enough to believe him."

Lanthrea swallowed hard and shook her head. "No, no…Mairen, he would not have broken his promise. I just came from him, and he….he…would never leave you alone."

Mairen suddenly jerked her head and stared directly into Lanthrea's eyes. "Oh, he wouldn't, would he?" she snapped. "Well, he, in fact, did."

She kicked over the tea at her feet in her anger, shattering the cup and sending the hot water sizzling into the fire.

Lanthrea, confused, tried to stay calm. She looked at Mairen and asked quietly.

"What happened to your husband?"

Mairen looked as though a knife had just gutted her. "He was killed. By a great cat. On the second night of our journey through. The cat came out of nowhere, glowing yellow eyes….I remember the eyes." She shuddered here at the memory before continuing. "He was dead before I could scream. Dead and gone. I, myself, managed to get away from the cat's claws, but barely." She lifted her skirt to reveal a terrible scarring on her legs before continuing. I buried my husband over by the stream." She paused here for a moment before saying, "And I've been here, utterly alone, since that time. The King has not come to help me. The King did nothing to stop his death. The King is a liar, and Palem is a place of empty promises. Empty…." Her voice trailed off, and she went back to staring at the fire.

Lanthrea stood up, suddenly feeling the icy fear she used to when Tenk whispered its warnings to her. She could hear it now, "*Warning, miss. The king lies. Danger, miss.*"

Her mind reeling, she slumped down by the fire in the darkened room and tried to think. The King promised he would help. The King promised he would be with her on her journey. Why had he not done so for Mairen? Why would he leave her here all alone and in such pain? It made no sense. Having no answers at all, she suddenly had a thought.

Whipping around to face Mairen, she blurted out,

"I'm here, Mairen! Come with me! We will journey together out of this place. I had a friend once who accompanied me out of a desert. Let me be that friend for you!"

Mairen stared into the fire still before saying. "Oh, you're not the first to come here to my home and offer such nonsense."

Lanthrea was quite taken aback. "You mean, others have come through. And met you? And offered to travel out with you?"

Mairen nodded slightly. "Many. Many have come. But what good would it do to leave? My life was my husband. And he is gone. I wish not to live without him. The King has never bothered with me. Such a liar. He has never helped me, not once."

Lanthrea immediately had another thought. A lightning bolt of a thought.

"But Mairen, what if the others that have come…what if *they* were his good help? Sent by his hand to take you home? What of that?"

Mairen sniffed, the tears coming again. "No. No. The King thinks not of me. He let the cat take my dear Mangan, and he abandoned me to this place."

Lanthrea felt herself getting increasingly desperate and not a small bit frustrated.

"But Mairen, even if Mangan is gone, you can leave this place. You do not have to sit here, alone in the valley. Come with me, I beg of you!! Come with me. We will journey together. Mairen, what if the King has sent *me to help you???*"

She was almost frantic by now, her voice pleading. She reached over to take the old woman's hand, but Mairen pulled it away angrily.

"Leave me now," she exclaimed vehemently. "Leave me."

Lanthrea found her eyes filled with tears. "Please, Mairen, come with me. I can help you go home. Or at least out of this valley and to a new home. Anyplace you choose. Come with me."

Mairen turned her face back to the fire. She said nothing more.

Lanthrea stood helpless. She would leave the old woman alone for today, but she would come back tomorrow. Yes, tomorrow.

She leaned over and picked up the shards of glass from the broken teacup and tossed them into a waste bin she found in the corner. In so doing, she saw something at the bottom of the bin: a book, tattered and ripped. Could it be? She pulled it out, seeing a tree adorning the ragged cover. The book! Whipping around, she was going to hand it to Mairen but then thought the better of it while the old woman was in such a bitter state.

She left the little cabin, heading back into the bright sunshine, but gently set the book on the table by the lantern before shutting the door behind her.

Wandering back to her camp, she found it hard to be hopeful about anything. Perhaps Elpin will perish here as well—maybe his wound won't heal well after all. Maybe she herself would be attacked by a great cat and wounded too badly to ever leave. Perhaps she, too, would be stuck in the valley. Shaking off the dark thoughts, she went back and spent the afternoon alternately foraging and applying more poultice to Elpin's wound. She could hardly sleep that night, so anxious was she for the morning and her return to Mairen's cabin.

Up before the sun, she grabbed her stick, and fairly ran through the forest until she found the deer trail and followed it to the little cabin. Upon arrival, she knocked at the door, calling out for the old woman. This time, no sound of a footfall, no opening of the door. She knocked again, louder this time, calling out, "Mairen, it's me, Lanthrea. I have come to visit again....Mairen?"

She tried the door latch, only to find it locked, once again, from the inside.

Lanthrea visited the cabin every day for a week until Elpin had healed enough from his wound to begin their journey out of the valley.

The old woman never again answered the door.

CHAPTER EIGHTEEN:
The Cliffs of Abalor

In preparation for the long walk through the valley, Lanthrea had decided a weapon was necessary. During the week of Elpinhoeve's convalescence, she had heard the growls from the great cats at least three times. Once, it might have been a coyote, but it didn't matter. She needed to be able to defend both herself and her horse from another attack from *any* predator.

Using the hunting knife and a sturdy pole she had cut from a young poplar tree, she laced the knife to one end of the pole, strapping it with a leather tassel she had cut from the saddle. It had been decorative, so served no function anyway. She would walk, leading Elpin behind her, and they would travel only during the day, making camp at dusk. Being mid-summer, there were almost ten hours of daylight, so they would be able to make good time.

Cleaning up her little campsite, she had looked towards Mairen's cabin once again sadly and said a prayer for her. She realized there was nothing she could do for the old woman if she didn't want help. With that paralyzing thought, she had turned and started toward the north.

The day was bright and sunny, promising to be hot as well, so they had begun their journey before dawn. There were plenty of animal trails along the valley floor, and they had their pick of the easiest paths and the most level ground. Elpin had all but lost his limp, and his wound had scabbed over well. Lanthrea had been able to remove the flap of useless skin that had been hanging off the wound with her hunting knife once it had withered and was no longer attached to blood or sinew. She had also been able to stick the saddle on his back, careful to cinch it as far behind the wither as possible and loose enough so as not to pinch. Elpin seemed fine with that and was doing well as they walked along together on this lovely morning.

Only once during their journey north had Lanthrea had to use her makeshift spear to ward off a cat, and it had been a small one, probably a cub, out practicing its hunting skills. It had proved no problem and had scampered off at the first thrust of the spear and a few loud shouts from Lanthrea.

Their first night, they camped next to a small lake fed by a rocky waterfall. The sound alone had delighted her, and she had slept well that night, lulled by its melodies as the falls splashed into the lake. The second day proved as uneventful as the first; their only nemesis being the hot sun, as it was merciless today, and no breeze to help cool its intensity. They must have made good time, for it wasn't even mid-day when she could see the Cliffs of Abalor rising above them, about a half day's walk away. They were there by dusk, and it was then, and only then, that Lanthrea saw the enormity of their situation.

The cliffs were like none she had ever seen. Even the Great Abyss had not been as steep nor featureless. Essentially, the cliffs were simply a slick, white stoned wall, rising at a right angle from the valley floor and continuing up about a thousand feet. There was not a path, nor a switchback, nor even a plant adorning their surface. It was, in fact, a great wall of stone. Going straight up.

Lanthrea pulled the saddle off of Elpin, made camp, and watched as the sun set over the cliffs, their shadows casting a dark, foreboding gloom over the valley floor.

There was no visible way up that stony wall. It would be akin to scaling a thousand-foot castle wall with no footholds in the stone nor ropes or ladders tossed down from above.

It was, in a word, impossible.

She pulled out the map and looked at it again, more carefully than ever before. Had the King included any helpful hints she had not seen? Was there another way up, over, or around these monstrous stone walls? She thought for a moment of Mairen and her hopelessness and sense of abandonment from the King. No. She would not give in to that temptation. He had promised to be with her, in the joy and in the danger. But had she known he would burden her with impossible tasks?

Deciding to sleep on it rather than try and figure out an unsolvable puzzle when she was this tired, she set up her lean-to, ate a bit of dried meat, and drank from her water pouch. Elpin found a little puddle of water left over from the rains a few days ago and drank as well, then set about his usual grazing. Lanthrea sat next to the fire for a long time, reading the book and looking at the illustrations, and thinking about painting them again properly. She hadn't painted in so long now: there really hadn't been any time for that during her stay at Palem, and she had no need of coin there, anyway. She flipped through the book, looking at all the pictures again. Tonight, the one that she was most drawn to (and one she avoided looking at the most) was a page with what could be described as no other than demon creatures on it. It was a picture that had always confused her— juxtaposed as it was to the beauty and tranquility of the others—but tonight, she couldn't stop looking at it. She had a vague memory of seeing things like these creatures when she had been afflicted by the sand tines. Dark, shrieking demons with sharp teeth and many arms—

some with dark, jagged wings and all with blood-red eyes. Usually, she skipped over this page, but tonight, she couldn't seem to move away from it.

She tried to pray but found it difficult. For some reason, between the memories of those horrid creatures and the sharp, impossible cliffs before her, all she could do was feel anxious. Unsettled. In a word, miserable.

Sleep came, but not easily. And her dreams were full of darkness and evil, winged flying creatures.

Morning came on early—the summer sun hot—only intensified by its reflection off the white stony cliffs under which they were camped. It felt like they were in an oven, a great outdoor oven. Elpin was already glistening with sweat on his chest and under his mane, and the sun had only just risen. Lanthrea, having not slept well anyway, was cranky—the heat making her even more miserable. She stood, hands on hips, looking up and the wall of rock before her, craning her neck to try and see the top of the cliffs, which disappeared today into the soft white summer clouds.

Shaking her head, she shrugged and pulled out the map again. Had she read it incorrectly? Did the King really mean for her to scale this impossible wall of stone? With a *horse*? Knowing full well there was no new information on the map, she stuffed it back in her pocket and grabbed a bit of cheese from her saddle pack for a morning meal. It would do no good for her to be hungry as well as cranky.

They were camped about a stone's throw away from the cliff, so after her meal, Lanthrea thought to go inspect the cliffside close up. Perhaps she had missed something. Leaving Elpin to graze, she walked a hundred yards or so until she could touch the white rock. It was already hot from the sun's rays and slicker than she would have thought. Almost a polished sheen to the stone—slick and impenetrable. She slumped down and leaned against it. This wasn't an improbable task. It was an impossible one. She thought for a moment of Mairen, safe in the shade of her cabin in the woods. Maybe it was best she had stayed her life in the valley. For most certainly, anyone attempting to scale these walls of stone would perish.

Convinced of her assessment, she walked back to Elpin and decided, for lack of any other option, to travel a bit along the base of the cliff just to see if there was any deviation from what she was seeing now—perhaps a cleft or a cavern (hadn't they found one that took them through the cliffs above the tundra on their way to Palem?)

She slipped the saddle and bridle on Elpin, gathered her things, and led him along, headed east, as that would be her ultimate destination anyway. They had walked about an hour when the sun became too hot to bear, reflecting as it did off the cliffs. They were going to have to move away from them if they were to continue moving at all. The forest was only about a mile away, and sadly (with a great deal of resignation) Lanthrea led Elpin back toward the green, welcoming valley forest. The temperature reduced considerably the further they went from the cliffs, and by the time they reached the woods, it felt like they had arrived in another season altogether. She took the saddle off Elpin, and he immediately had a roll in the cool, green grass, then stood, shook, and began devouring it. Lanthrea, too, lay down in the grass, looking up at the green canopy above her, and enjoying the cool embrace of the green. While laying there, looking up at the sky, she thought to pray. "Good King, there is no way I can see to ascend those cliffs. There seems no way out of this valley."

It wasn't a good prayer, but it was hers for the moment at hand.

It was only mid-morning, but Lanthrea had already decided they would camp here, at the edge of the forest, in view of the great cliffs for their third night of the journey. She honestly did not think there was any way to move forward and was planning on heading back to Palem in the morning, tail between her legs and a slightly wounded horse at her side. The thought, though embarrassing, was also a happy one, as being back in Palem would feel like a dream at this point. She had failed in her Return as much as Mairen had failed in hers. It was that simple.

She set up her lean-to, lay her makeshift spear by the door thereof, and didn't even bother with a fire. It wasn't needed this time of year even in the relative cool of the forest's edge. She found a small stream with fresh water nearby and led Elpin over to it, filling her own water pouches as well. A great many small, finger-sized fish darted here and there in the little stream, and she tried cupping her hands to catch a few to no avail. She would have needed a dozen of them for even a bite, anyway. Grabbing a few berries from some nearby raspberry bushes, she popped them in her mouth, enjoying the sweet, juicy dinner more than any fish. Once back at her tent, she pulled out the book and thought to read a bit. Smiling, she remembered her lessons in reading the ancient tongue the book was written in. Having thought it old Drymacian, she learned from her tutors (the very two women in blue who had attended her from her first day in Palem) that the language was actually far more ancient than that. It was written in the time before time, in Palecian, the language of the El-Gudan, High Lord of All. Hard to learn at first, but it became easier with practice, as all things do. But, unlike other languages or skills, this one seemed to be a part of her, as if she'd known it her entire life but had simply forgotten. Learning it was more like *uncovering* a lost language rather than learning a new one.

She flipped it open to the unsettling page with the demon creatures again but skipped quickly past it. She didn't need those images in her head again tonight. Instead, she found the image of the lovely young woman, the one she had named 'The Courtier' the first time she'd seen it. The image was as lovely as it had ever been, but as Lanthrea looked at it this time, it caused her no pain. She remembered how she looked at it before when it felt like nothing but a comparison. One in which she would never have such beauty and could only be envious of it. Envious and sad. But today, as she looked at the maiden with the long brown hair, she only felt a sense of kinship. She, like Lanthrea, was simply a daughter of the King. They were Sisters in a broader, deep, and loving family. She sighed happily and let her eyes fall to the words below the illustration.

"For you are now a part of the King's family, each one serving a part, every part beloved and unique."

She read it three times, wondering what part hers might be. Maybe to just go back and tell people about Palem. But how? Suddenly it occurred to her. Hadn't she *just* been thinking about painting again? Hadn't that been her means of making a living in Cenecal? She would paint! She would paint her own pictures of all the wonderful people and animals and things she had seen in Palem. It made such easy sense! She remembered Petrul and his carvings of Palem and the Solemn Memories. Hadn't that been exactly what he had done? Used his talent to express the joy and the stories of the King. She closed the book, thankful for these thoughts. Yes. She would paint again. And tell the stories of Palem through the images, being careful to keep the pictures different enough from the book's so as not to attract Bythim's attention.

The problem, however, still before her was: how was she to get back to Drymac? The cliffs still loomed above her, and she wondered when she got back to Palem if the King would show her another way home or be angry with her for not succeeding in this one. She spent the rest of the day gathering wood for the night's fire, finding a few blackberry bushes to pick clean, and figuring out the easiest way back through the hills and switchbacks they had just descended to get to this valley. They would start back to Palem at dawn.

She slept that night uneasily. Something was wrong with her thinking. She just couldn't put her finger on it.

The sweet song of summer birds awakened her, and she flinched. Her back ached today, something she hadn't felt in the longest time. Wondering if she slept wrong, she twisted and stretched in the morning sun. Elpin had wandered over to the nearby stream and was grazing in the shade of a giant oak tree, and Lanthrea had a morning meal of berries and a bite of dried meat with it for variety. Her heart was singing, even as her back ached. She was heading back to Palem today! The very thought of seeing the King in person made her almost giddy. She chewed her salted meat slowly, enjoying every bite when suddenly an odd feeling came over her. She couldn't identify it at first. What was it? An old feeling…an unhappy feeling. *Defeat*. It was defeat. As if she had been given a task and had simply…given up. It was unlike her to ever give up, headstrong as she had always been.

She slumped down in the grass, head in hands. She couldn't just give up and go back. The King had told her to go this way and had offered no other direction. He must know better than she. Groaning, she looked up and over at the Cliffs in the distance. They hadn't gone anywhere, and they were just as impassible as they had been yesterday.

She kicked at the grass, tearing up a small divot of turf and sending it flying. If she were one to curse, she would have, loudly and mightily. Instead, she screamed out at the sky.

"Good king, what do you want me to do? The cliffs are impassible, yet I don't want to give up. Show me how I can do this!"

There was no answer. No lighting bolt. No sudden revelation. Just the warm morning sun on her back, a wounded horse, and an impossibly steep cliffside blocking her way out of this valley, casting its shadow as though to taunt her.

She got up slowly and decided to try the cliffs one more time. Maybe she had missed something in the heat of the day yesterday. She tossed the saddle and bridle on Elpin, packed up her things, and led him toward the walls of stone. This time of day, the heat reflecting off them wasn't as intolerable, and she found she *could* think more clearly than yesterday. Not that it did her any good. The stone was still just as slick, the cliffside still tall, and no passageway could be found through or over. She led Elpin about a mile along the base of the cliffs, looking for something, *anything* that might prove promising. Nothing presented itself outside of one place where there were some slight variations in the stone - indentations, if you will - and she even tried to scale the rock for a few moments before dropping helplessly and hopelessly back down to the ground.

The thought occurred to her as they walked along the cliffside that they simply couldn't go on forever. Perhaps if she walked to the end of the cliffs (there must be one!) then a way around them might be found. It was the best idea that she had in the the past two days, and what could it hurt? Remembering the valley was about a day's ride across (according to the map) and with hand walking a horse, about two, she thought to just continue along the base until nightfall, then try again in the morning. She was not going to let this obstacle win. She would find a way.

They walked all day, the sun getting progressively angrier and impossibly hot as it bounced off the stone and reflected back on them, but they kept going. Stopping at dusk, she found the evening considerably more bearable, as they were now in the shade of the cliffs, and it cooled down almost immediately once the sunset. She made camp, turned Elpin out to graze (there were some sparse grasses growing here and there at the base of the cliffs), and fell asleep without evening meal, being exhausted and so wrung out from the heat that she was not hungry at all.

It was at about the first hour of the new day, just after midnight, when something awakened Lanthrea. A slight hissing of the wind perhaps, or a rustling of leaves—she couldn't tell. Once awake, she sat up in her lean-to and listened more carefully. It was whispering. Soft, but nearby and getting louder. The hair bristling on the back of her neck, she wrapped herself tightly in her blanket and tried to hear the words.

"She won't come, you know," whispered someone with a low voice "they rarely do." A higher voice, kinder (if that was possible to tell by the sound of it) responded. "But sometimes they do. We haven't even tried yet."

Lanthrea reached under her blanket and pulled out her hunting knife, slowly and quietly, so as not to be heard.

"It's your turn to talk, you know," said the low voice.

"I know, I know. I'm just trying to get ready. I want to make the very best impression," responded the other.

Lanthrea was having no more of it. She leapt from her tent, knife in hand, only to find herself face to face with two small creatures, standing about three feet tall, with extraordinarily large eyes and rather kind faces. She stood up to her full height, towering over them, knife brandished, and yelled, "Who are you, and what do you want?"

The two creatures both stepped back immediately but didn't leave. In the light of the dying campfire, she could see them more clearly now. They had short arms and legs but were well-proportioned for their height, round faces, and their ears appeared to be pointed. Both were wearing what looked to be hunter's attire: leather vests and leggings, each with a bow slung across their shoulders and a quiver of arrows on their backs. One was bearded (the low voice, she assumed) and the other was female, from the length of the hair and the little silver crown atop her head. They stood aways back from Lanthrea, blinking their large eyes and not saying a word.

"Well?" Lanthrea insisted.

The female spoke first. "Pardon, my lady. We were to have met you here a day prior but were delayed by the Drekkens. We were sent by the King."

"Yes," the bearded one nodded his agreement. "The King sent us to help you."

Lanthrea slowly let down her knife and tucked it in her waistband.

"Help me what?"

The male elf (for this is all Lanthrea could think they were) raised an eyebrow with an expression that looked like he was speaking to an imbecile or a pet dog and nodded in the direction of the cliffs. "To help you with *those,* of course."

Lanthrea looked at the silver crown on the female elf's head. It looked much like hers. It seemed most probable that they had, indeed, come from Palem, although she had not met any such creatures while there herself. She gestured toward the fire. "Well, then, forgive my outburst. Please sit down."

The two small creatures sat down, cross-legged by the fire. The she-elf spoke first.

"My name is Plaxi, and this (here she pointed at the bearded one) is Clink. The King sent us to meet you five days ago when he heard you had not arrived at the upper lands yet. You must have been delayed here in the valley?"

Lanthrea nodded. "My horse, he was hurt badly from one of the great cats that live here. It took a little over seven days for him to heal. And then, well…I've been trying for two days to find a way around these cliffs. To no avail, I might add."

Plaxi let out an understanding, "Ahhhhhh." Then turning to Clink, she nudged him with her elbow and said, "See? I *told* you there was a reason. She wouldn't just *give up.*"

Lanthrea reddened, glad of the night to hide that fact, and then admitted, "Well, the truth is, I almost did. I was going to head back to Palem but decided to try one more thing. I was trying to find the end of the cliffs and go around them tomorrow. There has to be a way, don't you think?"

Clink grunted. "There *is* no way around. In the morning light, if you were to continue along the base in either direction, you would find even more impassible mountains on both sides of them. The cliffs are the *only* way to the upper lands. Didn't you *read* the map?"

Lanthrea reddened again, but said nothing.

Plaxi broke the tension quickly. "Let us all try and get some rest. We will need it for the journey tomorrow. Is this not right, Clink?"

The elf grunted again, stroking his beard. "True, true. Yes, rest we shall, then."

"I have no room for more than myself in my lean-to," Lanthrea said apologetically, "But I imagine it would fit the both of you if I slept out here by the fire. Let me gather my things."

Plaxi started to protest, but Clink nudged her in the side again, and she acquiesced with a simple, "That would be lovely, thank you. We have been traveling for quite some time now, and the Drekkens were nothing to be trifled with."

Thinking to ask what she meant by that (as she had wondered upon the first time 'Drekkens" were mentioned) Lanthrea almost opened up the new topic of conversation, but tired as she was, assumed the two elves even more so, and let her question wait until another time.

The two elves settled into the tent, and Lanthrea slept on her blanket by the fire, letting the crackling of the wood lull her into an easy sleep.

She opened her eyes to find two pointy-eared creatures staring at her from only six inches from her face. She bolted upright.

"What? What is it?" She blurted, her heart pounding.

Clink spoke with his low, gruff voice. "Just waiting for you to wake up's all. Thought you were going to sleep all day from the look of ya."

Plaxi sighed and rolled her eyes. '*Clink*! Stop it. She's human. They need more rest than we, you *know* that."

Lanthrea rubbed her eyes and checked on Elpin, who was standing very still, eyes wide, tail flicking and staring intently at the two small elves. She didn't know if he was curious or frightened, so she made sure she soothed him with a few "E*asy, boy. It's alright*'s."

They had the little campsite loaded up in a few minutes, with no morning meal, as Clink had insisted they could eat as they traveled. Interestingly, they turned back south, back to where Lanthrea had originally confronted the cliffs, and all she could do was shake her head and hope these two knew how to scale an unscalable cliffside.

They arrived at a spot not too far from where Lanthrea had camped the night prior when suddenly Plaxi insisted upon taking Elpin's reins, turned him around, and began to lead him back toward the forested area away from the cliffs. Lanthrea hollered after her, "Do you want us to follow you?" But the little elf just shook her head and disappeared after a bit into the green. Assuming she was taking him to graze before the brutal ascent in the heat of the day, she waved her on.

Clink, on the other hand, was just standing at the base of the cliff, tapping his toe impatiently as though he was waiting for Lanthrea to do something. She looked over at him, confused and considerably irritated. "What?" She barked at him, frustrated at his impatience but also, secretly, at the taking of her horse.

"Well," Clink said, shaking his head in disbelief. "It's time to go."

Lanthrea looked up at the cliff before her and laughed. "Go? Go where? Up *that*? How?"

Clink exhaled a huge, exasperated sigh and glared at her. "Did you learn *nothing* during your time in Palem?" He asked. Then under his breath, "What *do* humans do in Palem besides eat rich food and sit about?'"

Turning back to her, he inhaled deeply, steadied himself (as though he might blow at any moment) and said, in a very measured tone, "You *ask*, Lanthrea. You ask."

She pursed her lips, a confused look on her face.

"I...*ask*..." she responded sarcastically, slapping her hands onto her hips in exasperation.

Clink threw his head back and sighed before answering, "Yes, human. You ask the King. Did you think you could do an impossible thing? Did you decide somewhere in that huge, gobbly head of yours that you could do something that was un-do-able? All by yourself?"

Lanthrea was quickly tiring of this elf's sarcasm and critical tone but remained silent, considering his words.

Plaxi was just returning at this point, saddle bag in hand, and entered the conversation.

"Clink. Stop it. She doesn't know what she doesn't know. Have some patience with her. She is new to the king's ways."

Grateful for the kindness, Lanthrea was about to thank her when she noticed that Elpin was not by her side.

Fear welling up inside, she fairly barked at Plaxi. "Where is he? What did you do with Elpin?"

Plaxi smiled. "Lanthrea, there is no way he could make this journey. I have left him in the forest with the Lady of Lanthor. She will ask the King for help to get him to the upper lands, for even we cannot do that."

"The Lady?" Lanthrea brightened. "She is here?"

Plaxi nodded. "Just beyond those trees. But she isn't here for *us* right now. Our job is to get you up these cliffs. And, we'd best get at it. The day won't stand still."

With that, Plaxi nodded at Lanthrea. "Well, then…you need to ask the king for help. Only he can get you up these stone walls to the top."

Lanthrea stalled. "But I have asked, Plaxi. I asked him to show me how to get over them. To show me a way. And there was no answer at all."

Plaxi sighed. "Did you ask *him* to get you up the cliffs? Or did you ask him something else altogether?"

Lanthrea screwed up her face, trying to think. "I…I didn't ask him, really. I told him I couldn't find a way."

Plaxi smiled, "Well, then…there you go! You asked to find a way. You. In your own power. But, Lanthrea, there *is* no way. Only the king can do the impossible. But you have to ask him."

Lanthrea pulled back, skeptical and a bit insulted. "You're telling me I have to ask some specific, exact thing in order to get help?" She shook her head. "Seems unlikely."

Clink, still tapping his toe and beyond himself with frustration, blurted out, "It doesn't have to be the words, human…it has to be your *concession*…that you can't do this thing. No, if's, and's, or but's. You have to admit that you are helpless."

Still uncertain, Lanthrea considered his words. She always wanted to think she could figure any situation out. Could maneuver and manipulate almost anything with her own intellect and abilities. This was a new thought that Clink was offering. *Complete helplessness and complete admission of it.*

She thought about his for a bit, then wrinkled her nose, closed her eyes and put words to this new thought. "Good King, there is no way up these cliffs. Yet you have asked me to go this way. I give up, and I give this journey to you."

Another simple prayer, but surprisingly honest. It felt like she had just discovered a deep chamber in her heart that she had never known existed.

Plaxi clapped her hands rather gleefully, and Clink simply nodded in agreement. "Now then, let's go," he said. They grabbed their items and turned to face the cliffs. The next thing that happened was one that Lanthrea would remember the rest of her life. For the cliffs began to crack. From the top down (starting high above their heads where they couldn't see for the clouds) the cracks ripped downward through the white cliffs toward the earth, causing the ground to shake and sending little rocks spewing here and there as the cracks widened. Then, with a great and terrible cracking sound, like that of an earthquake, the cliffside simply split in two—the ground shaking and the noise completely deafening.

Lanthrea covered her ears, closed her eyes, and ducked to avoid the stones that were being thrown down to the base of the cliffs before settling in a cloud of dust. When she, at last, dared to look, what she saw before her was, indeed, impossible. The Cliffs of Abalor had simply opened before them, leaving a small but passable passageway for them to travel. Noting that it was too small for a horse, Lanthrea was immediately glad of Plaxi's help by calling the Lady to take Elpin.

Clink waved the dust away and said, "Well, then. Daylight's a wasting. Let's be on our way." He hiked his quiver up on his back, rounded his shoulders, and was the first into the gap.

CHAPTER NINETEEN:
Naganthria - The Quiet

The passage through the cliffs had been surprisingly easy. Never would she have guessed that morning that they'd have managed the cliffs and would be making their ascent to the Upper Lands by evening. For, once through the cliffs, the land rose upward at a very manageable pace, and the hike to the top was more like a mid-summer's day walk than anything else. About half way up to the top, Lanthrea turned around and discovered she was able to look down and see the entire Valley from this vantage point. She gasped at what she saw. For there, scattered every so often, far enough from each other so as never to meet, were a great many cottages and cabins like Marien's. There were hundreds of them, maybe more, smoke rising from each solitary chimney. She hung her head. So many had refused to leave. So many had given up —given into whatever sorrow they faced. She looked at Plaxi and Clink, leading the way, grateful beyond words for their good help.

They reached the summit (if it could be called that) by evening meal, and Clink had used his excellent archery skills to secure dinner. They made camp by a small lake, all set about by tall green grass and clover that Lanthrea was certain Elpin would have loved. They ate their meal of roasted hare, sweet berries and wine, which Lanthrea hadn't had since her time in Palem. Clink had informed her that he never traveled without a wineskin full of "the good stuff", and had shared it freely. Relaxing as they were by the fire, its flames reflected in the lake and the clear sky above them, Lanthrea felt as though she was actually back in Palem. Good friends (even Clink turned out to be somewhat agreeable in his disagreeable-ness), good food and talk of the King made the evening just about perfect. She learned that Plaxi and Clink were often sent by the King to help those who were in need, and Clink's rough exterior proved only to cover his soft heart and good intentions. Plaxi was as bubbly and kind as she appeared on the surface and had enjoyed hearing of Lanthrea's travels thus far, hanging on every word as though the story was her own. Lanthrea sensed a certain but restrained sadness, maybe a kind of envy, from Plaxi—as though she had always yearned for such a journey herself.

The elves would be leaving Lanthrea in the morning, a fact for which she was unexpectedly sad, but they had other people they needed to help and were already late in getting to them. This brought up the conversation about the Drekkens, who had hindered them in getting to Lanthrea earlier. Plaxi hadn't wanted to talk about them, but Clink's eyes literally glowed with an inner fire as he spoke.

"The Drekkens, yessss…..a formidable foe, they," he had said, the starlight flickering in his eyes. "They are imps, really, no more, but they think themselves to be intractable demons. They come from the great caldera in the land of Kress—far to the south of here, living on the chasm's molten rock and thriving in its fumes. They love nothing more than to attack people or animals…they really don't care which. Their main objective is to terrify, immobilize, then, if possible, kill their prey. They can do no harm if they can't terrify first. Without their prey's fear, they are impotent. But they fight like hyenas, and we had a goodly battle with them on the edge of the Great Abyss."

Plaxi interrupted his narrative. "I wouldn't call it a *good* battle," she said sadly. The man they were terrorizing is a wonderful soul; he has just…lost his way. Azar had no power to help him, as the man had given himself over to despair. That is when the Drekkens attacked. The man was paralyzed by terror, and they almost had taken him by the time we arrived. We were able to scare most of them off and kill those who stubbornly refused to go. But the poor man…he is still there at the Abyss, agonizing in his indecisiveness and fear."

Clink grunted. "Aye, I guess we have to go back. Help the miserable sod."

Lanthrea smiled at his caring heart. She cleared her throat. "I hope to never meet these…creatures," she said softly.

Plaxi put a hand on her shoulder. "I will hope this with you, friend."

They slept well, from both the wine and full stomachs as well as the calm summer night. The next morning, Lanthrea had awakened before the others, even before sunrise, rather hoping to rub Clink's nose in that very fact.

The elves had awakened not long after, and Clink had pursed his lips at seeing Lanthrea already preparing morning meal, but said nothing. She had smiled coyly as she handed them both some sliced cheese with sweet blueberries she had found by the lakeshore.

"Plaxi," she asked as they ate their meal, "when will the Lady have Elpin brought to me?"

Plaxi shrugged. "That I don't know, my friend. All I know is she said that she would ask the king for his help and that he would give it. She had then taken Elpinhoeve from me and disappeared into the forest." She took a bite of cheese and added, "Don't worry. You'll see him again soon."

Lanthrea had no doubt of it, but it would be lonely headed north through this new land. According to the map, it was known as Naganthria, but the elves had told her it was known to the locals as The Quiet, which sounded both appealing and curious. No matter, though. It was through this land that the map said to travel. So be it.

The elves said their goodbyes after they had eaten and helped Lanthrea clean the camp. Plaxi had jumped up onto a stump and hugged Lanthrea tightly, kissing both her cheeks in farewell. Clink simply grunted, then turned and walked back toward the Cliffs of Abalor.

Finding herself completely alone for the first time since she had had begun her journey, Lanthrea sat for a very long time by the edge of the little lake and read from the book before beginning her journey. Today the illustration that drew her in was that of the forlorn and ugly tree. She avoided this chapter often for many reasons, not the least of them being the sadness she felt every time she looked at it. She had never read the chapter; the image of the dead tree haunted her so. The King had told her that this chapter of the book was the most important of all, a fact she found hard to believe. If so, then why the ugly image? The lack of color and life and everything good. It made no sense to her. She looked at the tree and the black, starless night drawn behind it in ink and felt the sadness again. A horrid, lonesome, fearsome, and deadly sadness, yet tinged with an indefinable and powerful love. The two emotions were juxtaposed in her heart every time she gazed upon it. Why was this even *in* the book, as confusing as it was? Her eyes fell on the words below the image, and she read them for the first time.

"Only the truest love could ever embrace the tree and all it holds."

Cryptic. She hated cryptic words. Once again, she found the page…*disagreeable* and far too weighty for her small heart. She shut the book, deciding it best to get going rather than to sit here pondering this puzzle. Gathering up her things (for Plaxi had brought the saddle bag back filled with her smaller necessities) she decided that her lean-to was far too much to carry without a horse, so she rolled it up, set a large stone upon it to hold it down from wind, and hoped it would perhaps serve another traveler one day.

She headed north, as the map had indicated, to travel due north until she came to a rough mountainous region, which would mark the end of Naganthria. The day was bright and sunny, and this land was lovely in every way. This place reminded her of a high alpine valley. Everywhere she looked was replete with beauty. Tall purple and blue foxgloves, white spiky lupines, purple heathers and a scattering of wildflowers laying low to the ground, surprising a person with every step. She found herself stopping every few minutes just to breath in the clean, heather-scented air and let the sun warm her shoulders.

The land was aptly named. For other than birdsong and a gentle breeze, there was no sound at all to rattle the senses. An occasion waterfall splashing happily into a cold lake would break the silence every so often, but other than that, the place felt like a physical representation of peace itself. Wishing that Elpinhoeve could be with her (he would have loved the sweet clover growing everywhere here) she decided to simply enjoy the gift and walk until she could walk no more, which happened at about sunset. Not having her lean-to any longer, she tossed the saddle bag aside off her shoulder, found some kindling and a few dry logs for a fire (it would no doubt get cold at this altitude) and plopped down to eat some dried meat and cheese.

She hadn't but begun the nibble on the cheese when she saw a figure leading a horse walking towards her from a small grove of trees to her right. Squinting, she saw immediately who it was. The Lady of Lanthor! And Elpin! She jumped up and ran to them both, hugging the Lady and kissing Elpin's velvet nose. The Lady smiled brightly. "I suppose he'd like his tack off. This clover looks inviting."

Lanthrea pulled off the bridle and saddle, then patted Elpin's haunches. He was happily ripping the sweet flowers off the clover within seconds after a quick roll in the tall grass, swishing his tail in joy.

"His wound is completely healed," she noted, relieved.

"The King saw to that," the Lady said, smiling. "And he told me to let you know he is proud of you. Not everyone makes it out of the Valley of Sorrow. Some choose to cling to their sadness and helplessness, and if so, there is nothing that can be done for them."

Lanthrea thought immediately of Marien. "I know, my Lady. I met one still there. Is there nothing that can be done for her?"

The Lady reached out and lay her hand on Lanthrea's shoulder. "Not unless she wishes it, I'm afraid. The King will not impose himself upon anyone who does not wish it."

"But is there hope for her?" Lanthrea asked sadly.

"There is always hope," said the Lady. "You can continue to ask the King to send more help her way. But, in the end, she must decide whether or not to let them in."

Lanthrea nodded. They walked in silence to the little campsite, whereupon she offered the Lady some food and drink, which she readily accepted. The two women talked until after the sun set and the moon rose, so joyful was this meeting and their time together. Lanthrea didn't want it to end.

It was about the tenth hour when the Lady stood and brushed the dust from her long velvet gown. "I must go now, child. Remember these words: Listen only to the King's voice as you travel north. His, and His alone."

Lanthrea stood and tried to stall her. "I will, my Lady. That will never be a problem again. But can't you stay a bit longer? I have some questions about the book....one page in particular. The tree. Could you tell me about that picture? It confuses and upsets me so." Thinking this would confound the Lady and perhaps make her stay, she was disappointed when instead she simply responded, "That is for another time, Lanthrea. Suffice it to say the tree was at the site of a great battle between the King and his enemies. There was death at that battle: death and righteous blood spilled. You will learn more of this later. For now, straighten your back, be of good courage, and let us say our goodbyes." Lanthrea straightened up, swept her hair back from her shoulders and smiled. "Thank you for everything," she said through her tears. The lady nodded, then began to walk back towards the grove of trees. Lanthrea's eyes followed her until she could see her no more, then she lay down next to the crackling fire and stared up at the stars until sleep overtook her.

She awoke at dawn, shivering from the cold mountain air, and quickly stirred her fire back to life. Hunching over it, warming her hands and face, she looked around until she found Elpin, who was rolling in the tall grass about a hundred yards from her. Smiling, she realized that she could ride him today now that he was healed! What joy it would be to gallop through these alpine meadows, smelling the sweet clover as they rode over it. With that thought in mind, she whistled to him, and he popped up from his roll, shook the dust off, and trotted over to her, burying his head in her chest.

"Glad to have you back, boy," she said softly, scratching under his forelock. He nickered softly and lipped her arm gently. She gathered up her things, saddled and bridled Elpin, then mounted and kicked him into a trot. It was as joyous as she had imagined. The perfect stillness of the place—the smells of the open meadows and clustered pines all were a delight to her senses, and she felt she would be overcome by it all. It was as they were walking through a very still glen, with aspen trees making a kind of natural archway for them to pass under, that she heard something break the silence. It wasn't quite a voice, but something like one. More like a thought, a loud thought, but somehow one she could actually *hear*. It was a very unsettling experience, and she kept shaking her head to stop the sound.

So bothered was she by this sensation that she finally pulled Elpin to a stop, dismounted and stood in the deep quiet of the meadow to just… *listen*. It was only then that she could hear the voice clearly.

"This Return is not what you think," said the thought-voice. *"You are being duped, going back to Drymac will be your death. Lord Bythim will find and kill you. This is the truth. Can you not see?"*

She blanched at the words. For, to be sure, she had considered since that day in the garden when the Lady told her of the Return that her entrance to Cenecal could, most certainly, mean imprisonment and possible death. It had, after all, been less than a year since she'd left, her house burned, and the Bythim's men looking for her. And Bythim had a long memory and a longer arm. Plenty of people knew her from the Market. It wouldn't take them but five minutes to find her once she was back, especially if she began painting again.

An old, terrible feeling crept into her heart. *Fear.* The same fear that Tenk used to bring as he warned her of potentialities and probabilities. Shaking it off, she tried to readjust her thinking. So much good and miraculous had happened. And the King had promised he would be with her. But what else had he said? "In the joys and *in the dangers.*" Her heart squeezed. It had been so easy to gloss over that part of his benediction the other day. She thought, just for a moment, of popping onto Elpin and riding south again. Perhaps the Cliffs of Abalor were still open to passage. She could live in the Valley. Find one of the many who had stayed there. Maybe even Marien would take her in. There would be room for two in her cottage....

Suddenly, she heard another even louder thought break her musings. "*Listen only to the King's voice.*" The words were gentle but insistent. "*His and his alone.*" The Lady's words. Shaking off the captivation of the other thoughts, she blinked, looking around, shocked. She must have been standing in this one spot for several hours. The sun had moved far across the sky, and she had lost precious time.

She found Elpin just a few yards away, resting in a little grove of trees, out of the sun. She mounted quickly and kicked him into a canter. It would be best to get through this place rather than linger and enjoy the beauty. For this was a truly beautiful, but subtly dangerous place.

Skipping midday meal, she rode until sundown, glad to have no more disturbing thoughts. Of course, she had worked Elpinhoeve fairly hard in order to attain this goal, the sound of his hoofbeats on the ground giving her something to listen to. But she was hungry, and he was exhausted by dusk, so she turned him loose to eat and rest, and she plopped down by a stream to drink and check the map. Evening in this alpine paradise was as delightful as daytime. The cooling air only accentuated the scents of heather, green grass and clover. Looking up, the stars sparkled like crystals, and, in the glen next to her, a group of fireflies lit up the evening with their soft, tiny lights.

She relaxed and watched them flitter about in the pines.

"They will hurt you. And no one will be there to help."

The thought-voice was back. Louder than before. She jerked up from her repose and shook her head to rid herself of the words.

"You have no friends there. Cenecal is a cruel place, and no one there will care for an old woman like you. You'll be tossed away in a dungeon somewhere, left alone. And you will be terrified."

She jumped up from the stream bed and tried to focus on something, *anything* else.

The thought-voice hammered away at her.

"You'll probably get sick in those dungeons. You'll have consumption by the first week in some damp, dark, cold place. Bythim's guards will offer no help. You'll die, but it will take a long time. And you will suffer so. All alone."

Lanthrea grabbed her head and began to cry. She had never in her life felt this helpless. "Stop it," she cried out. "Stop it, stop it, STOP IT!"

"All alone. You will be so frightened. And no one will help you."

Elpin had been watching his mistress acting strangely and had come over, nuzzling her with his velvet nose, nickering softly. Lanthrea felt his presence and tried to focus on him but was finding it almost impossible to think.

"Where was the king when you were growing up? When the marauders found you hiding behind the grain bin that day? When you were sick with the Great Cough that plagued Cenecal and lay feverish and gasping for air on the floor? He was never there. And he won't be with you in that dungeon of Bythim's, either."

Lanthrea was sobbing now and found she could do nothing to stop either her terror nor the voice causing it.

Suddenly, she felt a hand on her shoulder, and she jumped away, panicked, only to find herself looking into the kind eyes of Azar. He grasped her by both shoulders and looked into her eyes.

"Lanthrea. Listen to me. Listen to my words. The king has sent me to help you. Lanthrea…remember the King."

She shook her head and tried to focus. It took a few moments, but bit by bit the forest came back into view, as did Azar.

"There you are," he said, smiling. "Welcome back."

She looked up, shocked to realize the night had passed and it was morning already. The sun was up, and the birds were singing their appreciation of that fact.

"Azar. What….what…is happening to me?" She almost moaned the words.

"Here, let's get a meal into you," was all he said, leading her to a small table that was somehow miraculously set up in the middle of a little pine grove, the same the fireflies had played in.

On the table was simply a loaf of bread and two glasses filled with wine. "Here, sit," he said, motioning her to sit on the pine- needled ground, "I've brought you food." The scent of pine and bread were both intoxicating, and she hadn't realized how hungry she was. He broke the loaf in half and handed her part. Never had morning meal tasted so good…so *necessary*. She was completely depleted from the night's travails. Sipping on the wine, she let Azar talk— too tired was she to even speak.

"It is well known that the quiet of this place can overwhelm a person," he said. "The Lady tried to warn you. You must *only* and *intentionally* listen to the King's voice and call to mind his words while in this place. We are a people of remembrance. Each of our Solemn Memories reminds us of this truth." He chewed his bread slowly, then sipped the wine.

She nodded but still had no energy to respond.

They sat in silence for a long time before Lanthrea turned to him and asked, rather sadly, "How? How do I listen only to the king's voice? Azar, I honestly don't know what that means. The king isn't here. I can't see him, nor touch him, nor converse with him as I did in Palem. How on earth am I to listen 'only to his voice' when I can't even hear it?"

Azar nodded in understanding. "Lanthrea, tell me this. Was the voice you heard in your head - warning you of doom and death - was it from a person standing next to you?"

She thought of the assaulting voice and admitted, "No."

"Yet it was loud and distracting and, dare I say, convincing, was it not?" Azar was looking deep into her eyes.

"Ummmmm…yes…it was wholly convincing," she muttered softly.

"So, to quiet that voice, you simply have to remember the king's words to you and trust them completely. It is that simple. *And that difficult.*" Azar had great compassion in his eyes. "This place," he said, gesturing to the forest around them, "They call it The Quiet because it allows one to be still enough to hear. And it can lead either to hopelessness and madness or to hope and well-being. It really is the listener's choice."

Lanthrea sighed. "But how…"

Azar interrupted her. "By remembering his words to you and believing them. The more you remember and believe, the louder his voice will become. The Drekkens…."

She gasped. "These voices were from *them*?" She found herself shivering. I saw no such things. Where were they?"

Azar put her hand on her shoulder, "Peace, daughter. They were not here, per se. They have many abilities. One of them is to whisper dark terrors to a person from afar. Remember what Plaxi told you? It is their prime objective to incapacitate someone with fear. But Lanthrea, you need not worry. There *is* no terror in the King's economy. There is no fear that can exist with him."

She nodded weakly, remembering Tenk and how small it had become in the King's hands before disappearing altogether.

"But I gave Tenk up," she offered.

"Yes, and it was a first step. To not own a glottin, to put out fear is good." He reached out his hand and pulled her up. "Here is a certain help for you: if you sense terror and death in a voice, it is not the King who speaks. Do not listen to those voices."

"But that voice in my head was so loud," she argued. "How do I *not* listen?"

"Use the words from the book," Azar said gently. "Just say them out loud. Drekkens cannot stand the book. It hurts them in a way we can't really understand."

She took a deep breath, then looked at Azar with tears in her eyes. "I don't want to hear that voice again," she cried, realizing she was begging him.

"I know, child," he responded. "But you will. And you need to be prepared."

Azar stayed the rest of the day with her, helping find passages from the book that would stave off the Drekken's whispers. They then looked at the map together, Azar noting that it was not long now before she would arrive at the harsh mountains and summits marking the end of Naganthria—a day at most. He had hugged her tightly before leaving at sunset, heading south back towards the Cliffs of Abalor, his walking staff in hand and gray hair blowing in the wind.

Lanthrea slept uneasily that night and used a passage from the book to say over and over again as she fell asleep:

"Put the King ever before you, and he will protect you from fear."

CHAPTER TWENTY:
The Summit at Glastone

The next morning promised nothing but glory. Warm sun, shockingly blue sky and the ubiquitous aroma of alpine flowers wafting in the gentle summer air. Lanthrea awakened and first thing made certain she had morning meal so as not to get as hungry and depleted as yesterday. She saddled Elpin up and began her day's trip to the north.

Azar had told her much about the ragged mountain she was about to encounter: showing her the best (and in some cases, only) possible trails and passages through the glaciers, and even gifting her with a cloak, warm and thick, that she could wrap herself once needed. He warned her of the wild winds, the icy paths, and the snow so deep it would be impossible to get through unless she followed his directions exactly. He told her to stuff as much green grass and clover as she could into one of the saddle bags, as there would be little vegetation once they neared the top, and Elpin would be in need of food until they began to descend on the other side. The saddle bag full of grass wouldn't be near enough, but it would help. Few had taken this journey with a horse to feed, but there was no way out of Naganthria without hiking to the summit at Mount Glastone.

The rest of their journey through the Naganthria was uneventful. She thought once that she heard a voice telling her that scaling the summit 'would be an impossible task', but she had simply said, *"the King will protect me"* out loud and heartily, and the voice had stopped. It was about sunset when, coming around a small hill covered with heather and lupines, the Mountain came into view. She gasped. No alpine hike, this. It seemed to rise from the ground like a jagged, dark predator. She slumped down in the saddle and sighed. These were not like the mountains of Palem, with their low hills and easy grades. This was a high and craggy colossus of a thing: the tree line ending a few hundred feet up and the snow covering the entire rest of the rocky way to the summit. Dismounting, she let Elpin graze (he would need it) and looked up towards the top. Another seemingly impossible task. But this time, she remembered. She actively *remembered* what had happened at Abalor. After all, that had been impossible, too.

Although Azar had not mentioned it, Common sense told her there was no way to start the ascent at night. She would begin at first light.

The morning came on sweet and warm, a portent of a good climb today. Lanthrea filled one of her pouches with grass and clover and another with water. Azar warned her about trying to eat the snow, as it would freeze her slowly from the inside. Looking over, she was glad to see Elpin grazing in a tall bunch of grass.

"Eat up, boy!" She hollered at him as she packed up her little camp.

They were saddled and mounted and ready to go within a few minutes and began their ascent. The first few hours weren't bad at all. Azar had drawn on the map the best path to take: around this outcrop of rock, to the left of that glacier and follow the stream till the waterfall. Elpin had no difficulty on these lower slopes, as there was little ice and snow on the paths, so he had been rideable to that point. It was about the third hour of their climb when things changed. For one thing, the wind picked up at this altitude, and besides being bitter cold, wet snow began to blow around them, making it almost impossible to see. Pulling out her cloak, she wrapped it around herself tightly, pulling the hood over her head, and tried to keep riding. But within minutes, the pathway became icy and too slick to put extra weight on Elpin. She got off and began to lead him along the narrow path they were on, head down to the wind. The snow was not deep here, but the path was slick with ice, and it was getting increasingly difficult to stay on her feet. She was utterly exhausted after only a few minutes of this climb and found herself stopping every few yards to catch her breath, then heaving back into it.

Azar had told her of a small cave about half way up that would offer a break from the wind, but she hadn't seen it yet. Hoping she hadn't missed it because of the blowing snow in her eyes, she kept going, afraid to stop for fear of freezing to death. She looked back at Elpin, who was covered in a layer of icy snow that was sticking mercilessly to his head, chest, neck and withers. They needed to find that cave and soon. She whispered a small prayer. "Good king, please help us." It was all she could think of to ask. It was enough. A few minutes later, she thought she saw an indentation of sorts in the rocky crag they were traveling under. Within another few minutes after that, they had made it inside the cave, shaking and disoriented from the cold and exhaustion.

Elpin shook the snow off his coat and stood, head hanging, heaving for breath. Lanthrea, too, shook off her cloak and caught her breath before taking off Elpin's bridle and saddle and rubbing him down well with her hands to try and warm him a bit. Once she got her bearings, she was grateful beyond words for the protection of the cave. Just being able to *see* without the pelting ice and snow in her face felt miraculous. She thought about continuing up to the summit today and decided against it. They were both exhausted. They would stay the night here, protected by the cave.

Her first order of business was to find firewood and kindling with which to light it. This would be difficult, if at all possible, for there were very few trees this high up the mountain. She wrapped herself in the cloak and stepped outside to look. No trees, to be certain, but there were scrub bushes with plenty of dry branches that broke off easily. Gathering up an armful of these (the thickest she could find) she hauled them back into the cave and got a fire going within no time. Next, she pulled out her little wooden bowl and filled it with snow, then set it by the fire to melt. Ensuring she and Elpin both had a drink (she had to fill the bowl several times for the horse), she then grabbed a few handfuls of the grass and clover mix and let Elpin have a bite while she chewed on some dried meat.

"I'm sorry there isn't more, boy," she said as she patted his neck. "But we'll be to the top tomorrow and down the other side soon after that, I promise you."

She wrapped up in her cloak but found the fire was doing an adequate job of heating the small cavern so let it loosen around her shoulders as she took some time to look again at the map.

According to this (and just as Azar had shown her), they were just about half way up to Glastone Peak at the summit by now. They had made good time. She guessed it was probably about mid-afternoon, but there was no way to tell.

She busied herself for a few hours with reading from the book and with rest. She had learned from this journey that sometimes rest was an active thing. Cla'neen had taught her early on how to make your body rest because you need it, even if you didn't want to.

She went back out and grabbed another armful of bush branches, tossing them on the fire before falling asleep. It was probably only five in the afternoon when she drifted off, but exhaustion helped make sleep come easily.

She awoke with a horse's velvet nose in her face, breathing softly and nudging her awake.

"Elpin, good morning," she said sleepily. "Looking for some more grass, are we?" She stretched her neck and shoulders, immediately realizing how cold it was in the cave and how dark. The fire had gone out hours before (the bush branches not being substantial enough to hold a hearty, long-lasting flame), and the cave was freezing.

Wrapping the cloak around her tightly, she opened up the saddle bag, dumped the rest of the grass on the ground and let Elpin have it all. The next half of this climb would be harder than the last, and he would need every bit of energy. Likewise, she took a piece of bread and a small hunk of cheese from her pack and ate them slowly. She thought of making a fire for the morning but decided their time was better spent by getting back onto the trail.

Poking her head out the cave entrance, she was shocked by what she saw. For it had snowed last night and not just a little. Everywhere she looked was covered with a few feet of the white, fluffy stuff. It was beautiful and looked almost magical. But she soon realized it had also completely covered the trail, and beyond that, she had no adequate shoes nor boots to handle such a problem. Mercifully, the wind had died down completely, and she could see for miles from this high up on the mountain. Blue sky above, the tree line below—with the snow-covered pines looking for all the world like bumbly figures in puffy white clothing —it was truly one of the most breathtaking scenes she had ever had the privilege to witness. Under any other circumstance, it would have been idyllic.

Shaking her head and sighing, she turned back to Elpin inside the cave, saddled him up, packed her things, and flopped down on the soft dirt of the cave floor for a minute to gather her thoughts.

How would she find the trail under all this snow? And how would she walk in it without freezing her feet? There were no answers to these immediate problems. Suddenly, she remembered Cla'neen wrapping Tenk's feet in leather to keep them from burning in the desert sand. Could she do something similar here? She had no leather, but she did have the cloak. It was long enough that she could cut a foot or two off the bottom of it and wrap her feet in that. Jumping up, she grabbed her hunting knife and laid the cloak on the floor of the cave. She carefully cut two strips, each about a hand's width wide off the length of the cloak, then wrapped her feet with them, lacing the cloth on with two long decorative straps she cut from Elpin's saddle. Her feet looked clunky and ridiculous, but they were warm.

Checking that they were laced on adequately, she grabbed Elpin's reins and started out of the cave. Immediately she found that she was almost blinded by the brightness of the sun reflecting off the snow. Having no way to mitigate this discomfort, she squinted her eyes and stepped out into the deep powder.

Azar had informed her that, once past the cave, the trail would zigzag up the mountain, making it easier to ascend. The problem was she couldn't find the trail. Everything was just a flat, white table of snow, with few demarcations to identify what was where. Outside of several boulders and scrawny pines that had avoided being buried, everything looked the same.

She had a thought (it was a long shot) but it was her only plausible idea. Perhaps the *horse* could find the trail. His legs were longer, and he did, after all, have four feet to her two, plus an animal's uncanny instinct. She put Elpin's reins up around his neck and tied them together, then patted his hind end. "It's up to you now, boy. Take us up."

He looked confused at first, not knowing what was being asked of him, and turned his head towards her as if to say, "what are we doing?" but she pushed his hind end ahead of her, stepped behind him and clicked her tongue. "Just like pulling a cart, boy," she said encouragingly, "except I'll just be back here, walking." She clicked again, and he moved forward into the deep snow. Elpin did a remarkable job of finding good footing, and she realized after just a few minutes that he was, indeed, zigzagging up the mountainside, just as Azar had told her. Her feet were cold but not freezing, and the cloth wrapping stayed put. The sun was actually warm today, and without the freezing wind, their climb was almost enjoyable.

Within a matter of a few hours, she saw the summit. Glastone Peak, shining like a beacon in the bright blue sky, sharp and craggy, with points of naked stone here and there below the snow-crowned summit. A welcome sight for the two weary travelers. Pushing ahead, they made it to a huge rocky area in less than an hour—the base of the summit. Here, the snow was not deep—most had been blown off by the high winds, and because the icy temperatures at this elevation weren't as conducive to heavy snowfall. Whatever the reason, she was elated to get onto dry ground, even if rocky and hard to walk upon. This part of the summit was rather broad and flat, narrowing as they moved along it, finally turning into a large trail that encircled the base of the snow-capped summit itself. Picking their way through on the sharp rocks, they stumbled and clamored around the peak until, just past the top, a certain change appeared. Little blue wildflowers began to pop up here and there amidst the rocks, forcing their beauty right through the barren topsoil and opening to the sun. As they began their descent, more and more appeared until, at last, a bit of grass could be found on the side of the trail as well. Elpin was at it within seconds, and Lanthrea sighed in relief. They had made it.

They were now on the leeward side of the peak, somewhat secure from the snow and wind. There was a huge glacier to their right, but as long as they stayed on the rocky path, they would be able to walk down the rest of the way without difficulty. Finding a large stone to sit upon, Lanthrea let Elpin pick at whatever grasses he could find, and she opened her saddle bags and grabbed a hunk of cheese and some sweet dried berries left from the Valley. She drank from her pouch and offered Elpin a handful of water as well. They continued down the trail after their brief rest, and water no longer became a problem, as the glacial melt-off was running in small rivulets next to them, fast converging to become a stream, then a river, and finally, a crashing waterfall tumbling down a cliffside to the green valley below. Lanthrea enjoyed watching it grow as they descended and smiled as she watched it finally splash and leap off the cliff in the great waterfall. It felt to her as though she was watching life itself—each rivulet changing as it combined with the others—growing collectively into an entirely new thing.

By midway down the mountain, the air was warm enough for her to take off her cloak and handmade boots, and she shoved them both into her saddle bags, not knowing when or if she might need them again. They made good time, being of good cheer and finding the path easy to descend, and by nightfall, they had made it to the green valley at the base. She looked behind her, up at the peak, and found it hard to believe they had just scaled that monster successfully. She thought about herself just six short months ago, her body so bent and broken that it would have been an impossibility to even get to the tree line on the other side. Shaking her head, she whispered a prayer of thanks, not just for the safe crossing but for her stronger body and calmer mind.

They made camp at the base of Mt. Glastone, and both of them slept well until morning.

Lanthrea awakened early to a pale gray sky and a light dusting of snow that had covered the ground sometime during the night. She hadn't thought she'd see snow again on this trip, and certainly not at this low altitude. She wasn't pleased to see it at all, especially as a flake or two continued to float down, promising more. Elpin was, of course, off grazing already, and she decided to have her morning meal while he was having his.

She pulled out the map and looked at it closely. This next part of her journey was in a northeasterly direction, heading due east back to Drymac in a few more weeks. It wouldn't be long now. The odd thing was that the territory she was currently in had no name delineated on the map. It was just an irregularly shaped blob of land, with the Thetan Ocean on the far western side of it and the promise of a route to the East (and Drymac) on the right through what looked to be some rolling hills and a few lakes. Satisfied with that information, she neatly folded the map and stuck it back in her pocket. They began their journey in good spirits (Elpin was prancing and quite happy to gallop) and headed out. They were to travel north for about a day. Then the route would bend east towards the hills.

The trip was easy, the land was flat and dry, and Lanthrea was enjoying the ride. It was about two hours into the journey that the light snow that had dusted them overnight, and had accompanied them without causing even a slight hindrance thus far, began to change. First, the flakes became larger, then heavier and more dense, falling in what could be described as no other than big, wet clumps. It was piling up around them faster than Elpin could trudge through, and Lanthrea finally stopped him, found shelter under some pine trees and let him rest.

As it was mid-summer, there was really no explanation for a snow storm such as this, but as she looked to the north from the cover of her little pine grove, she saw nothing *but* snow. The entire land was covered with it for as far as the eye could see. This was no freak summer storm. For some inexplicable reason this place was still in a winter season! She threw back her head and groaned. She had *just* put her cloak and foot coverings away, hoping for a summer ride to the northeast today. Grumbling, she rummaged about in the saddle bags, pulled them both out and wrapped her feet up well. Throwing the cloak onto her shoulders, she climbed back onto Elpin and headed into the snow.

The clumpy, wet snow fell for only about an hour before stopping suddenly, a welcome relief. With visibility immensely better now, she took stock of their surroundings. The land was mostly flat but with a few rolling hills. There didn't seem to be any villages or cities, at least as far as she could see. This worried her, as the supply of dried meat and cheese was almost depleted, and she would need to acquire supplies again very soon. They stopped at midday, and she ate the last of the cheese (saving some salted meat for later) as Elpin pawed the snow to get to the grass underneath. They were, again, under a grove of pine trees, and Lanthrea was shivering from the heavy wet cloak. Taking it off, she thought to hang in from some branches and try and dry out a bit when her eye caught the sight of some smoke coming from somewhere beyond the grove. Curiosity getting the best of her, she followed it through the trees, until coming to a small hut in the middle of an open meadow, just beyond the grove where Elpin still stood, grazing. Feeling, as always, the apprehension of who or what might be inside, she decided to go inquire within, none the less. Approaching the little place cautiously, she stepped up onto the welcoming little porch and knocked on the door lightly.

"Is anyone home? I'm a traveler on my way back to Drymac. I mean you no harm."

At first, there was no sign of life other than the smoke billowing from the chimney, and she knocked a few more times to no avail. She noted unusually small footprints all about the property surrounding the little hut, so she knew someone was living here. The tiny prints reminded her of Plaxi and Clink and she smiled. Turning to leave the porch and check around the back of the place by the woodpile, the door suddenly opened, and she whipped around to see herself face to face with a little girl, no more than five years of age, with a freckled nose, bright green eyes, and long blonde, unkempt hair. Surprised, Lanthrea drew back a bit, then asked, "Is your mother home… or your father?"

The little girl said nothing but shook her head. "Are you home alone, then?" Lanthrea asked quietly. The girl nodded and looked down at the floor. "Will they be back soon, then? Your mother and father?" The little girl shrugged her shoulders, and Lanthrea noted a tear roll down her face. "Oh, no…little one…come here," she said, reaching out her arms for the child. "Don't cry now. There, there."

Completely unfamiliar with children, Lanthrea felt awkward. Her only experience in comforting something had been with Tenk. But this little child aroused a strange feeling in her….what was it? *Protective, motherly. That was it! Maternal.* The little girl practically melted into her arms, and she held her close for a long time before saying, "My name is Lanthrea. What is yours?"

Sniffing, the girl said, "Mysta. I'm Mysta."

"Mysta," said Lanthrea sweetly, "what a lovely name. It's nice to meet you, Mysta."

The girl looked up and smiled weakly.

"Do you know where your parents are, dear one?" Lanthrea pressed a bit more.

The little girl nodded, the tears coming once again.

Seeing she was clearly in need of help, Lanthrea picked up the girl and took her inside, where it was warm. She left the door cracked open a bit so as not to frighten her, being a stranger and all, then took her over by the fireplace and set her down by the fire.

"Mysta. What has happened to your parents?" The little girl looked up at Lanthrea, her green eyes shining with tears. "They never comed back."

Lanthrea was crestfallen. "Where did they go, child? And how long have you been alone?"

Mysta wiped her eyes and sniffed. "I been here…and the …the snow comed. And they left to go hunting. But they never comed back."

"How long has it been snowing, Mysta? How many days since your parents left?"

Mysta held up both her hands. "This many sleeps."

"You've been alone for ten days?" Lanthrea was struck to the heart. "Mysta. Have you had any food? Are you hungry?"

The girl's eyes lit up at the mention of food. "Yes!" she exclaimed, "soooo hungry!"

Lanthrea smiled at her and said, 'Well, now, let's see what we can find here, shall we?" Walking over the one wall of shelves in the tiny hut, she found a jar of jam, a basket of onions, and one bunch of saggy, rather old carrots.

"Well, there's not a lot here to work with," she said, "but let's see what we can do. Do you have a pot?"

Mysta perked up and pointed to the hearth, where a copper pot sat next to the hook.

"Very good. Now, let's get some food into you."

She walked out into the snow, grabbed a handful and tossed it into the pot. Pulling the greens off of the carrots, she put them in with the water, then peeled an onion and tossed it in as well. She found a small tin with some salt in it, and pinched a bit into the vegetables, then set the pot on the hook.

"There we go. That will cook up in just a few minutes, alright?"

Mysta nodded excitedly. "It smells good," she said after a few minutes as the onion began to soften, filling the hut with the savory aroma.

Satisfied that the little girl was comfortable with her, Lanthrea walked over, shut the front door, then sat down next to the fire with Mysta. "Now, then. Tell me what you've been doing. And tell me how you learned to build such a nice fire."

"I learned-ed that from mommy," she said. "Put the little sticks in, lantern for the flame, big logs next and watch - it - burn." She sing-songed the little poem, obviously memorized—something her mother had no doubt taught her. Lanthrea looked over at the little lantern burning on the one table in the home. "Is that where you get your flame?" Mysta nodded. Lanthrea got up and went over to it. The oil was almost gone. Mysta wouldn't have a 'flame' much longer to use for fire. This entire situation was becoming more and more of a mystery and complex. Where were the girl's parents? Had they abandoned her? Been killed by animals or had an accident of some sort? Were they out there somewhere needing help? There was absolutely no way of knowing their fate, but that of the girl's seemed to be falling squarely into Lanthrea's hands.

"Mysta," Lanthrea said, walking over and stirring the vegetables with a wooden spoon she found on a shelf. "Have you ever ridden a horse before?"

Mysta shook her head. "Nuh uh. But I seen 'em, though. They look pretty. I told mommy I wanted a pony, but she said we don't have 'nuff to feed one very good."

Lanthrea smiled. "Well, I have a really nice horse. His name is Elpinhoe….." She stopped short, looking down at the little girl. Elpinhoeve would be a mouthful for her. "His name is *Bray*. Would you like to ride him, Mysta?"

The girl's eyes lit up. "Yay, yay, yay! Can we ask mommy when she gets back?"

Lanthrea sighed. "Well, sweet girl, maybe we could go find your mommy and ask her together. Would that be alright?"

Mysta was already on her feet, grabbing her coat by the door. "Is the horsie outside?" She asked excitedly.

"Uh-huh. Just a bit from here. But let's eat our food first, yes?"

Mysta impatiently plopped down at the table as Lanthrea scooped out some carrots and onion into a bowl for the child. The little girl dove into the vegetables, hungry as anyone had ever been and ate every last bite. Lanthrea gave her the rest in the pot, and she ate that as well.

Poor little thing. She's starving, thought Lanthrea.

Mysta was back at the door, coat on before Lanthrea had even cleared the bowl from the table.

"Can we see Bray now, Lanthrea?" She was jumping and bouncing like a little dog wanting to go for a walk. Lanthrea found a small pair of leather boots by the door and a pair of mittens, and slowed Mysta down long enough to get them put on, then took her hand, shut the door to the little hut, and walked her back through the snow to the pine grove to Elpin, who was still digging under the snow for grass.

Mysta's eyes widened, and she bolted over and wrapped herself around Elpin's leg, hugging it tightly. "Horsie!" she yelled exuberantly. Lanthrea grabbed her just in case Elpin didn't approve of this unabashed affection from a tiny human, but he was nonplussed, outside of looking down at the little girl and sniffing her once or twice. Lanthrea went over and grabbed her cloak from the pine tree's limb and tossed it on before taking Mysta's hand. "How about we ride to go find your mother," she asked. "I don't think she'll mind if I'm with you, do you?" Mysta shook her head and jumped up and down in anticipation. Lanthrea smiled. "Here now, let me help you up. It's going to be really, really high, so don't be afraid."

Lanthrea lifted Mysta up and set her on the saddle.

"Now grab that hair there - that's called his mane, that's right. It's a good thing to hold onto, and he won't mind at all."

Swinging herself up in the saddle behind the girl, she turned Elpin back towards the little hut, hoping to find some tracks in the snow in an attempt to find Mysta's parents. Once behind the hut, she easily found two pairs of tracks heading into the woods behind the little home and followed them for almost an hour before finding anything of note. It was at the edge of a riverbank that the first sign of what might have happened to her parents could be seen. There was evidence of someone sliding, slipping most likely, down the steep bank, and then of the other running down, sliding, too, as they ran to the water's edge. The river was a monster—created by the same glacial melt that Lanthrea had watched form on her way down from Mt. Glastone. It was a high, fast-moving goliath, and at this spot was full of rapids and sharp waterfalls that dropped by levels to a large lake below. Dismounting, she tied Elpin's reins to a tree and turned to Mysta.

"Mysta. I'm going to go look at the pretty lake. You stay here and take care of Bray for me, yes?"

The little girl nodded, busying herself with Elpin's mane. Lanthrea walked along the high, steep bank of the river to an outcropping where she could view the lake beneath the falls. There was no sign of her parents, and she sighed in relief. Maybe they had made it out? She scoured the landscape for any sign of footprints in the snow below the place where they had obviously gone into the water. There was nothing. The snow was undisturbed. No one had walked out of this place. She continued to walk along the outcropping when something caught her eye. Hard to see because it was directly below her, she had to crane her neck to get a good view. Her heart sank. There, on the rocky shore, were two bodies. Both were in brown leather coats, face down, half floating in the water, half washed up on the shore. There was no movement or sign of life. The woman's long blonde hair was floating gently on the rising and falling on the current. Lanthrea hung her head and whispered a prayer for their souls, then turned and walked through the deep snow to Elpin and Mysta.

She would tell the little girl later. Somehow. Remembering her own agony and terror the day Plata, their neighbor, had come to tell Lanthrea that her parents had both succumbed to the plague, she shuddered. How on earth could she do this to this little girl? How could she shatter her entire universe into pieces with her words? Paralyzed to even consider it further, she thought to just put it aside for now and come up with something else to tell Mysta.

It suddenly occurred to her that the girl was now in her custody. Her responsibility. She would have to find her other relatives, and quickly. She untied Elpin, hopped on, and squeezed Mysta tightly.

"Mysta. Do your grandparents live nearby? Aunts, Uncles…. Cousins? Can you tell me where they live?"

Mysta turned around and gave Lanthrea a funny look.

"What's a cuzin'? She looked genuinely confused.

Lanthrea explained, "Your Auntie's children…or your Uncle's?"

Mysta was silent.

"How about your grandmama or grandpapa? Where do they live…do you know?"

Uncertain of a five-year-old's ability to know where anyone lived, Lanthrea was not expectant of a helpful response, but the response Mysta did give was entirely illuminating.

"It's just me and mommy and daddy. I don't have a nonna or poppa. They die-ded before." She looked back at Lanthrea solemnly, "I was sad."

Lanthrea squeezed her tighter. "And you don't have an Aunt or an Uncle? Are you sure, Mysta?"

The little girl shook her head vehemently. "It's me and mommy and daddy." She brightened. "Sometimes, there *is* a squirrel who comes and eats dinner with us. I feed him nuts. Mommy doesn't like that…she says we need the nuts for us, but I…."

Mysta rattled on with her tale, but Lanthrea had stopped listening as the realization hit her. This child, this little girl, was *indeed* now her responsibility. This little child, unless someone could be found, was *hers*.

CHAPTER TWENTY-ONE:

The Winterland

They rode back to the little hut slowly, Lanthrea dreading any conversation with Mysta. Once back at the hut, she pulled Elpin's gear off and turned him out to find grass. He rolled gleefully in the deep snow before shaking from head to rear end, then loped off to find food.

Mysta ran into the house before Lanthrea, but not before turning around a tossing a snowball at her, then giggling as she darted in.

Lanthrea felt her heart squeeze. How could she possibly do this? "Good king, give me words," she whispered. Once in the hut, she pulled off Mysta's coat and mittens, setting them by the fire to dry, then took off her cloak to do the same. She grabbed a log from the woodpile by the fireplace (there were only a few left) and tossed it on as well.

Mysta had already grabbed a small rag doll from a box and was pretending it was riding a horse across the floor. "Hold the mane like that!" She instructed the doll on the imaginary pony.

Lanthrea swallowed hard. "Mysta...how would you like to ride Bray some more?"

Mysta barely looked up but said, "Mmm huh".

"Good. … Good," Lanthrea hesitated, wondering what to say next.

"Would you like to come with me for a ride, then? Bray would love that, I'm sure."

No answer from Mysta on the floor, but Lanthrea was certain she saw her little shoulders tighten.

"Mysta. I need you to come with me today. We are going to take a trip."

Mysta set the doll down on the floor but didn't face Lanthrea, her back rigid. "We didn't find mommy," was all she said.

Lanthrea swallowed, her throat feeling as dry as kindling. "No, honey… we didn't. Mysta. Your mommy and daddy…they…uh…they…they aren't coming back. They had an accident in the woods. And Mysta…they …..they died."

Mysta was a statue. She said nothing for a few minutes. Then, in the weakest voice Lanthrea had ever head, she barely whispered, "Like nonna and poppa?"

Lanthrea nodded. "Yes."

There was nothing more to say now that the little girl could understand…at least as well as a small child could. She stood and walked over to Mysta, knelt down and wrapped her arms around her.

"But I'm here now, Mysta. You are not alone. I won't leave you. I promise."

The girl was rigid, frozen. Lanthrea felt the child's terror and grief as she remembered her own so many years ago when Plata had held her and whispered similar words in her ear. But Plata *had* left her, moved on. She had her own family to care for, and another mouth to feed was not something her husband had agreed to.

Lanthrea hugged her more tightly. "I won't leave you alone, Mysta. I promise."

She meant it.

They spent the night in the little hut, Lanthrea gathering up what clothing and supplies she could for the trip ahead. Some warm clothes for the child, some real boots for Lanthrea, a few scarves, a tin of salt, and another hunting knife. There was even a money box with a bit of coin in it, enough for some food if they could find a place to purchase it. She had slept next to Mysta, holding the child as she cried herself to sleep; both Mysta's tiny heart and Lanthrea's old one breaking with every sob.

In the morning, Lanthrea bundled Mysta up, grabbed the remaining onions and the jar of jam, tamped the fire down, and made certain the little rag doll was tucked safely under Mysta's arm. They left the hut—Lanthrea shutting the door slowly and reverently—and were on their way north by mid-morning.

Mysta hadn't said a word since last night but continued to alternately whimper and sleep against Lanthrea's warm chest as they rode. Lanthrea kept an arm wrapped around the child, even though it was harder to ride that way. By afternoon, her arm was cramped, and she knew they were both hungry. After what seemed like endless miles of white, flat, snow-covered land with no sign of life, they rounded a glen of trees to find themselves at the outskirts of a village! The inviting plumes of smoke rising from chimneys and the sight of houses, horses and people moving about brought tears to Lanthrea's eyes. Food, drink and warmth! She told Mysta to hold on tight, grabbed the reins with both hands and kicked Elpin to move out. They entered the town within minutes, Lanthrea noting immediately that the people here seemed friendly and welcoming. Nods and waves from almost everyone as they walked Elpinhoeve to what was obviously a market, where vendors had set up baskets and boxes in the snow-covered streets and were selling their wares. There were large metal bins set about the place, each filled with wood and burning brightly, where people would stop and warm themselves as they shopped.

Dismounting, she pulled Mysta off Elpin, tied him to a pole and grabbed the child's hand. "Stay with me here, and we will find some food, yes?"

Mysta nodded, still not saying a word.

She found a kind butcher (who reminded her of much of Maruk, her butcher friend in Cenecal) and was able to purchase a week's worth of salted venison. She then found a rather pretentious cheese monger (who called himself 'a purveyor of fine cheeses') where she had enough coin left to buy a small half-round of hard cheese.

Thrilled with their goods and hungry as she had ever been, Lanthrea made Mysta sit down by one of the fire-bins and gave her both meat and cheese. Lanthrea was pleased to note that Mysta ate well. It was a good sign.

Still not having said a word since last night, Lanthrea didn't try and push the child into talking. It might be awhile before Mysta decided to 'come back' to her new world. Lanthrea would let her stay where she needed and for as long as she needed.

After eating, she took Mysta's hand, and they walked together on the boardwalks of the little village. She had learned from the butcher that the place was called Matan and was one of the ten villages that made up a loosely knit decopolis called Hylandria. There was no central governing body over the villages per se, but goods and foodstuffs were procured and supplied to the ten towns from Hylandria's capital city, aptly named Hyland, about fifty miles away. It assured the outlaying villages like Matan always had fresh food, even in this cold season. She had also learned that this odd weather occurring during the high summer months was an aberration that no one could explain. Two years ago, the snow and cold had come and had not ever left. Growing crops had become impossible, and had it not been for the village's interdependence and Hylandria's vast arm of purchasing from surrounding territories, the people would have starved to death by now.

The Matanians (for this is what they called themselves) had, by and large, reverted to superstition and ancient rites in attempts to thwart the endless cold and inclement weather; to that end, altars to the various forest gods and goddesses could be found throughout the village. The entire land, from The Thetan Sea to the eastern forest, had been dubbed "The Winterland", and many people had simply packed up and moved away, worried that it might not ever end.

Mysta clung to Lanthrea's hand, squeezing it tightly as they walked around the little village, visiting with the local residents. Realizing at one point that it was probably all too much for the little girl, Lanthrea decided to get her away from all the people and all the talking. Slipping off to a side street, Lanthrea hiked the girl up on her hip. It reminded her of how she used to hold Tenk, and she shivered, remembering how miserable and afraid it used to make her feel. Mysta wrapped her arms around Lanthrea's neck and held tight, burying her little head in Lanthrea's long gray hair. It hadn't been but a minute or two before a door suddenly opened across the street from them, and an elderly woman, older even than Lanthrea, called out, "You. You there with the child. Come in, come in…it's miserably cold out there."

Lanthrea stopped, wondering why a stranger might be inviting them into her home, but Mysta was shivering from the cold, and Lanthrea had to admit she could use a sit-down in a warm place as well. *The kindness of strangers*, she thought before jogging across the road—only to be greeted warmly by the woman —who opened her door and motioned them inside. Shutting the door behind them, she turned and smiled broadly —the lines in her lovely face gently chiseled by many such a smile. She ran her fingers through her soft white hair, freshening up as Lanthrea looked about the place.

The little house was, in a word, charming. A roaring fire with two overstuffed chairs facing it, a little kitchen from which the smell of something freshly baked (Lanthrea couldn't tell what), and a small table on the far side of the room with four chairs. It was to the overstuffed chairs that the woman pointed after taking their coats, scarves and mittens and setting them by the hearth to warm.

Mysta wouldn't stay in a chair by herself and clung to Lanthrea, so the woman sat in one, and Lanthrea and the girl cuddled in the other together.

"There now," said the woman, "that's better, no?"

"Lanthrea took in the warmth of the fire like a sponge to water. "Thank you so much, friend. This is a kindness we hadn't expected."

"Thought as much," said the woman. "I'm Clesta. And you are?"

"Lanthrea and (hugging the child), this is Mysta."

Clesta deep brown eyes glowed with kindness. "Nice to meet you both. I heard there were a couple of travelers in town—a woman and a young girl. I just know how hard it is to be out there in this infernal cold, so when I saw you across the street….well, now, let me get you both some hot tea."

And with that, she was up and disappeared into the little kitchen, rummaging about with a kettle. She emerged but a few minutes later with two cups of steaming tea and handed one to each of them. Mysta held it in her hands for the longest time before finally taking a sip, then making a face. "Mommy puts honey in mine," she whispered sadly.

Lanthrea could have shouted. The first words she had spoken!

Clesta put her hands on her hips and said through her smile, "Is that so? Well, then…let's do it like your mommy does, yes?" She opened a small cabinet on the wall by the table and pulled out a jar of honey. Bringing it over, she plopped a spoonful into Mysta's tea, then joined her guests next to the fire.

"How long are you staying in Matan?" Clesta asked. She seemed genuinely interested.

Lanthrea took a deep breath. "Well, ten minutes ago, I would have said that we were leaving today. But now, sitting in your warm house and enjoying your hospitality, I honestly don't know."

Clesta chuckled. "Well, you are welcome to stay here as long as you like." She looked over at the child. "By Palem's throne, she looks exhausted. She could use some rest."

Lanthrea sat up, "Palem?" She blurted breathlessly. "You know of it?"

Clesta laughed out loud. "Well, of course, dear. I went there to meet the king when I was but a girl of sixteen years. I came back here shortly thereafter. To tell people about Palem. About him." She sat back in her chair and sighed. "Few listen, that's true, but the ones who do…." Her voice trailed off. "For those who do….isn't it all worthwhile?" She looked earnestly at Lanthrea. It was not a rhetorical question.

Lanthrea shifted in her soft chair. "I…I don't know yet," she said honestly. "I am just on my way back from Palem to Drymac. Just beginning the Return. I have yet to speak of this to anyone."

Clesta shook her head and nodded at the little girl in her lap. "Oh, I don't know about that," she smiled. "Our deeds speak much louder than our words."

Lanthrea held Mysta tightly. "Well. Maybe so…"

She looked around the warm little home, grateful for Clesta's kind deeds and suddenly she saw the telltale signs of Palem everywhere. There was the fireplace hearth for one—carved with the same Solemn Memories that Petrul had on his cane and table. Then there was the lovely stone mosaic, mounted on a shelf in full display…Clesta's crest, set by the king's hand. And then (how had she missed it?) on top of the mantle, sitting atop a lovely hand made lace doily, was the book. Larger than Lanthrea's small copy, but indisputably the book. The same tree on the cover, the same waxy pages.

She looked over at Clesta. "It wasn't just that we were new in town that moved you to invite us in, was it?"

Clesta laughed gently. "No, friend. Azar was through just the other day. He told me you'd be coming." She gestured at the child. "He did not tell me everything."

Lanthrea glanced down at Mysta, her tea with honey balanced precariously on her lap; her eyes closed in a soft and easy sleep. Taking the cup from her hands, she set it on the floor gently. "I did not ever think I'd be bringing a child on this journey," she whispered. "It's a long story."

Clesta nodded. "It always is…it always is." She stood up, "here, let's get the little one into bed, shall we? We can let her sleep until evening meal or beyond if she needs it. And you can tell me her story."

They laid the little girl on a trundle bed in a small bedroom, pulled the curtains, and shut the door quietly behind them.

"She may sleep a long while," Lanthrea whispered as the two women headed back to the fireplace and plopped down in the chairs. "I found her, quite by chance, in the forest, about a day's ride from here. She was alone. I found her parents—perished, I'm sad to say—in a lake….they had fallen into the river…a terrible accident while out hunting. Mysta had been alone for over ten days when I knocked on her door. By the king, I don't think she would have lasted much longer. There was little food in the house and even less oil in the lantern she was using to keep the fire lit." She took a sip of her tea, "And only three logs remaining in the woodpile. It was by chance that I found her just in time."

"Oh, I don't think it was by chance, Lanthrea," said Clesta softly. "Not at all."

Lanthrea pursed her lips. "I…I hadn't thought of that," she said. "I honestly hadn't thought of this as something the king had for me to do."

"Ah, once a member of his family, there is little that is not," Clesta said with a grin. "Now. Let's prepare evening meal together, and we can talk….about everything!"

Lanthrea was happy to be in a real kitchen, preparing real food, and found she was completely outdone by Clesta's kitchen skills. From handling and preparing a duck from the market to baking a cheese pie, her abilities were far beyond anything Lanthrea had. Of course, Lanthrea never had the coin for such luxuries as duck, butter, or even the soft cheese and spices going into the pie. It was as Clesta was rolling out the dough that Lanthrea couldn't contain her curiosity any longer.

Nodding at her full larder, she asked (and rather bluntly), "Does everyone in Matan have such luxury?" Realizing immediately that she was coming off as judgmental, she softened and tried to pull the words back a bit. "Oh, I don't mean to be rude, but you have such wonderful foods and spices. I'm…I'm just not used to such things in Cenecal."

"Not to worry, I take no offense. The answer is yes and no. Yes, in that Hyland sees to it that no one goes without. And it is no small feat, as the ten villages are spread far apart, and the roads have been closed many times due to this eternal snowfall. They somehow provide most of our basic goods, no matter the weather. And the 'no' rests on the fact that I am more blessed than most. My husband, rest his soul, was a very successful merchant. When he died, he left me and the children a goodly sum of coin. My oldest son has invested it well, trading with other lands and continuing to profit off the original inheritance.”

Lanthrea immediately felt embarrassed. “Oh, Clesta, I didn’t mean to pry…I shouldn’t have asked.”

Clesta stopped rolling the pie dough and looked her directly in the eye. “Coin is not an issue for me, Lanthrea. If you haven’t learned by now, the king’s people are not to be concerned with wealth except to the extent that we share what we have with others. My son’s earnings do supply me with many privileges, but I give most of my excess supplies and food away. After all, what need does one old woman have with an extra pound of butter?” She smiled. “Besides, all of this (she waved her rolling pin at the larder) allows me to fix a hearty meal for you today.”

Lanthrea nodded and continued mixing a spicy paste that was to go on the dough and said nothing more about the subject.

They put the duck, properly tied and herbed, into the open brick oven and let it begin its roast. Clesta showed Lanthrea how to finish off the pie by fluting the crust neatly, ensuring the cheese wouldn’t escape once put to flame.

Grabbing a bottle of wine from the cupboard, Clesta got out two lovely glasses and filled them almost to the rim before giving Lanthrea one and motioning her to the living area and the soft chairs. Sitting together next to the warm fire, they sipped the wine and talked as the bird roasted in the oven. The smell of it was overwhelming Lanthrea, and she was having trouble focusing on the conversation. They two women found they had nothing at all in common but Palem. Lanthrea, single, never married—an orphan living and working alone in poverty on the mean streets of Cenecal for a lifetime; Clesta, married with three children, wealthy and wanting for nothing or no one. Her children visited regularly, bringing her any supplies she needed, and almost always hauling the grandchildren over, much to her delight. In fact, she now had almost five great-grandchildren, a point she made at least four times as they waited for the duck to roast. At one point, Clesta got up and put the pie in to bake, letting Lanthrea know dinner was only a few minutes away now and wondering if they should awaken Mysta. Lanthrea had checked on her a few times as they visited, but the child had been sleeping soundly. They decided to let her sleep and would feed her whenever she awakened, be it this evening, middle of the night, or morning.

It was as they were setting the table for dinner when Clesta asked a question that Lanthrea had been secretly been considering ever since the 'great- grandchildren' conversation.

"Will you keep her then….Mysta? Will you keep her and raise her as your own?"

Lanthrea closed her eyes and froze. "I don't know," she said. "I promised her I wouldn't leave her alone, and I won't. But Clesta…I am not a young woman anymore. She opened her eyes and pointed to her face. "These lines prove it. Perhaps I can find some nice young couple that would take her."

Clesta laughed. "No, no…no. It's true you're not young. But if the girl came into your life, don't you think there is a reason?" She pulled the pie out of the brick oven, golden brown with cheese oozing out the sides, and set it on the table. "You've never had anyone. You know, the king is known for helping people find a family."

"So I've heard," Lanthrea tried to smile, "but I thought that meant the family at Palem…the family of those who know and love the king, not a….a….*real* one."

Clesta laughed again, wiping her hands on her apron. "Both are real, friend. One just takes more *work*."

Lanthrea forced a small laugh but found herself suddenly burdened and a not a small bit overwhelmed. Finding someone to care for the child was one thing, actually caring for her was altogether another.

"Well, no matter…I'm going to go check on her again," she said, leaving Clesta to pull the duck out of the oven. Opening the door to the little bedroom, she tiptoed in, and sat down gently on the side of the bed. Little Mysta, with long blond hair, a handful of freckles, and bright green eyes, now shut peacefully in sleep.

Lanthrea leaned over and kissed her forehead. "Oh, how I pray your dreams are as sweet as you look right now, dear one. May the horrors of the past day be swept from your heart by love."

She kissed her again, then rose and left quietly. "Good king," she asked, "help her through this time. Heal her broken heart. Let me be what she needs, and let me lead her to you…as no one was there for me…" It was as she said these words that she closed the door leaned against it, and began to cry.

For no one *had* been there for her. She had had to do it all alone. It had been terrifying, exhausting, and so, so confusing. Living on the cruel streets, protecting herself from dangers at every turn, living in constant fear, and embracing a glottin who demanded even more. Always hungry, never knowing any worth at all, no one to even….(and here her cries turned to sobs) brush the tangles out of her hair.

Reaching up, she touched her soft hair, now pinned with the butterflies given her by the Lady and her two helpers at Palem. No, she had had no one to help her find her beauty and worth. No one to hold her in the middle of the night. No one to speak life to her broken little soul. She thought of Mysta, her innocence and sweet spirit. No. She would not, she *could* not leave her alone nor pass her on to someone else.

Wiping her eyes on her sleeve, she straightened her skirt and walked to the dinner table, knowing deep in her heart that she now had a *daughter*.

Mysta had awakened just as the two women were about to share after-dinner tea by the fire. Wandering out, hair mussed, eyes sleepy, and dress rumpled, she rubbed her eyes and walked right over to Lanthrea and fell into her lap. Lanthrea stroked her hair and whispered, "are you ready for some dinner?" in her ear. The little girl nodded, still rubbing the sleep from her eyes.

Clesta started to get up, but Lanthrea put up her hand. "No, please. "Let me," she said. Clesta smiled, nodded, and sat down for her tea.

Lanthrea walked Mysta into the little kitchen, sat her down at the table, and pulled the pie from the shelf and the duck from the outside kitchen windowsill, where Clesta had put it, wrapped in about five tea cloths to keep animals from smelling it. "The cold temperatures keep it fresh enough," she had explained when Lanthrea had raised an eyebrow. Remembering how her butcher friend Maruk used blocks of river ice for the same purpose, she thought it one advantage of a perpetually cold land.

She filled a plate for Mysta with a slice of the cheese pie and the leg of the duck (she had saved it for her specially). The girl had devoured both in a matter of minutes, and Lanthrea had given her a cold mug of milk (kept on the same windowsill) for her dessert. Mysta hadn't said anything while she ate, and Lanthrea didn't push her to talk. It was as she was finishing her milk, upper lip covered with the thick, white stuff, that she spoke.

"I want my mommy and daddy." Her little voice was weak, and she sounded broken.

Lanthrea nodded, her eyes filling with tears. "I know you do, Mysta." It was all she could say.

"They won't come home?" She was looking up at Lanthrea, her eyes desperate for a new—a *different* answer.

"They won't, dear one." Lanthrea let the words do their work. She added nothing to them but reached out and held Mysta's hand.

"I am here for you now. I am here, and I won't leave you. You are safe. You are safe with me."

The little girl blinked and pulled her hand away.

"You're not my mommy," was all she said.

"No, I'm not. But I am here for you, and I will take care of you. And we will miss your mommy together."

Mysta put her mug down. Her eyes glazed over as though she was in a different world altogether. A world where this wasn't happening. A world, *her* world… where she would awaken in the morning in her little home and hear her dad singing his Morning Song in his big, bellowing voice and her mother laughing at him as she tended to the fire.

Lanthrea left her to her thoughts but stood and stroked her hair for a few minutes until Mysta looked up at her and said, "I wanna go to bed."

Lanthrea nodded. "A good idea, lovely. Here, I'll carry you." She lifted her up and carried her into the bedroom, laying her back onto the trundle bed. Gently kissing her forehead, she watched helplessly as the little girl rolled over, back towards her, and pulled the blankets up over her head. There was nothing she could do to ease her sorrow. She knew this, but oh, if she could have, she would have taken all the girl's pain onto herself in that moment.

She slogged back to the big chair by the fire and flopped down. "I wish I could help her through this," she said, looking helplessly at Clesta.

"You are, dear. You are. Time will be a good help as well. Time and love. Yours and the king's. For your job will be to lead her to him. As you weren't ever really alone, she needs to know she isn't, either. The king is there, *has* been there…for you both."

"So he told me," Lanthrea said. "It's hard to believe….." Her voice trailed off. There were some things that still hurt her heart.

Clesta slapped her knees and got up. "Time for you to get some sleep, as well. There is a bed in my daughter's old room. It has blankets and a pillow. It is yours for as long as you need."

Lanthrea emitted a little laugh. "A warm bed and a pillow. You are speaking my language."

Leading her to a back bedroom, just beyond the tiny one Mysta was in, Clesta left her to rest, but not before bringing in a soft sleeping gown (her daughter's) along with a towel and a basin of water.

"Morning Meal is at eight bells," she said, her voice trailing down the hall to her room, where she blew out the hall lantern and left the house in darkness.

Lanthrea fell into bed, feeling both overwhelmed and grateful. She slept soundly, having dreams of riding Elpinhoeve with Mysta in a lovely green forest.

***

"You haven't touched your oatmeal."

Clesta was gently chiding Mysta as they sat at the table for morning meal. The girl said nothing but pushed the grain around in her bowl with a spoon.

Lanthrea and Clesta exchanged glances. Lanthrea took Mysta's bowl and walked to the larder. "Here, how about I add some honey and cinnamon to it for you? I'll bet you've never tasted *anything* like cinnamon before." She brought back the bowl, added a touch more cream and handed Mysta the spoon. "Just try it."

Mysta dipped her spoon in the oats and took a bite. Her face lit up, but she scowled again as if to hide it. Another bite, then another, and she had finished the entire bowl within a few moments, her scowl gone. Looking up and licking the spoon, she asked, "Is there any more?"

Clesta laughed heartily, "Indeed there is, dear." She stood to get a ladleful more from the pot, added the honey and cinnamon and set it down on the table. Mysta added her own cream and continued to eat through an entire bowl again as the women talked.

"Tell me about the weather here," Lanthrea asked as she sipped on her tea.

"It is a strange thing, indeed," Clesta answered with a shrug. "It was two years ago now when the snow came in late spring. We thought it just an aberrant storm, but the melt never came, and the snow never stopped."

"And no one knows the reason?" Lanthrea was dumbfounded.

Clesta shook her head. "No one does. But I have my suspicions."

Lanthrea looked at her as if to say, 'go on'.

"Well, just about two years ago, the king of this land made a pact with a neighboring royal family. The pact's details are not known to we commoners, but all know it had something to do with the cessation of power and a re-naming of our kingdom. We were not always just known as The Winterland, you know. For as long as there were people here, this land, from the Thetan Sea to the eastern forest, was known as Thetonia."

"Thetonia," mused Lanthrea. "It's funny, but the map the king gave me had no name for this land. It was left blank. I wondered as to the reason for that omission."

"Well, that's why," Clesta sighed. "Our name was removed, our identity with it. It wasn't long after that the snow came. I can't help but think the two things are connected." She paused, sipping her tea. "Ever since, people have simply named it what they wanted.

Winterland, Icehaven, Land of Ice…whatever. It feels as though we have….lost ourselves."

"Who rules the land, then?" Lanthrea inquired.

"The King of Nycia. It is a territory far to the west of us. A powerful military realm, with little concern for its native citizenry, and even less for its acquisitions - whether gained through war or negotiation. The Nycian King is known for his dabbling in dark magic, a fact of which our king (a weak and fragile man) was well aware. When Nycian armies began to posture at our borders—threatening invasion —I think it was out of blatant fear and cowardice that our king simply handed Thetonia over. Little blood was shed. Outside of a few good men who tried to hold the Nycian soldiers at the border, there weren't even any major skirmishes. But a terrible price was paid none the less."

"And you think the perpetual winter is because of this treaty?" Lanthrea asked, "I mean, how does a military acquisition cause…"she looked out the window, gesturing at the snow, *this?*"

Clesta just stirred her tea and nodded. "I don't know how. But I believe it did. The perpetual snowfall, the lack of our own sense of Thetonian identity, the fragmenting of our very soul as a people." She set her tea down and lowered her voice considerably, almost to a whisper. Leaning forward over the table, her eyes narrowed as she spoke.

"You know…I've heard that the King of Nycia not only toyed with black magic, but also made alliances with the *Koth*, far to the south. The evil rumored to come out of that region—a land named Kress—is well renowned. I think that that alliance, more than anything else has brought this enchantment upon us." She took another sip of her tea before continuing.

"There is one thing I've learned from being a follower of the good king and a sojourner to Palem. Things are often connected at levels we just don't understand. I think there are powers behind these earthly ones…powers we know nothing of. Sitting up straight she pursed her lips and smiled coyly. "But then again..what do I know?" She sat back in her chair and shrugged. "Anyway, this is how it is here now, and we have no idea if or when the freeze will ever end."

Lanthrea sighed and pushed back from the table. Mysta was playing with her rag doll on her lap, having consumed two full bowls of oatmeal, and Lanthrea was glad to see it.

"We should get going," she said, watching Mysta play. "It is about time for us to get back to Cenecal. Although, speaking of powers, Lord Bythim, who rules my land, may still be looking for me. I don't want to bring a child into that if I can avoid it."

Clesta's eyebrows raised. "You are wanted by the King of your land, this Bythim?"

Lanthrea nodded. "Lord…He prefers that title, but yes."

Clesta pressed in. "What on earth for?"

Lanthrea chuckled. "Well, for having a copy of the book. And the funny thing is, I didn't even know what it was. I made the mistake of painting some of the illustrations onto cloth and selling them at market, not knowing what they meant. But Bythim's men did, and the paintings led them to me…well, my home. I left that day and haven't been back since."

Clesta clucked her tongue. "Oh my. Well. Do you think they will still be looking for you? You've been gone for how long now?"

Lanthrea took a moment to figure it up… "about four months, all told," she replied. "And I don't know if they are still looking for me. They have to know by now that I have left town. Cenecal is too small a place to hide for long. They would know that." She tapped her fingers on the table. "Perhaps they have forgotten about 'the old woman who sold pictures from the book' by now."

Clesta nodded, "By the king's land, we can only hope."

The women cleaned up the table and let Mysta play with her doll by the fire while Lanthrea packed up their things. Clesta gave them many parting gifts and supplies, the most gracious thing being money. She handed Lanthrea a small bag filled with coins, reminding her 'she had plenty more where that came from'. Overwhelmed with gratitude, Lanthrea had hugged her tightly and promised to look her up if they were ever in Thetonia again.

Elpinhoeve had been warm and comfortable all night in Clesta's small barn. He had been given a stall, water, a large flake of hay last night and again this morning, and Lanthrea had given him a bucket of oats as well. He nickered happily when she and Mysta came into the barn and saddled him up for the ride ahead.

Leading him out to the front of Clesta's house, she hoisted Mysta up on the horse, then hugged her new friend tightly once again.

"Maybe next time we see each other, our land will be green again," Clesta had said, tears in her eyes.

"We can hope and pray," Lanthrea had added and kissed her new friend on both cheeks before climbing up on Elpin and turning him East, out of Matan and towards Drymac.

CHAPTER TWENTY-TWO:
The Glen at Darrow Falls

Mysta had been quiet all morning as they rode towards the forested land the map referred to as Braydenland. There was nothing of note on the map about this place, no topographical hindrances like cliffs or mountain passes, but it did show the land was heavily forested, a fact for which Lanthrea was glad. She loved riding through forests and was looking forward to seeing green again.

The snowy, cold climate of Thetonia gave way slowly to the summer the further east they traveled. Mysta's quiet began to melt away with the snow, and she became increasingly chatty the further out of the winter climate they went. By midday, the temperature had climbed to a normal mid-summer high, and Lanthrea had to stop Elpin to get off and pull all of Mysta's and her winter clothing and have a bit to eat. The little girl was more interested in the hot sunny weather and all that it brought than eating and kept chasing every butterfly she could find, giggling and jumping about. She squealed with delight as she picked handfuls of wildflowers, sticking them in her hair or shoving them next to Elpin's mouth and trying to get him to eat them. Lanthrea smiled, her heart full to see the girl so happy. Realizing Mysta probably didn't even remember a time when the sun shone and the summer danced, she was grateful beyond words to see her enjoy it so much now.

"Lanthee…Lanthee…look!" She would holler as she tumbled on the soft green grass or did cartwheels in the wildflowers next to

Elpin, who would step sideways and look at the girl curiously with every flip she made.

"I'm looking," Lanthrea said over and over and over again, amazed at how persistent at five year old could be. Most happily, she loved that the girl was asking for her attention and the name she called out. *"Lanthee."* It was perfect, and it meant Mysta had somehow, at least a little bit, appropriated her into her life, and given her a name. It felt like what had happened in Palem when she had been given her new name there—it felt like….family.

She pulled out two pieces of the cheese pie that Clesta had packed for them and called Mysta. She came running over, red-faced and happy, gobbling up the pie. They drank from the water pouch, Mysta draining it, thirsty as she was from all the exercise in the hot sun.

"Well, now. We're going to have to find some water, aren't we?" Lanthrea said, shaking the pouch to see it was empty.

"Can I play some more?" begged Mysta.

Lanthrea stroked her hair. "Of course! Go play and tumble. Stay here next to Elpin, and I'll go to check for a stream."

Mysta nodded happily, then scampered to a large patch of grass and started skipping around in a circle, then falling down every so often, laughing. Elpin looked up from his grazing at her, then returned to the grass. Lanthrea swore he was rolling his eyes at the child and laughed out loud.

"It's what children *do,*" she yelled at the horse, who ignored her summarily.

She wandered down a little hillock, happily finding a small, fresh stream at the bottom of it and filled the water pouch. As she slid the cork into the pouch, she thought she heard a sound not far from her. Unwilling to go any further into the trees without Mysta at her side, she walked back up the hill and interrupted Mysta's play to hoist her up on Elpin, leading them both down towards the sound.

"There, do you hear that?" She asked the girl, who was still catching her breath from dancing.

Mysta listened and said, "Uh-huh. It's coming from over there. It sounds like singing. Daddy did it all the time."

They followed the sound, coming at last to a lovely glen of aspen trees, their leaves fluttering in the summer breeze, wildflowers all about. Here the stream made a sharp turn and pooled up, gently falling in a cascade of iridescent water into a pond within the glen. The singing became louder the closer they got to the little waterfall until, at last, they were able to peek between the tree branches to see the source.

It was an old, old man wearing a long, white robe and a garland of ivy on his equally white hair. He was standing all alone with his back towards them in the middle of the glen, and he was singing a lovely song. His voice, though old, held the certain timbre of a much younger man, and the tune he was singing was completely captivating. Hearing it made Lanthrea think of spring flowers, freshly baked bread and good wine all at the same time.

Hearing them approach, he suddenly stopped his song and turned to face them.

"You've come at last!" He exclaimed.

Lanthrea pulled Mysta from the saddle and held her hand tightly.

"You were expecting us?" She asked, hesitant to step any closer to the man and placed a protective arm in front of Mysta.

"Indeed," he said, smiling. It was a most winsome and inviting smile, and it put Lanthrea immediately at ease. Relaxing her grip on Mysta a bit, she continued to stay firmly planted where she was.

"Who are you? I think that's a fair starting point, yes?" Lanthrea asked.

The old man smiled. "My name is Innatus. I am the Keeper of Darrow Falls…and these woods. And you are most welcome, Lanthrea and Mysta."

"You know us?" Lanthrea was taken aback.

He nodded. "I do. The King told me to await you here. For it is time."

"Time?" she responded curiously, glad to know the king has something to do with this encounter.

He nodded again, then waved his hands in a circular motion. Blinking, Lanthrea saw there were now two ornately carved golden chairs in the glen where none had been before.

He motioned to them. "Come, sit. Let us begin."

Mysta, still exuberant from this sunny summer day and excited as any child could be, darted away from Lanthrea and toward the man. Before she could say a word, the girl had plopped down in a chair. "Come on, Lanthee!"

Lanthrea moved toward the man and the chair hesitantly.

"Time for what?" She asked again before sitting down next to Mysta.

"For the Becoming," he said plainly, as if she ought to know what that meant.

With no further explanation, he turned his back to them and there, in his hand, appeared a flask full of what appeared to be either water or oil, Lanthrea couldn't tell. Lifting this up toward the sky, the old man began singing again, his voice soaring towards the heavens, the melody lifting Lanthrea almost out of her chair. The song was at once thrilling, solemn, mysterious, calming, and….holy. She couldn't bring herself to do anything but listen, and for a moment, it felt as though heaven and earth had somehow coalesced, as though this man was summoning the very stars down to this exact place in the forest. Perhaps he was. There was no other way to explain the song except that Lanthrea felt she could listen to it forever and never tire of it. Mysta had a different reaction. She became very calm, and then she began to cry. She wept there in that chair as the man sang his song, and the summer sun winked at her through the aspens.

Suddenly, he stopped singing and turned to face them. "Welcome, daughters of the King. To this place—to this very song — you have come and may always come. Let this song heal you, revive you and guide you always. For it is given you by the King's own hand as solace for your journey."

He then tipped the little flask and poured the contents over first Lanthrea's, then Mysta's head.

"Become one with the king's family and one with each other today."

Lanthrea bowed her head, hardly understanding his words but somehow knowing this was a sacred moment. She sat for a time, absorbing the feeling. When she, at last, looked up, she and Mysta were alone in the aspen glen. The old man was gone, and where he stood, there was something on the ground, sparkling in the sun that filtered in through the trees. Mysta jumped up and grabbed it before Lanthrea could even move.

"It's a necklace!" She squealed excitedly. "Look, Lanthee! Look!"

Lanthrea looked at the tiny golden chain in the girl's hand. It was one of the most delicate and lovely things she had ever seen. About to put it on Mysta's neck, the little girl suddenly pointed and yelled, "Look! There's one for you, too!"

Lanthrea looked over, and sure enough, another sparkling necklace lay on the soft brown earth where the old man had stood. She leaned over, picked it up and began to cry. For there, in her hand, was a perfect silver necklace reminiscent of the crown the king had given her. It had a little silver charm dangling from the clasp. She turned the charm over, and there, engraved upon it, was a butterfly. Touching the pin in her hair, she was overcome. The Lady of Lanthor's touch, to be sure.

She secured Mysta's necklace and then hers, gently touching the charm and whispering a quiet thanks to the king and the lady. Having felt she was part of a family in Palem had been one thing. Something about what she felt this day was altogether another. She was not just *part* of a family. She *belonged* to one, as now Mysta belonged to her. It was as though they both had been melded into something more ancient and immense than either could ever have imagined.

She and Mysta left the little glen quietly. Neither of them felt much like talking. When they sat down to have another drink of water from the stream before they left, Lanthrea noted that Mysta's eyes didn't seem to hold the same depth of sorrow they had before. She was still sad, to be certain, but the sense of desperation and loneliness seemed somewhat lessened. It wasn't something that Lanthrea could quite put her finger on, but she was certain of the change in the girl and grateful for it.

They got back onto Elpinhoeve and rode eastward through the forest, talking and laughing as they watched the rabbits and deer bound around them and Mysta enjoying each breath of the warm summer air.

It was late evening when the sun gasped its last, the days being so long this time of year. Mysta had trouble falling asleep, so excited was she to watch the sunset, something she hadn't seen before, as the constant cloud cover at home had always obscured   the horizon. When at last she shut her eyes, cuddled close to Lanthrea by the fire, it was past midnight, and Lanthrea was exhausted. She touched her silver necklace and smiled sleepily. It seemed every time she turned around, the king had a new surprise for her: a new gift. Her only sorrow was that she had not come to know of him until her seventh decade. So much time lost.

She shook off that particular sadness and let herself fall to sleep, a daughter in her arms and her new family in her heart.

Mysta was up before Lanthrea could even open her eyes. The morning was warm and sunny, the flowers blooming, the soft scent of summer everywhere. Mysta had never before in her memory awakened to such glory. She was outside! And she didn't even need a coat!

Running over to see Bray, she patted him to say good morning, then ran into the meadow to pick flowers again. They were the most beautiful things, and she had only seen pictures of them that her mother had drawn with charcoal on pieces of wood. Her mother told her what spring and summer used to be like, and Mysta hadn't quite believed her. Until now.

She stopped for a moment and picked up a small daisy. She ached for her mother. She couldn't put words to it, but it hurt deep inside. Like something was tearing her apart. Tears welled up, and she didn't even try and stop them. Lanthee was nice, but she was so old. Like her nonna had been. Nice and old. But her mommy. With her golden hair, pretty lips and the most beautiful face in the world. And her daddy. Tall and handsome, stronger than any man in the village. The best hunter, too! And the best hugger. She began to cry and then cried until she didn't have any more tears left. Sniffling and wiping her eyes with the hem of her skirt, she reached up and touched her new little golden necklace. It made her feel a bit better. She didn't know why. It just did.

Jumping up, she ran back to Bray and petted him all over again.

Lanthrea felt the tugging at her sleeve.

"Lanthee….Get up, Lanthee! Time to get up! Time to eat…it's good for you…Lanthee…"

She opened her eyes and yawned. "Oh, good morning, little sunshine! I'll bet you *are* hungry. Have you been up for long?"

The little girl nodded and pulled at her sleeve again. "C'mon! Let's eat! I'm hungry. Don't you wanna eat?"

Lanthrea sat up, stretched her arms and yawned again. "Morning meal, then. Here we go!"

They decided upon a meal of bread, butter and jam from Mysta's own home. Mysta was overjoyed to see the little jar when Lanthrea pulled it out from the provision bag. "My mommy made that!" She had squealed before suddenly becoming very quiet. "I miss mommy and daddy," she said simply with the brutal raw honesty of a child.

"I know you do, lovely," Lanthrea said, smoothing her hair gently. "Do you want to have the jam later? We can just have bread and butter this morning if you want."

"No. It tastes good. Mommy makes the bestest jam. You try it too, Lanthee."

They sat under a big elm tree and ate bread, butter and jam until they were stuffed. Lanthrea pulled out the map while Mysta played with a caterpillar she found on a leaf. According to the directions, they were not far from Drymac now. Braydenland was the last of the outer territories before they would reach the Great River of Sherhall, which marked the westernmost border of Drymac. The map showed that the only way across the formidable river was a bridge that could be found by locating two tall pinnacles of the Ciracian Range notated as 'The Twins'. The bridge was located in the valley between those two mountain peaks. Once crossed, the map showed what appeared to be a relatively easy passage through the Ciracs and then another easy drop down into Drymac. Cenecal was in the central portion of the kingdom, and Lanthrea knew well the way there.

She closed the map, folded it and put it in her pocket.

They would be home soon.

Lanthrea saddled up Elpin, packed up their belongings, and then swung Mysta up on the saddle before swinging herself up behind her. Her goal was to get as far as the Ciracian foothills by nightfall, making camp one last time before heading into Drymac proper. The day was as bright and sunny as the morning had promised. Mysta rattled on and on at each new thing she saw, amazed at the colors, sights, smells and sounds of another lovely summer day. Her continual running commentary delighted Lanthrea, and she found herself taking joy in Mysta's joy.

"Lanthee, look at all the green leaves on that tree?" "Look, Lanthee! Butterflies!" "The flowers are so pretty, isn't they, Lanthee?" "Can you smell them? I can. They smell so goooood."

The funny thing was, Lanthrea was finding that she hadn't really seen *any* of these things, nor appreciated them, in a long, long time. Having Mysta was like seeing the world through brand new eyes; the girl's sense of wonder was infectious.

It was barely evening when Elpin seemed to slow his pace a bit and, even though she planned on going further, decided that the extra weight on the horse earned him an early break from travel. She could see the Ciracian Range in the distance, about a half day's ride away. It wasn't as far as she wanted to go today, but it gave her pause to look at the Ciracs from a distance. Sharp, jagged, rising from the lowlands like gigantic claws, she recognized immediately why Drymac had few visitors. Nothing about the Ciracs was inviting.

She pulled Mysta out of the saddle and laughed as she hit the ground, literally running, jumping and tumbling about. *Oh, to be young again*, she mused, stretching and cajoling her old stiff legs back to life. Letting Mysta play, and Elpin graze, Lanthrea made camp, then pulled some rations from the saddle bag. Clesta had packed them quite a few luxuries, and she decided to serve a few of them for dinner. There was, of course, the last piece of the cheese pie and then a hunk of wonderful sourdough bread. She unwrapped the treasure of the night: some smoked venison—peppered and salted to perfection. Laying the food out on a blanket, she called to Mysta, who came running over and plopped down, breathing hard and wiping sweat from her face.

"I runned fast, didn't I, Lanthee?" she was grinning from ear to ear as she began devouring a hunk of bread.

"You did!" Lanthrea laughed. Now, let's say thanks for our meal, yes?"

Mysta looked confused but simply finished chewing her bread and, swallowing, said, "Who we gonna thank, Lanthee?"

"Well," Lanthrea said, wiping a crumb from the girl's mouth, "We can thank Clesta…for making us this good food, and we can thank our good king for helping us find her."

Mysta just nodded, and Lanthrea took her hand. "Good king, thank you for leading us to Clesta and for her kindness."

Mysta looked at Lanthrea sideways, her hand hovering over the cheese pie, ready to pounce.

"Go on, eat," She laughed. "I'll tell you more about our good king later after evening meal. I even have a book with some pictures to show you."

They ate well, Mysta recollecting her day all over again, and Lanthrea delighted and amazed at how excited a person could be about a blue sky and a field or two of flowers. After the meal, a campfire was built, and Mysta snuggled into Lanthrea's lap to look at the book. Having not ever seen a book before, let alone colored illustrations on paper (her mother's charcoal drawings on wood had been amazing enough!) her eyes were the size of saucers as she looked at each picture. Her favorite was that of the great winged horse. She simply could not get enough of that image, as she would look at it, then over at Elpinhoeve, then back at the picture. Lanthrea didn't tell her much of the king that night except to let her know that she had once met such a beast as the flying horse named Garanthor in his land, and maybe Mysta could meet one someday as well.

With this thought as a bedtime benediction, Mysta curled up in her blanket, her face towards to fire, the flames dancing in her eyes.

"Lanthee," she said sleepily. "Can I go to see the big horse with wings soon?"

Lanthrea leaned over and kissed her forehead.

"I hope so, dear one. I hope so. Sleep well."

Mysta drifted easily off to sleep, her dreams full of butterflies and flying horses.

CHAPTER TWENTY-THREE:
The Bridge Over Sherhall

Clouds moved in sometime during the night. Mysta was sorely disappointed that the 'blue wasn't out' but had happily eaten her morning meal of grains and berries all the same. Lanthrea looked towards the east and towards the peaks of the Ciracs. Dark, ominous billows were hanging over the summits; the mountains were making their own weather. She bit her lip and decided, once again, not to worry about it. It was hard, as she knew rain down here in the lowlands would mean snow up there at the summits. Glad this time that they both had *real* boots and coats, she packed up camp and loaded Mysta up onto Elpin's back.

It took the entirety of the half-day's ride she had calculated to reach the foothills. The clouds spit at them now and again, but at this elevation and temperature, it was more of an annoyance than anything else. They stopped for a midday meal at the base of a foothill that led straight up to a low glacier around which they would have to navigate. There was no taking Elpin and a small child through that deep snow. Not if she didn't have to.

She pulled out the map while Mysta ate. It showed clearly that they had to find the twin peaks in order to find the bridge across the Sherhall River. She looked up. Peaks aplenty, but nothing resembling 'Two Twins'—just irregular and disparate summits of craggy stone, each one foreboding in its own way. She folded the map, secured it in a saddle bag and had a bite to eat. Just as she was finishing her piece of cheese, the rain suddenly decided, after a morning of teasing, to let go and assault them. She quickly packed everything tightly away and pulled out Mysta's coat and hat, wishing they were made of something other than wool. They'd be soaked and heavy before they got halfway up the hill, and there would be no drying them unless the sun reappeared before nightfall.

She scratched her head. This wasn't going to work. Her own life was one thing, but she had a *child* with her now. Pulling Elpin under some trees for cover, she set up a little tent (big enough only for one) that Clesta had scavenged from her from her eldest son's things and made Mysta go sit inside. Happy to be out of the downpour, the girl pulled out her rag doll and played.

"I've seen rain before," she hollered out at Lanthrea. "It makes snow!"

Lanthrea sighed. As if she didn't know.

She had so wanted to make it to the 'Twins' by nightfall, and it was now looking as though they'd be lucky to get past that low glacier up ahead. Groaning, she thought to simply wait out this cloudburst and hope for the best. Standing under the trees, listening to the rain pelt the leaves, she absentmindedly reached up and fiddled with her necklace - the one left for her at the Falls of Darrow Glen. Touching the little charm with the butterfly on it, she thought of the Lady of Lanthor and smiled. So much help the Lady had given her. And hadn't the old man in the glen said they 'had all become one family' now? Pondering that idea, she thought to simply ask the lady for help. What could it hurt?

Very quietly, under her breath, she whispered, "Good lady, I don't know if you can hear me. I only know that you are kind. Could you ask the king to help us? I know only that if you can, you will."

Leaving it at that, she sat down and leaned against a tree trunk to wait out the storm. She found the cloudburst wasn't in a hurry to leave, and after several hours of the wet, pelting rain with no end in sight, she realized it was too late to travel any further this day. She turned Elpin out, made certain Mysta had a good evening meal and huddled under a tarp for the rest of the cold, miserable night. Her dreams were unsettling and dark. She was being assaulted by the winged creatures with jagged teeth—screeching and howling with their unearthly voices. She awakened almost every hour just to rid herself of the dreams, but each time she fell asleep, the demons would haunt her. So disturbing was her dreams that she finally gave up and attempted to light a fire, but any wood she found was too wet to hold a flame. She sat up, shivering against the tree trunk, as frightened and shaken as she ever remembered being. She didn't need Tenk to tell her that there was danger ahead.

The sky lightened only to reveal another cloudy day. But the rain had stopped, and the temperature was warm, leaving the ground steaming. Mysta was still sleeping, but she would have to be awakened soon if they were to forge ahead and find a way past that glacier before midday. There was no way of telling if the clouds held any more rain, but one thing was certain: time was of the essence. Her nightmares still at the forefront of her thoughts and coloring her emotions, she was exhausted before she even whistled to Elpin, calling him over to saddle him up. To make matters worse, Mysta was cranky and complaining about everything from the weather to the morning meal (which, for expediency's sake) was only a piece of bread and butter.

They started up the foothills, miserable to a person, Elpin being the only creature happy to ascend the mountain this morning. The first few minutes were non-eventful, and once to the glacier's edge, even more so. Lanthrea was surprised and relieved to find a distinct path around the icy perimeter forged by wildlife looking for an easy way around. It only took a few hours to navigate around the entire thing. Once they managed that task, Lanthrea relaxed considerably, having been worried about it for the last day. The truth was, it hadn't been an issue at all. It reminded her of what the king had taught her. Worrying about something before getting to the thing itself was not only fruitless, it only proved to be discouraging. *"Most importantly, a person is usually wrong in their assumptions."* How many times had he told her that? She shook her head at her own stubborn heart and continued on up past the glacier. Finding a stony outcrop above the snow, they dismounted, and Lanthrea prepared for the midday meal, promising Mysta more than bread this time. It was obvious that the girl had been crying, a fact Lanthrea hadn't noticed until now, so intent was she on finding her way around the glacier. Taking time to sit with her, she let Mysta cry, not even asking what was wrong, as her snuffles and *"I want mommy, I wanna go home's"* said it all. There was nothing she could do but hold her tightly. It gutted her to hear Mysta's broken heart and deepest longings, and strangely, it brought up some of her own. Suddenly she was five again, sitting outside what had been her family home, sobbing inconsolably for her mother. But no one stopped to wipe her tears. No passer-by slowed to ask her about her needs. She was completely alone, and there was nothing that could be done about it. She remembered being terrified and how Tenk had bounded up to her that very day (a young glottin at the time) and snuffled its long snout in her chest. It had told her that 'things will get worse' but that it would be there for her to warn her of the dangers to come. Grateful for the company and the protection she had taken Tenk into her life that very day. Oh! If she had only known another way back then. If she had only known there was a loving king and a family that were waiting for her. Lanthrea squeezed Mysta tightly. She would make sure this little girl knew, and she would do her best to fill her heart with hope and love.

With one arm firmly around Mysta, she pulled out her map and looked at it once again. Once past the glacier, the path through the foothills looked relatively easy. They would circle around until she could see the twin peaks and hopefully find the bridge by nightfall. Satisfied with her plan, She squeezed Mysta tightly and let her cry until she was asleep. They could stay here a few more minutes. She would let the child rest. Rocking her back and forth on her lap, she began to hum an old Drymacian folk tune, one her mother used to sing for her at night. The memory brought tears to her eyes, and she sang softly, letting them fall gently down her cheeks.

Mysta awakened after a half hour, bleary-eyed and red-cheeked but rested. After giving her a bite of bread with butter and jam, Lanthrea loaded Mysta onto Elpinhoeve and situated herself behind her in the saddle. The path around these foothills was flat enough not to have to lead the horse; the two could ride until they found the peaks. Mercifully, the black clouds above them hadn't decided to dump the rain they held, and Elpin picked his way carefully on the rocky path until they found themselves staring up (quite suddenly) at two enormously sharp, tall peaks. *The Twins!* They had to be! She swung off Elpin's back and pulled Mysta down to let the girl stretch her legs. Spying a tiny blue wildflower amongst the path's stones, Mysta was off and running to smell it. Smiling, she looped the reins over Elpin's neck and let him find some grass on which to graze while she surveyed the landscape. She saw no evidence of a bridge. For that matter, the great river Sherhall was nowhere to be seen, either. She shook her head. These had to be the Twins. Two perfectly shaped peaks, side by side? She knew it was pointless, but pulled out the map again anyway and scanned it for any minute detail she might have missed. It showed the two peaks and, directly below it, the Sherhall River and the bridge. She exhaled roughly (more of an irritated growl than anything else) and stuffed the map back in her pocket. Where was the river? It had to be close. Checking once again on Elpin and Mysta, she walked to the edge of the path, where a slight drop-off showed her how far they had climbed. They were, at best estimates, about a quarter of the way up the mountain by now. They had made good time. But no river could be seen below her. She walked on a bit further up the trail and heard something. Peering over the edge, she saw nothing but scrub pine and fallen rocks, the latter presumably from the bare granite peaks above. Continuing on up the trail, the sound got increasingly louder until, at last, she made a sharp turn on a switchback and was stopped in her tracks. The noise was now a roar, and below her, straight down the rocky cliffside, was the Mighty Sherhall. She had never seen anything like it in her life. It was more a surging wall of water than a river—at least any river she had ever seen. As wide as a small lake, but raging and leaping down the valley below, white water foaming over every rapid. It looked as mean and formidable as anything she had ever seen.

The bridge was not visible from this position. She looked up. The peaks were directly above her head now. The bridge had to be here somewhere. She turned and jogged back to Mysta, got settled on Elpin's back, and nudged him slowly forward on the path. Turning the corner, Elpin spooked at the river's roaring, jumping sideways about two feet, almost dislodging Mysta from his back. Lanthrea tried to calm him but found her heart racing as well. "Easy, boy…easy. Take a good look at it. It can't hurt you…at least from here." She nudged him forward, and they continued up the next series of switchbacks, the river's roars becoming quieter with each foot they ascended. It wasn't until they were about halfway up the mountainside that she finally saw it. The bridge! It was not far from them as the crow flies, but it was below them a considerable distance. She saw no way to get down to it from here, and there had been no lower paths that she had seen. Looking ahead, the path only went up. Looking back, there was only the glacier and another dead end. She saw no way down to that river bed, let alone the bridge, nestled as it was below the cliffside. It was as she was pondering this conundrum that she felt a drop of rain on her face. Then another, and another. "Lanthee…it's raining…Lanthee…I'm gonna get cold." Mysta was snuggling as close to her as she could, and Lanthrea pulled the girl's hood over her head. "I can't stop the rain, dear one," was all she could say, but before she could even get off Elpin and pull Mysta's coat and mittens out of the saddlebags, the sky let loose. Within moments the rain was coming down in blinding sheets, pierced with ice. This was merciless stuff: sharp, painful and numbingly cold. Elpin's ears lay flat against his head, and he was prancing nervously on the slick rocks. "Easy, boy. Easy….whoa now, we'll get out of this storm, easy now."

Lanthrea was trying to calm both Mysta and Elpin, but in actuality, she was terrified. She couldn't see the trail any longer, the sheets of rain obscuring all visibility, making small rivers of their own at their feet. She tried turning Elpin around. They had to get back down to the glacier. At least the land was open and flat there. They could get their bearings and their coats.

Elpin was rearing up a bit as she pulled him around. The trail was narrow, and he couldn't see anything either. He crow-hopped a bit, trying to find his footing on the slick rocks and mud when the unthinkable happened. The earth simply gave way. The little narrow switchback on which they were standing crumbled suddenly and viciously, turning in an instant into a stone-flecked river of mud. Elpin screamed—an unearthly sound that only a terrified animal could make—whereas Lanthrea had no time to. She remembered the sensation of falling, of grabbing for Mysta, of feeling the weight of the horse crush them both as they slid down the mountainside. She remembered mud and rock in her mouth, and then she remembered no more.

She awoke, or at least she thought she was awake (it was hard to tell) feeling nothing but pain. Her head, her back, her arms and legs. Screaming, shrieking pain. Aware enough only to know she wasn't aware enough, she tried to call out for Mysta. She wasn't even sure if her voice was audible. Feeling something on her chest, she looked down and saw the child, crumbled in a bloody, mud-caked ball, laying across her. She tried to lift an arm but shrieked in pain. Quieting her panic as best she was able, she felt the gentle rise and fall of Mysta's breath against her. She was alive! She tried to lift her head to get a better look at the girl, but found she couldn't. The rain was still coming down in sheets, and it was impossible to get her bearings. They were lying somewhere close to the river bank, for the roaring of the rapids was earsplitting. She winced in pain as she tried to sit up. Still nothing. She couldn't move at all. Suddenly aware of the probability that she could be paralyzed, her heart began to race, and her mind whirled in terror. She called out for Elpinhoeve, hoping to hear a sound back. Nothing. The child was beginning to moan and stir, and Lanthrea tried to calm herself.

"Mysta. Mysta…are you alright?"

The girl moaned again and lifted her head.

The minute her eyes caught Lanthrea's, she dissolved into wailing tears of both terror and pain. She said no words, just screamed and cried at the top of her lungs.

Lanthrea exhaled. The girl could move! How badly hurt she was would be told in time, but she could move and cry and breathe!

"Mysta. Mysta dear. I'm here. I'm here, and you are with me. Mysta…Can you tell me where you hurt?"

The girl stopped screaming and began gasping for breath in between huge sobs.

"Tell me where it hurts," Lanthrea said again, as calmly and gently as she could, doing her best to quell her own terror.

"My leg…it hurts," the girl sobbed.

"Anywhere else?" Lanthrea coaxed.

Mysta shook her head. "My leg, Lanthee….my leeeeeeeeg!" She broke into sobs again.

Lanthrea breathed a sigh of relief. A broken leg. If that was the worst of the little girl's injuries….

"Mysta…do you see…do you see Bray anywhere?"

Mysta sat up, cringing as she grabbed her leg and tried to wipe the rain and blood from her face. "He's over there, Lanthee….over there…in the water."

"Mysta," Lanthrea tried to keep her emotions in check, "Is he standing up?"

Mysta wiped the rain from her face again and looked.

"Nuh uh…he's sleeping."

Lanthrea felt as though her heart had just collapsed in her chest or that it might escape from her body and explode somewhere in the rain-drenched sky. Not Elpin. Nooo….

"Mysta…is he moving? At all? Look again."

She looked over, wincing again and grabbing her leg.

"No, Lanthee, he's asleep…my leg hurts…." Her tears and sobs began again.

The rain was beginning to let up a bit, and Lanthrea could see around her more clearly. She realized she could turn her head but not lift it. Everywhere she looked was just mud and rock, and parts of the fallen cliffside splattered around them in chunks and muddy piles. She tried wiggling her toes. Yes. She could move them. And her fingers as well. But her arms and legs proper wouldn't respond to her, no matter how hard she tried. And the pain in her head was formidable. She licked her lips and tasted blood. No doubt her head or face had been cut, but she couldn't tell and didn't want to ask Mysta for fear of frightening her.

"Mysta. I need you to go over to Bray and get some water and food from the saddle bag. Do you think you can do that?"

Mysta shook her head. "My leg hurts too bad, Lanthee."

"I know it does, dearheart, but we are going to need some water and food for the evening meal, aren't we? And…I….I'm…stuck in the mud."

Mysta's face screwed up in concern. She looked at Lanthrea, her brows furrowed. "Lanthee…you look hurted."

"I am, dearheart, but I'll be fine. Let's just get some food and water in us. I'm sure I'll feel better. I'm just ….hungry."

The truth of the matter wasn't hunger at all, for Lanthrea couldn't have eaten if she'd been forced. But she was afraid the foodstuffs and water might be washed away with the horse if he was indeed lying, most likely dead, near or even in the river. Mysta would need the food soon enough, even if Lanthrea didn't.

"Mysta. Can you try and stand up for me?" Lanthrea tried to speak calmly and quietly, but it was hard to over the roar of the river. "It's important, dear. We need the food, and I can't get up right now. Do you understand?"

Mysta sniffled and nodded her head. "I'll try," she muttered. Pushing herself off of Lanthrea's body, she whimpered in pain as she tried to stand up.

"Can you stand on both legs?" Lanthrea asked, unable to see much from her prone position.

"It hurts!" Squealed Mysta.

"I know it does, but ….can you?"

Mysta made some little squeaking noises, then began to cry again. "I can walk, Lanthee, but it huuurrrrts," she wailed.

Lanthrea exhaled. Maybe the leg wasn't broken after all.

"Alright, then. Why don't you try hopping over to Bray? Like when you played in the forest the other day. Hop like a bunny on one leg. Can you do that?"

More sniffling and cries from the little girl.

"It's too muddy. It's too slick, too. Lanthee…Help me go see Bray."

"I can't, dearest," Lanthrea sighed deeply. "But you can. And listen to me, Mysta. You *must*."

She heard the child whimper and then heard a hopping sound for a moment before being overtaken by the roar of the rapids. *"Please, good king, don't let her slip into the river."*

It was probably only a few minutes later, but it seemed like an hour when she could once again hear the slushy hopping of the little girl. Mysta flopped the food bag and a water pouch down next to Lanthrea, then plopped down herself.

"I gotted it, Lanthee" she exclaimed exuberantly.

"You did! Such a brave, good girl," Lanthrea said, wishing she could hug her child.

Mysta looked at her, concern again in her eyes. "Get up, alright? Get up, Lanthee, and let's go get Bray, alright?"

Lanthrea swallowed hard. "When you saw Bray, then…Was he ….was he ….did he get up?"

Mysta shook her head. "Nuh-uh. He's still sleeping. Let's go wake him up, Lanthee, alright? Come on!"

"I'll tell you what," Lanthrea said, "Why don't you help me sit up. Can you do that?"

Mysta nodded. "Sure. I'll help!"

She grabbed Lanthrea's hands and tried to pull. But her arms were in no way strong enough to lift a dead-weight adult from the sucking mud, and she gave up after three tries.

"I can't lift you. You get up, alright? You do it."

Lanthrea was shivering all over by now. Not only from the cold but from the injuries. She knew this, and she knew it was not good. What were they to do? She closed her eyes and whispered a cry for help.

"Good king, we need you. Sweet lady, can you hear us?"

The roar of the rapids and the light drizzle remaining from the downpour was all she could hear in response.

They were alone, grievously injured, at the bottom of a ravine, next to an impassable and angry river, with one bag of food and a severely injured or dead horse. She thought of Elpin and began to cry. She couldn't help it. Her friend, her help, her companion, her strong Braydenthall…her Elpinhoeve…hooves of hope. She groaned. There was absolutely nothing hopeful about their situation now. Nothing at all. She knew she had to stop crying, lest she frighten Mysta, but she just couldn't. The tears ran down her cheeks into the mud.

Mysta crawled over and huddled next to her. "Lanthee….Lanthee…what's wrong? Lanthee…you're scaring me. Get up, alright? Let's go now, yes? Please, Lanthee."

Lanthrea inhaled deeply and tried to compose herself. It would do no good to terrify the child. She might have to get to the bridge by herself and would need all the encouragement that could be given. Lanthrea realized that she was getting very sleepy, and wondered if her head wound might be more severe than she had hoped. She was having trouble keeping her eyes open and, worse, had noted the pain in her body had almost stopped. She knew this wasn't good but was helpless to fight it.

"Mysta. I need to have some rest now," she said slowly. "You have something to eat from the bag. Anything you want, alright? Anythin….."

She fell into complete blackness, Mysta's terrified face being the last thing she saw.

The first thing she felt was pain. The second was the soft nuzzle of a horse on her cheek. "Elpin," she whispered.

Her eyes fluttered open to see the face of a horse, but it was enormous, and it wasn't Elpinhoeve.

"Garanthor!" she cried out weakly, almost unable to believe what she was seeing. The gigantic animal was standing over her, wings folded on his back and Mysta by his side.

"Lanthee! You waked up now? Look, Lanthee, it's Gaarn…Garanth…It's Gara-something! And he *talks,* Lanthee, he can talk!!"

The enormous beast bent his head low and whispered in Lanthrea's ear. "The king sent me. And none too soon, I see."

She smiled up at him and tried to sit up, but the pain stopped her once again. She realized, however, that she could move her arms a bit and could shift her legs in the mud. "I think I might be hurt too badly to move."

He nodded, his magnificent black mane catching the light rain and sprinkling her with water. "I see that, human. But I am going to try and help you."

Lanthrea looked over towards the river. "Elpin… is he…is he…"

Garanthor closed his eyes for a moment and sighed. "He is very near death. But the Lady of Lanthor called for as many of my kind as are left. We flew here to help *all* of you, even our cousin, the horse. He has been taken back to Palem. He was lifted out of this canyon on a sledge, slung between my brothers Gorath and Klestfeather. The king will see to him, but we do not yet know the outcome. Nor is that your concern now. Come, let's see if I can help you sit up. Grab ahold of my mane if you can."

Her heart lifted in hope at the news. Elpin was in Palem. Live or die, he was in good and kind hands. That was enough. Taking a deep breath, she attempted to lift her arms and reach out for Garanthor's long mane. Her first try was futile, but on her second, she was able to grab on, and Garanthor slowly raised his head until she was pulled to a sitting position. The pain was bad but tolerable. Mysta ran to her and hugged her. "You alright, Lanthee?"

She tried to wrap her arm around the girl and hug her but found her arm unresponsive. "Garanthor," she said quietly. "I don't think I can get up."

The huge beast simply nodded and said, "Trust me."

What happened next was nothing short of a confusing blur of activity and movement. Lanthrea remembered being pulled to her feet as she clung desperately to the horse's mane, and then, with a swirl of feathers and whooshing of wind, felt herself being gently lifted onto his back, one wing gently caressing her until she caught her breath. Once on Garanthor, she realized she was lying across his back crosswise, like a dead deer on a hunting trip. Her arms and legs were still screaming in pain, and hanging her head down was almost unbearable.

"It's not a perfect solution," said the great beast gently. "But it is what we have."

Lanthrea nodded weakly, the blood rushing to her wounded head, but immediately thought to ask about Mysta.

"My girl," she said, "Where will you put her?"

Garanthor whinnied—a wild, free, happy sound. "She has already chosen a seat," he said, "behold!"

He let his wing unfurl till the tip of the feathers touched the ground. Mysta simply stepped onto it and was scooped immediately up to his neck, where she gleefully grabbed handfuls of his long mane, turning and grinning at Lanthrea. "Look, Lanthee! I'm riding a BIG horsie!"

Lanthrea breathed a prayer of thanks to the king and the lady for their good help and closed her eyes in exhaustion.

Garanthor looked back at Lanthrea. "Listen carefully. You will need to use those hands of yours to hold onto the cinch around my belly. I have no way of strapping you on. It is not the best solution…as I said, but it is…"

"What we have…" Lanthrea finished his statement. She reached down and felt for the cinch, a large leather band with metal rings on it. Thankfully, the rings were about the size of her fist, and she slipped her hands through them like bracelets, then hung on for dear life.

"Here we go, then," Garanthor announced and began to trot (the hardest part for Lanthrea), then canter, and then, with a magnificent leap and flourish of his wings, he took to the air. Mysta let loose a squeal of delight and yelled, "I'm fllllyyyyyinnnng!"

Once airborne, Lanthrea found it easy to hang on. It was as though she was floating through the sky. It felt absolutely delightful and the delight eclipsed her pain. Under any other circumstances, this would be like a beautiful dream. She looked down on the valley, watching the bridge recede into the distance. Once her only way across the mighty Sherhall River, it now looked more like a little toy on a tiny stream, getting smaller and smaller as they climbed. They crossed over the great river and flew between the Twin Peaks, the mighty wings of Garanthor working rhythmically, keeping them suspended in the air (although it felt more like magic as they swirled and dove amongst the clouds.)

It wasn't but a quarter-hour before Garanthor began his descent into a small valley on the Drymacian side of the Ciracs. It was green and lush, and as they lowered, Lanthrea could see a small dwelling come into view. Garanthor slowed, his wings folding back a bit, then quickly spreading almost backwards as they pulled against the air and slowed him to the ground, where he landed lightly as a feather and trotted to a stop in front of the little hut.

Before his feet even hit the soft earth, the door of the place opened, and an old man with long white hair came running out to greet them. Lanthrea recognized him immediately. Innatus, the Singer from Darrow Falls! It was he! Even without his white robes and ivy garland, he was easily recognizable. He ran to Garanthor's side, and with incredible strength (not looking as though he had much at all!) he pulled Lanthrea from the horse's back and carried her into the hut.

Without the distraction of the flight, immediately the pain came screaming back into her consciousness, and she moaned and flinched as he lay her gently on a bed next to a roaring fireplace. He looked her over, examining the various wounds on her body, gently touching her head and her limbs. Then he loosened her clothing, pulled a warm blanket over her and went to a cupboard. He returned with a flask, looking very similar to the one with which he had anointed her at the Glen, and poured some of the contents into his hands. He then placed the liquid on her forehead, her arms, her shoulders, her legs and everywhere else he had found damage. It felt like oil, smelled like the finest spices, and was cool to the touch, but as it sat on her skin, it began to warm. Then became warmer still, and then, in a crescendo of pain, it burned as though it was setting her on fire. She screamed in agony, and then, in a second, it was over.

The pain…all of it…was gone.

The man sat down at her side and took her hand in his.

"I'm sorry about that," he said meekly. "But there was no other way. You were wounded through and through. The potion saves, but it purges as well. You need to rest now." He waved his hand over her eyes. "Sleep now, Daughter of the King."

She was out before he finished speaking.

Garanthor and Innatus stood together outside the hut for a long time, speaking in low voices as Mysta played nearby with a toy horse she had found. In the end, Garanthor had bowed to the man, who had placed his old hand on the horse's forelock as if in blessing. Garanthor then trotted over to say goodbye to Mysta, letting her pet his nose before turning from the hut and, with a great whinny, began his canter and lifted off into the sky.

Innatus had taken Mysta's hand as they waved goodbye to Garanthor, then walked into the hut together.

Lanthrea was awake, sitting up in the soft bed, and Mysta ran to her and jumped on her lap.

"Lanthee! You're up!"

Lanthrea kissed the girl's head and smoothed her hair. "I am, sweet girl. And I see your leg is better now, yes?"

She smiled. "Uh-huh. The man putted some med'cine on it. It hurted, but it's all better now." She burrowed into Lanthrea's chest and made intentional little happy noises. Lanthrea laughed. "I'm glad to see you're better." She looked up at the man.

"How did you know we'd be coming?" she asked quietly, a nascent understanding growing that when the King and the Lady were asked for help, she could count on it.

Innatus puttered over the fire, adding another log. "The king sent word. And Garanthor came here before flying to you in the valley. It was I who put the cinch on him. I had no saddle large enough for such a beast. But then again, who does?" He chuckled to himself, and moved over to the little kitchen, opened the cupboard and brought out a round loaf of bread and three glasses. Setting them on the table, he then laid out three heavy stone bowls and fetched a copper pot from the fire. Grabbing a ladle, he poured a thick, hot soup into each bowl, then lit the candles on the table, poured wine in all three glasses (a half finger's worth for the child) and bade them sit.

Lanthrea found herself stiff but not in pain as she hobbled over to take her seat. Mysta was bouncing on her chair, so hungry was she. She started to grab some bread, but Innatus held up his hand and nodded at her.

"We will give thanks first," he said quietly, not in a reprimanding fashion at all, just an informative one.

Mysta perked up. "Who we thank *this* time, Lanthee?" She said, remembering her lesson of late.

Innatus smiled warmly. "Well, we will thank the good King and the kind Lady for sending Garanthor to help you." He winked at Mysta. "And we can thank Garanthor as well."

After saying their thanks, they ate their meal in joyous fellowship; the Singer telling wonderful tales and stories of Palem, reminding them of the King's words; making everyone at the table yearn to go there.

After evening meal, Innatus bade them both sleep well and left the hut, disappearing into the starry late summer night as Lanthrea and Mysta cuddled in the soft bed by the fire and slept as though they had never slept before.

CHAPTER TWENTY-FOUR:

Drymac

Mysta was up before anyone else, and the little house in the green valley seemed to come alive, as though smiling at her childlike energy. Tremendously excited to see the blue sky and sunshine, she ran out the door to pick wildflowers even before the sun's rays began to warm the earth. She was bounding back in the door with an armful of them when Lanthrea awakened, stiff, sore, but deliciously alive.

"I brung these for you," she squealed in delight, shoving the makeshift bouquet in Lanthrea's face. Lanthrea took them and inhaled deeply. "Mysta. They're lovely. Thank you. Let's see if Innatus has a vase for them."

Checking about the little house, they didn't see the old man anywhere. "Well, then, let's have a look around, shall we?" Lanthrea got up, stretched her neck and back, then walked over to the wall of cupboards near the kitchen area. "Hmmmm….bowls, plates, cups….ah! Here we go!" She pulled out a lovely, slightly blue-colored glass vase, blue like the pale morning sky. "Perfect. And I don't think Innatus will mind us using it, do you?" She asked the girl.

Mysta shook her head. "Uh uh…he'll think it's pretty," she said earnestly.

Finding the water jug, Lanthrea poured a bit of water into the vase and put the flowers in, fluffing the petals a bit to arrange them nicely.

"There," she said, smiling. "What do you think?"

Mysta grinned. "Put 'em on the table, Lanthee. For morning meal!" Just then, the door swung open, and Innatus walked in. He looked notably different than he had the night before but in a subtle way. Lanthrea couldn't put her finger on it.

"Good morning, you two," he said in a cheerful voice, "I see everyone is up!"

"Uh huh…and we brung you flowers!" Mysta announced gleefully, pointing at the vase.

Innatus whistled. "Oh. And lovely they are, lovely they are."

Lanthrea watched him walk over and take a sniff, then straighten up and put his hands on his hips. "Well, then. Morning meal." He clapped his hands together and began digging in the larder. His movements were more fluid than yesterday. As if even walking was easier. That was it! He seemed…younger. Looking carefully, Lanthrea saw other tell-tale signs. There were now a few strands of black peppered into his white hair, and his shoulders were straighter. He even appeared a bit taller than he had in either the Glen the other week or yesterday here at his house.

Lanthrea furrowed her brow. "Innatus," she said slowly, "You seem….different this morning." She thought not to mention youth, lest she insinuate that he was 'older' the day before and insult him.

He looked up and raised an eyebrow. "I should think so," he practically bellowed. "I have just returned from the lake to which I go every night. And each time I go, I am renewed again. Such it is with those who go to the waters. Every morning my youth is returned to me, little by little." He looked directly at her and grinned, pointing at his still-quite-white hair. "To be sure, it's a slow process."

She smiled and touched her gray hair absent-mindedly. He looked over at her and, intuiting her thought, replied, "Yes. Yes, it would be the same for you. And, haven't you noticed that your youth seems to be returning to you ever since you began your journey to Palem?"

She thought about it carefully. It was certainly true that her muscles felt stronger, and her back no longer ached as it had before. "But I've been to no lake," she posited, looking at him questioningly.

"You were washed in the waters of Lake V'esta, were you not?" He asked, "and again in the bath at Palem?"

"Well, yes, but…"

"The king uses any and all things to revive his own. You will see this as you journey on." He slapped his knees. "In the meantime, we need to ready you for your return to Cenecal. And in the immediate, we need to get morning meal started and that little girl of yours fed!"

They ate a wonderful meal of hot porridge with cinnamon and honey (Mysta's new favorite meal) and drank something that neither Lanthrea nor Mysta had ever encountered before: hot chocolate. Mysta was leaping about the house for quite a while after drinking it, begging for more. Innatus promised she could have some more tomorrow if she would behave herself today and listen well to more stories from the book. He had then very reverently opened a small cupboard near the fireplace and pulled out the loveliest tome Lanthrea had ever seen. The cover was of silver, with inlaid stones that created an intricate mosaic of a lion. Lanthrea and Mysta both sat in childlike wonder at Innatus' feet, amazed at the incredible illustrations (far more lifelike and detailed than those in Lanthrea's book) and bewitched by his reading of the text. He often sang the words, as he had in the glen that day, his voice lifting their hearts towards the heavens. The parable he read to them was of that of the Beautiful Young Maiden (the illustration of which Lanthrea had called The Courtier, and the story of which reminded her much of her own). His voice captivated them both as he read:

Exhausted, she fell to the ground, her sword falling helpless at her side. The lone Rider who approached her that day carried no weapon, but she knew as he approached she was entirely at his mercy. She had no strength left with which to fight, and her body was broken and battered by enemies she had tried to route singlehandedly.

He dismounted and knelt by her side in the mud. "You are wounded," he said plainly. She began to cry, for these words alone were a greater kindness than anything she had ever experienced in her entire life. "You have been alone here, at this outpost, guarding it with everything you had. But it was not yours to guard. This battle was never to have been yours."

She blinked, not comprehending his words. "There was no one else," she said, tears forming once again in her eyes.

"There was me," the Rider said. "I have been here every day, but you couldn't see me thrashing and slashing about at your enemies as you were."

"You never came," she argued softly. "No one has ever come for me."

"You are wounded. Let me soothe your wounds and comfort you," was all he said in response.

"You will hurt me," she said, fully convinced her life was about to end.

"I will not," he replied. "I am here to heal you, help you, and take you home."

"I have no home," she said. "I have been here, alone, since I was but a child."

"You were never alone. I have been here every day," he responded gently. "You couldn't see me for the terror in which you lived. But you see me today. Let me take your sword."

"You will run me through with it," she whimpered.

"I will not," he replied, "but even if I did, would it be worse than living like this, fighting on alone day after day?"

She paused. She was exhausted and grievously wounded. Glancing at the sword in her hand, she began to release her grip on the hilt. It tumbled from her hand into the mud next to her.

He smiled and picked it up. "Look at it," he said.

She looked up. Her battle sword was made of wood, ragged, chipped and dull. "It was all I had," she said.

"It was not enough," he responded. "Here, take my hand."

Shaking, she reached up and grasped his hand. He pulled her from the mud, and she immediately felt life return to her broken body.

"No one has ever come to my aid," she cried out.

"Yet, here I am," he said, smiling. "As long as you held that sword of yours in your hands, you effectively kept my good help from

you. Now, rest in my care, and know the comfort of the King." From that moment on, he took her into his home, tended her wounds and disfigurements, and dressed her in the most beautiful garments. Her beauty became known throughout the land, and her gentleness, faith and wisdom were known to all.

He gently closed the book. Mysta sat for a moment in silence, then began to clap wildly. "More! More! Read us more!"

Innatus laughed. "Perhaps later today," he said. "Now we have work to do in preparation for your journey home."

They spent the rest of the day helping Innatus clean his little home, prepare food for their journey, and wash and dry their clothing, covered in mud as it was from their fall from the cliffside.

That night, after Mysta had been put to bed (but not before yet another good parable from the book had been read) Lanthrea and Innatus took the time to walk to the lake. Sitting at the edge of it, listening to the water gently lap up on the shore, they looked up at the stars together.

"They are so bright tonight," Lanthrea mentioned casually, "although not as bright as in the Prathian Desert."

Innatus smiled, the starlight reflected in his eyes.

"No, I'd think not," he nodded, "nor in Palem, for that matter," he added. She smiled, remembering the lake in the center of the palace grounds where the king would often sit with her and whisper truths about her heart that she had never been able to comprehend, broken as she was.

Innatus nodded at the water, lapping at their feet. "If you enter in, you will be renewed." He smiled. "At least in part."

He stood, reached out his hand and grabbed hers, lifting her from the sandy beach. "Come, refresh yourself. You have a long journey ahead of you tomorrow." He produced a small vial from his cloak, then turned from her, facing the water, and lifted it to the sky. A song softly came from his lips, the same melody she had heard that day in the glen. As the song rose, his voice, like before, became younger and more vital, and she closed her eyes from the sheer glory of it. Once again, it was as though he was summoning the heavens to earth, as though she was being lifted up while the heavens were being brought down. Opening her eyes, she gasped, for the entire lake was truly alight with life and light, as though the stars had simply tumbled from their home in the sky and fallen into the lake, lighting up the waters with their beauty. It was completely irresistible. She lifted her skirt gently and stepped in, letting the sparkling water wash over her feet and ankles, feeling the life course through her body. It was only a few moments later when he stopped the song and turned to face her, his face dancing with light.

"Remember this when you get to Cenecal. You may always come to the king's waters —and all waters are the king's. They will always heal you in both body and heart. Promise me you won't forget?"

She stepped back onto the beach out of the sparkling waters. "I promise," she said. He nodded. "Good. Now, let's get back to Mysta. And you need some sleep as well. Morning will be here before you know it."

They walked silently back to the little house, the smell of the green grass under their feet and a spring in both their steps.

***

Lanthrea awoke refreshed, noting immediately that the lilt in her step last night was even more noticeable this morning. Innatus caught her looking at herself in her little golden mirror (a miracle it had remained in her pocket during the fall) and winked at her. He then pointed to his hair, which was considerably thicker and darker than it had been the day before. Smiling at her own small vanity, she shut her mirror, wishing only that she had not lost the golden hairpins the Lady and the Attendant had given her. (For unlike the mirror, they had fallen out of her hair somewhere back in that muddy valley.) Sighing, she tucked the mirror back into her bag and secured it for the trip ahead.

Mysta was up and begging for both oatmeal and another story from the book by the time Lanthrea had packed all their things for the journey. The three of them ate a hearty (somewhat heavy) morning meal of not only oats but fried sausages and quail eggs, which Innatus had collected before sunrise. "You'll appreciate it as you walk today," was all he had said (as Lanthrea had tried to refuse another sausage he flopped onto her plate). Mysta ate the oats but skipped the eggs completely, wrinkling her nose at the yellow, runny yolks. She grabbed a piece of sausage and asked if she could take it with her out to play, which Lanthrea had said was fine. It was another blue, perfectly warm and sunny late summer day, and Mysta simply could not get enough of this weather.

"It's going to be hard keeping her in the house," Lanthrea said, nodding at Mysta as she practically leapt out the door.

"Uh huh," Innatus responded, nodding as he finished up a hunk of sausage. Swallowing, he continued, "Where, then, *do* you think you will live? Your home is gone, and you dare not go back to the Market Quarter, I'd imagine."

Lanthrea groaned, patting her full belly and leaning back in the chair. "I don't know. I honestly don't. If Bythim's men recognize me, or if someone else does…" She sighed. "I was not well known in Cenecal but known well enough."

Innatus bit his lip. "Do you know any of the king's people there?"

Lanthrea started to shake her head, then stopped suddenly. "I…I *do!* Petrul and Marinda! They live in Old Town, and…and…Oh, Innatus!!! I'm certain they will take us in, at least for a time!"

Innatus clapped his hands together. "Well, I don't know them, but I know Old Town. The King has protected it from the worst that Cenecal has to offer for many a year now because so many of his people live there. And if you two folks who reside there…" He stopped and looked at her directly. "And you are certain they are trustworthy?"

She nodded vehemently. "Oh, yes. I'm certain of it. They were so kind to me and tried to tell me of Palem, even when I wouldn't hear of it. I had been…quite rude to them. Marinda had wanted me to put my glottin out, and I was furious with her at the suggestion." She stopped, inhaling deeply. "I was so frightened back then." Looking over at Innatus, her eyes suddenly filled with tears. "I had no one but Tenk. I honestly thought its warnings and constant fear mongering were for my good. I knew no other way but to embrace it. To embrace *fear*. I missed so much….so very much…..”

Innatus pursed his lips and emitted a sigh. “I’m so sorry, dear,” was all he said. It was all he *could* say. They sat for a moment in silence, then he straightened up and slapped his knees.

“Come, then. Let’s get you and your little one home.”

The walk through the Ciracs today would be an easy one. This little home of Innatus (he had another, more majestic residence near Darrow Falls) was in a valley mid-way down the Drymacian side of the range, with easy slopes and plenty of alpine-like meadows, streams and berry bushes. They would not go hungry nor thirsty on this last leg of their travels. Lanthrea’s biggest concern was the simple fact that Mysta was only five, and her little legs could not carry her as far as an adult’s, childlike energy notwithstanding. They would have to stop many times for both rest and nourishment. Lanthrea looked up at the late summer sky. What did it matter? The weather would be good, the days long, and what with Innatus had packed in their bags, they would not go hungry. Looking at the lush green grass of the valley, she felt her eyes fill once more with tears. Elpin would have loved it here. How she missed her dear friend. No word had yet come to them on his condition, and she had been holding him in her heart every moment. He was in the best of hands. That was all she knew. And it would have to be enough.

Innatus had packed their things in a mountain pack, easily affixed to Lanthrea’s back, freeing up her hands for whatever Mysta might be up to as they traveled. Hauling it outside and leaning it against the house, Innatus called Mysta from her play.

"One more story from the book, eh?" He smiled as he patted his knee. She popped upon his lap happily and begged for the Courtier story again.

"Not this time," he said quietly. "I think this time we shall read the parable of the Robin who Wanted to Fly."

Opening the book to an illustration of a bright red-chested robin, he cleared his throat and began to read.

"Once there was a robin, just hatched, who knew in his heart that he was meant to fly. For weeks he had watched his mother and father fly to and from the nest, and he knew he, too, had wings that folded neatly upon his back. One day, flapping them wildly, he decided he was ready to float through the sky and so climbed up onto the edge of his nest. Opening his wings, he flapped them three times, then began to leap into the air. It wasn't but a moment later, just as his claws were letting go of the nest, that his mother swooped in and grabbed him with her beak, pulling him back into the safety of the nest. The baby robin screamed in anger. "Let me fly! I was made to fly!" He protested.

His mother looked at him with knowing and loving eyes. "You were, that is true," she said softly. "But look below," she said.

The baby robin looked over the edge of the nest, whereupon he saw a giant black cat slinking about the base of the tree.

He looked as his mother, his eyes wide.

"You are not yet ready to fly," she said gently. "Look at your wings. The feathers have not yet come in full. And your muscles aren't strong enough to hold you up in flight. If you had tried to fly today, you would now be in that cat's belly."

The baby robin stopped crying and settled in next to his mother.

"But I'm meant to fly," he sniffed.

Mother robin preened him and fluffed his feathers.

"And you will," she said, "when you are ready. And that is for me to decide, not you, for I know what is best for you. All you have to do is trust my timing. And then I will push you out of this nest myself, and you will fly like the eagles do!"

Innatus gently closed the book and raised his eyebrows as he looked at Mysta. "Does this story make sense to you?" He asked.

Mysta nodded quietly, and then she began to cry. "My mommy isn't here anymore," she sniffed.

Innatus wiped a tear from her face. "No, dear child. She is not. But Miss Lanthrea is. And she will help you know what's best for you, just like mother robin. Trust her, Mysta. She is a gift to you."

Mysta snuffled a bit, then nodded but said nothing more.

Lanthrea and Innatus exchanged glances. The little girl had much healing yet to do; none of it would be easy, and all of it would take time.

The three of them stood, and Innatus helped Lanthrea secure the pack onto her back. They tied a sweater around Mysta's waist in case the walk became chilly, and Innatus blessed them both by placing his hands on their foreheads, as he had done with Garanthor.

Shifting the pack's weight on her shoulders, Lanthrea smiled at Innatus, grabbed Mysta's hand and turned toward the mountain pass that would take them home.

The first part of the journey was an absolute delight. Mysta had energy for the walk and didn't complain once about her feet hurting or the sun being too hot, nor the breeze too cold. Lanthrea found carrying a backpack considerably easier than using either a waist pack or her shawl, as she had done on her way to Palem. The weather was perfect, the wildflowers scented the air, and the music of many a bubbling brook cheered them along the way. They were full into the kingdom of Drymac by mid-morning, and it was midday, the sun almost straight up above their heads, when they finally stopped for a meal and to rest their feet.

Lanthrea had a minute to pull out the map the king had given her (also miraculously still intact after their calamitous fall) and check their bearings. They had but one pass through these Ciracian mountains, then would begin their descent into Cenecal on the dusty back roads that Lanthrea (then Myka) had played on while her parents had gathered mushrooms or hunted hare on long, lazy summer days much like this one. She knew these roads well, and it would only be a day's walk before they would be able to see the lights and colors of Cenecal. She thought of it now. The noise, the crowds, the marauders, the danger. She groaned. The Returning had seemed a grand idea while back in Palem, but now, with this little girl as her ward, returning to such a place made her feel nothing but apprehension and an odd, poignant sorrow. She even wondered for a moment if the King hadn't been mistaken about sending her back. Looking over at Mysta, she noted the girl was happily playing with a caterpillar she had found. Such innocence and such sadness, all wrapped in a five-year-old little heart. Oh, how she hoped Bythim and his men had forgotten all about her and her paintings by now. She wanted not one more sorrow or pain to haunt her little girl.

They picked up their picnic after eating a light midday meal of bread with butter (still full from their morning meal) and started again through the pass. Lanthrea estimated they would be to the first of the backroads by nightfall, and, were they to continue down those roads, they could be in Cenecal this very night. But there was no hurry and absolutely no good reason to enter the town under cover of darkness when the gangs and drunkards did their worst. No. They would camp at the end of the pass, in the forested area, and begin their descent into the town tomorrow morning.

Mysta was being an absolute delight. By dusk, Lanthrea knew her little feet were getting tired, and yet she never complained even once. In fact, it was Lanthrea's feet that finally gave out, the weight of the pack straining her old back and causing her to call Mysta to make camp. Mysta came skipping back (having gone on ahead a bit) and plopped down on a fallen log.

"Time for evening meal?" She asked excitedly.

"Not only that but let's camp here for the night, yes?" Lanthrea answered her as she slid the pack off her aching shoulders.

"Can we have oatmeal and honey?" Mysta asked, smiling and dancing about on the log.

Lanthrea laughed. "I'm afraid Innatus didn't pack us such a treat." She dug around in the pack. "But ho! How about this?" Pulling out a meat pie, she watched Mysta's eyes grow wide. "Oh, yes, please!!!" The little girl squealed as she jumped on and off the log in excitement. "Can I have a whole piece by myself?"

Lanthrea grinned. "Of course! By tomorrow night, we will be home, and maybe my friend Marinda and I can make an entirely new pie for dinner then!"

She cut the pie into four slices and handed Mysta hers. The girl ate happily while Lanthrea set up a little lean-to, reminiscent of the kind Cla'neen had taught her to make. *Innatus thought of everything*, she mused as she put the canvas on the poles.

She made the fire, then sat down on the log to eat a piece of the pie herself. The fire danced and crackled; the embers floated up on the smoke towards the deep black, starry summer sky. *Innatus would love this,* she thought and smiled. He was no doubt back at the lake right now, calling down the stars and letting the waters renew him one more time. Finishing up her meal, she coaxed Mysta from her after-meal-dance by the fire and helped her wrap up in a warm blanket. She then put her into the lean-to, tucking her in and kissing her forehead gently. Tomorrow they would start their new life together in Cenecal. How she wished she could get a message to Petrul and Marinda before they arrived—to let them know she and Mysta were coming. Sighing, and with that slight frustration on her mind, she wrapped up in a warm blanket herself and stretched out by the fire. Petrul was a good man. Marinda was a gracious and welcoming hostess. They would be welcome without proper advance notice. She sighed again. *Tomorrow. Home.* She was asleep before she could think about another thing.

It was the slight snuffling that awakened her with a start. A little wet nose was tickling Lanthrea's cheeks, and she jumped up to find a small red squirrel next to her, standing on its two feet and pawing at the air.

"What….what….what in the kingdom…?!" She stammered, shaking the sleep from her groggy brain.

The squirrel stayed upright, balanced on its tail, its little nose and whiskers twitching. Gaining her senses, she knelt down next to it.

"Well, hello, little one," she said softly. Are you looking for food?"

The squirrel cocked its head a bit, looked straight at her, and *spoke*. "Not food, exactly," it said, "But I was looking for *you*." It went back onto all fours, its tail curling up over its back. "And if there were to be some food involved with finding you, I wouldn't be opposed."

Its nose wrinkled and twitched, as did its fluffy tail.

"I, uh…I…" Lanthrea rubbed the sleep from her eyes, "You are a *talking* animal?"

The little squirrel shook its head and twitched its whiskers again. "Are you deaf, then? Of course, I'm talking. I'm talking to *you* at the moment."

Lanthrea furrowed her brow. "But we are….we are in Drymac now. And you wear no crown. Besides, there are no more talking animals here…they were all hunted —if you will pardon me— to..to..extinction."

The squirrel shook its head and fluffed its tail again.

"Well, as you can see, that is not the truth. For, in point of fact, here I am. And can you imagine wearing the Palemian crown here in Drymac? We would be dispatched immediately. By the king, you humans have no sense at all."

Lanthrea cleared her throat. "Indeed. Yes. Well, then, let me introduce myself. My name is…"

"Myka. Your name is Myka. Or Lanthrea, I guess, as the king's messengers said you are now called. New name and all." It shook its head and twitched its whiskers again. "Never understood the new name thing, but….either way, I know you. And I was sent to warn you."

Lanthrea pulled back a bit. "Warn me? Of what?"

The little squirrel bounced up on the log by Mysta's tent, assumed a most proper position and cleared his throat. "Uhm hem. My name is Randeen. I am the Emissary of the Drymacian Council of Creatures. I have been sent to warn you that Bythim's men are still looking for you. You must be very wary as you head into Cenecal proper." He relaxed. "There. Thank you for your time, and good day."

He turned on his tail and began to flounce away, but Lanthrea yelled at him. "Randeen! Please, don't go yet. Please. I have so many questions."

The little squirrel stopped and, with a great sigh, hung his head for a moment and drew a deep breath before turning around and bounding back, whereupon he jumped up on the log and twitched his nose.

"What? I did my job. They said, 'find Myka…er…Lanthrea…tell her about Bythim'…la la la….you heard the rest. I really *must* be going now."

"Yes. I heard you well. And thank you. But my questions aren't about me or my safety. They are about *you*." She stopped here and looked at Randeen, who was tapping his little sharp claws on the log impatiently. Lanthrea noted this and barreled on. "How many of you are there left? Does anyone in Cenecal know? Does Lord Bythim himself know?"

He rolled his eyes and answered. "Many. Yes. And No. In that order."

Lanthrea paused. "Right. Alright then. To whom do you hold allegiance? And who told you to warn me?"

Randeen stopped his toe-tapping. "We all honor the king of Palem, of course. Most of us are from that land originally. And it was Azar himself who told us to find you."

Lanthrea's heart skipped a beat. *Azar!* So the king and his people were still watching over her from afar.

As if sensing her thoughts, Randeen offered, "Of *course,* those at Palem are watching over you." He turned to go again but stopped short. "Oh. And there is one more thing. Elpinhoeve sends his love…er…as well as a non-speaking beast *can,* that is." He tapped himself on the head a few times. "How could I have forgotten that? Bad Randeen, bad." With that, the little red squirrel bounded back into the woods just as Mysta was crawling out of the tent, rubbing her eyes.

"Who you talkin' to, Lanthee?" She asked, yawning.

Lanthrea could barely contain her joy. "Elpin is alright, Mysta!!! Elpinhoeve is alive!!!"

She started jumping around, grabbing Mysta by the arms and twirling her about.

Mysta squealed with delight and then, when the dancing and twirling were done, looked up at Lanthrea and asked, "Who's Elp…Elhoooo…Elpi?"

Lanthrea threw back her head and laughed. "Bray! Bray is alive. I call him Elpin sometimes…and well…Bray is alive!"

Mysta jumped up and down in joy. "Yay! Can we see him? Can we?"

Lanthrea shook her head. "I don't know, dear one. I don't know. Maybe. But for now? For now, we eat morning meal!"

The warning Randeen had brought literally melted away in the face of the good news about Elpinhoeve, and Lanthrea ate one of the best morning meals of her life, albeit in the absence of a table, plate, or cup so great was her joy. They were now only a half day's walk to Cenecal, and having been warned that she was still a fugitive, she thought to take a back road into town. It was one of her favorite logging roads as a child, as it had a bridge over a little creek where she loved to play while her parents would gather mushrooms. It led directly into the Dwelling Quarter of the town, not the Market Quarter, where people were more apt to know her. Always crowded and with a swath of people constantly coming and going—almost assuring anonymity—the Dwelling Quarter would be a good entry point to the town.

Mysta ate her piece of bread hastily, so excited was she to get going. She hadn't been in a large town ever in her life and was anxious to see all the 'people and things' in Cenecal. Hoisting the backpack on her shoulders, Lanthrea led Mysta a bit to the east of their current path through the pass, nudging them closer to the old logging road that would take them into town. It was a lovely late summer day, clear and bright, and they came upon the road within an hour. Mysta, still having boundless energy, loved the flat road and began skipping along, singing a little song that went something like: *'people in town, people and things, bright* shiny *things, people and people.'* Lanthrea laughed every time she emphasized the word 'shiny' with her little voice. Thinking on it, she realized Mysta had never seen the inside of a shop of *any* sort, let alone the kind of shops that Cenecal boasted in the Market Quarter. Bythim was a tyrant, to be sure, but the trading in Cenecal was known throughout the region. From small things like Lanthrea's painted cloths to exotic woven rugs from the far south to sweet shops with delicacies flavored not only with honey but spices like nutmeg and cassis, cardamom and (Mysta's favorite) cinnamon. Lanthrea was almost as excited as Mysta to share these treasures with her. As long as they didn't get caught.

It only too about two hours (once they hit the logging road) before they crossed the little bridge Lanthrea had loved as a child. Suddenly, the town of Cenecal could be seen through the trees. From this altitude, it looked almost charming. The town itself—with its circular shape and spoke-like streets made each Quarter look like rather like a piece of a giant pie. Except for the Forbidden Quarter (which was worn by age and crumbling), the buildings and streets of the other quarters were considerably impressive in size and sheer number. Old Town, of course, stood out like a diamond from here. The magnitude of the place, unlike anything Mysta had ever seen, seemed to mesmerize her, even from this distance. The girl stopped in her tracks, staring down at the town and emitted an uncontrolled 'ohhhhhhhh'.

"Is that it?" She said quietly, her mouth open and eyes wide.

Lanthrea ran her hand through the girl's hair. "It is. Are you ready?

Without saying a word, Mysta suddenly leapt forward and began running down the road as fast as her legs could carry her. Lanthrea laughed as she straightened the backpack and jogged along behind her. "Wait for me!" she yelled, knowing it would do no good whatsoever. Mysta's excitement propelled her down the road, and it wasn't until they met a group of travelers heading out of town that the little girl stopped short, ran back to Lanthrea and grabbed her hand. The travelers, two men and a woman, nodded and greeted them kindly, with no incident at all, but Lanthrea was glad of Mysta's sudden shyness and willingness to stay close by. They walked that way, hand in hand, into the town, Mysta's eyes wide as saucers at each new horse, or carriage, or dwelling place bigger than the one before. Lanthrea had wrapped her head and face in a light blue scarf (Innatus' suggestion) and was wearing her long gray hair in a soft, loose braid—something she had never been able to coax the tangled mass into before. She was aware of the fact that her gait was smoother than before she had left; she was no longer hobbling and bent over in pain. She was also aware of the fact that she was thinner than before and stronger with more muscle. What she didn't know was exactly how appreciable these changes were, nor if they were enough to secure her safety from recognition. The blue scarf offered a degree of anonymity, and the little girl clutching her hand yet another. For a while, many knew her as the 'old artist who painted on cloth'. No one knew her to have a grandchild, let alone a child. Breathing deeply, she held tightly to Mysta and tried to enjoy the girl's fascination with each person and place they passed by. The Dwelling Quarter was rather lacking in points of interest, at least in Lanthrea's estimation, as there were no shops or marketplaces here. But the sheer number of people, animals and buildings was enough to captivate Mysta, and she kept pointing and exclaiming every time a group of interesting people would walk by. A group of florists headed to the Market Quarter with a wheelbarrow full of flowers, in particular, had her completely gobsmacked. "Look at all the flowers, Lanthee! *Look*!" And so it went throughout the morning, with Lanthrea continuing to feel apprehensive about someone recognizing her and sweet Mysta elated at every new sight and sound.

They made it through the quarter in good time and entered into Old Town at about midday. Lanthrea felt herself relax the minute she smelled the roses from the first garden, a large one that adorned the welcoming gate to Old Town. Mysta even dropped her hand and ran over to stick her nose in every bloom, flowers being the most captivating part of summer for her still. They walked slowly through the streets, enjoying the hanging gardens, the cats and dogs lounging on welcoming porches and the nods of the elderly folk who, to a person, greeted them with a smile. They found the center court fountain in no time, and Lanthrea even pointed out the Robin's Egg— her grandparent's little dome-shaped house—as they walked. Remembering Petrul and Marinda's place was just a short block away, she quickened her pace. She couldn't imagine how surprised they would be to see her and hear of her journey. She found the little red brick house easily, fairly leaping up the steps to the wooden porch. "Mysta, these are friends of mine! They are going to just love meeting you, and maybe we'll make you that fresh pie tonight!" She knocked gingerly on the door, excited to see Marinda's smiling face.

The door opened slowly, and to Lanthrea's surprise, a young woman dressed in simple garb, tattered dress, hair wrapped in a cloth, with a rag in her hand, stood staring at them.

"What you want?" The woman barked gruffly, her eyes cold, her demeanor icy.

"Oh, excuse me," Lanthrea said, "but I'm looking for Petrul and Marinda. Do I, do I… have the wrong house?" she said, looking around to see if she had lost her bearings somehow. She had, after all, only been here once, and that was after dark.

"Right house." The woman said. "But they ain't here no more. Now, I have cleaning to do before the new ones move in, so if you don't mind…" and began to shut the door. Lanthrea stuck her hand in between the door and the frame to stop her.

"No, No…I mean, what do you mean 'they aren't here any longer?' Did they move? Did they….were they sick..did they, did something happen to them?"

Her mind was reeling. They were both well advanced in years, but only a few months ago had seemed in good enough health.

"Don't know," the lady said, pulling at the door. "Got me work to do, is all I know." And with that, she slammed the door shut. Lanthrea heard the lock click.

Mysta looked up at her, questions all over her face. "Are they gone, Lanthee?"

Lanthrea swallowed hard. "I guess so, Mysta. I don't know…."

She took Mysta's hand and walked slowly off the happy little wooden porch, feeling as though her feet had weights on them. As they headed toward the street, she saw a few wooden boxes out front by Marinda's lilac garden stuffed with thrown-away items, things the cleaning woman must have pulled from the house. She walked over and picked through some of the items to look for anything that might explain what had happened to her friends.

Nothing of any note in the first box: a broken picture frame, some broken pottery, some ripped towels and a few broken cups. The second box was filled with a rolled-up carpet, thin and long - probably a runner. She lifted it up and gasped. There, covered in the dust from the rug, were two ceramic-type platters, each adorned with lovely stones in beautiful mosaic patterns. She remembered seeing them lovingly displayed on the open shelves in their living room. Of course, she hadn't known what they were at the time. There was no mistaking them now. They reminded her much of her own—the crest the king had made from her journey stones. Hers, of course, had been lost in the fall, but these must be Petrul and Miranda's, made by the king as well. Their stories in stone!

Looking around and seeing no one nearby, she pulled them out from under the rug and slid off her backpack. Making room, she slipped them inside, set the rug back in the box and put the pack back on.

There is no way anyone would purposefully throw out their journey crest. Something awful had happened to her friends, she knew that now. There was only one way to know what it was. She would have to risk revealing herself by asking someone. It was necessary.

They walked back to the center court and sat down on the brickwork surrounding the fountain. Suddenly, Lanthrea felt old again and somewhat hopeless. They had nowhere to stay here in Cenecal without Petrul's help. But worse, her dear kind friends were gone. Either dead or ….well, she couldn't imagine.

An old woman was just emerging from her little home across from the fountain and was walking toward them. She was carrying a bucket, obviously to draw some water, but was struggling to lift it and was stopping every few feet to set it down. Lanthrea got up and walked over, took the bucket and offered the woman her arm. "Here, let me help you. This bucket is a heavy one." The old woman looked up thankfully and smiled. She was at least ninety years of age, probably more, wearing a colorful scarf tied over her hair and a simple peasant's dress over her short, round body. "I do thank you, friend", she said. "I guess I'm getting too old to be fetching water."

Lanthrea laughed. "A task for the young, indeed—it's hard for me as well." Mysta was dancing about on the rim of the fountain's brickwork and called out, "Is that your old friend, Lanthee?"

Lanthrea brushed the hair out of her face and walked slowly toward the fountain with the old woman on her arm. "No, but it is a new friend," she yelled back, giving the old woman's arm a squeeze.

She led the woman to the brick wall and helped her sit down. "This," she said, nodding at the dancing girl," is Mysta. And my name is Lanthrea. May I ask yours?"

The old woman caught her breath and answered. "My name is Plen. And thank you for helping me today." She shook her head. "I couldn't have hauled any water back, even if I'd made it over here to the fountain. Don't know why I even tried. I'm just feeling so weak today."

"Well, no worries. I'm glad I was here," said Lanthrea as she dipped the bucket into the fountain's pool and filled it. "I'll carry it back to your house for you as well when you are rested."

Plen nodded and patted Lanthrea's hand. "So, who are you here to visit?" She asked. "You're too young to be livin' here in Old Town. Mysta mentioned a friend?"

Lanthrea smiled. "I'm not too young by much," she said, pulling the blue scarf off her head and face and revealing her gray hair. Plan chuckled. "Well, I wouldn't be knowin' it by watching you. You move as a much younger woman." She sighed. "I used to be strong, too…and honestly, usually, I can fetch my own water. It's just that today…..I'm so tired."

Lanthrea patted her back. "We all have our days, Plen." She sighed. "And insofar as your question, I'm here to visit Petrul and Marinda. But…they are not at home. Say, do you know them?"

Plen's shoulders tightened, and the smile fell off her face. "Oh, dear. Oh, dear. Oh, dear. You didn't know?"

Lanthrea felt her heart squeeze. "Didn't know what, Plen? I've been gone a few months. Didn't know what?"

Plen cleared her throat, then spoke softly, almost under her breath.

"They disappeared about two months ago. Just…poof! Like that. No one knows for sure what happened, but there is talk."

Lanthrea bristled. "Talk?"

"Yes," the old woman nodded, "Bythim's men. They done a raid here in Old Town awhile back. They ain't have bothered us in years…decades. But one day, late last spring, a whole bunch of 'em come into Old Town. Sitting on their horses, all shined up in their armor. Said they were looking for anyone who had 'the book'. Said there had been talk of people readin' it again. Reminded everyone that it was forbidden. One had even waved a cloth around, a yellow one with a picture of a deer on it. Said some old woman had painted it straight out of the book. Figured from her age, she might be hiding here."

Lanthrea froze. The doe. The painting Bythim's men had taken from the woman at the market. The painting *she* had made.

"Did anyone come forward?" Lanthrea asked softly.

"Of course not!" Plen answered. "None of us admitted to having …." She stopped suddenly and looked deep into Lanthrea's eyes, "and of course, I don't know anything about no book….never have seen one…." Her voice drifted off, and Lanthrea knew she was being asked an unspoken question.

"I do not hold to Lord Bythim's rule…I am a follower of another king - a good one." Lanthrea said plainly. "You do not need to hide anything from me."

Plen exhaled. "You are? You know the Good King? 'Tis a mercy to find another who has met him. Not many of us left here in Cenecal now." She eyed Lanthrea carefully, then satisfied, continued. "Well, then. None of us come forward, and none of us said a word to the men. But then," Plen shuddered, "Then one of the soldiers saw Petrul's cane. He walked over and grabbed it, examined it, and the next thing we knew, he had hit Petrul with it. Right on the head. Asked him what he knew about the book, who might have one, and where the old woman who painted the deer might be. Petrul said nothing — not one word —brave soul that he is —and you know he must have been hurt badly. The soldier had taken his cane, broke it in two in front of him and tossed the pieces in the warming fire. All those beautiful carvings of Palem….." Her voice trailed off. "We thought that was the end of it. But about three days later, Petrul and Marinda…just…disappeared." Plen looked up at Lanthrea plaintively. "We don't know if they left or if they were taken. We just don't know."

Lanthrea thought of the mosaics in her pack.

"I think I do," she said sadly.

Plen looked at her with questioning eyes. "You do?"

Lanthrea watched Mysta playing on the rim of the fountain. "I'm afraid I do. I found their mosaics, their crests made by the king himself, tossed in the waste in front of their house. There is no way they would have left those to be thrown out. Someone has taken our friends….you can be certain of that."

Plen groaned. "Oh, I was so hoping they had left town before it come to that. There is little hope for them now, I suppose."

Lanthrea started to agree but pulled herself up short. Had not the King and the Lady sent Garanthor to save her and Mysta in the river valley just a few short days ago? By every miraculous means possible? No. No…there was always hope because the king was always good. She grabbed the bucket, helped Plen to her feet and called for Mysta. She turned to the old woman with tears in her eyes. "There is great hope, Plen….always."

She walked the old woman back to her little house, made certain the water was poured into her jugs for use and gave her a hug.

"If you need anything, let me know," Plen said as Lanthrea and Mysta stood on her porch to say goodbye.

Lanthrea squeezed her hand and took a deep breath. "We may be in need of a place to stay soon. If so, would we be welcome here for a time?"

Plen smiled widely, showing all her teeth, even the missing ones. "Of course. Just knock. I'm always home. The king go with you, Lanthrea!"

"And with you," Lanthrea returned the blessing, squeezing her one more time before wrapping the blue scarf around her head and face, then walking hand in hand with Mysta past the fountain. They would go to the Market Quarter next. The Market Quarter, with its color and life and danger. The Market Quarter, with the Constabulary right smack in the middle of it, and hopefully Petrul and Marinda somewhere therein.

CHAPTER TWENTY-FIVE:
The Beginning of the End

It was mid-afternoon when they made their way into the Market Square, and Mysta began to ask for something to eat. Lanthrea had completely forgotten about midday meal, what with all the happenings today. It didn't help that every shop and street vendor was open for business, and the smells of baking bread, roasting meats, and a thousand other delights were wafting through the air. A few hungry glottins darted here and there in the streets, hopping from waste bin to waste bin, and Lanthrea felt herself sadden. It wasn't that she missed Tenk. It was that she missed so much life *because* of Tenk. These glottins would, no doubt, be taken in by someone. They would be fed and strengthened and would keep their keepers locked in fear, thinking there was no other way to live and no better company to keep. Sighing, she pulled Mysta close to her. This little girl would never know that kind of loneliness and fear. Not if she had anything to do with it.

At one point, they walked right past Lanthrea's old crook in the market wall—where she kept her booth. It was now being used by a young woman selling clay pots, and the butcher and the purveyor of religious trinkets were still on either side, a long line at the one and only one at the other. Pulling her scarf tightly around her face, she put her head down and quickened her pace. They made their way through the crowds easily and arrived at her friend Maruk's tent just as Mysta had begun to whine in earnest for food. Lanthrea found a bench for her to sit on, slipped off her pack, and rummaged about in it for the last of the meat pie Innatus had packed. She handed it to Mysta, along with the water pouch, and smiled as she watched Maruk and his son Banum hauling out a box of meats from behind their booth. She felt like it was just yesterday and yet a million years ago that she had seen them do this very thing. It was that day Maruk had told her to get rid of the book. He had warned her, but it had been too late. Now, she was going to have to talk to him and trust him with her very life. She felt she had very few options. The butcher was not only her friend, but he knew everything that happened in the Market Quarter. If anyone knew anything about Petrul, it would be he.

She told Mysta to stay put and, keeping an eye on her, walked up to the booth and waited for Maruk.

Pulling some fresh lamb out of the box, he noticed Lanthrea standing there.

'Ma'am. Can I help you? See anything you'd like? I have a good portion of smoked venison sausage still in back if that'd interest you."

Lanthrea swallowed hard, her throat dry. Slowly unwrapping her head and face, she looked back at Maruk and smiled. "I'm not here for trade," she said softly. "But I do need your....your help."

Maruk jutted out his chin and straightened up, wiping his hands on his apron. "I'm always one to help a lady," he said, "what is it that you need, Ma'am?"

"Maruk. It's me." She said softly, almost whispering.

His eyes scanned her carefully, and he pursed his lips.

"Ma'am?" Was all he said.

"It's me...don't you recognize me?" She responded.

He looked carefully at her, and slowly his eyes lit up.

"No," he protested. "No, it can't be! Myka?"

She laughed, "Yes, it's me. I need your help. Can we talk in the back?" She wrapped her face and head again, then glanced over again at Mysta, still happily eating her meat pie on the bench.

"Myka. You've changed," he said, reaching across the table and hugging her neck. "Yes, of course, of course, here…come on back."

He motioned her to come around the table to the back storage area behind the tent. Lanthrea called Mysta over, and she came running, licking pie crust from the corners of her mouth.

"Maruk, this is Mysta. Mysta, this is my friend, Maruk."

'Nice to meet you, Mysta," the big man said as he opened the tent for them both. "Come, and have a seat."

He pointed to a large box with the words "Sausages" scrawled across the side and a blanket tossed over the top. Shrugging, he laughed. "It's the best we have back here."

Mysta climbed up on the box, swinging her legs, and Lanthrea sat down next to her.

Maruk couldn't stop staring at Lanthrea. "I'm sorry," he finally said, "but you don't look at all like you did when I last saw you, no offense intended."

"None taken," she laughed. "Much has happened."

He nodded at Mysta. "I'd say so," he replied, his eyes wide.

"It's a long story," Lanthrea said, "one best saved for another time in a less public place. For now, I need your help."

"If you mean Bythim's men, they haven't stopped looking for you," he said, exhaling deeply. "They know who you are. Too many people knew you and your cloths from the market. I think they found your house right off."

She nodded. "Oh, they did. That very day you warned me. They burned it to the ground. I left that day. Haven't been back since." She fiddled with the scarf on her head. "Till today."

"Why on earth would you come back here?" Maruk asked imploringly. "You should have stayed away. I'm certain you'd be safer….well, wherever you were than here."

"Hmmm….safety isn't my priority right now. There are so many things I'd like to tell you, Maruk. But there are two other friends of mine that are in danger right now. Truth be told, they may already have been dispatched by Bythim's men…I was hoping you might have heard something."

"Ask away," the big man said, untying his apron and tossing it in a ball onto another box.

"Two elders from Old Town, they might have been taken into custody a few weeks ago. Their names are Petrul and Marinda. Have you heard anything?"

Maruk closed his eyes and clicked his tongue. "Petrul…Petrul…." He opened his eyes and shook his head. "I've not heard that name. But, Lanthrea, a whole slew of people from that Quarter were rounded up in the past few months since you left. Those paintings you made. They riled 'em up real bad around here. Bythim has doubled down on anyone reading or even mentioning that confounded book you had." He looked at her and narrowed his eyes. "Tell me you got rid of that thing, yes?"

She pursed her lips. "I can't tell you that," she said.

He rocked back on his heels and whistled. "Oh, my dear woman…you don't have it in that pack of yours, do you? Because if you did, I'd be obligated to report you, Myka. I don't want to do that."

Lanthrea said nothing but stared at him intently. "We are friends, Maruk. Please remember this fact."

He inhaled deeply. "Right. Right. And I don't see a book anywhere on your person, so….. there's nothing to tell. Right. Nothing to tell."

"Alright. These people are rounding up. I'm assuming they are all at the Constabulary?"

Maruk shook his head. "No. They have taken them out of Cenecal. Isolated them all at an encampment almost outside of our territory, near the foothills. Not far from an outlying village named Glarren…Glanner…Glanet! That's it…near a village named Glanét."

Lanthrea's heart raced. Glanét! The village she and Tenk took refuge in. Good people. Decent people. Hated glottins. There is no possible way they would be a party to this sort of thing. It gave her hope.

"Are you certain of this?" She asked.

"I hear everything," he said, grinning, "like you said." He motioned to the girl, one eyebrow raised. "Do you want to tell me anything about your past few months?"

She smiled. "As I said, another time, another place. For now, it's best that I stay out of the public eye for a while." Looking at him earnestly, she pulled off her scarf again. "And you're certain I'm not recognizable any longer?"

He nodded. "I never would have known you had you not told me yourself. You look younger, more vital. It's hard to explain." He smiled and kicked the dirt around. "Even your hair…well, it used to be….well…"

She threw her head back and laughed. "I know. A mess. I know."

"I didn't want to say…." He smiled at her. "Well, then. I have to get back to work now, Lanthrea. It was good to see you. I mean that." He turned to Mysta, still swinging her legs on the box. "And nice to meet you, pretty girl," he said, bowing low before her. She giggled and patted him on the head as he did.

He grabbed his apron, tied it back on, and turned to Lanthrea. "Please be careful. But I don't think you have to worry about being recognized. Still. That scarf seems a good idea."

With that, he opened up the curtain and headed back to the booth and the public. Lanthrea hoisted Mysta off the box and knelt down by her. "Did you get enough to eat?"

Mysta nodded. "But can we stop and get a sweet? From one of the shops you tolded me about?"

Lanthrea laughed. "I think we should. Come, let's find a good place with just the right thing for a hungry little princess."

"Princess! I'm a prinnnncessss," squealed Mysta, twirling around and around till she got silly dizzy and dropped to the ground.

Lanthrea felt her heart warm. This sweet little girl was, in fact, a princess to her, just as she, Lanthrea, was to the king. Twirling the little silver crown ring on her finger, she smiled. Royalty, both of them. She would not forget.

Shifting the backpack on her shoulders and checking to ensure her face was covered, they walked together out into the bright sun. First, something tasty for Mysta. Then, off to find Petrul and Marinda after a good night's rest at Plen's little house in Old Town.

****

Mysta sat in the big chair in Plen's little house, licking the honey and cinnamon off her fingers. Plen had given her an old rag doll that one of her granddaughters played with after they had eaten dinner, and Mysta was happily involved in a scenario about a princess and a pony as the two older women talked.

"And you're certain your friend Maruk won't talk to the court or their confounded soldiers?" Plen asked as she sipped her tea.

"I am," Lanthrea answered. "He is a good man. I can trust him."

"Well," said Plen, stirring her tea with her finger, "either way, he doesn't know anything about me or where you are tonight, so I'm certain we are safe."

Lanthrea took a sip of tea. How horrible that no one could trust anyone any longer. Cenecal was always a rotten place, full of darkness and evil, but this sort of evil was of a most insidious stripe. The type of evil where brother betrays brother—neighbor betrays neighbor. It was hard to take, even for hardened Cenecalians.

"You think, then, that Petrul and Marinda were taken to this…this camp?" Plen asked.

"I have no reason to think otherwise. And I've been there…well, near there… to the village Glanét. I know the people. I think they will be glad to see me again. They are certain to have nothing to do with Bythim's business. In fact, if they knew about it, they most certainly would do what they could to stop it."

Plen nodded. "Then, will you enlist their help once you get there?"

Lanthrea threw her head back. "I honestly don't have a plan." She looked up at Plen imploringly. "I don't have….a plan."

Plen sighed. "Then we shall simply ask the king for wisdom and guidance. That is the best thing we can do."

Nodding in agreement, Lanthrea motioned to Mysta. She came bounding over, smelling of cinnamon and honey and crawled into her lap. Plen waddled over to a bookcase and shuffled a few books aside, at last pulling out a small, black book from behind them.

"I hide it. Not too well, but well enough," she smiled.

She sat down in the big chair now vacated by Mysta and opened the book. She turned it around so Mysta could see the illustration. It was that of the tiny doe with the silver crown. Mysta sighed in appreciation.

"Let's see," she said, running her finger down the page. "Ah. Here. A good passage for us today." Clearing her throat, she read from the page:

"And when it is dark as the darkest night, and when you have no good help, ask the king, and he will guide you. Ask again, and he will send help. Ask thrice, and he will go with you himself, for he cannot forsake his own."

Mysta shook her head. "I don't get it," she said plainly. "Lemme see the deer again!"

Plen turned the doe to her and let her look for a long time.

"It just means you are safe and loved and protected, just like the little deer in the forest," Lanthrea said. "You are never alone, Mysta. Ever. Do you understand me?"

The little girl nodded, but Lanthrea saw the tears forming in her eyes. "But mommy and daddy lefted me alone, Lanthee."

Lanthrea winced. There was no way to avoid this topic. She hugged Mysta tightly and pet her hair. "Yes, that is true, princess. But they didn't want to. They would not have if they could have possibly helped it. And then…then….the good king sent me to find you that day. Because he knew you were alone and scared and sad. And it broke his heart. So, he sent me from so very far away to find you. So you would learn of him. So you would know you never have be alone again."

Lanthrea stopped. Too many words. Too large a concept for so small a heart. She quieted herself and simply held Mysta close.

Plen closed the book and looked over at Lanthrea, eyebrow raised. "I dare think you were speaking to your own heart just then."

Lanthrea felt the truth of the old woman's words. Since she had been Mysta's age, she had no one. It was difficult to know, deep inside, that this was no longer the case. Looking back at Plen, she said quietly, "Please read the passage again. Please."

Plen read it three more times, Lanthrea savoring every word. She realized by the end that Mysta had fallen sound asleep in her lap, rag doll in hand, honey on her face. Carrying her to the small bed Plen had made up by the fireplace, she tucked her in, pulling up the blankets and placing the rag doll on the pillow next to her.

Plen hid the book back behind the others on the bookcase and said her goodnights, waddling down the hall to the one tiny bedroom in her small house.

Lanthrea curled up in the big chair, pulled a soft blanket over her, and stared out the window at the moon. It was so peaceful here in Old Town, just as she remembered it as a child at her grandparent's little egg house. Back when she had a family. Back when she first felt safe and loved. She whispered to the sky, *'please, good king, let me know your love tonight. And let Mysta know mine.'*

Pulling the blanket tighter about her shoulders, she drifted off, the moonlight bathing her in a benediction of light.

The smell of bread baking woke her up. She forgot for a moment where she was until she saw Plen puttering in the kitchen area.

"She awakens," Plen said in a sing-songy voice, her smiling face putting Lanthrea entirely at ease. Stretching, she got up out of the chair, folded the blanket, and walked over to help Plen. "Anything I can do?"

Plen shook her head as she pulled a tray of hot biscuits out of the small brick oven next to the fireplace. "Got it all ready for you two," she said. "My mother's recipe," she pronounced as she placed the biscuits in a steaming pile on a plate. "You're going to love them."

Lanthrea's mouth was watering. "Let me go see if the princess is awake yet," she said, sweeping her hair up into a loose bun and finishing it with a pin she had borrowed from Plen. "Don't eat them all yourself!" she quipped.

Plen laughed, and Lanthrea could hear the clink of dish-ware going onto the table as she tip-toed over to the little bed and pulled the blankets off Mysta's face. She was drowsy but stirring. The minute the smell of the biscuits hit her, her eyes popped open, and she bolted upright.

"Mmmmm….morning meal?" She asked, grinning. "It smells like what mommy used to make."

Lanthrea smoothed her hair. "Well, then. Let's get you up and go see what Plen has for us."

Mysta nodded happily, bounced out of bed, and ran over to the table.

"Biscuits!" she hollered happily. She whipped around to Lanthrea. "Do we have any of mommy's jam left?"

Lanthrea sighed. "I'm afraid that was lost in our fall." She looked over at Plen. "But I'll bet Miss Plen has some for us?"

Wiping her hands on her apron, Plen nodded to a small larder. "Go look in there, Mysta. See what you can find."

She bounced over to the little open cupboard and dug around. "I founded some!" She yelled happily, producing a jar of raspberry jam and holding it up like a trophy.

"Well, then. That's what we shall have," Plen said, plopping a huge scoop of butter onto a plate and setting it by the biscuits. "Now. Everybody go get dressed and washed up. The biscuits are gonna get cold!"

After a very satisfying morning meal (Lanthrea had to admit, Plen's mother's recipe was one of the best she'd ever had) Mysta went to play with the rag doll, and Plen and Lanthrea talked about the next steps.

"So, you will journey to the foothills today? How far is the trip?"

"It takes only a day," Lanthrea answered. "And I'm in much better shape than I was seven months ago. I'm certain to get to Glanét by nightfall."

"But you'll come upon the encampment prior to reaching Glanét, yes?"

"Uh huh….but I can most assuredly get around it and to Glanét without being seen, especially under cover of darkness."

"What if the people in this village…this…Glanét have been taken by Bythim's men? What then?"

Lanthrea bit her lip. "I don't see why Lord Bythim would bother attacking a neighboring village in another province. It would mean more work for his men and more control for the guards. I'm hoping that Glanét has been left out of this for now."

They sat in silence for a few moments. Plen put words to what they were both thinking.

"You should leave the girl here," she said, at last, whispering so Mysta couldn't hear.

Lanthrea nodded and looked out the window, avoiding eye contact with Plen.

"She'll be safe here," Plen added. "You know this is best."

Lanthrea nodded again but said nothing.

"You should talk to her," Plen urged.

Looking over at the little girl, Lanthrea sighed. She stood slowly and went over and sat down next to Mysta on the floor.

"You like that doll," she said quietly.

Mysta nodded. "She's pretty."

Lanthrea smoothed the girl's hair again. "She *is* pretty. Like you."

Mysta flashed a grin, then went back to playing.

"Mysta, how would you like to stay here for a while with Plen? You could play with your doll anytime you like. How does that sound?"

Mysta kissed the doll and smiled. "Are we gonna stay here for always?"

Lanthrea swallowed hard. "Well, I don't think so. But for a while. How does that sound?"

Mysta lifted the doll up and danced her in the air. "As long as you are here, too."

Lanthrea cleared her throat. "Mysta. You would be here with Plen for a while without me. I have to go do something and….and it wouldn't be safe for you to come with me. You'd be here, safe and sound, with Miss Plen. Is that alright?"

Mysta kept playing.

"Mysta?"

She looked up at Lanthrea and said only one word.

"Nuh-uh."

Lanthrea bit her lip. "Mysta. I can't take you with me. I'll be back very soon."

Mysta held the doll close. "Mommy said that, too."

Lanthrea felt her heart burst. That had been her biggest fear. That the girl would fear abandonment again. But it was right to leave her here with Plen. And necessary. She would need to be strong for both of them.

"Mysta. Look at me."

The little girl looked up, tears in her eyes.

"I'll be back very, very soon. I have to help some other friends of mine. And Plen is here for you," she looked over at Plen imploringly. "Aren't you?"

The old woman finished cleaning up the table and put her hands on her hips. "I am. And Mysta. You can help me. I'll even teach you to make biscuits."

Mysta sniffed. She looked up at Lanthrea. "You promise you'll be back soon?"

Lanthrea nodded, knowing full well she couldn't promise anything but knew of no other way to give hope to the girl.

"I'll be back as soon as I can."

Mysta stood up and walked over to her little trundle bed. She jumped up on it and laid the doll on the pillow. The conversation was over.

Lanthrea took the next few minutes to pack her backpack with a few necessities and emptied it of the non-essentials. Bread, cheese, and some dried meat, along with a full water pouch, went in. The stone mosaics stayed behind, Plen tenderly tucking them into a drawer between layers of clothing. There was no need to take any coin. There would be no trading on this journey.

Wrapping the blue scarf around her face, she kissed Mysta and Plen goodbye and left quickly, allowing for neither fanfare nor tears.

She made it out of town quickly and found the wide road leading down to the foothills an easy walk. She remembered her first trip this way with Tenk. She was absolutely exhausted every step of the way. Granted, the glottin was heavy, but she was also weak and completely out of shape. This time was remarkably different. She had plenty of food and water, the weather was good, and the days long. Outside of stopping for a bite to eat and drink every so often on the grassy knolls that dotted the road, she walked throughout the day, reaching the bottom of the foothills and the wide plain, still within the border of Drymac (but barely) by dusk. Glanèt was just about an hour from here, and Bythim's camp had to be close. It had to be within Drymac itself. There was no way Bythim would make an incursion into an outlying territory. There was no need, and Lord Bythim was, if nothing else, not an expansionist. He cared little about acquiring new land and had thus far shown no interest in war or conquest. Dominating another people group or territory seemed like too much trouble for his court, content as they were with getting rich off the backs of their own. Spending *any* of the palace gold on a bloody campaign held little interest for a small man like Bythim.

Lanthrea found a nice grove of trees to rest in. The moon and stars were just about out, and her plan—that which it was— necessitated the cover of night. She ate a bit of cheese and nibbled on one of the biscuits Plen had made this morning. She could imagine Plen and Mysta at the little table right now, enjoying evening meal together. It made her heart smile.

She went over her plan again and again in her head as she ate. It would, of course, depend upon the setup of the camp, which had yet to see. Maruk had said they had taken many of the elders from Old Town to this place, but how many were 'many'? Hundreds? Tens? Her entire plan would depend on details she did not as yet have but went something like this: she would get past the camp to Glanèt sometime before midnight. Relying upon the good graces of Neruk, the chieftain there, she would enlist their help. A few men to help guard the area for her as she snuck into the camp to find Petrul and Marinda. The assumption being that the people interred within would be both helpful and quiet. And a further assumption that there would be no locked gates or cells within the camp itself.

It was a plan that was practically no plan at all. She was fully aware of this fact. She finished up the last of Plen's biscuit and put her pack back on. The outer border of Drymac was only a few miles from here now, and the camp must be close. Time to get moving.

Staying off the wide main road, she walked along the side, using the trees and brush as cover. It was only about a quarter-hour later that she saw lights. The camp! She stopped and found a rock to climb up on to get a better look at it. Mercifully, it was just a single tent…large, but not even as big as some of the traveling animal and juggling shows she had seen in Cenecal. There seemed to be only a few guards outside, laughing, drinking, and smoking pipes in the torchlight. Of the three she could see, not one of them looked to be interested in their duties. No doubt, the elders inside were not much of a problem. This would work in her favor. The guards wouldn't be expecting trouble of any sort.

She stayed far from the tent, slipping by easily without notice, and made her way past the camp towards the village of Glanèt. It was about another half hour later that she saw the welcoming fires outside of their round huts, and within a few minutes, she found herself entering the village proper.

Everyone was asleep, and Glanèt had no guards or tower keepers, so few were the visitors here. She remembered vaguely which hut belonged to Neruk and made her way there quickly. Knocking on the door, she heard rustling inside, then the door opened. There stood Neruk, tall, handsome (although disheveled at the moment), rubbing his eyes and squinting in the darkness.

"May I help you?" he growled, his voice heavy with sleep.

"Please, Neruk. I don't know if you remember me. My name is Lanth..my name is Myka. I was here in the spring…with my glottin. Do you remember?"

Neruk rolled his shoulders and rubbed his eyes again. "Myka…Myka….oh, yes! The glottin. I remember. You left here quite in a huff. Do you still have that thing with you? You know how I feel about boarding them here."

"No, no. It's gone. But I need your help. May I come in?"

From inside the hut, a woman's voice called out. "Neruk, does someone need help? Neruk. For heaven's sake, let them in."

He shrugged and opened the door. "Come in, then," he said, yawning. "Come in."

A lovely woman with long black hair was just lighting a lamp in the corner of the hut. She straightened her bedclothes and smiled at Lanthrea.

"Welcome. Myka, isn't it? I remember you. You were not pleased with us for taking your glottin." She paused. "I do hope you'll forgive us. It was for your good, you know."

Lanthrea exhaled. "I do know…now. And," she paused here and took a deep breath, "I thank you for trying to help me. I didn't know then what I do now."

The woman extended her hand. "My name is Th'rena. I am Neruk's wife. I had no chance to formally greet you last you were here. Welcome back, Myka. But what on earth brings you here in the middle of the night?"

Neruk motioned to a large soft pillow on the floor. "Sit, sit," he said. "Th'rena, get our guest something to eat."

Lanthrea protested. "No, no. There is no need. Nor is there time. I have a long story to tell and no time to tell it. Perhaps I could make this easier. Do you remember when I was here last, I told you of Cenecal and Lord Bythim?"

Neruk nodded. "Oh, yes. I remember being grateful we had no such tyrant ruling over us here."

Lanthrea nodded. "Yes. Well, he has done a terrible thing, and I need your help. He has decided that all the people in Cenecal who have the book" she paused… "do you remember that story I told you…about my book?"

Th'rena nodded. "I do. Something forbidden about it, wasn't there? Didn't they burn your home for having some paintings from it, if I remember? "

"Exactly," Lanthrea urged, "Exactly. Well. They didn't stop there. They have taken some elders from our town and imprisoned them just north of here. They have them in a tent…an encampment of sorts. I don't know what they plan on doing with them, but I know it can't be good. I have two friends being held there. I need your help to get them out."

Neruk stroked his beard. "You must remember that we are peaceful people. We have few weapons and no fighting men. How can we possibly be of assistance?"

Lanthrea shifted her weight on the pillow. "Well, I think that if you could spare a few men to help watch the guards, I can get into the tent and try and get my friends out. I've already seen the place.

There are only a few guards, and they seem completely uninterested in their jobs." She sniffed. "There's not a person in that tent that hasn't seen their eighth decade already. I'm certain that Bythim's men have paid them no mind at all."

The beard stroking continued as Neruk considered her words. After a few moments, he pursed his lips and turned to Th'rena. "I think we should help our friend."

She nodded but said nothing. Rising, she walked over to the wall and pulled an ornately decorated robe off a hook. She carried it across the room and laid it over her husband's shoulders, leaving her hands resting gently on him.

"You will lead them," she said softly. "Call the council together."

He patted his wife's hands and stood.

"Ring the bell," he said resolutely. He turned to Lanthrea. "My men will gather. They will also have good ideas that might assist you in yours."

Lanthrea exhaled, not realizing she'd been holding her breath for the last few minutes of discussion. "Oh, thank you. Thank you so much." Her eyes filled with tears of gratitude, and she bowed her head to Neruk.

The Council of Glanèt met in the gathering area for a very short amount of time. Within minutes, a group of five men, led by Neruk, approached Lanthrea, who had stayed with Th'rena back at the hut.

"These men and I will accompany you," he said. "We will take our long spears with us. They are used for decoration and protection only, but they may be needed for something else altogether once there."

The five men bowed low before her, and Lanthrea felt tears come again to her eyes. Such honor and kindness from near strangers. It was far more than she had hoped for.

She left her pack with Th'rena so as to be unencumbered for the journey and hugged her tightly. She, after all, was offering her husband up for a dangerous task. She was offering her best.

The six men and Lanthrea made it back to the camp in a quarter of an hour—the men's strides being much longer and faster than Lanthrea's. She had to jog to keep up. Once there, they spread out, each taking a position on the perimeter of the tent, each one about a stone's throw from the guards. One of the three guards Lanthrea had seen earlier was already asleep, and the other two were still talking and drinking in the light of a campfire near the tent's entrance.

Lanthrea had no intention of attempting to breech the entrance to the tent. Instead, her plan was to slip in the back and crawl under.

Upon Neruk's signal, she quietly ran to the far side of the tent, hoisted the heavy canvas, and, finding it unsecured by tether or rope, ducked inside. The interior was almost pitch black, and she couldn't see a thing. However, her senses were assaulted immediately by noxious odors. The captives were obviously not given a proper place to relieve themselves, and the interior of the tent had the repulsive, sickening scent of both urine and feces and, worse, of death. Resisting the urge to gag, she wrapped her blue scarf tightly over her nose and mouth and tried to let her eyes adjust, and her stomach stop lurching.

It was only a moment or two before she realized there was a light source not far from her. A lone lantern, dimly lit, was flickering just a few feet away. Starting towards it, she felt her foot hit something and tripped, falling face down on the ground. The odor was overwhelming, and she turned to see what she had tripped over. Eyes widening in horror, she realized it was a body. The frozen stare of a corpse looked up at her from the ground. It was an old man, and he'd been dead long enough to have begun his journey back to dust; his flesh almost gone. She wretched, but managed somehow not to scream. Standing up, her eyes now adjusted somewhat, she saw there were dead all around her. Here, fallen on top of each other, lying bloated and swollen in various degrees of decay, were the elders of Old Town. She picked her way through the corpses, wondering if any were still alive. Why would there be guards posted at what was essentially a morgue?

Another light source was coming from a few yards away, from behind a curtain that separated the room she was in from another. She made her way there and pulled back the curtain. Eight pairs of eyes made contact with hers. Eight elders, lying on the ground, turned their miserable heads towards her. Too weak to react much, one old woman managed to reach her arm up to Lanthrea.

"Help us. Please," was all she could get out between rasping breaths.

Lanthrea glanced around the room. Sallow faces, sunken eyes. If Petrul and Marinda were in here, there was no way of recognizing them. Mind racing, she suddenly realized she had no plan left at all. None of these people were in any condition to escape this place on their own except through the doorway of death. She would have to report back to Neruk. There was nothing more she could do.

Making her way back through the partition, she held her breath as she made it to the tent wall, lifted it, and gulped in the fresh summer air. She ran as fast as she could back to Neruk, who was waiting for news.

"There is nothing I can do for them," she gasped, breathless, sobbing. "There are but a few left alive, and they are too weak to move on their own. I have failed. I have failed….Oh, Petrul….Oh..Marinda….I'm so sorry…" her sobs quietly filled the night air, and Neruk put a hand on her back.

"Then. We will bring them out. How many are there?" he asked, his voice firm; resolved.

"Eight," she sobbed, but they would have to be carried."

"I understand. Wait here."

He disappeared for a few minutes, and she heard an odd sound akin to a bird call—no doubt a signal to the others. All six men were gathered back together within a moment of the signal. Neruk's eyes shone in the moonlight. His face was stern as he spoke.

"Men. Tonight you shall have to fight. You may have to use your spears to kill. If you are not willing to do this, I understand, for it is not our way."

The men said nothing, but each grabbed his spear and plunged it into the ground at Neruk's feet. He nodded in understanding at this signal of solidarity.

"Let it be so," he declared. Turning to Lanthrea, he spoke quietly.

"My men have agreed. I do not want you to see this. This is not for you. You have been brave enough. Once the guards have been dispatched, we will again have need of you. There are only seven of us and eight of the elders. We will need your strong arms."

She nodded, wanting to thank them, but held her tongue. This was a sacred moment. She recognized it as such. Words would be hollow, if not crass.

She sat down on the soft grass and bowed her head. She would ask the king and the lady for their help and hoped they could hear her call.

Within moments, she heard the scuffles and groans of the guards. As it turned out, there had only been the three of them, and the fight had not lasted long. Neruk waved to her after it was finished, and she ran down to the tent. They entered in, found the eight elders, lifted them each out of their putrid cage, and carried them outside. Laying them down on the soft grass, the old men and women took their first breaths of fresh air in what had to have been months. Neruk quickly ensured they each had a drink of water, then checked them for wounds or broken bones before assigning a man to each for transport back to Glanèt. One particularly huge man was assigned two of the smallest and most frail women to carry, and Lanthrea was assigned a man. She couldn't lift him, of course, so Neruk had made a kind of dragging sledge for her from his ceremonial robe. "A better use than hanging as a decoration in my hut," he had said with a smile. They had the elders back to Glanèt within an hour (Lanthrea and the fragile elders slowing them down considerably, and Th'rena had already awakened the women of the village who were waiting with water, food, medicine, and warm blankets. The elders, each assigned a family, were quickly taken into the huts and given everything they needed…everything that could be done for them. Lanthrea still had no idea if Petrul or Marinda were among the survivors. And it didn't matter. Those that remained had been saved.

The Council had met all night after that, not emerging from the gathering area until morning light. They all agreed that they had most likely just opened themselves up to the wrath of Drymac and Lord Bythim. They also agreed that there was nothing else they could have done. It was right. It was good. And it might possibly forever change the destiny of their peaceful little village.

With weary faces and furrowed brows, the Council had returned to their family huts that morning, not knowing Glanèt's future for the first time in their lives.

Lanthrea had slept in Neruk and Th'rena's hut—if sleep is a proper description. She mainly tossed and turned and cried and wondered. She wondered how long before Bythim discovered what they had done tonight. She wondered if she had done the right thing by asking Neruk to put his village at risk. She wondered if she should have come at all.

By morning, she had no answers to her questions, but she had the light of day. Perhaps she would find her friends amongst the survivors this morning. Perhaps.

CHAPTER TWENTY-SIX:
From the Ashes

The morning brought no good news. Two of the eight elders had perished during the night—two women, neither of which was Marinda. The only solace to Lanthrea was that they had died in a clean place, with caring arms attending to them.

The other six elders were barely alive. They had been denied food for so long that their stomachs could not take in much, and they were so weak and sick that the medicines Glanèt had were of little use.

Lanthrea had gone from hut to hut, still hoping to find Petrul or Marinda, but she had already seen five of the elders this morning and had found neither of her friends. She entered the hut where the sixth Old Towner was being attended to by a lovely family of the clan Bar'ath. The children were being extremely good and quiet, much to the credit of their patient and kind mother, Shaleen. Shaleen was helping the old man who had been assigned to them. Lanthrea walked in and stooped down by the pile of pillows and blankets the man was laying on. She looked, and looked again. Could it be? The old man's eyes fluttered open and met hers. It was. It was he. It was Petrul! He was emaciated, covered in bed sores, with parched lips and bruising on every limb. Lanthrea literally dropped to her knees. "Petrul. Oh, sweet man. Is it you?"

The old man, gasping for every breath, looked back at her, but no flash of recognition crossed his face.

Lanthrea held his bruised hand gently in hers. "Oh, Petrul. You don't need to think. I only met you once at your house. My name was Myka back then. You told me of Palem. Oh, Petrul, it is *good* to see you." She sat there, tears pouring down her face. The old man closed his eyes again, and she saw a tear form in the corner of one and slip down his cheek. She gently lay his hand back down. Turning to Shaleen, she said, "This is Petrul. He is a wonderful man. You are blessed to have him in your home." Standing, she left the hut and let her feet carry her to the gathering area, where she sat down on a bench and looked up at the late summer sky.

So blue, so inviting, the sun shining as it did every summer day, yet today it all felt different. Like a certain evil had invaded her world, one she had never known before. One she could never have anticipated. One worse than the marauding gangs in Cenecal or the drunken beatings one risked by walking through the Market Quarter at night. This was a darkness that threatened to snuff out the sun. She couldn't explain it. She just knew it. None of this made sense. In Palem, the king had told her of the Return. To go back to her home here in Drymac and tell others about him and his good kingdom…to anyone who would listen.

How was that to happen now? Why had he even sent her back? She had seen the full depth of Bythim's cruelty on the frozen, anguished faces of the dead last night.

Suddenly, she jerked herself free of these thoughts as new, more immediate concerns pushed to the front of her mind. Mysta! Mysta and Plen! They were alone in Cenecal. She had to get back to them. It was assured that once Lord Bythim found his guards dead and the elders escaped, he would redouble his efforts to find any who followed the king, exacting his petty vengeance upon them. She rose quickly and headed to Neruk's hut. She needed to get back to Cenecal.

Explaining her situation to him, Neruk was in complete agreement that she would return home immediately. He had not known of Mysta until today, and, once hearing of her, agreed Lanthrea had to go back. He and his council had decided the only way to avoid conflict with Bythim's men was to ensure the elders were well hidden away if (and no doubt, when) they came to inquire as to the happenings at the tent. There was no definitive proof as to who had killed the guards and nothing other than the elders themselves to connect Glanèt to the situation. But secrets were hard to keep, even in a tight-knit village such as theirs. They had to be ready to face anything. Assuring Lanthrea they would do everything they could for the old ones, Neruk had blessed Lanthrea's travels and promised they would talk further upon her return. At this point, Lanthrea saw no way she could keep Mysta safe in Cenecal. For, without knowing who had struck the encampment, Bythim would never again suffer any more 'readers of the book' in his town.

Lanthrea left for Cenecal at midday, but not before stopping to say goodbye to Petrul and check on his condition.

To her surprise, he was sitting upright, leaning against the wall, and a bit of color had come back into his face.

"He was in need of fluids," said Shaleen, "And in considerable pain from his wounds. I put this ointment on, and his breathing improved as his pain diminished."

Lanthrea knelt down by him again. "Petrul. I'm so happy to find you doing better. I'm so sorry for all you've been through…"

He opened his eyes, a small smile cracking his parched, dry lips. He motioned to her to come near, leaned up, and whispered in her ear. "The king is good. And good is always right, but often brings suffering."

His head dropped back to the pillow, and he closed his eyes, the smile still on his face.

Lanthrea patted his hand and rose. Turning to Shaleen, she said softly. "Take care of him. I'll be back soon to help."

Gathering her pack, she wrapped her face in the blue scarf and headed back up the foothills to Cenecal. She would be at Plen's house by nightfall. And Mysta would be safe in her arms once again.

CHAPTER TWENTY-SEVEN:
The Inner Court

"Lord Bythim, whose countenance is as that of the sun, I bring news from near the southern territories."

Bythim shifted his small body in his gigantic chair and intoned in a most melodramatic fashion, "Continue…"

Gareth cleared his throat. As Lead Guard, this announcement fell upon his shoulders. He would deliver the news well.

"The encampment of which you, Lord and Master, have generously provided for your subjects from Old Town—even though they lack any honor for you and disregard your ordinances,—has been ransacked."

Bythim stood slowly from his golden perch, his heeled boots clicking on marble with his feathered cape swirling about his feet.

"What is this? Explain."

"As you wish, Sire. We sent a change of guards to the encampment. They found that those posted there had been dispatched, and we are certain that some of the Elders you so kindly were providing for there… have escaped."

Gareth watched as Bythim's face reddened, his porcine eyes narrowing.

"How many have escaped?" was his only response, mentioning nothing of his murdered men who had been posted there.

"We think perhaps as many as ten, sire. But maybe less. Our numbers....our tally of how many had been taken there was not particularly… accurate, sire." He swallowed, his mouth dry, and added, " The people there were very old and frail. Even with your highness's good and excellent care, many of them had perished of natural causes and old age." He swallowed again, thinking to punctuate the positive one more time. "We think it only ten or less, sire, who escaped."

Bythim sucked in his cheeks and sat back down, petting one of his glottins as he did.

"And you, Guard, thought it appropriate to sully my good day with this news?"

Gareth straightened his shoulders.

"The duty fell to me, my lord."

Bythim sniffed. "That is most unfortunate, then, for you."

Gareth closed his eyes. He thought of his wife, his two children, and his small home on the outskirts of Cenecal. He only had a moment to think of them before his head lay on the ground, rolling toward Bythim's golden throne.

"Clean that up," Bythim growled. "It's staining my marble."

The Court Guards, having done their unholy duty, bowed and picked up the body. Three courtesans, dressed all in the dark blue of Drymac, appeared from the back of the room with buckets of water and rags. The mess was gone within minutes.

Bythim pulled one of his glottins onto his lap. "Is there anything else?"

The remaining Court Guards stepped forward. "Nothing, my Lord," they said in unison.

Bythim leaned down and listened as the glottin in his lap whispered to him.

"Yes. Yes, I know. It will be handled," he cooed in response.

"Bring me the scribe," he shrieked to the women at the back of the room. "I have an edict to write."

The women scurried out a small side door. Within moments, the ornate doors opened once again, and a small man with long gray hair on which sat a blue felt cap, entered the room. He was carrying a box made of wood.

"Sire?"

"Take this down," Bythim said, irritated with his robe again and blowing the feathers out of his face. The little man set the box on a pedestal near the throne and opened it, pulling out parchment and an ink pen.

As the doors to the Inner Court swung shut, Lord Bythim dictated his will to the scribe. All of Cenecal - all of *Drymac*- would know of his will by morning.

***

Lanthrea made it to Plen's house from Glanèt before the sun had set. It was a hot, muggy late summer day, and though having to stop frequently along the way to refill her water pouch from a stream now and again, she still had made good time. Mysta was overjoyed to see her, running and jumping into her arms the minute she opened the door. Plen had given her a hug and put Mysta to bed so Lanthrea could rest from her journey.

As they sat in the living area, Lanthrea in the big chair and Plen in a small rocker, they said nothing for the longest time. Plen, noting the sorrow in Lanthrea's eyes, finally rose, made a pot of tea, and handed her a cup.

"You did not find your friends?" she asked quietly, unsure if she should say anything at all.

Lanthrea inhaled, then exhaled slowly, never giving Plen eye contact.

"I found Petrul," she said, then said nothing more.

Plen saw there was to be no more discussion this night. She stood up, took the cup from her friend, and pointed at a pile of pillows and a blanket she had set on the floor.   "You need to rest," was all she said.

Lanthrea recognized a directive when she heard one. Sleep sounded like a good idea anyway, having not rested well in the past several days. She nodded and lumbered over to the pillows.

"This is nice," she said, then added quickly, "But I could just use the chair again, you know."

Plen shook her head. "Whichever you want. Get some rest, dear. We'll talk in the morning."

Lanthrea arranged the pillows on the floor as she had learned at Neruk's and lay down. She found herself staring at the ceiling as she listened to Mysta's gentle breathing. They would leave in the morning for Glanèt. She only hoped she could convince Plen to make the trip.

Her dreams were full of the winged demons again. Vicious, ugly things darted at her over and over, attempting to tear at her flesh. She awoke at first light, bolting upright and batting at invisible enemies. Mysta was already up and came running over. "What you doin', Lanthee?" She asked, bouncing up and down on the pillows.

Lanthrea shook off her sleep, took a moment to clear her head, and grabbed Mysta. "Tickling *you*," she laughed as the girl squealed in delight. Plen came waddling down the hall only a few minutes later.

"What is all this noise so early?" she asked, her smile betraying any real irritation.

"Plen! Lanthee has got me, heeeeeelp!" the girl wailed, laughing.

"I think I'll just make morning meal, if you don't mind," Plen grinned as she waddled into the kitchen.

Mysta flopped down on Lanthrea's lap, breathing hard from laughing. "I'm glad you comed back," she said, snuggling against her chest. Lanthrea kissed her head. "I am, too," she said. She let Mysta pull her to her feet, and they wandered over to the little kitchen table together. Plen had already set out bowls for each of them, filling them with a hot grain and pouring a little cream into each.

"You feeling any better in the light of day, Lanthrea?" She asked, setting the little pitcher of cream on the table.

Lanthrea took a bite and chewed slowly, looking up at Plen. "It wasn't good," she replied.

Plen nodded. They talked about the weather and Mysta's new adventure with her rag doll (who had lost her pony in the woods and had to go find it) until Mysta finished eating.

Lanthrea tousled the girl's hair. "How about you and Ragdoll go out on the porch and play for a bit?" she suggested.

"Her name is Bryta," Mysta corrected as she jumped up from the table and ran out the front door.

"Leave the door open," yelled Plen," So we can keep an eye on you and Bryta, yes?"

"Uh huh!"Mysta yelled back.

Plen turned to Lanthrea. "Your friend Petrul. He is alive?"

Lanthrea sighed deeply. "Barely. But I'm afraid Marinda perished in the camp before I could get there. As did many of the elders." She looked up at Plen, tears in her eyes. "They were left there to die. In the heat of that tent. In their own filth. I honestly can't believe *any* of them survived."

Plen took her last bite of hot grains. "As it is with man's cruelty."

They sat in silence for a long time, Lanthrea, at last, breaking it.

"We have to go from here, Plen. It won't take Bythim long to decide to punish any others who follow Palem's way. He'll find you, Plen. He will. I'm certain of it. We have to go."

Plen drew back. "Go? Go where?"

"To Glanèt. Neruk said we are all welcome there. He understands. He saw."

Plen shook her head. "No. This is my home. I'll not be run off like a common marauder."

Lanthrea nodded. "I understand. But the thought….the thought of you being thrown into that tent." She stopped and swallowed hard. "Plen, please."

Plen stood up, picked up the bowls, and walked into the kitchen. Pouring some water from the jug into them to soak, she turned and faced Lanthrea.

"I'm old, Lanthrea. Much older than you. I have no energy for —nor interest in even a short journey. I have no desire to spend my last days in a foreign land. No. I'm staying here."

"But Plen, they won't let you," Lanthrea begged.

"Then I will show them I am unafraid. And they will have to carry me to my death if that is what they want."

Lanthrea exhaled, closed her eyes, and nodded. "I understand. But we need to warn the others in town. Any of them that wish to leave can come with me. We need to let them know."

Plen gently bowed her head before looking up at Lanthrea. "Agreed. Now, I be knowin' almost everyone in Cenecal who holds to the book. I will get the word out this very morning, but it'll be takin' a few days for people to gather their things and ready themselves. You, on the other hand, need only to get Mysta ready to go."

"That will take no time at all. Let me help you warn the others. Tell me what to do."

Plen nodded. "A good idea." She looked up at Lanthrea. "We can start now. Follow me."

Pushing away from the table, Lanthrea once again wrapped her head and face in the blue scarf, helped Plen to the door, and grabbed Mysta's hand. They spent the cool of the morning walking through Old Town, knocking on the doors of the elderly living there, informing them of the current situation. Only a handful agreed to leave Cenecal. Most, like Plen, decided to stay and face whatever opposition might come. This was their home. These were their roots. If they were to leave, they would have to be taken from this place.

Exhausted and somewhat frustrated by midday, Lanthrea made the three of them sit down under a tree by the center fountain to rest. Mysta ran across the square to Plen's house and brought back a loaf of bread from the kitchen. They tore the loaf and shared it, the soft late summer sun and the sparkling water of the fountain belying the gravity of the situation. It was a lovely break from reality.

Plen ate her bread slowly, reflecting upon the people in town. "There are a few more," she said. "In the Dwelling Quarter. "I know of at least three families that hold to the book. We need to be tellin' them, too. They might have children, I can't remember. They may want to go with you."

Lanthrea swallowed her last bite of bread. "I'll go. It's a long walk. Just tell me where."

Plen pushed herself up from the ground with a grunt without assistance and dusted herself off. Smiling, she looked at Lanthrea and curtsied. "Didn't think I still had it in me, did ya?" she laughed.

"Oh, you are what I hope to be when I'm your age," Lanthrea grinned back at her. "Now, where do I go to find the others?"

Plen told her the streets and family's names, then took Mysta's hand and walked her back to the house. "Be back by evening meal, yes?" she had waved to Lanthrea from the porch. Promising to do so, Lanthrea had turned, ducking underneath a lovely hanging garden as she headed to the Dwelling Quarter.

The town was less crowded than when she left last spring as the Festival of Ciracus was heating up. Looking around, it was obvious that the brilliant hues of summer were quickly melting into the muted tones of Autumn. It was quite lovely. The air was crisp; the trees alive with colors that offered a last gasp of life before giving up their leaves, letting them flutter to the ground. She pulled at her blue scarf, letting only her eyes be visible to any passers-by. Only a few of Bythim's men were out and about today, and none took any notice of her. Even so, each time a group of them walked by—their armor flashing in the fall sun, their dark blue capes swirling pretentiously in the breeze—her heart would begin to race. It would take several steps before she could breathe normally again. She made it to the Dwelling Quarter within half an hour. Streets here were not marked with signage, but the spoke-like configuration of the town was easy enough to navigate. Plen told her that one family lived on the second spoke and the other two on the fourth. The houses were all three marked by porches with a chair or two out front (not a common occurrence in Cenecal, where no one was particularly welcoming). They should be easy to find.

The first family she met had proved more challenging than she anticipated. The wife just kept saying, "What book? I don't know what you're speaking of." The husband simply darted into the back of the house and never re-appeared. Lanthrea had left them the news (although truncated, not giving any details other than they should be aware and leave town if possible) and left feeling somewhat defeated. They certainly didn't feel safe to entrust with discrete information about Glanèt and the welcome they would find there.

The second family had received the news gladly, had invited Lanthrea in for tea, listening carefully with discernment. However, they decided to stay in Cenecal and do what they could to help any others who might need it. Their children were nearly grown and had agreed to this plan as well. The last family (she had thought them not home but had happily found them in the back, digging in their vegetable garden and harvesting some early fall squashes) had small children. They agreed it best to leave Cenecal and arranged to meet Lanthrea and Mysta at Old Town Center in the morning. Lanthrea had begged them to meet her this very night, but they felt it best if they had the day to gather their belongings, maybe even bring some food along for the others. Acquiescing in the end, Lanthrea had so agreed, and they decided to meet just prior to dawn at the fountain. Dragging her feet on the way back to Plen's, Lanthrea felt defeated. Musing upon her lack of success in convincing everyone to leave town, she thought about how hard her message might be to apprehend. A stranger, coming to your door, telling you of Lord Bythim's plans to take you from your home—you, living in peace in Cenecal. You—doing no one harm and keeping to yourself. Why would Lord Bythim even consider you? Hers was a hard declaration to make and an even harder one to believe.

It was almost dusk by the time she made it back to Old Town. The scent of the rose gardens and lavender stands had come alive in the cool evening air, and just breathing them in did her heart good. It was as she was closing her eyes to enjoy these last scents of summer that everything went black.

There was no lavender to revive her when at last she opened her eyes. Fighting to focus, she was vaguely aware of something quite the opposite: a musty odor—dank and putrid—and the fact that she was lying down on a cold and wet surface. Sitting up, she rubbed her head where she had been (unbeknownst to her) clubbed quite viciously. Her head ached in a way she had never known before, and the dizziness quickly overwhelmed her stomach as she emptied it on the wet ground beneath her.

Fighting to stay conscious, she tried to calm her lurching stomach and her labored breathing, to no avail. The air here was almost thick with mold and vomit and the putrid stench of death.

Leaning against a wall, she tried to assess her situation. It was dark, save for one torch, lit outside her room, or what seemed a room, perhaps more a cage. There were bars across the front of it, and the walls and floor were seeping with water, no doubt groundwater. She was underground. That seemed obvious, but where?

Retching again, she sat back and tried to calm herself. She was alone in this place. That much was certain.

It was over an hour—or more—it was impossible to tell without the movement of the sun to guide her, that she heard footsteps. Wet, sloshing things coming towards her from the left. She sat up as best she could.

"Welcome to Kraleck. Lord Bythim sends his best."

The man was tall, thin, and dressed in the finest linens with a dark blue court cape over his shoulders and a long, sharp nose, the most prominent feature on his hawk-like face.

"Where….where…." Lanthrea was unable to speak properly—no doubt a result of the head injury.

"I just told you that, don't you listen? Another strike against you." The man rolled up his sleeves before reaching over and checking the bars of the cell, then wiped his hands on his cape.

"Wha…What…am I doing here?" she managed to get the words out.

"Oh. You and I both know the answer to that. But, honestly, had it not been *for you*, we would never have found you. You have changed, Myka. Not quite the ragged old thing we were looking for…" and here he smiled, "yet here you are. And talking to people all day long. Warning them about *us*? Tsk, tsk. Not a very clever woman, are you? We were informed of your presence by the very first family you made contact with. We had you in our sight before you had even made it out of the Dwelling Quarter."

Lanthrea's mind was racing. Disoriented as she was, she couldn't hold a thought, let alone understand the man's dismissive lecture. He continued talking, but she couldn't make sense of his words. His tone, however, was easy enough to understand. And she *did* know of Kraleck. It was a prison: a series of tunnels and cells deep beneath Bythim's palace that was reserved for the kingdom's enemies or anyone of whom Bythim wished disposed. It was deadly and inescapable. She drifted off into unconsciousness, the cell tipping sideways as she slid down the damp wall to the floor once again.

She awakened. Her head was clearer, the pain less intense, and the man—gone. She could now focus her eyes and wished she couldn't. The place was abysmal. The odor alone was enough to choke a person, and the slimy walls and floor made her gag. She was already cold to the bone, and there was obviously nothing to be done for it, as there was no window for sunlight and no blanket—even the thin, rough, muslin kind she used to have—for warmth. She seemed alone, but she could hear someone, not far away but too far away to see, moaning and rasping for air.

She was about to ask if her fellow captive needed help when she realized the folly of such a question. It was only a moment after that realization that she felt her heart almost leap out of her chest. *Mysta!* Mysta had to get out of Cenecal. *Oh, Plen. Realize something has happened to me. Get Mysta to safety. Please, Plen.*

She whispered her plea into the thick, dank air of her cell, then curled up into a ball and sobbed.

CHAPTER TWENTY-EIGHT:
The Alone

It had been almost two weeks now. No one had brought food or water. She had realized, after the first few days, that she was going to have to lick the walls and floor of the place if she wished to live. There was enough water seeping through the cold clay that it would sustain her. If she could gag it down. She managed, although the first time she tried, her body rejected it, and she retched for hours. It got easier, and as her hunger abated after a time due to deprivation, so did her thirst. Having no sense of day or night, the moments were just a blur of horror. The quiet, endless horror of isolation and starvation. She assumed she would die here, and there was nothing to challenge that assumption.

In the beginning, she thought of Palem—of the King and the Lady. She thought of it and them often. For the entirety of the first week, she had constantly begged for their help, but none had come, and the dark and empty and lonely simply rattled on. Her hair had once again become a knotted mass, but who was to care? Not she. Leaning against the cold, clammy walls, she let time wash over her, staring helplessly and hopelessly into the darkness of the place. Her thoughts after awhile became jumbled and confused, but when they held any coherency at all centered around only one thing—rather one person— Mysta. She was no doubt frightened and sad. The little girl had lost so much already. Lanthrea had promised she wouldn't leave her…she had *promised*. Imagining Mysta's sadness was shattering her. In truth, the breaking of her body in this cell could not, by any degree of magnitude, compare to the breaking of her heart. Adding to her sorrow, the only other soul down in this pit with her had perished sometime during the last few days; his or her groans and gasping breath at last giving way to silence. She would be next. She would never see Mysta again. And so, with nothing left of herself but a fractured heart and a whispered prayer on parched lips, she awaited death.

Certain that her time had finally come, she had awakened one day from a wretched sleep and found she was struggling to see. The light was dimming all around her. Assuming this was the end, she closed her eyes and awaited the inevitable. But death had not come. In fact, she had opened her eyes to find that it was simply the lone torch in the hallway near her cell sputtering out. Unattended, it had flickered its last, and within minutes the entire dungeon was pitch black. She couldn't even see her hand in front of her face, so thick was the darkness.

She was surprised by her own reaction, for she had laughed. A cynical laugh. Of *course,* the torch would burn out. What creature comfort would be afforded her here? Certainly not that of light, of sanity itself. Not even the cruel mercy of death would be offered her today.

After a few days of sitting in the inky blackness, her mind had begun to play tricks on her. One time, she thought she saw Elpinhoeve in the cell next to her, happily grazing on clean, fresh hay. He had looked up at her, mouth full, and nickered happily. Once, she had seen Mysta, crying and holding out her arms to be comforted. Attempting to reach out and hold her, Lanthrea's heart had shattered as that image dissolved back into the blackness. She had slumped against the cold walls of her cell and cried, her body racked by gut-wrenching sobs. Mysta's suffering hurt her infinitely more than did her own, and she felt she could bear no more. She prayed again that Mysta was safe. That perhaps Plen had found a good family to take her in. Prayer was all she could do. Perhaps it was the best she could do.

One day—or night (it was impossible to tell)—when she was particularly defeated and quite resigned to certain death, she had awakened to find Innatus, his long, white hair crowned with a green garland, standing next to her. He was holding up a golden cup toward the sky and singing to the stars. She closed her eyes (even though it made no difference) and tried to listen to his song. She could almost hear it…

When at last she opened her eyes, the image was gone. But she remembered something Innatus had said to her back at the Lake of Lights. "The king can use any waters to refresh his people." *Any* waters. Maybe even these filthy, clay stained, musty rivulets that came through the walls? Was it even possible?

She got up on her knees and faced the wall, both hands out as she leaned against it, and let the fetid water trickle over her fingers.

"Good king. I have no strength left. Please use these waters to help me."

Slumping back down on her haunches, she hung her head against the wall and cried—tears pouring down her face. How could she even have any tears left? That, in and of itself, was a small miracle, and she let the tears themselves soothe her aching heart. No other help came to her, but, were she to admit it, would have to say that she *was* somewhat refreshed. Inexplicably and almost imperceptibly, she felt her heart buoyed by the warmth of an ember of hope. She curled up on the cold floor and slept peacefully, a mercy unto itself.

***

It was on the seventeenth day that the torch was relit. The flame, which would have been weak and dim to anyone outside of this place, had pained her as badly as looking directly into the sun. She closed her eyes against the assault.

A voice broke the silence, almost as painful to her ears as was the light.

"Not much left of you, eh?"

She looked up, grimacing as she tried to open her eyes. The image of a man came into view. Tall, thin. The Hawk.

"I've brought you food. Although I doubt you can eat it." He laughed sardonically. "By the way, Lord Bythim sends his regards."

The clank of metal rattled on the floor as he tossed a tin plate through the bars of her cell. The food, whatever it was, slid unceremoniously off the plate and landed in the sludge.

With her eyes now adjusting somewhat to the light, she thought for a moment to crawl over and pick up the food. But she had lost all sense of hunger a few weeks ago and had no energy to crawl the two feet from the wall to the plate anyway.

Slumping in resignation, she simply let the light from the newly lit torch bring reality back to her. The darkness had forced her to live in her imagination, where nothing was real, and everything was tenuous. Looking now at the cell—seeing the bars, the wet walls, and even the spilled food on the floor—felt good. Tangible. Real.

Suddenly, her stomach squeezed. Surprisingly, the sight of even this meager ration had forced her body to respond. She *was* hungry. In fact, she was starving to death. Could she eat?

Using all her energy, she lurched from the wall and crawled toward the food. It was some sort of cheese and a piece of flatbread, both now immersed in the dank water of the floor; the bread soggy, the cheese stained by the tannins of the groundwater. She thought to try the water-soaked bread first. Lifting it to her lips, she tried to nibble it. The first bite was impossible to swallow. Her throat was either too dry or too swollen to push it down. She placed her finger into a small puddle of water on the floor and licked it off, moistening her mouth. Trying again, she put the soggy bread to her lips and tried to chew and swallow. This time it worked. A tiny piece of the bread went down, and with it, her hunger was awakened. Like a sleeping beast, she suddenly found she could not stop, nearly shoving the rest of the bread down her throat. It was but two seconds later that she felt the urge to retch, but she suppressed it. She had to keep this down. After a few minutes, she picked up the cheese and nibbled on it. Salt. Milk. She could taste every element, each ingredient in it. Nothing in all of the universe could or would ever again taste this good. She ate but a few bites of it, then put the rest in her pocket for tomorrow. If she lived that long.

On the twenty-ninth day of her captivity, someone new came to her cell. The Hawk had inexplicably come every few days with the same bread and cheese as he had on the seventeenth, and once even with a gourd of fresh water. That water had tasted like ambrosia, so sweet and clear and refreshing. If she lived through this, never again would she take fresh water for granted.

So today, expecting the Hawk, she was surprised instead to see a woman standing before her. Young, beautiful and dressed all in black, with long dark hair tumbling down like silk from an ornate headpiece.

"You must come with me," was all she said.

Lanthrea blinked and groaned involuntarily. Surely this was another illusion.

"The King has sent me. You must come. Now." Producing a set of keys from under her black robes and fumbling with them, she finally inserted one into the cell lock until it clicked. She pulled the door, and it swung open.

"Come. Now."

Lanthrea groaned again. She hadn't been on her feet for more than a minute or two in the last month. Crawling over to the bars, she grabbed hold and pulled herself up. Her legs wobbled but held steady.

The woman in black took her arm. "Lean on me. I'll get you out."

The next few minutes were a blur. Lanthrea was still unsure if she was dreaming, mad, or…dead. On and on they walked, Lanthrea being supported by the woman through the dark tunnels, always going upward, until at last, there was a light before them. The woman then grabbed Lanthrea's hand and pulled her toward that light. Blinded by it, Lanthrea shut her eyes and let the woman lead. Suddenly, she felt the warmth of the sun on her body. Even with her eyes closed and twenty-nine days without it, she knew. Like the warmth of a hug or the comfort of a soft blanket, this was *sunshine* that was penetrating her skin. She tried to open her eyes but found she could not. It was just too bright. The woman, still leading her by hand, pulled her a bit farther down what seemed a rocky path and then told her to sit. Glad of this directive (her legs shaking from un-use), she collapsed onto what felt like a soft, crinkly bed. Feeling about her, she realized it was no bed at all. She was in a pile of leaves. She could tell from the smell alone. Fall leaves. Unmistakably fragrant in sweet decay, crackling under her fingers as she moved her hands over them.

It took another few minutes before she could open her eyes properly.

She was in the middle of a grove of aspen and birch trees, her favorites—white paper bark peeling off their trunks, with a few tenacious gold and rust leaves yet hanging onto the branches. She was sitting in a pile of the many that had already fallen to the ground. The woman sat down next to her in the leaves and handed her a flask.

"Here. Drink this. It will strengthen you."

Lifting it to her lips, she tasted what seemed like wine but more potent and considerably sweeter. Whatever it was, it warmed and strengthened her entire body, satiating her thirst and hunger simultaneously.

"It is the king's libation," the woman explained, intuiting Lanthrea's question. "It is given only to those in great peril. Here. The rest is yours. Drink of it as you feel the need. It will heal you."

Lanthrea took another small sip and indeed felt the life pouring back into her, both in body and spirit.

"Wh..who…who are you?" she struggled to speak. Words had left her several weeks ago. She forced her mouth and tongue to put sounds to her thoughts. Sipping the drink she awaited the answer.

"My name is Bethstra. I am from Palem." She stopped here and smiled for a moment as she remembered. "I used to be an attendant there. Perhaps you remember our kind? We welcome those new to the king's land and help ready them to meet him."

Lanthrea's heart quickened. The two women in blue who cared for her there! Of course she remembered.

"But …wha…what are you doing here?" Her voice was like gravel. It hurt to talk.

"Oh, I volunteered," Bethstra said happily, then, suddenly, her face fell. "I had no idea what it was like outside Palem's boundaries. "So much harder than I thought…so much…*sadder*."

Lanthrea continued to drink, and as she did, found it easier to speak. "How did you get into Kraleck? Or the keys to my cell?"

"The king provides," Bethstra replied, offering no further explanation. "Now, we need to get you out of Cenecal. This part of the city, behind the palace, is not guarded well. There is little need as no one can gain entrance here. But we have to leave, as the few guards that do patrol will make rounds soon. Come. Your legs should be stronger now."

Extending her hand to Lanthrea, she pulled her to her feet. It was true. Her legs were no longer shaking and weak.

"Now, take my hand. They cannot see you easily if you do."

Lanthrea wondered what this could mean but took Bethstra's hand obediently and let herself be led amongst the trees away from the palace grounds. It was as they were about to leave by the ornate gates at the back of the high walls that surrounded the palace, that a small group of guards appeared from around the corner of the building.

"Halt." One yelled loudly, pulling his sword from its casing and running towards them. The other two walked leisurely over, these two women obviously proving no real threat.

Lanthrea's blood went cold, and she simply closed her eyes and awaited the man's blade. Bethstra squeezed her hand tightly.

"Where are you going?" The soldier asked, his tenor at once both demanding and demeaning.

"For my morning trip to the Market Quarter," Bethstra said softly, "at Lord Bythim's good pleasure."

"And this is the gate you use?" the man said, a touch of disbelief in his tone.

"Not always," she responded, "But today, yes. I was enjoying the fall leaves back here."

Lanthrea was holding her breath, wondering why the guard had not yet struck her down. Bethstra continued to squeeze her hand as she tried to figure out why they weren't apprehending her. Maybe they thought her a servant. Maybe the men hadn't recognized her. For, in truth, only the Hawk had ever visited her in the cell.

The guard sheathed his sword. "I thought I saw someone else with you," he said at last. "But I see I was mistaken. Carry on."

He turned and joined the other two, continuing their rounds.

Lanthrea exhaled and opened her eyes.

"Say nothing," Bethstra whispered quickly, under her breath. "Stay silent."

Lanthrea didn't need to be told. She followed Bethstra out the gates, finding themselves at the top of a long, cobblestone road that led from the palace (situated in the dead-center of the many 'spokes' of Cenecal) down to each of the quarters. Bethstra walked slowly but deliberately, continuing to cling to Lanthrea's hand. They passed another set of guards, manning a station nearer town but no others. These guards, as the other three, spoke to and questioned Bethstra but didn't seem to notice Lanthrea. It was inexplicable.

The two women came to the junction that led to the Market Quarter, but Bethstra turned in the opposite direction, leading Lanthrea towards Old Town. They stopped only once, resting for a moment so that Lanthrea could take another sip from the flask. Strengthened once again, they continued until they entered the gardens of Old Town. The walk had taken almost half an hour, and Lanthrea's legs could hold her up not one minute more. Happily, Bethstra took her just a few more steps up to a little house (smaller even than Robin's Egg) and knocked on the door.

An old man opened the door, his eyebrows raised in surprise and eyes wide at the women before him. Frozen in disbelief for a brief moment, he quickly shook free of his stupor, bowing low before Bethstra and beckoning them inside.

"Quick, quick…before they be seein' ya," he muttered, obviously somewhat still flustered.

Once inside, Lanthrea suddenly felt the intensity of her weakness; her knees buckling as she collapsed near the door. "Help me get her to the bed," Bethstra commanded. The old man helped as they picked Lanthrea up and laid her gently on a bed in the corner of the room.

The man then bowed again before Bethstra and went to put on a pot of tea in the fireplace. He fumbled with the pot in his excitement, almost dropping it twice before finally affixing it on the hook.

The woman in black sat on the edge of the bed and lifted the flask to Lanthrea's lips once again.

"You'll need to keep drinking this," she directed. "It is most efficacious when most needed, but it will do its good work even when not."

Not quite understanding the woman's cryptic words, Lanthrea simply nodded and continued to drink. Nothing about this woman nor what had just transpired made any sense. It was probably not even real. But the bed was soft, warm, and dry—and she was broken and exhausted. It only took a minute before she fell into a deep, restorative sleep.

The man brought a cup of tea to Bethstra and bade her sit in the one good chair in the place. He waited for her to sit, then grabbed a stool for himself. His cheeks were ruddy and his eyes were shining.

"Who is she….the one you have brought?"

Bethstra sipped her tea. "Her name is Lanthrea. She has been in the bowels of Kraleck for nigh on a month now. She will need much time to recover. I have given her a libation. It will assist her in healing. You must help her get to a small village named Glanèt once she is able. Can you do this, Mellick?"

The old man almost jumped off his stool. "You know my name?! Who would have thought it? You know my *name*?" He stammered, blushing, before composing himself. "And yes, yes… anything for the king," he exclaimed. "And may I say again what an honor it is for one such as you to grace my door."

Bethstra smiled gently. Reaching over she patted his hand, her long black hair softly swaying in the sun. "If only you knew, you might say the honor is mine. We all serve the same king—each in our own capacity, no?"

Mellick shifted on his stool. "To be sure, to be sure. But it is rare that a…a…*klestara* such as yourself comes here to Cenecal."

She shook her head. "Oh, I've been assigned here for a long time, Mellick. It is heartbreaking work." She looked up and smiled. "But it is the king's work, and I am honored to do it."

Setting the cup down, Bethstra stood. "I need to get back to the palace. I leave this one" (here she nodded at Lanthrea) "in your charge. Again, the village is named Glanèt. It is just outside Drymac on the foothills. She knows the way." She stood and walked towards the door of the tiny home. "And don't forget to make her drink from the flask. It will greatly speed her recovery."

Mellick nodded, bowing again before Bethstra. "At your command," he said.

She smiled at him, then turned and swept out of the room, closing the door behind her.

Mellick fell back onto his stool. Never in his life did he think he would ever see a klestara, let alone have one grace his humble home. "You live long enough," he muttered happily to himself.

Picking up the teacup, he thought for a moment about keeping it on a shelf and never washing it again. Shaking his head at his own silliness, he set it in the washing tub and walked over to check on his guest.

She was sleeping soundly, her breathing deep and steady, a good sign. He took a hard look at her. She was old but not as old as he, and thin as a rail. All bones, no meat. The prison had done its work. Her long gray hair was tangled up into a solid mass, and her skin was gray and sallow, almost translucent. The smell of her was overwhelming, and he winced both at the odor and the indignity of it. How could Bythim do this to any soul, let alone a daughter of the king? Wondering what she might be able to eat after such an ordeal, he thought to make an easy-to-digest meal: oats with honey. He would have it at the ready when she awakened. Grabbing a pot from a low shelf by the fireplace, he set about making the oats, still shaking his head over the fact that a real, live klestara had just visited his home.

Lanthrea awoke the next afternoon. Having no idea where she was and thinking she was dreaming, she sat up in the soft bed and let her eyes feast upon all she saw around her. A lovely fireplace, a tiny kitchen and table, a rocking chair, and cheerful windows letting sunlight pour into the room. She must be out of her mind. She was, no doubt, in her cell and quite mad. Closing her eyes, she took a breath. The air smelled sweet and clean, and what was that? Food? A very detailed dream, this. Opening her eyes, she was surprised to see the scene before her remain the same. A fireplace, a kitchen, a table. This didn't seem like a dream. It was too static, solid. She pushed herself to a fully upright position just as the door to the place opened, and an elderly man walked in.

"Oh, I see you're up!" the man said with a smile.

Lanthrea didn't respond. She rarely did in dreams.

"I'll wager you are hungry, yes?" the old man in her dream rattled on. "I made a pot of oats for you yesterday. Had to throw em to the pigs down the street when you didn't awaken. But I made a new batch this very morning for you." He walked over and lifted the lid off of a pot hanging over the fire. Steam and the delicious smell of hot oats filled the room. "Do you think you can eat?"

Still not answering, Lanthrea sighed. How cruel of her mind to create such a lovely illusion. Or perhaps it was a mercy. Perhaps her mind would keep her forever in this sweet fantasy, never again letting her open her eyes to the putrid cell.

She closed her eyes. Feeling a tap on her arm, she jolted.

"Lanthrea, isn't it?" the man was at her side. "Do you think you could eat?"

She sat for another moment, her mind reeling. He had *touched* her. She could *feel* him. This wasn't a dream.

"Wha….Whe….where?" Her voice was raspy again. She took a moment to form the words. "Am I…am I really here? In this place?"

Mellick grinned. "Oh, yes, dearie, you are really here. And you are in my home…in Old Town." He tapped her shoulder. "See? It's really me….er…my name is Mellick."

Suddenly, a blur of jumbled memories flashed through her mind. A woman, dressed all in black, a drink—tasting like sweet wine—guards, walking through town. An old man opening a door with a smile….

She looked at Mellick. "I remember now. Mostly. Where is the other one…the woman?" And then, as the reality of the situation sunk in, her heart leapt in her chest. "Mysta! Did she tell you anything about my Mysta? Her whereabouts?"

Mellick raised his eyebrows. "No mention was made of a 'Mysta'. Lanthrea tried to get up. "I have to find her…I…" She felt the weakness overwhelm her and crumpled back onto the pillow. Mellick lay his hand on her shoulder. "There, now. We shall have to find her once you are stronger." He saw the worry in her eyes. "I'll poke about and get information on her whereabouts. I promise." With this oath, he walked back to the fire and checked the oats again. "And, in answer to your question. I don't know exactly where the woman has gone. Back to the palace, I'd imagine." He placed his hand over his heart, "A klestara. Can you believe it? Here? In my home?" He almost giggled. "Did you know she knew my *name*? Oh, it's all too much."

Lanthrea furrowed her brow. "Klestara? I've heard of them, but…I think the woman yesterday said something about my attendants in Palem being just like her. It's all just a blur." She paused for a moment before trying to sit up again. "Mellick, I really *have* to find my Mysta…my daughter."

Mellick gently reached over and helped lay her back onto the bed. "I promised I will help you," he said reassuringly. "You're in no shape to find anyone right now. I'll make inquiries myself this afternoon. Your job is to rest." He turned, walked over and grabbed a bowl from a shelf.

"I'm certain someone will know about your daughter. If a klestara got you out of Kraleck, I'm sure someone helped your girl."

He fiddled with the pot over the fire, filling the bowl with hot oats. "And the klestara, yes…I'm not surprised you met a few in Palem. They're helpers of the good king. Magical sorts, capable of all kinds of good, they are. And assigned to different places—some there, some here, some in other lands, I'd imagine. Yours was named Bethstra. Didn't she tell you that?"

Lanthrea let her head fall back onto the soft pillow and groaned. "I don't remember much. Just images, snippets, really. I honestly thought I was dreaming. I'm still not sure I'm not."

Mellick laughed heartily, adding honey and cream to the bowl.

"I assure you, you are not. Here. Eat this. Go slow. Your stomach will thank you for it."

He handed her the bowl. The smell almost overwhelmed her. She dipped the spoon into the hot grain, and put it to her mouth.

In that one small moment, it felt as though all of time simply stopped. Chewing the oats slowly, savoring every bit of texture, flavor, and smell, tears began to well up and roll down her cheeks.

"I never thought I'd make it out of there. I really didn't. I didn't believe the king would help me." She looked up at Mellick, her eyes begging for understanding through her tears. "I thought he had left me alone to die. I gave up hope. I…I….stopped believing he…." She stopped suddenly before finishing her sentence. She couldn't bear her own dark thoughts.

"Oh, daughter," Mellick patted her shoulder gently. "That's the thing, isn't it? We are weak creatures, we are. Made of dust. But know this, child, the king has compassion on us. He has mercy on our frailty. Even on our thoughts." He paused, letting his words do their work. "Now. Try to eat," he said, leaning over and patting her shoulder again, "and slowly!"

Lanthrea pushed herself upright in the soft bed and lingered over every bite, gazing gratefully out on the bright fall day and, even though broken in body, feeling more alive than she ever had before.

CHAPTER TWENTY-NINE:

The Healing

She slept on and off for the next few days, awakening only to eat, drink and attempt to walk about the tiny house. Mellick had seen to it to find information on Mysta as promised (the young family that was to have met Lanthrea by the center fountain had been charged with taking her to Glanèt) and knowing this calmed her heart enough to let her body heal properly. Perhaps Mysta was safe, after all.

The libation Bethstra left was almost gone, but it had proved an absolute miracle. In only a matter of days, Lanthrea's emaciated and weak body had strengthened and healed. Her color was back (at least according to Mellick) and she could feel life returning to her each time she drank from the flask. She had even felt well enough to attempt brushing her tangled hair but had made little progress against the knotted up mess. The thought occurred to her to shave it all off and start fresh, but each time she set about doing just that, something stopped her. She resigned herself instead to wrapping a scarf over her head and focused on getting stronger.

The news Mellick brought day by day was both good and bad. Bythim had not as yet connected the villagers of Glanèt to the elder's escape, which was a mercy and a miracle. But he felt that the escape colored him somewhat a weak fool and this enraged him. In his paranoia and fury, he was taking it out on anyone in Cenecal that was even remotely connected to belief in Palem. People simply rumored to have the book were rounded up and taken away on the slightest innuendo; no proof necessary. Case in point, the vendor next to her old booth (the man selling religious trinkets) had been taken 'out of caution for the civic good', though he, himself, had never even *heard* of Palem. One thing was obvious. Bythim would not suffer any form of allegiance other than to him.

In the midst of all this, Mellick had somehow escaped notice. Having decided early on that he would not leave his home (he had not been home the day Plen and Lanthrea had come through warning of Bythim, but had heard it from a neighbor none the less) he had watched helplessly as his friends had been taken one by one, in the middle of the night. But by the king's mercy, Bythim's men had not come near his little house. The 'cleansing' of Old Town had stopped after about two weeks, and no more incursions had been made to the quarter by the time Lanthrea and Bethstra had shown up on his doorstep.

It was on Lanthrea's fifth day with Mellick that he managed to get news about Plen. The information was given to him by one of her neighbors, having watched the entire thing herself. After safely handing Mysta over to the young family that bright morning a month ago, she had stayed behind, defiant to the end. The soldiers in the blue capes had come to her home the very next day, and she (as promised) had refused to go on her own. The commander had become enraged with her resistance and had run her through with his sword. She died on her welcoming little porch with a smile on her face and forgiveness on her lips.

It was on her tenth day with Mellick that Lanthrea felt strong enough to begin considering her trip to Glanèt. He thought it best she wait another few days, but she was anxious to see Mysta and so decided to leave at dawn. They spent the day packing up a very light bag for her to carry and talking late into the night. Lanthrea had fallen asleep easily and dreamt of Mysta dancing in the late fall leaves and romping in the squash patches outside of Glanèt.

She awakened early, before dawn, and readied herself for the day's journey. Knowing she was still considerably weaker than the last time she made the trip, she wanted to make sure she had plenty of time before nightfall, darkness coming much earlier in autumn. She wondered if the tent was still being used to hold those who had been incarcerated or if Bythim was using a new space. Mellick had been unable to find out anything about that. No information, not even a rumor, was circulating about where they had been taken. That, in and of itself, was bad news. Either people weren't surviving to tell the tale, or the secrecy and security around those taken had risen to a new, more dangerous level.

She slipped over to the chair where Mellick was sleeping and kissed him on his head. "Thank you," she whispered softly, watching as he stirred slightly, then settled back into sleep.

Opening the door quietly, she tiptoed outside and slipped the pack onto her back. The moon was still out, and the center fountain, as she walked by, was sparkling in its glow. '*Please let Mysta be safe with Neruk*', she whispered to the sky, watching as the stars blinked away one by one, the dawn gently enveloping them.

The hike out of town was completely uneventful. Not even the town crier was as yet doing his rounds, and she saw no blue-caped men on patrol. What she did note was that her muscles and lungs were not as strong as she would have liked. She found herself stopping every so often just to lean against a tree and catch her breath. The sun rose after about an hour of walking; about the same time she came upon the wide, welcoming road that led down the foothills and out of

Drymac. There was no one else traveling today, which was a blessing that allowed her to walk slowly, taking her time and resting as needed. Not fully aware of her own level of exhaustion, it was on one of these stops that she sat down at the base of a pine tree just to rest for a moment and fell fast asleep.

The dream was vivid. She was at Lake V'esta, alone. The sun was sparkling on the lake, and she felt the warmth of it on her face. Startled by a rustling behind her, she turned to see the Lady of Lanthor in her woodland gown of brown velvet with the pearled bodice, her long brown hair softly blowing in the breeze coming off the lake.

"You're tired," she said, the proclamation both telling and comforting.

Lanthrea nodded and closed her eyes again to face the sun.

"You can be honest," the Lady said quietly.

Lanthrea opened her eyes. "About what?"

Th Lady sighed deeply and placed her hand over her heart. "About this," she said.

Lanthrea felt her eyes fill with tears. "I cannot. I…can..not."

"But you must. Your heart is as knotted up as your hair. I can't help you if you won't tell the King how you feel."

"I have no right," Lanthrea cried out, wishing this conversation would end.

"None of us do," the Lady responded gently," Yet he asks it of us. For our healing."

Lanthrea took a deep breath. "He…He cannot be trusted." The words felt like acid in her mouth. "He cannot be, or he wouldn't have let me be taken to that prison to suffer so. He would not have let Mysta be abandoned by yet another person."

The Lady smiled, her face becoming as light as the sun reflecting off the lake, but said nothing.

"And there's more," Lanthrea cried out, her voice breaking along with her heart. "I didn't just stop believing he would get me out of that place. I stopped believing he was *good at all*."

"Ah. There it is," the Lady said, her face showing nothing but compassion. "Look into your heart, Lanthrea, as deeply as you can. See what you find there."

Looking down at her chest, suddenly, Lanthrea could see through skin, sinew, and bone. And there, her heart was beating, sure and steady.

"As is your heart, so is he," the Lady whispered. "And even more so. For your heart will one day fail, but his sure and steady love never will. He is always there, never failing, even if you can't perceive his presence or understand his purposes. He is a King like no other. He is not a man like the other rulers—even the good ones—of this cruel earth."

"No," Lanthrea whispered quietly, shaking her head. "No. I was alone in that prison. You do not understand."

The lady shook her head. "If your eyes could only have seen the truth behind the darkness of those days, you would have seen him there, me there —a myriad of klestara all around you in that hole. No. You were never alone."

Lanthrea's voice broke into a sob. "But I couldn't see. And….it…broke me. Don't you see? I'll never be whole again."

The Lady of Lanthor reached out and touched her shoulder. "It is a journey, sweet daughter. And you are more whole now than ever before, whether you know it or not. You cannot now understand the reason of your time in Kraleck, nor see its benefit. There are times here in this place of shadows when trusting the King is all you will have. But you can—and must —be honest with yourself and with him. Otherwise, you might as well have stayed in that cell. You can tell him, even now, of the truth and the depth of your sorrow."

Lanthrea took a breath between sobs and closed her eyes again. Could she dare tell the king of her faithlessness? Of her anger? Of her heart's pain? She sat for the longest time in silence, then began slowly —hesitantly —to speak. "King of Palem. I was so hurt. I was so frightened…so terrified. And I could not bear my daughter's pain, yet could do nothing to help her. I thought you had left me to die alone. Why? Why would you let this happen to Mysta…or to me?" Her voice was heavy with sorrow, cracking with each syllable but she couldn't stop. "You are not who you say. You cannot be. You cannot be good… for you promised never to leave me." At first, her words were met with only silence, and she feared she had said too much.

But then, suddenly, she saw in her mind's eye a picture of herself, huddled in the fetid water of the cell, emaciated and broken. She saw herself, and then she saw the Others. The King himself was there, kneeling by her side, his arms around her, protecting her from the cold. The Lady was there, stroking her hair and comforting her as would a mother. There were three other women there as well, protecting her from harm, whispering to and cajoling the Hawk to bring her food. Looking closely, she recognized them! Two were her attendants from Palem, and one was Bethstra, who had unlocked the cell and led her out. She gasped at the sight and opened her eyes.

"You were there!" She exclaimed, her heart full of wonder. "All of you, you were there *all along*."

The Lady nodded. "The king never leaves his children, nor do those who are assigned to their care. Lanthrea, you have never been, nor will you ever be, alone. Even if you had perished there, in that place, we would have been with you and carried you to the Forever Land. Live or die, it is all the same love."

Lanthrea awakened with a start under the pine tree, blinking for a few moments in order to get her bearings, feeling a certain joy and ineffable lightness in her heart. Even though just a dream, it felt as though it were real, as though the Lady had actually been with her. Reveling in that feeling for quite a while, loathe to leave its warm embrace, she at last turned to put on her pack. It was at that moment that she saw something flashing in the sunlight on the ground in front of her. She reached down and plucked it out of the dirt. It was a golden hairpin, similar to the one the Lady had given her, lost in her fall from the mountain trail. Turning it about in her fingers, she gasped as she lovingly traced the image of a butterfly engraved upon it. In wonder, she reached up to stick it into her messy hair.

Shocked, she found her hair was smooth and soft, not a knot nor tangle left in it. Tears falling like rain, she gently coaxed her long gray hair into a soft bun and affixed the pin. She rose and faced the road before her. Live or die, suddenly it didn't matter. Though she may not understand her sufferings—for in humility she would accept that there were things beyond her comprehension—she knew that she was not alone or unloved in any of them. Never was. Never would be.

Picking up her pack off the ground and tossing it on her shoulder, she continued down the road toward the far southern border of Drymac.

Toward Glanèt and Mysta.

It was dusk when she came upon the Drymacian prisoner encampment. The original tent was still standing, but a wooden structure had been added to it. A long structure with no windows and a pitched ceiling. There was one chimney at the far end of it, and even though a cool night, Lanthrea noted that no smoke arose from it. Bythim had increased the guards. Whereas last time there had been but three, now there was at least one entire squadron of ten. And none of them were sleeping or smoking pipes this time around. These men were on full guard. Lanthrea hid behind a small group of trees, keeping her body close to the ground and barely breathing for fear they would hear her. It would not be easy to get around them. How did the others do it? Her eyes darted around the area, surveying her options. It was just then that she heard a noise behind her in the bushes. She froze. No doubt they were monitoring the road out of Drymac. She had been seen. Heart pounding, she turned slowly to face her certain demise only to find, instead of a blue-robed soldier, a young man dressed only in leather. He was motioning her to come and was completely silent.

Confused, she slid on her belly towards him in the dirt.

He said nothing but scooted towards her until he had taken her hand. He then pulled her towards the bottom of a hill, both of them sliding down together. Still not speaking, he stood and motioned her to follow him, then quietly began running toward a group of trees a good distance from the road.

Motioning her to sit, they leaned against the trees and caught their breath.

"I am Manut." The young man whispered. "From Glanèt. I've been assigned here for a few weeks now but haven't had the chance to help anyone until now." He smiled. "You're my first," he said proudly.

"I'm Lanthrea," she responded, whispering so as hardly to be heard. "And I thank you."

Manut's eyes widened. "Lanthrea? Did you say your name is *Lanthrea*?"

She nodded, still afraid to speak.

He grinned broadly, his white teeth shining in the rising moonlight. "We have all been waiting for you. Hoping you were still alive. Mysta has been…"

"Mysta!"Lanthrea interrupted, her heart leaping for joy, "she *is* here, then?"

Manut nodded. "Oh yes. She's here. And your old friend Petrul is still here as well! Come, we must go. Those soldiers can hear a branch drop off a tree from a thousand paces."

They got up and ran quietly through the brush until cresting a hill. From there, they could look down into the valley and see the welcoming fires of Glanèt. Manut grinned. "Home," he pronounced happily.

Having now crossed over the Drymacian Border, they both relaxed a bit, but Lanthrea didn't stop holding her breath until they entered the village proper. Many of the residents had already taken to their beds for the night, but a few were out and about. Manut raised his arm to the sky and made a fist.

"We have another one," he declared, "and her name…her name is Lanthrea!"

In a matter of moments, all up and down the village streets, the doors to the huts flew open, and people came running out to greet them. Neruk was among the first, sweeping Lanthrea into his arms and swinging her around. He had just set her down gently on the ground when another set of arms wrapped around her waist. "My rescuer," said a vaguely familiar voice. Turning around, she came face to face with her old friend Petrul. Looking thinner than he had in Old Town but considerably healthier than when she had last seen him, she simply grabbed and hugged him tightly, letting the tears come. It was but a moment after that happy reunion that she looked up to see Neruk's wife, Th'rena, approaching, holding the hand of a little girl. It took only the blink of an eye for Mysta to see who it was, and she pulled away from Th'rena and flew into Lanthrea's arms with her squeal of "Lantheeeeeeee!" making everyone present either shout for joy or dab their eyes or both.

After a time, Neruk clapped his hands together and pronounced, "To the gathering place, all who wish! It is time to celebrate!"

The crowd moved to the open area, but Lanthrea stayed back for a few minutes with Mysta, holding her as tightly as she could, unwilling to let her go. Her prayers had been heard after all. Mysta was safe, and safe now in her arms.

"You've grown," she said through her tears. "Just *look* at you!"

Mysta clung to her and sobbed. "I thought you die-ded. Like mommy and daddy."

Lanthrea held her close. "I'm so sorry you were scared. I would have come sooner if I could have. I *promise* you that. I promise you…"

Mysta sniffed and looked up at her. "I know. Petrul tolded me."

Lanthrea smoothed her daughter's hair and smiled. "I'm here now. And, with the king's blessing, I'll not leave you again, alright?"

Mysta nodded, then looked over toward the Gathering. "Can we go over with everybody?"

Lanthrea hoisted her up to her waist and Mysta wrapped her legs around.

"You've gotten so *big*," Lanthrea laughed, exaggerating her huffing and puffing as she carried the girl over to the others.

The night was spent in joyful celebration. No talk this evening of Bythim or encampments or soldiers. Just good wine, good food (left over from evening meal) and good company.

It felt, to Lanthrea, like Palem.

CHAPTER THIRTY:

Rumblings

He had never before known such a place. Not even in his imagination could he have dreamed it. The busy shops, the crowds, this palace. Even the ornate doors through which he was about to enter. Never in his imagination. Why had he not traveled here before?

Tapping his toe impatiently on the marble floor of the enormous hallway, Rethan awaited his turn. The woman in blue had told him it 'would not be long a wait'. She had been wrong. He had been here now for hours. This angered him. He had seen the Merchant Quarter on his way through the city and was anxious to return as soon as possible. Fine leathers, good meats, and strong libation all awaited him. And he would soon have the means for any or all of them.

He heard a muffled shuffling behind the doors, and a moment later, they swung open, revealing the grand room before him. It was breathtaking. How any structure could be so large and house such opulence? Golden chandeliers, wall tapestries in the finest silks, the patterned marbled floor, not to mention the voluptuous courtesans draped here and there on luxuriant furnishings. And the throne! Gold, dripping with some sort of clear, sparkling gemstone, and larger than the bed he slept in.

He stepped into the hall, lowered his head as he had been told (hard as it was to stop feasting his eyes on the opulence), walked forward the required six steps, and waited. The woman had informed him of proper protocol earlier in the day, and although he found such formality a waste of his time, he submitted. He knew what he had come here for.

"Speak," the command came.

Lifting his head, it was all he could do to suppress a laugh. For there, seated on the gigantic, oversized throne, was a tiny balding man dressed in a fur garment and cape that made him look rather like a mangy badger. Two glottins lay curled into balls lay at his feet. He was wearing a gold crown on his head, and the few wisps of hair he had left straggled out from underneath it at odd angles. Lord Bythim looked ridiculous.

Maintaining his composure, the man bowed low and began.

"My Lord, it has been rumored that there would be a… um….there might be…compensation for anyone bringing information on how the elders escaped from your good care lo a month ago. I have such information."

Bythim said nothing but leaned down and listened to one of his glottins whisper in his ear.

"I *know* that," he hissed at the creature, which simply yawned and settled back down into a nap at Bythim's feet.

"My glottin warns me that you may be employing a deception of some sort. Many others have come here, claiming information, looking for coin. They have paid the price for their impudence. Can you refute this as a possibility?"

"My refutation comes only in that I bring the truth. For it was my own village, sire, that not only dispatched the guards that were stationed there but released and now house the few old fools they found therein."

Bythim sat up, interested. "You say your village?"

The man nodded. "Yes. It is called Glanèt. It is not in your province, sire. You were most certainly not aware of it. We live near the southern border of Drymac, in an independent territory."

"Go on," Bythim said, licking his lips.

"We have others who have come to our village seeking refuge as well. Our leader is weak-minded and doesn't understand that outsiders can bring nothing but trouble. More mouths to feed and bodies to clothe and house. I am of the opinion that you should have them back. Do with them as you wish. They, to a person, irritate me. Fools, all of them. Prattling on about a book, and magic writings and a king." The man paused, then punctuated with, "A king other than *you*, sire."

Bythim swallowed. "And you are of the opinion that I should take them back, are you?"

The man cleared his throat. "Well, if it be your good pleasure, sire."

Bythim raised an eyebrow. "It may well be that your opinion and mine align on this point." He waved a page over and whispered in his ear. The man left, returning only a moment later with something in his hand.

"Approach," Bythim pronounced in an exaggerated voice.

The man stepped forward, moving within arm's length of the throne. Bythim tossed him a small blue bag.

"Your coin," he said.

The man smiled. "My liege," he replied, careful to say nothing more.

A woman in dark blue—the same as that of the soldier's cloaks—suddenly approached him and took his arm. Leading him out of the hall, he realized his audience with Bythim had concluded. As the great ornate doors behind him closed, he tossed the little velvet bag up and down in his hand. He, Rethan of Glanèt, had finally come into what he always knew he was due.

The Merchant Quarter, with its plethora of pubs, were to see his coin tonight.

***

The order had been made before the man from Glanèt had left the palace grounds.

Several squadrons of Bythim's considerable army was to leave for the outer territory by end of week. No one was to be left breathing in this village of rag tag barbarians, this Glanèt. They would feel the full wrath and precision of Drymac's military power.

Until today, Lord Bythim had never been given to expansionism of any sort but he was beginning to rethink this. Perhaps starting with this village, his men could then march further south. There had been rumors circulating in Drymac for decades that the lands beyond the Outer Territories held great treasure. The Prathian Desert, for instance, was said to hold great stores of gold under its sands. There for the taking. Yes, Bythim was beginning to think his regime needed to expand. This small conquest of an inconsequential village would be just the beginning. He called for his generals. There was much to decide.

***

Lanthrea awoke with a start. The demon creatures with jagged wings and sharp teeth had assailed her dreams for most of the night. By now, she knew them to be Drekkens, feeding on her fears when she was at her weakest. Bolting upright, she reached over to check on Mysta. The girl was sleeping soundly on a pile of soft pillows—her breathing steady and tussled bedtime hair covering her eyes like a soft golden spiderweb. Lanthrea brushed it away from Mysta's eyes and smiled. Seeing this sweet face with ruddy cheeks, the longest eyelashes imaginable, and a spattering of freckles on her nose simply melted her old heart every time. How blessed was she to have found family this late in her life. And not just Mysta. But Neruk, Th'rena, and all the good people of Glanèt. This was not just a place to find sanctuary from Drymac. These people were family. This place was becoming *home*.

Yawning, she arose to go meet the other women at the well a prepare for the day. She and Mysta had been given a small, private hut at the edge of the village. It had belonged to an old man, a tribal elder, who had passed not long before. Having no heirs, his hut, as was custom, was given to the most needy. Being that Lanthrea had a young child, it had been awarded her. The other new families who had come - refugees from Cenecal—had all assisted in making their own huts in a lovely tradition involving the entire village and an all-day building ceremony. The remaining six elders, rescued from the encampment, had chosen to stay with their host families for both comfort and practicality. Most needed help with daily activities, and all, save Petrul, had returned from that ghastly tent with physical limitations of one sort or another. All told, by the time Lanthrea arrived, there were twenty-two new citizens of Glanèt, with one more, a baby, on the way due mid-winter.

It wasn't a huge group, and already the little band of new-comers had become one with the villagers—adopting their lifestyle (cooking their spicy vegetable dishes, eating communally, living as one family) and sharing theirs (the people of Glanèt were fascinated by the book,) and cheese was a new and delicious addition to their fare (as many Cenecalians had brought goats with them.)

Leaving Mysta to sleep, Lanthrea wandered down to the well, bucket in hand, breathing in the crisp fall air. The trees had all but lost their leaves by now, and there had even been a dusting of snow the night before. The portent of a hard winter. She was actually looking forward to her first winter outside of Cenecal. The villagers were well prepared already, having put up root vegetables, salted cheeses, and kegs of good beer, enough to last the season. Humming to herself, she realized she felt safe for the first time in her life outside of her stay in Palem. She was in full-throated song by the time she got to the well, where she grabbed her friend Tr'ineth and twirled her about, both of them laughing at their silliness.

She filled her bucket and walked slowly back to the hut, sloshing icy water on her feet every other step or so. She laughed again. Nothing bothered her today. Today she and Petrul were going to meet in the gathering place and read a chapter or two from the book. They had made this a weekly practice, one which they both enjoyed greatly and one which was frequently attended by a handful of villagers. Often, Petrul or Lanthrea would share stories of their time in Palem, the others listening to every word. *Well, it isn't Cenecal as I planned, but I* am *telling any others that will listen,* she mused to herself as she sloshed into her hut.

Mysta greeted her with a running hug, splashing more of the water onto the floor. "Lanthee! Can we go deer- peering today?"

Lanthrea set the bucket down and put her hands on her hips and smiled. "Again? We just looked for deer yesterday."

"But I love 'em, Lanthee. They remind me of Bray."

Lanthrea smiled. Oh, dear Bray, dear Elpinhoeve. How she wished she could see him today and take a ride out into the frost-covered forest floor.

She took a cup of water and put it and a handful of grain into an iron kettle, setting it on the hook over the fire. "You know what? Let's *do* go deer-peering today. After I meet with Petrul, yes?"

"Uncle Pete!" Mysta squealed. "Can I come, too?"

Lanthrea grinned. "You only love him for the sweets he brings you, princess!"

"Nuh-uh," Mysta grinned. "I love him for his hugs, too."

Lanthrea laughed. "Well, he loves you as well. Of course, you can come." She stirred the grain as it began to boil. "We'll be reading some of the book today, though. Can you be quiet and listen?"

Mysta screwed up her face. "I guess so. I know all the stories though," she said as she struggled to braid her own long blonde hair, "but I like 'em all."

Lanthrea finished off her braids, securing them with some ribbon Th'rena had given them, and they ate their grain sitting next to the fire. Mysta had honey and cinnamon in hers; Lanthrea, instead, added a pat of butter in the traditional Glanètian manner.

They both bundled up in warm clothes in preparation for the 'deer peering' excursion and walked hand in hand to the gathering place, where Petrul and a handful of others were already seated.

The reading today was from the chapter with the horrid, dark picture of the demon creatures. Lanthrea hated this part of the book and avoided reading it whenever she could. It reminded her only of suffering and nightmares. But it was Petrul's turn to choose the reading, and this was what he had chosen.

Opening the book, he cleared his throat and began.

Stand firm, be not terrified. Evil has no power lest you leave the king's side.

He closed the book. Everyone, even Lanthrea looked confused.

"That is all today, Petrul?" she asked.

"That is all for today," he said, standing. No one said a word, but each looked at the other, questions on their faces. Usually the readings lasted for over an hour, with plenty of discussion and questions. This was an awkward moment, an uncomfortable moment.

Petrul turned and walked slowly back to his hut. No explanation was offered. No friendly banter or discussion employed.

It made Lanthrea very anxious. Taking Mysta's hand, they walked slowly through the village to the edge of the forest and began their deer hunt. Lanthrea was completely preoccupied with Petrul's odd behavior, but Mysta was bouncing along the trail, certain she saw a deer behind every bush and tree. As it was, they found no deer at all this day and were about to head back when there was a rustling in the bushes to their right. For some reason, it startled Lanthrea, and she jumped sideways. Mysta laughed. "It's just a bunny, Lanthee," she squealed happily. "Look! It's up on its back feets!"

Lanthrea looked down to see a completely adorable little brown and white hare sitting on its haunches, wrinkling its nose in its rabbit-like fashion.

"Well, aren't you a fine one?" she said, squeezing Mysta's hand. "Isn't he a fine bunny?"

Mysta nodded and leaned over to try and pet it.

The rabbit jerked back but didn't move. What it *did* do surprised them both.

"I don't appreciate being touched," the rabbit said firmly.

Mysta jumped up and down, clapping her hands. "Lanthee! It's like Garanthor! It talks!"

Lanthrea smiled and knelt down. "Do excuse us, dear rabbit. We didn't know."

"To be sure, to be sure," the rabbit brushed away her apology. "I am Fliver. I come from the Drymacian Council of Talking Beasts. I've come an inordinately long way to give you warning."

"Warning?" Lanthrea questioned. "Of what?"

Fliver looked to his right and then his left before speaking. "They are coming. You need to be ready."

Lanthrea felt her blood run cold. "They?" She asked slowly, not really wanting to know the answer.

Fliver thumped his back feet quickly on the dirt, the sound reverberating on the forest floor. "Bythim's men. They are coming to Glanèt. You have little time. They have been seen marching out of Cenecal this very morning."

"Forgive me, good rabbit," Lanthrea said, "but how do you know this?"

Fliver's nose twitched. "How do I know? How do I *know*? There is a vast number of us in my clan, from Drymac and the Circacian Range to the edge of Prathia and the Great Desert. My own *kin* have seen the men. And heard their words, which they sent on to me. And I ran, as I said, a long distance to meet you here. These men, they are headed to Glanèt." His nose stopped moving for a second. "And they are armed for battle."

Lanthrea froze for just a moment—a brief second as the world seemed to slow to stop around her. Then, faster than ever before in her entire life, she grabbed Mysta's hand, spun around, and ran. Mysta cried out more than once, but Lanthrea just kept pulling her along until they reached the outskirts of the village. Lanthrea ran to the center well and frantically rang the bell hanging over it as loudly as she could.

From all over the village, people appeared, running towards her and the sound of the bell. Neruk was among the first.

"Lanthrea. What on earth has come upon you that you sound the alarm on such a lovely fall day?" He was smiling, although confused.

She panted for breath and, in between gasps, managed to get out the words.

"Bythim's men. They are coming. Here. They will be here by nightfall." She looked up at him, her eyes desperate and terrified. "Neruk…they come today."

Neruk's face fell, then blanched as an audible gasp went through the crowd. For a moment, no one said anything, and then, as if one organism moving in concert, the women ran to their huts and the men to the gathering space.

Lanthrea leaned against the well, sliding slowly down to the ground, and cried. She couldn't think of anything else to do.

Neruk gathered with the men and raised his hands to calm them.

Saying nothing for a few moments, he finally began. "We knew this was a possibility from the start. It is nothing short of a miracle it took them this long to figure things out."

A short man in the back shouted out suddenly, "No! They would not have connected us to this had someone not told them. We have been betrayed. That is the reason they come."

The men began to murmur in protest. Neruk again quieted them.

"Of what do you speak, Galen?"

The small man stepped up onto a bench. "It was one of our own. I was uncertain of it until this moment, but now am convinced. Rethan has been unsettled and angry as of late. He complained to me about the elders we brought here. He complained about the food they ate, the clothing we provided them." He stopped for a moment before continuing, "He also has been taking more than his share of both firewood and water for a few weeks. Something in him has…changed."

"Or been revealed," added another voice. A young bearded man standing quietly in front of the men interrupted Galen.

"I have known Rethan since childhood. Always has he been small and petty. He knows neither how to forgive nor to care for anyone but himself."

Neruk clapped his hands. "Enough. We will not disparage one of our own who can not speak for himself. Where is Rethan now? Let him speak."

Galen jumped off the bench and approached Neruk. "That is the thing, Neruk. He left here three days ago. Said he was going to gather herbs to preserve his fall crops. He has not returned."

Neruk's shoulders and face fell.

"Then. It is most likely so," he said softly. Standing in silence for a moment, he then straightened up and addressed the men, his voice strong and loud.

"We have few choices against The Drymacian men. They are armed. They are trained to fight. This is their sole purpose. We have neither the training nor weaponry to resist them. I am, at this moment, in need of your good council."

The men muttered amongst themselves for a bit when a loud voice cut through the noise.

"We will fight."

The men quieted and turned to see who spoke.

It was Petrul. He stood up from his place on a bench and repeated himself. "We *must* fight. I have seen the evil of this kingdom firsthand. I have lived in Drymac for almost ninety years. I know well the deadly fruit of Bythim's reign. Evil like this does not die on its own, nor does it stay contained. It grows like a sickness. If Bythim is willing to come here, what is to stop him from going beyond us? This is a man and a kingdom that cares not for its people. That incites and encourages violence and malice. That has no heart for the good....*any* good." He took a deep breath. "We must fight him."

Neruk hung his head. When he looked up again, his face held a certain steely resolve. "What weapons have we?"

"Only our ancestral spears—each man his own," said a tall, lanky man. "Decorative, but functional." The others all nodded in agreement.

"Then we must find some other means as well," Neruk said. "Ideas?"

"A trench," Galen suddenly blurted out. "A well-placed trench around our village, then covered with brush. It would slow them considerably. Give our spears a chance."

Neruk bit his lip. "Make it so. Each man to his home. Bring all implements, tools...anything that can break soil. We begin immediately."

The men ran from the gathering place and began their task.

Petrul alone stayed on his bench. He lifted his eyes to the sky. "Good king, this task is as impossible as climbing the Cliffs of Abalor. The outcome of this battle is a foregone conclusion without your help. For the sake of these dear people, who have taken us in and loved us well, save them."

He stayed there on that granite bench for a long time, eyes closed, lips moving silently in battle against the enemy that was coming.

CHAPTER THIRTY-ONE:
Of Blood and Earth

The women of Glanèt had already begun preparing themselves and the children for what was to come. Packing bags of food and clothing, they would be ready to leave when and if Neruk gave them the signal. A few of the younger women, unmarried or without children, were readying themselves in a completely different manner. Sharpening their cooking knives, wrapping themselves in leathers, and braiding their long hair tightly to their heads. They would join the men in the fight.

Lanthrea had pulled herself together and was helping the elder refugees gather provisions. She was to lead them out of town as soon as possible and keep them well hidden on the off chance Bythim's objective was only to find and retrieve them. The idea was that if they were not to be found, perhaps the men would retreat peacefully. It was almost fantasy to even consider such an outcome, but all outcomes must be considered, even those that contained wild hope.

The men and every able-bodied woman who wasn't nursing took to the task of digging a trench around the village perimeter. There was no conceivable way to encircle the entire place, but there was only the one road into Glanèt, so only the front of the village would need trenching. This would be manageable by dark. All told, there were two hundred and fifty villagers, excluding children, who numbered forty-nine. Almost three hundred souls were at stake in this endeavor, and each soul knew it well.

They had the trench, about four feet deep and two feet wide, dug and covered with brush by dusk. Backs ached and sweat stained every brow, but the task was complete. It should prove a good deterrent for the soldiers, provided they entered the village from the road, which was a reasonable assumption. Neruk and a small entourage would greet them in front of the trench to determine the direction of the day—whether they would have to fight or not. The other villagers, armed with their spears (and some cooking knives), would be hidden behind the huts, ready to engage. Either Bythim's men would show restraint, searching the village and leaving (not finding their escaped prisoners) or make some sort of ultimatum and attack. Neruk was not one to lead even Bythim's men into an ambush without knowing their intentions first. He would not employ evil if no grief was intended for his people.

The villagers had all gathered for a late evening meal, perhaps for the last time. It was a crisp, clear fall night, stars blazing across the sky and a full moon making a spectacle of itself for all to see. They ate together that night the best of their fall foods—hearty bread, butter, cheeses, and their unique spiced vegetable dishes that warmed a person to their toes. Voices were low. Hands were warmly grasped, kisses on cheeks given freely. It was sometime during this meal that Neruk nodded to Lanthrea and the other women. It was time for them to leave with the children and elders, getting them to safety. Lanthrea bowed her head in acknowledgement, gathered the five elders who would be leaving with her, and started out of town into the wooded area. Petrul, even in advanced age, had chosen to stay and fight. The women and children headed due south toward the Prathian Desert (were they to make it that far), where one family had a cousin who would help them find refuge. Petrul walked over to Lanthrea and, kissing her on both cheeks, held her face in his hands. "This is my second chance at life because of you. I will not waste it, friend. I promise. For the king and all that is good." She let the tears pour down her cheeks. "For the king," she said softly, hugging him one last time.

He watched her lead the others away in the moonlit night until the shadows from the trees enveloped them, and he could see them no more. Lanthrea led her tiny group deep into the woods by a stream that ran underneath a large stone outcrop that would provide both shelter and cover. It was unlikely anyone would find them here unless they knew where to look. They were to stay here until or if someone was sent to bring them back. If no one were to come, they would know the village was gone and head south into Prathia and join the others.

Mysta was very unsettled, crying every now and again about 'wanting to sleep on her pillows at home'. Lanthrea knew her girl. This was less about sleeping arrangements and more about sheer anxiety. They all felt it. They were choking on it. They made a nice, dry camp under the stones, but Lanthrea forbade a fire. No telltale signs of smoke or light this night. Everyone agreed and wrapped themselves up in layers, sitting close to each other for warmth. Lanthrea looked up through the canopy of trees and asked the King and Lady for help. She twirled the ring on her finger and touched the necklace given to her at Darrow Falls gently. Tokens from her family in Palem. She remembered her lesson from prison. They were not alone. She took solace and great comfort in this truth. Pulling Mysta close, she distracted her by telling the story of how she received her little silver ring from the king—her crown. "One day, you will receive yours," she told Mysta, whose eyes were shining at the thought.

They all sat in that place, huddled together, each one hoping for peace and all of them asking the good King for his help.

Back at Glanèt, the villagers continued to make ready for battle. Having no armor, they wrapped themselves with thick leather and sharpened the tips of their spears, checking to ensure the blades were affixed well to the wooden shafts. They created makeshift sheaths in which to carry and conceal knives on their persons. It was all new to them, and it was all too little—they knew this.

Bythim's men would, no doubt, be well-armed and armored with both spear and sword, and possibly bows. The villagers knew they would be no match for either their weaponry or training. All of them, to a person, could only hope that this display from Cenecal was simply to extract the elders. That the traitor Rethan had perhaps not incited Bythim to revenge but recovery. None of them believed this, but it was a good hope.

They all mingled about the village square by the well, speaking quietly—some seated, some pacing nervously, all exchanging silent glances; their silence speaking volumes.

It was about midnight when they heard the jangle of horse's breast collars and the uniform rhythmic marching of the soldier's feet. Neruk inhaled deeply, rolled his shoulders back, stood to his full height, and walked out in front of the brush-covered trench, unarmed.

The full moon provided good light, and he could easily see the number of those who had come. It was about five squadrons, each with ten men. One squadron was mounted, the others on foot. All were wearing shining armor with long blue capes affixed. He saw both sword and shield on each man. If there were archers, he could see none.

The men pulled their horses to a stop, the great beasts pawing and snorting from the restraint. These animals were meant to charge, and they could sense the excitement and apprehension in their riders.

A very tall man on the lead horse dismounted and walked toward Neruk, his blue cape swishing with each step.

"You come to meet us at the apex of the night?" he quipped sarcastically, nodding to the moon. "You are not asleep in bed with your wife—your family at your feet—at this hour?" His lips twitched, a smirk forming. Pray tell, how is it you knew of our coming?"

Neruk did not answer his question, instead announcing, "I am Neruk. I am chieftain of Glanèt, before which you now stand. You are no longer in the province of Drymac. By what right do you march on our land?"

The tall soldier sniffed. "By the might and declaration of our Lord Bythim. Perhaps you have heard of him?"

Neruk said nothing.

The soldier spat on the ground. "This village is inconsequential to us. As are its occupants." He stopped here and glared at Neruk. "As is your wife and family."

Neruk stood firm, not taking the bait to respond defensively. "Tell us why you come to our land. That is owed us."

"We owe you exactly nothing," the soldier almost growled. "You have taken from us. You have taken the lives of our soldiers and have assisted in the escape of our prisoners." He smiled. "But surely, you are aware of these facts, no?"

It was at this moment that Neruk knew his flagging hopes of these men retreating had been dashed. He bowed his head and looked down at the ground. The soft, rich earth of Glanèt. Where his ancestors had lived and loved for generations. This very life-giving earth would swallow his people's blood tonight.

Raising his head, he looked into the soldier's eyes. "You are not welcome here. Go back. Tell Bythim we have no interest in a fight, but we will also suffer no injustice as was done to the elders. This is our way."

The man looked at Neruk for a moment in disbelief, then howled with laughter. "I don't think you can offer much of a fight. And Lord Bythim would be unimpressed with your small declaration or 'your way." With this, he walked back and mounted his horse.

"Make your people ready. They either surrender now or die momentarily. The decision is yours."

Neruk nodded, then turned and walked back to the village, careful to cross the trench on some well-placed boards covered with thorn bushes. Reaching the well, he said nothing to his people. He didn't have to.

It as only a matter of minutes before the shrill cry of the Drymacian battle horn was heard, followed by the thunder of horses' hooves and the unsheathing of swords. The villagers let out a shout in unison and ran as one out to meet the enemy.

The horses in the first squadron charged, tumbling immediately into the camouflaged trench, the animals screaming and the men falling off or being thrown to the ground. The next group of soldiers—realizing the ruse —tried to break formation and get around the trench, but everything happened so quickly that a good portion of them fell down through the brush as well. The villagers were upon them all in seconds, using their spears to dispatch any unfortunate enough to be stuck in the trenches or trapped under a horse. All told, about fifteen of the soldiers perished in that first volley, the trench doing its work well.

The remaining soldiers broke ranks and got around the trench, coming up in the middle of the village and swarming through.

They were met with the spears of the Glanètian men or the sharp knives of the women, untrained people simply fighting for their lives. The soldiers, however, once they regained their footing, were beginning to inflict real damage. Their swords killed an entire line of village men who were trying to hold them off with mere knives and stones, their spears having been used irretrievably on others. Neruk found himself fighting the tall leader of the enemy, the soldier's broadsword slashing through the shaft of Neruk's wooden spear like kindling, leaving him defenseless. Ducking and darting, Neruk did what he could to avoid the blade, and had it not been for Th'rena's nephew, who had run the soldier through from behind with his wife's hunting knife, Neruk would have been killed on that very spot. The villagers continued to fight fiercely, surprising the soldiers with their resistance and creativity. Hiding in their huts, they employed surprise attacks whenever the soldiers would near. The women were fighting in teams—one luring a soldier into conflict (what harm could a solitary woman be?) then several others attacking from behind. Their spears, used in the first volley, had been retrieved and used again fiercely as the villagers felt the battle turn in their direction.

In fact, the entire conflict lasted only about half an hour, and, in the end, it was the sheer number of villagers (along with their unusual methods borne out of necessity, determination and grit) that had won the day. The remaining thirty or so soldiers not lost in the trench now lay dead or mortally wounded on the rich brown earth of Glanèt.

Neruk ordered the dead to be pulled to the outskirts of the village to be burned. Those mortally wounded were dispatched mercifully so as not to prolong their suffering.

By dawn, the entire thing was over. The dead of the village numbered forty men and women. The casualties numbered more.

Most every person in the battle had been wounded to one degree or another.

These were being attended to as best they could, the more able helping those in more grave condition. Now that it was known they had won the day, Th'rena's nephew (the very one that had saved Neruk) had been sent to retrieve the women and children before they got too far south towards Prathia. They needed the women's ministrations and knowledge of herbs and poultices for the wounded. A young woman named Birnah had been sent to bring Lanthrea and her lot back.

Lanthrea was still awake when Birnah arrived at the stone outcrop, panting yet exuberant.

"Could it be?"Lanthrea asked excitedly. "Does Glanèt still stand?"

Birnah fell to her knees, smiling from ear to ear. "It stands," she said between breaths. "It stands, indeed."

The two of them woke Mysta and the five elders and helped them gather their things, then walked them back into Glanèt. Lanthrea took one look around and immediately began attending to the wounded, applying cloth, washing wounds, and making splints and bandages from anything she could find. It was exhausting and heartbreaking work, and it wasn't until mid-day that all who needed had been attended to. It was also around that time that the women and children returned, flooding back into Glanèt; their presence felt to those wounded like that of klestara as they helped with poultices, preparation of food, getting potions and tinctures into the wounds and mouths of all who needed. By nightfall, Glanèt was calm once again. Of those wounded that day, only three would succumb to their injuries and be buried with the others in the forest graveyard of their ancestors.

Neruk, although exhausted and wounded himself, went hut to hut for the next day and a half, checking on his people and offering any assistance he could give. It took Th'rena to finally put him to his bed, where he slept nigh onto two more days, awakening only to eat, drink and partake of a potion made to strengthen him.

Lanthrea was given a duty that no one else could help with: handling the Cenecalian war horses. Of the ten that had been in the battle, five had been killed (or mercifully destroyed shortly thereafter to alleviate their suffering), three had run off, and two had remained at the side of their fallen masters, both of them in need of care and wide-eyed with trauma. No one in Glanèt had ever worked with a horse, and Lanthrea was assigned the task. It was as she was tending to the animals that Petrul walked alongside her in the forest three days after the battle.

"Is your leg healed?" she inquired of him as she watered the horses at a small stream.

He patted his thigh. "It's coming along," he said quietly. "You understand these beasts well," he commented, patting the largest one's glossy black neck.

"Even as of a year ago, I had never so much as haltered one," she admitted. "But I was…adopted by a horse on my journey to Palem. He has become family to me."

"And you didn't bring him here?" Petrul looked confused.

"He was wounded on my way back to Drymac. He is in the King's care now. His name is Elpinhoeve" She looked up at the big black horse and the slightly smaller dapple grey mare before her. "I miss him so."

She tied the horses to a tree branch, brushed the frost off a stump, and sat down.

"This won't be the end, will it, Petrul?" She gazed out into the forest, not daring to look at him.

"You know the answer well enough," he replied. "His men never returned. It is most certain that because of that, a second, more pernicious plan has already been made. It is only a matter of time."

"What can we do, then?" she asked, afraid again to look at her friend.

He shook his head. "That I do not know."

They and the horses stayed in the forest for another few minutes until an icy wind suddenly blew through bringing a dusting of snow with it. They walked slowly back to the village, Lanthrea showing Petrul how to properly lead a horse and enjoying the soft snow falling on their shoulders. Under any other circumstances, it would have been a joyful outing for them both.

Neruk and the men of Glanèt that were able to meet had been discussing their situation. No one was celebrating their small, even though significant, victory. There was no time, and a great shadow now hung over them. Everyone knew that Bythim would not tolerate his squadrons' defeat. What no one could know was what he might do next.

They had, in effect, awakened a sleeping giant by simply defending their home.

The timing was the other unknown. How long would it take Drymac to assemble another group of men? Did Glanèt have days? Hours? Their wounded were still fragile; their dead only just buried—

the Burial Canopy from the Rite of the Dead not yet even been taken down. Talk of picking up and moving the entire village to a new location, perhaps in Prathia, had been brought forth. But few were in any shape for such a journey, either physically or emotionally. But battles are rarely waged on the ready, and a decision had to be made quickly. In the end, it was decided that, ready or not, they must retreat. They must become refugees in another land, provided they could find a people who would take them in. And they would have to move quickly.

The decision being made, much had to be done. The horses had proven a great spoil of war, for, with them, they had a way to haul a wagon. This would need to be built and would carry the most severely wounded. It would also take the most time in that Kennan, the blacksmith, had never made wheels as large as would be needed. He began immediately by taking all the metal from every small implement and melting it all down in the foundry, then building the molds. Several of the men proficient with wood and hammer began on the wagon body, and the leather workers created the harnesses for the horses. The people of Glanèt didn't rely heavily on acquisitions of any sort, so each family was packed and ready to leave within a day. The autumn had given way in the past few weeks to early winter, and the snow was building up on the road leading south. This, more than anything, worried Neruk and Lanthrea, for while the two horses could easily pull a wagon on a dry dirt road, pulling one through snow would prove impossible.

By the third day of preparation for their exodus, the snowfall was so heavy that there was no option left. Kennan finished the wagon wheels, but they would not be immediately used. Instead, the woodworkers were tasked with making sledge runners. This would put their departure back at least another day—maybe two—and spirits were beginning to lag as anxiety hovered over each home. Neruk was quick to remind them that their obstacles would also mean obstacles for Drymac. The snow would make it more challenging for Bythim's men to reach them, no matter if on horseback or foot. The road down the foothills would be slick and almost impassable by now. This bode well for Glanèt.

Mysta and the other children were enjoying the snow, and everyone worked at keeping the inevitable anxiousness from them, instead encouraging the building of snow castles and snowball fights to pass the time. There was not much else to do now that their family's scant belongings were packed up in bulky bundles awaiting the strong backs of their parents on the day they would leave the only home they had ever known.

It was exactly eight days from the battle that they were finally ready. The gravely wounded (fewer now after a good week of healing) were loaded onto the wagon, the horses harnessed (after a few practice runs to ensure they would not spook), and everyone else bundled up, hoisted packs onto shoulders, and met at the center well. It was a quiet morning, the sky white with snow, soft flakes falling all around them as they stood for one last time together in Glanèt. No one said a word, letting the silence be the salve in each heart until a voice (a lovely tenor voice belonging to a young man named Narth), began singing. The voice was soon joined by others until the entire village lifted up their song to the heavens.

Sun and sky, come what may, each of us apart,

Thus we go, even tho', here we leave our heart

Journey made, on this day, despair is never known,

Moon and stars hold our place, no matter 'ere we are.

The ancient tune floated up to the sky as the snow fell around them. As many times as this song had been sung, none had ever sung it with full knowledge that they might never return home again. This time, every soul knew that certain sorrow.

Neruk led the caravan of travelers from the village, and they began their long journey south, toward Prathia and the warmer climes of the desert.

CHAPTER THIRTY-TWO:
The Pond at Prathia

Lanthrea and Petrul rode on the buckboard of the wagon: Lanthrea driving the horses, and Petrul holding Mysta on his lap. The sledge worked well, and the horses pulled it easily through the deep snow—the ride smooth for the wounded in the back. Neither of them spoke until they were a good hour out of Glanèt. The snow had stopped, and the wind had come up a bit, whipping hair about, making people bundle a bit deeper into their coats.

Mysta had fallen asleep on Petrul's warm lap, and it was he who broke the silence.

"Had it not been for us, these people would still have a safe home." He said the words but avoided eye contact with Lanthrea.

She clucked at the horses. "Perhaps. Or perhaps only for a bit longer. Bythim would have taken note of Glanèt at some point."

"We don't know that," he countered.

"We don't," she responded softly. They were quiet for a good time again before she turned to Petrul, her eyes sad. "Tell me of Marinda. What happened?"

Petrul sighed. "They took note of us because of my cane. Beat me with it…if you must know. Then, three days later, they came during the night. Took us from our beds. Threw us in a wagon, not too dissimilar from this one," he said, nodding behind them, "and we were taken to the encampment."

He sighed again before continuing. "We were fed and given water at first. But after about a week, the food stopped. We were given water only once a day after that, and it was rancid stuff. Marinda came down with a cough not long after that. She died in my arms, raging with fever, begging for water. I gave her my daily ration, but it was not enough." His eyes filled with tears. "There was nothing I could do for her. Nothing."

Lanthrea inhaled deeply. "I'm so sorry, Petrul." She clucked at the horses again as they navigated a rather deep drift of snow. "I don't understand why the King didn't send help to you."

Petrul gently stroked Mysta's blonde hair and turned to Lanthrea. "He did. He sent you."

She bit her lip and said nothing more. It all seemed too little and too late. She didn't want to argue with him about this, though, so remained silent.

"And you?" He inquired. "Tell me of how you come to know of the king. When you left our house last, you were…unreceptive to talk of Palem."

She looked over. He was smiling. How could he smile about any of this? She shook her head. "Another time."

He nodded and pulled his coat tighter against the wind.

"They are going to need a rest," he said after a few moments, motioning to the villagers. "All of them. The horses, too."

Lanthrea scoured the landscape ahead of them. They were coming into the land of Prathia soon, the trees giving way to more arid scrub brush and a few low-growing cacti that poked their way through the ever-lessening snow.

"I remember a small pond not far from here," she said, recalling her trip through last spring. There is fresh water to refill our flasks. Waterfowl, also, if anyone wishes to hunt."

Nodding, he motioned for Neruk, who was walking directly behind the wagon. Telling him of the plan, the word spread quickly through the villagers, who were soon buzzing with relief and excitement over the thought of rest. Slogging through the snow was exhausting. It was only about an hour later when Lanthrea urged the horses off the main road, turning left and edging down a small ravine, the bottom of which sat the pond. The snow wasn't nearly as deep the further south they traveled, more a dusting than anything else by this point. It was time to change out the runners for wheels, as the horses were now more dragging the wagon through sandy soil than sledging over snow.

The temperature was still cold here, but the pond wasn't as yet frozen over, as it was still too early in the season for a hard freeze. There were (just as Lanthrea had remembered) a good number of ducks and other waterfowl on the banks of the pond, huddled together for warmth. Glanètians, on the whole, were not hunters, preferring their spiced vegetable dishes to meats, but this was an unusual situation. A few of the women and children simply ran through the ducks and geese, easily grabbing a number of them, goose nips being endured as the price paid for a hearty evening meal. Fires were made, and a makeshift camp was set up. They would rest here, eat, fill water pouches and change out the sledge runners. They encircled the pond, facing outward, just in case. No one was expecting trouble, but no one was at ease, either. Within minutes, the geese and ducks had been dispatched and were roasting over fires here and there in the camp. The snow had all but stopped, and there was a bit of blue sky peeking through on the southern horizon towards the desert. The desert.

Where Cla'neen had saved her life. Where Braydenthal had been found. Lanthrea thought now of Cla'neen and wondered how she was. Had she ever gone back to her people, to her arranged marriage? Or had she remained in the open desert, enjoying the purple sunsets and white sand as it sparkled in the sun? She took a moment to wrap her hair in a bun, using the Lady's golden pin to hold it into place and smiled. Her journey had brought her so many good friends and good things, yet also much sorrow and an almost equal measure of pain. But, though it all ran a silver thread of joy. A certain, almost palpable hope that all things were headed in a right and proper direction. Even the pain and sorrow was subsumed by this hope. She inhaled deeply, whispered a prayer for Cla'neen, and unhitched the horses from the wagon to let them graze.

It was about the fifth hour past noon, as the group was settling down for evening meal, and the late fall sun was disappearing behind the foothills, that the horses stopped their grazing and began to prance uneasily. Lanthrea, more aware of this than the others, walked over and patted them, speaking low and calmly in their ears.

The stallion particularly was unsettled. Pawing the ground, nostrils flared and eyes white, Lanthrea was having trouble calming him down. She looked around for a predator, remembering the golden cat that had attacked Bray and shuddered. She hadn't remembered seeing any wild beasts when last she was here. But something had the horses' attention, of that she was certain. Tying their lead ropes to a tree, she walked up over the hill to check the higher ground. She hadn't taken three steps past the crest of the hill when she saw them. It was Bythim's men. On sledges, horses and foot. They were but a few minutes from the pond and moving fast. And there were at least two hundred of them. She froze for a moment not willing to believe her eyes, terror rising in her throat, then turn and flew as fast as she could down to the pond and the villagers, screaming as she ran into their midst.

"They are here! They come! They…come!" Breathless, it was all she could get out.

In what could be considered nothing less than a frenzy, the evening meals were tossed to the frozen ground, the men grabbing weapons, the women and children running for the far edge of the pond, where they huddled together as had the ducks and geese, and just as vulnerable. As quickly as they had been built, the fires were extinguished, but the unmistakable smell of roasted goose hung over the camp like a marker. Even if they were not seen, they would be found.

Neruk had rallied the men who could fight into a line formation, behind which were the women and children. They flipped the wagon over (having moved the wounded to the ground) and as many as could were were hunched behind it, using it as a shield.

There had been no time for words to be spoken to rally the people. There was no time now.

It was only minutes before Bythim's men were upon them. The first volley was by the archers, a complement not used in the last battle at Glanèt. Several of the villagers were killed in that first spray of arrows, crumpling helplessly to the ground, their blood reddening the snow. The war horses came next, their riders slashing relentlessly at anyone who stood in their path. The deepening night made it hard for anyone to see well, but these men were on a mission, and nothing was going to stop them this time. Even in the darkness, their weapons found purchase with anything they could. Neruk and his men were holding off a group of horsemen with nothing but spears and a few hunting knives. It was a lost cause. Pushed back, they retreated further, screaming at the women to run as the soldiers moved closer to them. Bythim's men on foot had now swarmed into the fray with long swords and battle axes. The Glanètian fighters were dropping to the ground by the dozens. No amount of wild determination and grit could save them this time. And no retreat would be afforded them.

Lanthrea had Mysta's hand and was leading a group of women away from the pond as fast as they could run. The moon suddenly popped out from behind a cloud, mercifully lighting the way for them as they headed into some scrub brush and tall cacti that lay past the far side of the pond. The screams of the men, the clash of metal, the horses shrieking as they were pierced with sword or spear; it was all too much. Mysta was screaming herself, and Lanthrea suddenly became numb. Too much fear. Too much running. Too much pain.

She dropped Mysta's hand, pushing her into the arms of a village woman with two other small children, and told them to run. Turning, she headed back towards the battle with nothing but a prayer on her lips and crazed fury in her heart.

Tripping over the body of a soldier, she grabbed his sword off the ground. It was almost too heavy for her to lift, but she managed to swing it up, cold metal shining in the moonlight. She would fight this time, not run. Enough was enough. Standing for a moment, catching her breath, her eyes tried to make sense of the chaos unfolding before her. It seemed as though time had slowed to a standstill. Horses rearing, men slashing, blood pouring from heads and throats. She stood for a moment, or maybe more (it was impossible to tell) with her blade flashing in the starlight. Then, with a shriek that almost shattered her voice, she charged headlong into the fray. The bodies of the villagers were all around her. Some were dead, some dying, their glassy eyes reflecting the moonlight before dulling in death. Upon seeing a soldier about to run a young village man through with his spear, she ran towards him and thrust her sword with all her might into his back. Never had she felt anything like what she felt at that moment. The thud of metal tearing through flesh and bone. The resistance of the blade to muscle and sinew. She couldn't even pull the sword out of the man's body but fell to her knees and vomited. The young man's life being spared, he managed to nod to Lanthrea before turning to face the next sword that was upon him.

She sat in the blood-soaked soil and tried to make her legs move but found she was frozen. As though her limbs were glued to the earth. It was as she was on the ground that she saw something move to her left. She turned slowly to see a rabbit. It hopped by her, seemingly unafraid of the chaos all about it. Then another, and another. Shaking her head and blinking, she looked behind her. A veritable swarm of animals were flooding into the battle. Squirrels, rabbits, mice, and behind them larger animals: bobcats, stags, foxes, and coyotes. Leaping past her, they were throwing themselves into the fight, biting the legs of Bythim's men, leaping up and scratching at their faces, clawing arms until weapons fell to the ground.

The soldiers were confused by this sudden and bizarre attack, and the confusion gave the villagers an opportunity. With many of the weapons being dropped as wrists were bitten or legs mauled by sharp teeth, the men and women of Glanèt turned with a new ferocity on the enemy.

Lanthrea was struggling to make her legs move, and as she was rising from the ground, she heard something in the air above her head. Dark though it was, she could see, outlined in the moonlight, the shape of great wings. Within seconds, the shapes landed all around her. They were gigantic. Struggling to believe her eyes, she realized it was Garanthor and his kin! With a great sweeping motion, the flying horses (fifteen in all) began to slam the enemy to the ground with their strong wings, then rear up and strike them until they resisted no more. By this time, Bythim's men were completely confused and frightened, and quite a few were beginning to retreat back to the road. The flying beasts pressed onward, pushing the ranks towards the road, dispatching as many as came near. The villagers, by now, realized they had help and, although as confused as the soldiers, accepted the good fortune and pushed on. It was as Lanthrea was struggling to her feet, still quite helpless in her shock and amazement, that the most wondrous thing happened. From the south, shining in the moonlight, came a woman riding on a horse. Lanthrea looked at the horse, then looked again. It was Elpinhoeve! And upon him, arrayed in the most flowing and beautiful gown she had ever seen—translucent in the light of the stars and the moon—was the Lady. Behind her was an entire cavalry of men and women on horseback, each wearing the golden insignia of Palem on their armor and each holding aloft a great sword. The Lady herself gave the order, and the horsemen and women galloped into the battle. The Drymacian soldiers, seeing this onslaught and themselves now vastly outnumbered, literally turned and ran for their lives. But the armor-clad warriors overran them in an instant, and within minutes, not a soldier from Bythim's court remained standing, except for two that had escaped early on and run for their lives back into the foothills.

The moon was full now, and the clouds had moved on, casting a luminescent glow on the ground below. Everywhere were the dead and dying. Those remaining stood for a few minutes, catching their breath, stunned at the carnage all around. The whimpers and cries from the children were the only sounds that could be heard for a moment. Then, suddenly everyone, as though on cue, sprang to life. The women ran out to help the wounded. The great flying horses were helping people to their feet, using their wings as lifts. The men and women of Palem were everywhere, giving aid in any and all forms.

The smaller animals were scurrying here and there, dragging water bags to people with their teeth or laying on top of a suffering person to keep them warm until a blanket could be found.

The Lady of Lanthor was walking among the wounded, gently and lovingly leaning over each one and giving them sips from a flask similar in appearance to the one Bethstra had given Lanthrea.

Lanthrea was helping move people to dry ground and get the fires restarted for warmth. She wanted more than anything to reunite with Elpinhoeve, but this was not the time. Besides, he was busy, as were each of the animals. In their shock and sorrow no one seemed a bit concerned (nor even amazed) that there were wild beasts helping them, and only a few (and these were mainly children) were staring at the giant flying horses as though they were seeing phantasms.

It was dawn before the battle scene was cleaned up, the wounded tended to, and a morning meal ready to distribute to all. Every woman and every man that was able made certain each person had a bowl of hot oats, having been prepared in giant cooking pots set atop the fires that were scattered about the camp. The children and the wounded were also given a piece of flat bread that had been made during the night and baked on stones heated by those same fires. Neruk had stood in the center of the people, next to the pond, and spoken to them all, thanking them for their bravery and honor, then taking the first bite of food before anyone else did. This was an ancient tradition in Glanèt done at celebrations and harvest time. It seemed appropriate this day.

It was as Lanthrea walked over to talk to the Lady that she felt a soft nose on her arm. Turning around, she saw the big brown eyes of Elpin. She immediately threw her arms around his neck and cried for joy as he nickered and breathed softly on her chest. "You look so good, boy," she cried, patting him from head to hoof. "I could not have missed you more than I have." He nickered softly and closed his eyes as she petted his forelock and scratched under his mane. He walked by her side over to the Lady, who was seated in the sandy soil next to the pond, watching the ducks waddle into the waters. Elpin bent down to drink, and Lanthrea leaned on his warm flank. The morning was clear and bright, the temperature mild, as was often the case at this time of year this close to the desert. Cloaks and hats were being folded and packed back into the bundles, and the children were having a hard time eating, so fascinated were they by all the beasts. Most had never been eye to eye with a fox or a coyote before, and certainly, none had seen anything like Garanthor and his kin.

"You came," Lanthrea looked at the Lady through thankful eyes.

The Lady sighed. "We would have been here sooner had we not encountered Drekkens just outside of Palem. They were not aware of our destination or purpose, but they hate us all and try to deter us no matter our mission. Once they saw us, armed and ready for battle, they attacked. They thought us easy prey. Most armies are terribly frightened as they head into battle. Drekkens love to take advantage of this." She looked up and smiled. "If only they knew us better."

Lanthrea shivered. "I've only heard their voices. They attack me in my sleep. That is bad enough. I still hope never to meet one." They both looked up as Neruk approached them and bowed. He cleared his throat before speaking.

"I am unfamiliar with whatever land from whence you have come," he began, "but I recognize royalty when I see it." He said this quietly, hardly looking up.

The Lady reached out and took his hand in hers. "I can see it standing before me as well."

He reddened with the compliment and his eyes began to fill with tears. "We would certainly have perished last night had you not come."

The Lady nodded. "This is a fact, my son. We are only sorry we didn't get here earlier." She motioned to a large rock. "Please, sit down. Join us."

Neruk sat down and let go the Lady's hand. "As grateful as I am, your arrival raises more questions than not. Will you tell me who you are? Why you came?"

She looked over at Lanthrea who busy watching Elpin graze. "Did your friend here ever tell you of the book?"

Neruk nodded. "I know it brought her much trouble, and has brought us all of ours. I don't understand it. I don't know how words could have the power to inflame kingdoms to such malice."

Lanthrea shifted her weight in the sand. "It also has the power to inflame kingdoms to great good, as the Lady of Lanthor here has brought to us."

The Lady stood up and placed her hands on Neruk's head. "Your questions will all be answered soon, child. For now, we have much to do, and many wounded yet to attend."

Neruk nodded and rose to his feet, bowed again, and, noting a young man, hurt badly, who was struggling to eat his bowl of oats with his one good arm, ran over to help.

Lanthrea looked up at the Lady. "His questions will be answered soon?"

The Lady smiled and patted Lanthrea on the arm. "Soon, indeed."

The rest of the day was spent in a flurry of wound cleaning, changing of bandages, food distribution, and mourning the dead. It was decided that the deceased would be buried on the flatlands south of the pond, and the Glanètian Rite of the Dead would be employed the next day at sunrise. The Drymacian dead were, as before, placed in a funeral pyre and set ablaze. Of the two hundred men who had come from Cenecal, almost all had perished in the battle, but for the two that had escaped, presumably heading back to Cenecal to report their loss to Lord Bythim. Only a handful were wounded too badly to escape during the night, yet still lived by morning. These were being held by a contingent of village men; each Drymacian soldier in disbelief that they were being fed well and their wounds treated. By night, the air had turned cold again, and another light dusting of snow had fallen, but the spirits of the people were high, and a good group of geese had once again been caught and roasted that night for evening meal along with several hearty pots of grains. The various families all gathered around the fires, not only warming themselves, but finalizing words to be spoken over their loved ones during the funeral rite in the morning.

Lanthrea had found a dry place and a blanket on which to lie down, and had retired early. She was feeling every year of her sixty this night, and had lay there, looking up at the sky, wishing it were cloudless so she could see the stars. She closed her eyes instead and mused upon the words in the book that had always given her comfort.

Set the king ever before you and he will protect you from fear.

She inhaled deeply, as her heart inhaled the words. It was odd, but she hadn't been afraid at all during the battle. Tonight however, in this relative calm, she was shaking from head to toe. She knew she was exhausted. In mind, body and spirit. It honestly felt as though she could take no more of this life. No more sorrow, or battle or heartache or loss. Trying to ask the king for courage and strength, she instead fell asleep before even getting the words off her lips.

Neruk was awake before any others the next morning. He had seen to it that the Burial Canopy be built yesterday, and was double checking the frame in the predawn quiet.

He sighed, looking over at the fresh graves dug just beyond the canopy. Had he made a mistake helping Lanthrea and the elders? It was, after all, his decision that had lead to these disastrous consequences. The lives of his beloved people. The blood of good men and women. It was on him. Every drop.

The sun was just beginning to rise in the east, its first rays cresting over the rolling hills—the entrance to the Prathian Desert. He stood to let the sun warm his face when suddenly it became so bright he winced and closed his eyes. The intensity of the light was overwhelming. This was no ordinary sunrise. Heart pounding, he tried to cry out for help. This must be another attack from Bythim's men— a new weapon of some sort—and his heart couldn't bear it. He managed to open his eyes to see what was upon them, only to find, coming in the light of the sunrise, not an army, but a man. A solitary rider, on a magnificent horse. He was dressed in the finest armor, and wore on his head a crown that was reflecting the brilliance of the sun, scattering light in all directions. The horse and rider came closer as the sun rose, light seeming to follow them, or emanate *from* them; it was impossible to tell which. They came near, until Neruk could have almost reached out and touched them, had he wanted. Instead, he fell to his face on the ground. He didn't know why, but he knew he had no choice. He felt a hand on his shoulder.

"Rise, son," the rider's voice was gentle.

Neruk lifted his head, his whole body shaking, and dared look upon the face of the man. The rider's eyes were gentle, yet fierce; his countenance simultaneously majestic and humble. Neruk quickly lowered his head. He felt he had no right to look upon this man.

"I say again, rise, son."

Neruk kept his head down, but rose to his feet.

"We have much to discuss," said the rider. "Come with me."

Had anyone else been awake, they would have seen their beloved leader and the resplendent rider walking together into the early morning light, heads down and deep in conversation.

CHAPTER THIRTY-THREE:
The Reclaiming

Lanthrea was awakened by Mysta right after sunrise. She was bouncing up and down on a blanket and asking about morning meal. Lanthrea smiled. Children offered such hope and life, even in the shadow of death. Stretching, Lanthrea grabbed Mysta and pulled her close, kissing her on both cheeks before letting her loose to go run down to the pond and chase ducks. It wasn't until she stood up that she knew something was different. It was ineffable but noticeable. A certain sense of change in the air, a crystalline clear sense of hope she couldn't explain. Looking around her, as everyone began to awaken, she noted others felt the change as well. It could be seen in their faces. A sense of wonder, the kind one gets on the morning of a fall festival or a winter solstice gathering. Almost to a person, the villagers that were able were all walking towards the eastern side of the pond, where they stood, as though expecting the arrival of something or someone as yet unknown. Of even more interest were the animals. From foxes to rabbits to the giant flying horses—all of them were also headed to the same side of the pond where they were nestled, burrowed, or sitting on haunches in and amongst the humans—noses and whiskers twitching in the bright morning sun. It was just as the sun burst fully forth over the foothills, flooding the entire little valley in light, that they saw them. Neruk and his companion walking side by side back towards the pond.

It was at that exact moment that the strangest thing happened. The animals, to a one, bowed down to the ground—snouts and whiskers in the sandy soil. The horses gracefully bent one front leg down and arched their necks low to the ground, the flying ones lifting their wings above their backs like giant sails glittering in the sunlight. The people of Palem all bowed low to the ground, their hands over their hearts.

It took Lanthrea a few moments before she recognized him. The King! It was he in the flesh. Resisting the urge to run to him, she looked over to see that Petrul, too, looked ready to run, his eyes wide and tears pouring down his face. The few elders that had survived Bythim's camp had fallen to their knees, arms around each other in sheer joy.

Neruk and the King stopped as they neared the pond. Silence fell upon the crowd as Neruk raised his arm for attention, cleared his throat and began. "My people. Not long ago now, I made the decision to help some outsiders. It has cost us dearly. I have questioned my leadership. I have questioned my decision to help the elders at the request of Myka...of Lanthrea, who came to us for aid. I have questioned whether or not the price we paid was too high. And I know many of you have questioned this as well. As you have buried your loved ones. As you were forced to leave our beloved home. As you now tend to your wounds. I had no answers to these questions until this very morning. For, in truth, I did not know for whom or what we were fighting. I didn't know if the life of these strangers was worth the lives of our own. Until now. I know I have asked much of you. I now ask of you one more thing—to listen to this man." With this, Neruk stepped aside. A hush came over the crowd, and the animals lifted their heads to listen.

The King stepped forward, his crown glittering in the sunlight as though on fire.

"Please sit," he said, motioning them gently. He drew a deep breath. "I am A'lam, King of Palem and the son of the High King El-

Gudan. My kingdom is not far from here, but each of my followers carries it in their hearts wherever they go. It was several of my followers —the elders—that you, in your mercy and kindness, rescued from Bythim's hand. And, as Neruk has said, you have paid the ultimate price for your charity." He stopped and looked at them, his gaze penetrating each person's heart. "This is the highest law in my kingdom—that of charity. You have fulfilled it well, even with no knowledge of me. There is no higher good for a people than this. To give without any expectation of recompense. It is because of this that I have come here to honor you."

It was at this point that the most remarkable thing happened. A'lam took off his crown and, holding it in his right hand, knelt down on one knee, and bowed his head to the crowd seated before him.

To a person, every soul present felt a sudden sense of their own unworthiness, a profound humility, and then, on the heels of that, a wave of love and acceptance such as they had never known. After a few moments, A'lam stood to his feet but then turned to Neruk, took his crown, and placed it upon the chieftain's head.

"Behold, your leader. It was his love for truth and your sacrificial charity for others that led me to you, and now, each of you to me." He turned to the crowd and smiled the broadest smile that anyone had ever seen. "All hail Neruk!"

The villagers took but a second before they began to roar their approval, chanting, "Neruk! Neruk! Long live Neruk!" A'lam smiled, and, laying his hand upon Neruk's shoulder (who was quite red in the face by now) stood by his side as the people cheered. Even the animals joined in; their barks and neighs and yips and (in the rabbit's case) stomping of feet echoing in the still morning air. Within minutes the cheering died down, and the people dispersed to set the fires for morning meal. Many of the people began clamoring to meet the King as well. He strode amongst them, ignoring none, but attending first to the wounded. Each one he touched was healed instantly, and it mattered not if they had missing limbs or a gashed belly. Their pain was gone, and they were completely whole before he left their sides.

Lanthrea awaited her turn and, while waiting, enjoyed watching the people as they laughed and hugged and reveled in the miracles. She noted, at one point, that Neruk, Th'rena, and the Lady were deep in discussion over by one of the cooking fires, and she smiled. It was just last night that the Lady had told Neruk he would have answers soon, and so he had. It was as she was watching Th'rena laugh (so hard that she bent over, grabbing her belly) that she felt a tap on her own shoulder. Turning, she found herself looking into the gentle eyes of the King.

"Lanthrea." He said softly.

She said nothing but collapsed into his arms and cried. He let her, stroking her hair and holding her close to his heart for the longest time.

When at last she spoke, she didn't know what to say, let alone what she felt. It was a mixture of joy, sorrow, relief, anger, and disbelief. That is all she knew. She didn't try to untangle her feelings.

"I didn't know your name," she said finally, deciding on simply stating on simply state the obvious.

"Ah, yes. It isn't something I use often in Palem. My title there is enough for those who come."

Lanthrea nodded, then averted her eyes.

"You needn't hide anything from me, child. You can tell me the truth," he said quietly.

"Thus said the Lady," Lanthrea remarked, "but I have my doubts you will forgive what I have to say."

He smiled. "Why don't you try me?"

"It's all been too much," she blurted out at last, her throat dry and her lips trembling. "The fall off the cliff, Elpin's grave wounding, losing the elders, losing Plen, being thrown into that prison, the battles, the death…I cannot bear it, sir."

"And you think I should have stopped all this, yes?"

She looked up, suddenly aware of her fury.

"Yes. You should have." She fairly spat out the words. "You *could* have. But you didn't."

"And you know the entire story of all these things, all these people, and all these intertwined events and their ultimate end?" he said, looking at her with very steady eyes.

She said nothing, feeling suddenly that she had nothing *to* say.

He continued. "And you know that your ideas of what should have happened would be for the best—the absolute best—for all involved?"

She remained silent.

"And you are certain, in your heart, that because these evils occurred that I do not love well or rightly?"

She bowed her head.

"Lanthrea. Look at me."

Looking up, she swallowed hard as he spoke.

"I have never, for one minute, forgotten one of you. There is not one thing that has happened that was outside of my love and provision for each of you. But this is a dark place; this is not the Forever Land. These things, these events, like a beautiful painting of which you can only see a small bit now, will only make sense once you are there and can see the canvas in its entirety. Here, you must learn to trust me. I am always with you. And all is for good."

She nodded, knowing his words were true; deep in her heart, she knew. But she still was angry, hurt, and confused. Looking at him, she also knew that her cluttered emotions were acceptable to Him. They were honest, and he had just asked her to be truthful, not to be wholly settled in her feelings. She decided, in that moment, to fall on the sword of her own pride, and let her mind continue to be unsettled if need be. Her heart, however, would believe and trust her King. In an act of sheer will, she bowed down before him.

"I do not know about these things. I do not always know what is right and good. But I know *you* are, and I will trust you."

He stood back a step, his eyes wide, his smile like the sun. "This is a great gift you offer me, Lanthrea. The gift of concession. Of your trust. Of surrender of your will. This is indeed an auspicious moment." He looked at her with love and what she could only identify (as she mused upon it later) as pride. "Here then, hand me your ring."

She looked down at the little silver ring on her finger. Slipping it off, she handed it to him. Turning from her, there was a sparkle of light, and when he turned back, the ring had once again become her crown. Only this time, instead of just the delicate woven silver, it had in it a dazzling array of crystal stones, each one sparkling in the sunlight.

"One for each of your sorrows," he said, placing the crown gently on her head. "Oh, and I have one more thing for you." He reached inside his bag that was strapped over his shoulder and pulled out a platter-shaped item. "Your journey. I've taken the privilege of adding a few more stones to it for you." Smiling, he handed her the crest.

"But I lost this in the fall," she said.

"Indeed," he replied, but I found and increased it. For as you have increased, so has it. Your sufferings have produced glory beyond your imaginings. Look, it is more beautiful than ever before."

She turned it around and around in her hands. Truly, the stones he had added were far more lovely than any she had gathered herself. The stones he had chosen were of unearthly, indescribable colors, each one radiating with light.

"Thank you. It's…beautiful," she stammered.

"I have watched over you and cared for you every moment, Lanthrea, as I do all of my children. I have not missed nor been inattentive to one detail in your life. Let this mosaic remind you of that fact. Now, I have others to attend to." With this, he leaned over and kissed her forehead, then strode away purposely, headed toward a young woman who was bent over her newborn, convulsing in wails of anguish having just lost her husband the night before.

Lanthrea rose and called to Mysta, who was playing tag with a few rabbits and squirrels by the pond. A rather large rabbit with floppy brown ears and a positively brilliant pink nose came hopping over with her to Lanthrea's side.

"Lanthee, this is Pubbles. He's my friend." Mysta brushed her hair from off her face, grinning from ear to ear.

Lanthrea smiled and reached down to pet him, whereupon he pulled away, hopping off a bit.

"I think not," he said. "I don't like to be pet, you know. Not unless I know ye better."

Lanthrea grinned. "Oh! You are a talking beast. Forgive me, good sir."

"Not at all," he said with a hop closer. "We, all of us here, have come at the request of the Lady of Lanthor. She came to the Council of Talking Beasts and made her plea. Hearing of your plight at Glanèt, we thought of nothing but to come immediately."

"And we are grateful," Lanthrea replied earnestly. "No doubt we would have lost many more had you not come."

"Tis most likely true," Pubbles said. "We wished we could have been more, but the Lady came in the middle of the night, and we had trouble getting out the word."

Mysta interrupted the conversation. "Can we go play again, Lanthee?"

Pubbles looked at Lanthrea with an expression that said, 'this child is wearing me out', but twitched his pink nose, turned, and hopped away quickly, calling out, "Catch me if you can!"

Mysta squealed with delight and ran off to chase him., leaving Lanthrea to sit and look at the stone crest in her hands.

The day passed like a dream, the good kind where your heart feels free and light, and you awaken comforted and filled with hope. The king attended to each hurting soul and every aching body. After all had been attended to, the Burial Rite was done with great solemnity, and the King himself blessed the dead and gave great hope to the people that they would see their loved ones again one day. This idea was new to the Glanètians, and the joy it caused only added to the day. After the Rite, the animals and children were left free to play and romp in the early winter sunshine. By evening meal, even the previously wounded were ready for a celebration and had begun preparing the most delicious Glanètian dishes they could, what with the sparse supplies they had brought on the journey. Happily for the animals, Glanètians rarely ate meat (the geese had been an aberration) and the dishes were of the sort that everyone could enjoy: spiced squashes with flavored oils atop, hot grains with the savory and unique spices used only for celebrations, and good wine that A'lam himself had provided (no one saw where he had found it.)

They created a makeshift 'gathering place 'in which to eat, and Neruk rang a bell someone had brought from the village to call everyone together for evening meal. Everyone came together, brotherly arms on shoulders, some hand in hand, and smiles on every face as they sat down in front of Neruk.

"A'lam has taught me a new blessing," he announced, his voice echoing over the waters of the pond. With this, he turned his back to the people and raised a jar of oil to the sky. He began to sing a song, one which Lanthrea recognized immediately. It was Innatus' melody, the one she had heard first at Darrow Falls. Neruk sang the words, and as it had been with Innatus, so it was now. The stars, just beginning to sparkle in the sky, seemed to come suddenly alive—twirling and darting in the darkness—then, like a glittering waterfall, began to cascade to the ground. The heavens once again descended and met the earth, each soul present feeling the wonder of it.

After this blessing, A'lam himself passed out the bread to each family as the women began to set out the bowls of spiced grains and vegetables on a few makeshift tables set here and there. The night was clear and cold, and everyone bundled back into their coats and cloaks and hats, and each found a fire to settle down next to as they ate. Never had there such a joyous meal, never in the annals of Glanèt's long history—even though they weren't at home in their beloved village. After everyone had eaten their fill, two of the men from Palem who had brought their stringed filistas along began to strum some folk melodies. The strumming got louder, and a few voices joined in. Within minutes, bowls had been overturned and made into drums, and the villagers began to dance and sing together in the firelight. This went on long after the children and animals had gone to sleep, the dancing and the joyous celebration of a people who had, at long last, found their King.

Lanthrea sat out the revelry, choosing instead to take a moonlight ride on Elpinhoeve. Mounting him bareback (finding she had to use a stump as her muscles weren't as strong as the last time she had ridden) she turned him down the road towards the Prathian Desert and rode along in the moonlight. His warm back nearly melted her heart, and she found herself crying out of sheer joy as she felt his side-to-side rhythm and heard the clip-clop of his feet on the rocks. She pulled him up to a stop next to a straggly group of bushes and just sat there, looking up at the moon and breathing in the cold air. How could anyone be so blessed? A sweet daughter sleeping safely under the watch of the valiant Lady and her good King. A new family, an entire village of good people who were now on a journey with her. She suddenly realized the truth in the deepest way possible. She was no longer alone. At all. Ever. She lay forward over Elpin's silky mane, hugged his neck, and cried.

This journey had been so very hard.

This journey had been worth it all.

She turned Elpin back towards the pond and her people and, once there, slipped off Elpin, turning him out to graze, and made her way to Mysta. She was sleeping soundly under a pile of blankets. Lanthrea lay down next to her, pulled a blanket over herself, and watched her daughter sleep. No matter what came next, she would always remember this night. If she'd been so inclined, she would have found a stone to commemorate it, but instead, she let sleep overtake her. She would leave the stone gathering to the king from now on.

Everyone in the camp awakened late the next morning, so great had been the merriment the night before. The men gathered before morning meal with A'lam and were deep in discussion by the time Lanthrea awakened. By the looks on all of their faces, she knew the topic was gravely serious and in stark contrast to the joy of yesterday. The women were quiet as they made their morning meal, everyone knowing the probable topic at hand. Bythim had now been gutted. Twice. And his ego was not one to handle such a routing, even once. They also knew that even with the snow in the foothills slowing them down, the men who had escaped had surely made it back to Cenecal by now with information of their defeat at the pond. This was something everyone knew in their hearts but had put aside yesterday.

By the time the men dispersed and headed back to their families to break bread, word had spread quickly through the camp. They were to march on Cenecal. The decision had been made. The women were nigh onto panicked upon hearing this news, and it was only in the revelation that the King himself would be addressing everyone at midday that calmed them enough to have an appetite for their morning meal.

Lanthrea fed Mysta, then let her ride bareback on Elpin as she led him along the road. With no saddle, Mysta simply grabbed onto his mane and held on tight, squealing with delight as she bounced along, sliding side to side with every footfall. Lanthrea was having trouble smiling. She knew that she should be feeling light of heart and confident regarding the decision to move on Cenecal, but she didn't. At all. How could it possibly be that their rag-tag group of untrained, unarmed, and barely functional villagers could possibly attack the great city of Cenecal and Lord Bythim with all his wealth and unlimited manpower? For even if his soldiers were of small number, Bythim counted each citizen of Drymac as his own property, and therefore any of them could be conscripted on a moment's notice. Perhaps she needed to speak to A'lam. Perhaps he did not know the length and power of Lord Bythim's arm.

"Lanthee, Lanthee, I said I wanted off," Mysta's voice broke into Lanthrea's thoughts. Tossing aside her dreadful musings, she turned her attention to her little girl. "Can I get off now?" she whined.

"Of course. I'm sorry. I wasn't listening." Lanthrea pulled her off Elpin, tied his reins to a bush, and let Mysta run around on the road. Her long, blonde hair flying, her little freckled nose red from the cold winter morning. Such innocence and sweetness in this child. She had been through more than most people would go through in a lifetime, yet she remained content and trusting. A smile broke on Lanthrea's face. Yes, children *were* reminders of all things good and hopeful. And it was for that hope that she would talk to the King today. She was the only one in the group, outside of Petrul, who had actually lived in Cenecal. Perhaps her words would find a way to change the course of their current trajectory. She would first speak with Petrul, and perhaps he would accompany her to A'lam.

She let Mysta play for a few more minutes, then hoisted her back up onto Elpin, found a fallen log on the side of the road, and used it to swing herself up behind her, then clicked Elpin into a run. Mysta laughed uproariously as she bounced along, holding on for dear life as they galloped off the road and down into the ravine to the pond. Mysta slid off at Neruk's campfire, and Th'rena took her hand and sat her down by the fire to warm. Lanthrea nodded her thanks, then walked Elpin over to the other horses, who, though excited by the battle the other day, had not participated in it and were happily grazing on some tough grasses that grew by the pond. She then looked around the camp until she found Petrul, who was sitting by a fire with the other elders, smoking a pipe and whittling on a large branch.

"Another walking stick?" asked Lanthrea as she neared.

He looked up and grinned. "Indeed. And this time, I'm adding my own stories to the Solemn Memories." Lanthrea sat down next to him. "I've never known what they are. The Memories. No one has ever told me."

"No? "Petrul seemed surprised. "Here, then, allow me." He pointed to the first rudimentary carving on the branch. "This is the First Memory. The sun. For as the sun gives light and life to us, it reminds us daily of El-Gudan as the creator of all." He pointed to the next carving, which was of a winged creature with sharp teeth, looking somewhat like those Lanthrea saw in her dreams. "This is Darkness, which tries to overcome creation and stamp out the light of good. This is the Second Memory." She nodded, and he continued. "The third is that of the heart. For it is only through love that the Darkness can be overcome. The fourth Memory is the most sacred. It is the Tree, where A'lam and the Darkness fought the Great Battle for us all and where love conquered death. And the fifth is one you already know —the Book. Remembering the words of our King and El-Gudan is the most important thing." He brushed some of the sawdust away. "Of course, I have much detail yet to carve." She reached over and ran her fingers over the delicate engravings. "It's lovely." He smiled and puffed on his pipe. "It's a good story. One that is an honor to carve."

"You're going to add some of your own to it?"

He nodded. "Down here, at the bottom, the story of my escape from Bythim and the two battles we have won."

"I hope to see it when it's finished," she said, squeezing his shoulder.

He looked at her and patted her hand. "Now, then. You didn't come over here just to take a gander at my whittling, did you?"

Shaking her head, she sat down next to him. "No. I...I...I am concerned about Neruk and the King's decision to head into Cenecal. Petrul. They do not know the place, as do you and I. We need to tell them."

Petrul took his pipe out from between his teeth. "Well. It's true Neruk has no concept of what awaits him there. But, Lanthrea, A'lam knows well the place, as well the hearts of those we will face. Better than you or I."

She took a deep breath. "Then why would he ask these good people to attempt the impossible? It will be the death of every soul here."

Petrul set his pipe down on a rock and looked Lanthrea directly in the eyes. "Have you not yet learned anything? He is the King. He knows what is right and good. And in case you haven't noticed, he does rather impossible things all the time."

Lanthrea sighed. Perhaps she *had* learned nothing. In spite of all of this, she still felt she knew best. Her perceptions seemed right to her. And fear often still spoke louder in her heart than hope. Petrul saw her face fall and reached over, patting her knee. "Daughter. Trust the king. No matter what happens to us here, he will never leave us. And even if we are all to perish for his good name, it would be our honor to do so. Better a free and courageous death in the light than a fear-filled life in the darkness."

She nodded, although somewhat lackluster in her agreement to his words, and stood up to go. Petrul looked up and pointed at her crown. "I see you are wearing it. Have you looked at it lately—really looked? It isn't the same crown he gave you at Palem, you know. And it is from these hard things in following him here that have afforded you those new stones. Lanthrea, your crown now sparkles as you do. He knows what he is doing with our lives, daughter."

She reached up and touched the crown. She had forgotten she was wearing it. Pulling it off, she turned it around and around in her hands. The crystal stones sparkled and shimmered in the winter sunlight. *These things are to remind me*, she said quietly to herself. Smiling at Petrul, she put it back on her head. *He knows what he is doing with our lives*. Petrul was right.

She headed back to Neruk's campsite to pick up Mysta, her heart a small bit lighter than it had been just this morning.

It was getting on to midday meal when Lanthrea saw A'lam, walking through the camp, stopping now and again to hold children on his lap or laugh with the men that were standing about warming their hands over the fires. At one point, he glanced up at Lanthrea and Mysta, and after hugging an old woman who was sitting all alone on a blanket, he walked over to them.

"And who is this lovely girl who graces my presence?" He said, bowing to Mysta in a grand gesture.

"Mysta!" She yelled happily.

"Well, Mysta. Let me see you. Come stand here beside me."

The little girl pushed her hair off her face, looked at Lanthrea for permission, then walked closer and took A'lam's hand.

"You look like my daddy," Mysta said, her voice hovering between happy and sorrowful.

"Oh, sweet child," he said. "I am so sorry your daddy had to leave you. And your mother, too. They did not want to. Did you know that?"

Mysta nodded, her eyes filling with tears. A'lam looked up at Lanthrea. "May I walk with her for a bit?"

Lanthrea held her hands over her heart and nodded. If anyone could comfort her daughter, it was the king.

They turned and walked toward the pond, Mysta's tiny soft hand in his large, strong one. When they returned but a few minutes later, Mysta came bounding up and jumped into Lanthrea's arms.

"The King tolded me things. *Good* things. Mommy and daddy miss me, and they will see me again one day. Did you know that, Lanthee? Did you?"

Lanthrea couldn't help the tears rolling down her cheeks. "I do now," she said, looking up at A'lam and whispering a silent '*thank you* ' to him.

Suddenly, her idea of informing him of the dangers of a move on Cenecal seemed completely inconsequential. Looking at him, with love and kindness permeating even the air around them, she knew that she could trust him. With anything.

She and Mysta walked over to Neruk and Th'rena's camp and helped make the midday meal. They would eat as a family today.

CHAPTER THIRTY-FOUR:
The Preparation

Everyone had eaten their fill just as the sky was becoming overcast, and a few snowflakes were beginning to fall.

All attention was on A'lam, who walked down by the pond and directed everyone to sit and listen. Wrapping up in blankets and coats, all the villagers gathered to listen, each heart feeling the apprehension of the forthcoming announcement.

"My people," he began. "What we are about to do may seem foolhardy to many of you, terrifying to others. But listen to me. Bythim will not stop. His pride has been pricked just as sure as his soul is mortally wounded. There is nothing now but blackness in him. He will not relent on coming against you again, for to his dark heart, nothing but your annihilation will suffice. And it will not stop there. He will continue south, into Prathia, into the Dunes of Martauk, into the Forest of Landor itself. He would spread darkness over all the lands if we do not rise against him." He stopped and drew a deep breath. "And I have chosen you to help me stop him. As you have shown both bravery and love, you have also shown yourselves worthy of being my soldiers. And, though small in numbers, you are mighty in valor." He was quiet for a moment and smiled, the snow stopping and the sun pushing suddenly through the white winter sky. "And, besides…look! For help has come to aid you in this battle! Behold!" He turned around and looked to the east, beyond the pond. At first, there was nothing, but then, over the hill, came a solitary giant golden cat, similar to the one that had attacked Elpin in the Valley of Sorrows. Lanthrea felt her stomach tighten until she saw the small golden crown on its head. Next came a few more of the great cats, then more and more. Next came the horses. Hundreds of them, all a bit larger than Elpinhoeve but not as gigantic as Garanthor's clan. They came trotting over the hill, their manes flying in the breeze, their nostrils flared, legs lifted high in battle prance. The next group was led by two small creatures, both dressed in leathers with small silver crowns on their heads and bows and arrows strapped to their backs. Lanthrea squeezed her eyes to focus. No, it couldn't be! It was Plaxi and Clink! Behind them, a huge number of other elves and pixies of various sizes and shapes, each armed with bow and arrow and dagger, and each with a determined yet whimsical expression on their faces. The next to arrive were the bears, all the forest bears of Landor. Brown, Black, and Grizzlies - their silver tipped fur shining in the sun. Lumbering toward the king, they opened their mouths and growled in unison, a clarion call of battle. Finally, behind the great bears came two men. Both were dressed in white, their gray hair flowing behind them as they walked toward the king with broad smiles and a steady gait. It was Innatus and Azar! Innatus was considerably younger and taller than when Lanthrea had last seen him. The Lake of Lights had well rejuvenated him. He caught Lanthrea's eye and winked at her as he crested the hill. Barely able to contain herself, Lanthrea was about to burst with joy, but just then, as she thought nothing more could surprise her, she saw a woman coming over the hill. Long black hair, wearing a head-to-toe robe with the certain markings of the desert. It couldn't be. Lanthrea jumped to her feet, unable to contain them any longer, and ran toward her. It was Cla'neen! With a smile almost as broad as the King's, she ran toward Lanthrea, the two colliding like stars as they embraced, laughing and crying simultaneously. When Lanthrea, at last, looked up behind Cla'neen, she saw a veritable army of Prathian soldiers. Desert men and women, dressed for battle, each with the short, curved sword of the tribe in their robe's sashes and a bow and arrow on their backs. Cla'neen laughed. "My clan," she said, gesturing to the people behind her. "Word had spread to us that Bythim was considering a march on our beloved desert for the treasures underneath our sands. That was enough for us. A rabbit told us you were gathering here. We have come to join in your effort… if your king will have us."

A'lam turned and opened his arms to the Prathians. "Let your people be mine," he bellowed, and a great cheer went up from everyone, Glanètian and Prathian and those from Palem itself. The smaller animals, foxes, coyotes, rabbits, and the like, along with Garanthor and his clan, all fell into place with the others. The number of people, elves, and animals now numbered in the thousands; a great, diverse army unlike any ever assembled before.

A'lam motioned everyone to settle.

"Send a representative from each clan, group, and kin to meet with Neruk and me at the gathering place before Evening Meal. We will make our plans together. For now, everyone! Rejoice and celebrate!"

Suddenly, at each person's feet, there appeared a goblet of wine. On the ground near each animal, there appeared a morsel of their favorite food. They picked up their cups and snapped up their food as yet another great cheer erupted. "To the King!" They all shouted as they toasted to their newfound alliance and the one who had brought them all together.

Later, Lanthrea and Cla'neen walked arm in arm toward one of the fires to warm. Mysta was tugging at Lanthrea's arm. "Who is she?"

"This is my dearest friend Cla'neen. Cla'neen, this is my daughter, Mysta."

Cla'neen looked confused but said nothing. She took Mysta's hand and held it to her heart in a traditional greeting. "Aren't you a pretty one?" she said to the girl. Mysta giggled and asked if she could go play with her friends. The two women watched her go. "It's a long story," Lanthrea laughed, responding to her friend's unspoken question. Cla'neen smiled. "So, a *daughter*. And do you still have Brown Horse?"

Lanthrea laughed and pointed to the three horses grazing by the pond. "There he is, with the others," she said. "His name is now Elpinhoeve."

"A noble name," Cla'neen said. She nudged Lanthrea in the ribs. "Did you ever learn to ride him?"

Lanthrea laughed and nudged her back, nodding. "And ride *well*," she said. "I'll show you one day."

"And..so… did you marry your betrothed?" Lanthrea asked, almost afraid to hear the answer.

Cla'neen rolled her eyes. "That was never going to happen," she said firmly. "I finally went home to my father, and I told him so. It took a while, but in the end, it was my mother who convinced him to free me from the engagement. It is good to be back among my people. Living alone in the desert was fine, but not as fine as having family." She squeezed Lanthrea's arm. "As I see you have found."

The two sat down by the fire, the rest of the evening spent in telling tales of their adventures and reminiscing about their journey through the desert together. Cla'neen couldn't get over how healthy

Lanthrea appeared and how calm her spirit was without Tenk continually terrifying her with its words of warning and danger.

"You were certainly smitten by that creature, that glottin," she remarked as they prepared evening meal together.

"I had no one else for so long," Lanthrea responded. "I thought it was *for* me. I didn't know its job was to destroy me. It is hard to see that those things which we won't let go of can control us. It took the King to help me be freed from its lies."

Cla'neen nodded, understanding little of what she heard.

"I just thought it was a nice pet for you," she remarked, "even though a bit …fearful." She looked at Lanthrea and quickly added, "And what is this of your name, Myka? They seem to call you by another?"

Lanthrea nodded, explaining. "Given me by the King as well. Lanthrea is the name he gave me. It's funny. I don't even know what it means. But it is the name he gave me, so I gladly accepted it."

Cla'neen pulled the hood off her head and shook out her long black hair. "If you say," she said plainly. "I do not understand, but it is not for me to understand. I honor your journey. And your new name. We can share more in time."

Grateful for her friend's kindness and acceptance, they baked flatbread together on hot stones, and Cla'neen made some date paste in honor of their time in the desert together. They slathered the hot flatbread with the sweet paste and ate it joyfully, Mysta eating every bite of the sweet meal and asking for more. They spent the rest of the evening sharing their experiences over the past year and discussing A'lam. Cla'neen was interested in this King of Palem but not yet ready to assign him the import that did Lanthrea. Mysta fell asleep bundled under a pile of blankets, two of which were the soft, colorful weaves of the desert—both of which delighted the little girl. The two women finally drifted off after a night of talking and laughing as only old friends who had shared a wild adventure could.

In the morning, Neruk rang the bell and awakened everyone just as the sun rose. The women and several of the elves, who were known to be good cooks, headed to make morning meal for the huge assembly. Gathering food and drink from each family—elven, Prathian, or Glanètian—they used the goods to begin the meal. The animals were on their own for food, each either foraging or grazing to their heart's content. Representatives from each group gathered again with Neruk and A'lam after everyone had eaten to plan their incursion into Cenecal. Surprise was to be their most salient and potent ingredient in the attack. No doubt, Bythim would not even consider the possibility that the remaining villagers and a handful of rabbits left alive in the second battle would dare to attempt such a thing against Drymac. This would play greatly in their favor. Armament, however, would prove a problem. The villagers from Glanèt had little or no weaponry before the first attack, and all but a few spears had been lost in the last. The elves volunteered to help with this. Expert with iron and anvil, they were to make swords for any able-bodied soul that could wield one—male or female. This was to be accomplished by forging anything of metal left in the camp—from the wagon wheels to the sledge runners to the cooking pots and garden shears the villagers had brought along. Anything and everything would be used. The campaign was to begin in two days hence, giving everyone (especially the elves) little time to prepare. But if surprise was to be their main weapon, time was what they had the least of, and every second counted.

The Lady of Lanthor was busy training an entire corps of women for battle. Any woman not nursing and having less than fifty years could volunteer, but none were forced. Using bow and arrow, the Lady was showing them how to shoot straight and hit targets from a goodly distance. Lanthrea wanted to join but was told she was 'too aged 'by the corps lead archer—a beautiful, strong woman from Palem named Graetha. "It is not your battle this time," Graetha had said gently, compassion in her eyes. The truth of her age stung, but she had agreed compliantly, thinking more of Mysta than her own hurt pride. She deserved a mother around for many more years.

The men were training for more intimate battle: close contact with sword, dagger, and spear. Azar and the King himself were in charge of this training, and it was rigorous at best and soul-crushing at worst. Not a man nor elf didn't wish he were in better shape and hadn't lifted so many a pint as he had in the past few seasons. The animals were being coordinated by Garanthor. With his clan's long history of being in battles, he was best suited for training those who had not.

From sunrise to sundown, every person and beast trained hard, and those either too young or, like Lanthrea, too old, did the work of cooking, preparing poultices for those who inevitably would be wounded, and creating makeshift shields and spears—a job needing no forging, thus more suited for humans than elves.

The first night, every soul in the assembly literally fell into bed, many skipping evening meal altogether for sheer exhaustion. On the second day, everyone knew this was their last before they marched up the Circacians into Drymac. The mood was tense and almost frantic. The elves worked at a feverish pace, turning out as many broadswords and arrowheads as they could. The women's arms were strained and cramped from the sheer amount of archery practice they undertook, and the men were bruised and exhausted from the battle play they endured. It was just after midday meal that A'lam rang the bell and called the assembly together. He told everyone that the physical work was ended. The rest of the day and night would be spent in less vigorous activity, joining the elders and young in affixing arrowheads to arrows, spear tips to shafts, and helping fill water bags and the like. Everyone was to eat a good evening meal, and to a person, each was to attempt to sleep as well as could be expected right after they ate. He would not acquiesce on these points and had even chided a group of young men, who, after eating, had tried to skirmish in the field behind the pond.

By the time the moon rose, the entire camp was quiet. Few were actually asleep, but an uncanny sense of rest and peace came upon them all. Neruk was still awake at midnight, laying on a blanket with his beloved Th'rena when he saw the King walk up the hill from the pond, his form silhouetted in the moonlight. Neruk watched as he knelt down, lifted his face to the sky, and spoke. He couldn't hear his words, nor did he really understand to whom he was speaking, but he knew it was a sacred moment, and he rose from his bedding to his knees and joined A'lam by turning his face to the sky as well.

The night passed quickly, and by morning light, almost every single man, woman, and child was awake. The mood was solemn. There was little speaking. Morning meal was hearty and shared with good tidings, but no one was smiling, and shoulders were tight with tension. The Prathians were up before anyone else and had wrapped themselves in their head-to-toe flowing garb, but today had cinched it at the waist, wrist and ankle. The others, elves and humans alike, had wrapped leather around wrists or across chests as makeshift armor of sorts. The snow had begun falling again, dusting the foothills with about an inch of white powder, but nothing that would inhibit their climb up to Cenecal. A'lam had mounted his warhorse, his white stallion named Brynthall, and his polished armor shone in the diffuse winter sun, even through the snowfall. The camp was broken down in a matter of minutes, almost every item being used for the battle to come, and nothing but sleeping blankets and personal packs left to carry.

The assembly moved as one from the relative safety of the pond up to the road that led into Drymac. They swarmed over the road, spreading out like ants, a greater army having never been assembled in this region in all its history. Once on the road proper, A'lam stopped and turned to address the crowd.

"I have rarely been so proud of a people or so grateful for them. The march to Cenecal will take but a few hours, but first, we will pass the encampment where many of my people are currently being held. This will be our initial task. Those with food and medicines, these captives will be in your charge once we free them. If the guards surrender, take them with you. Do not run them through. Remain noble even if the enemy is not. (It was at this point that the few Cenecalian soldiers who had been captured hung their heads. For in all their years, they had never met an enemy who had treated them so well, almost inviting them into their lives. The King's words seemed to humble—or perhaps shame them). A'lam looked at the assembly and smiled sadly. "It is for all people that I offer freedom from tyranny. Do not forget this. Once we enter Cenecal, expect no resistance until we approach Bythim's palace. He will not be expecting us. The battle will take place there. Use your training. Be as deadly as you must, as merciful as you can. And leave Bythim for me."

With this, he turned and nudged his horse forward. The light snow continued as they marched west. They made it to the tent where the others were being held in a matter of minutes. There were ten guards surrounding the long building that had been recently built, attached to the original tent. They saw the crowd approaching them, A'lam in his armor at the lead. Opening their mouths as though dumbstruck, they simply dropped their weapons and ran. The captives, most of them elders from Old Town (but a few younger families from the Dwelling Quarter as well), were in bad shape. Several had to be carried out, and sadly, one very elderly man had collapsed and perished as they tried to walk him out, so great was his anguish and weak his body. A small group of women and one man who was an expert in tinctures and salves stayed behind for quite a while, attending to them until they were ready to travel. They would follow behind the rest and not enter Cenecal but stay on the outskirts until the battle had ended.

Sometime along the way, about halfway up the foothills, as the snow was getting deeper and morale a little thin, Th'rena's nephew Narth, the one with the lovely voice, began singing an old Glanètian folk song. The words and melody were easy, and everyone joined in after a few verses, smiles breaking out on faces for the first time all day.

"Ho, ho, on we go,

joined in song for evermore,

Far, far, far from home,

still we love and journey on"

The elves, it was discovered, had an incredible musical sensibility, and soon the entire assembly was singing in three and four-part harmony, with descants and a thundering bass line adding to the melody. Several of the elves had drums amongst their goods and pulled them out, making a steady beat to their marching as they sang. Lanthrea felt there had never been an anthem so inspiring or beautiful in all the world.

Up they climbed, marching to the beat of the drums and making good time up the foothills. They navigated the road into Cenecal readily enough. The music stopped only once the city could be seen from the road. A moment of silence was held, then hands were held momentarily over hearts before the group moved forward into the city. The elderly, the young, and those rescued from the camp stayed behind on the road just outside of town, where a few fires were built to stave off both the the cold and from the snow, which was still falling lightly.

Lanthrea, staying behind with the others, wished she could have been with the assembly. The sheer number of them pouring through the streets would have been joyful enough to see, as there wasn't a marauding gang in the world that would attempt to stand against this army. The mere thought of it filled her with delight. The drunkards, the vile, the gangs. Not one of them could possibly stand in opposition to the group that now traversed their city streets. Resigning herself to her situation, she settled for gathering a group of children around her and pulled out the book to read. Choosing the chapter with the illustration of the little doe with the silver crown (one of Mysta's favorites), she began to read aloud.

"For the king will go before you, and behind you and beside you. When all seems most sorrowful, rejoice! For the king is with you always."

The children seemed to like the verse, but they liked the illustration even more, and in the end, Lanthrea stopped reading and settled on showing them every single picture in the book and letting the drawings impress what they would upon the children.

Petrul was tending to the elders taken out of captivity, as he well knew their suffering and anguish, having experienced it himself in the tent. The Lady had left him a jar of healing balm, which he was applying to their wounds liberally as he comforted them with his tender understanding and empathy.

It was midday when everyone who had stayed behind with Lanthrea and Petrul heard the sound. A horn, is used by Bythim's men to announce danger or battle. The sound of —low and deep and resonant, dripping with evil— gave them all chills. They held their collective breaths for a moment.

It had begun.

CHAPTER THIRTY-FIVE:

The Battle At Cenecal

He kicked the glottin across the room, sending it flying, its sharp nails skittering on the marble floor as it tried to gain enough traction to run away. The other glottin leapt from its place at the foot of the throne and ran for its life, hiding under a table at the far end of the hall.

"I have had *enough* of 'danger 'and 'warning 'from you!"Bythim bellowed at his two most trusted advisors, both of whom he had invited into his life when he was a child. The glottins whimpered pitifully from their hiding places in the Great Hall but kept their eyes on their master just in case he moved on them again.

"If anyone else has any bad news for me, they should speak it now, for my mood is unlikely to get any better this day," he bellowed again.

Everyone in the room, from the courtiers dripping with gemstones, to the blue-robed soldiers standing guard, averted their eyes and said nothing. It fell upon one lone soldier, who had just entered the hall from his post on the palace wall to break the silence. He spoke breathlessly.

"Sire. A great army approaches, Sire. They are almost upon us even as we speak."

Bythim was just about to order his head on a platter when several other soldiers came running into the room so fast they slid on the marble floor before being able to stop, bowing down before the ridiculously garish throne once they were able to do so.

"Lord, a great army is just outside our gates. Our horn has been sounded. Your orders?"

Tossing off his feather robe, Bythim stood to his full height (even with his stacked heels, he stood only five feet in all), his eyes wild and his crown askew.

"What is this?" he screamed at the men prostrate before him.

"An army, sire. They are at our gates. An unusual lot—men, animals, women, and horses….um…horses with wings."

Bythim straightened his crown and began to smile.

"Ah. I see now. A joke. Very good. Well executed. Was this Wyeth's idea, then? Good old Wyeth. Always was good for a laugh."

The three guards at his feet did not dare look up. Only one dared speak.

"No, sire. This is not a joke. We saw this assembly with our own eyes."

The smile fell from Bythim's face, which quickly turned an odd shade of greenish white. He bit his lip and stood silent for a moment. Then, suddenly, he whipped around, jumped down from the throne platform, and ran from the room, disappearing out a back door and leaving the Great Hall with a few soldiers and five lovely young women in silken gowns, looking greatly confused.

The soldiers regained their composure quickly and, drawing their swords, ran out to face the enemy, leaving the courtiers to fend for themselves.

Outside, it was chaos. Once the battle horn had been blown, the soldiers on the palace walls had hardly time to load the trebuchets with stones before the great army of A'lam was upon them. Bythim's bowmen did the most damage, as they were at the wall within moments and sending volleys of arrows into their attackers, but even that was too late.

Garanthor and his lot made short order of them, flying up to the walls and knocking them off the palace with their great wings. Bythim's men did get a few stones off the wall, sadly crushing two of the bears and mortally wounding one of the horses.

The swordsmen of Cenecal came next, and only then did any real engagement occur. Bythim's men were well-trained and vicious to the core. They were considerably outnumbered, having only five hundred men at hand, but fought valiantly. The women archers, trained by the Lady of Lanthor, began their volley into the swordsmen, killing or wounding a great number in their first thrust. Next, the fighting men and women of Palem in their shining armor advanced, battling hand-to-hand with the Cenecalian soldiers. While Bythim's men fought unfairly, lopping off hands and slicing Achilles 'tendons, the swordsmen and women from Palem fought cleanly, with quick and merciful dispatching of the enemy. Any soldier who dropped his arms was left standing, to be dealt with later (a fact, once realized, had many of the Cenecalian soldiers simply dropping their weapons and running for their lives). Those brave enough to remain fought hard, but by the time the Prathian people came upon them with sharp scimitars and long swords, they honestly had little chance of winning, let alone doing much damage. The war horses and other animals did their parts by confusing the enemy: biting, striking, or clawing, and in the end, it all proved too much for the blue-robed men of Bythim. The entire affair was over within a matter of minutes—Bythim's men bound and grouped together with the bears guarding them.

A'lam approached the leader of the men and dismounted.

"Your lord, Bythim. Where is he?"

To their credit, in a rare moment of loyalty, not one of the men disclosed anything— but A'lam happened to look up at the palace just as several Courtiers were darting out of a back door.

He quickly got back onto Brynthall and kicked him into a gallop, cutting the young women off from the back gate of the palace yard.

"Your lord," he said. "Where might I find him?"

The three young women, completely terrified, could hardly speak. One finally screwed up the courage to respond with a "He left but a few minutes ago. Out the back. There." She pointed to a small door exiting the palace hall onto the gardens.

"Your truthfulness is well appreciated," A'lam said sincerely. "You will not be harmed. Do not be afraid to approach my people. They will treat you well." He stopped and looked at the three young women in their diaphanous and revealing sheer gowns. "And with dignity."

With this, he kicked Brynthall again into a gallop, turning him into the gardens behind the palace.

It was only minutes later that A'lam reappeared, dragging Lord Bythim behind his horse by a rope: his hands tied and his mouth gagged.

A cheer went up from the assembly, and several of the squirrels managed to climb up the bell tower of the palace and start pulling the ropes on the bells, their glorious tones beginning to ring over the entire town.

A'lam and Lord Bythim disappeared into the woods behind the palace proper just as the snow began to fall heavily, draping the entire place in white and covering even the blood from the fallen. The people of Cenecal, to a person, had all left their dwellings, merchant tables, or pubs and were walking or running up the hill to the palace. Straining to see what was happening, they were lining the streets, up on each other's shoulders, and climbing trees to get a view. Most had no love for Bythim's rule, oppressive and terrifying as it was, but quite a few had vested interest in seeing his reign continue —offering as it did cover and incentive for their wanton activities. Both sorts were now clamoring for a look at what had happened, having seen the huge army marching to the palace and hearing the subsequent ringing of the bells.

Lanthrea, Petrul, and the others had also heard the bells and had no idea what their tolling might mean. Was Bythim announcing a victory? Was it a warning of some sort? Had the King taken the day? All they could figure what that the battle was over, and to a soul, they decided to risk the trip into Cenecal to see what had happened.

Rounding up the children, they began the walk toward the palace in the center of town. Lanthrea surprisingly found herself quite nostalgic as they passed the Merchant Quarter today and then, a few blocks later, the remains of her old home. Having been burned to the ground, all that was left was her door (which had fallen into the debris but hadn't burned) and a few tiles from the roof. The place had not been rebuilt, presumably as a warning to others. The roads in this part of town were nearly empty, and they made good time to the Center, where the crowds had already assembled. There was to be no pushing through this mass of people today. Not with the wounded and the children. Instead, they came upon a few empty benches near one of the wells and decided to sit there and wait for news. The bells continued to toll for a good long time, and when they finally were silent, everyone listened for a word —good or bad—as to what had happened.

Had they been closer to the palace, they would have seen the bears ambling about as they guarded Bythim's men, who by this time had given up any pretense of soldierly behavior and were all seated directly on the snowy ground (or sitting on their helmets), eyes wide with wonder at the sights and sounds all around them. Not a one of them appeared frightened, long since realizing that they were being treated well, and, outside of the indignity of having immense hairy creatures guarding them, it seemed to them none were to come to an ignoble end at the tip of anyone's blade. The members of Bythim's court had been trickling out of the palace since the bells began to ring: guards, messengers, courtiers, cooks, butlers, and the like. Walking out into the soft falling snow from the gigantic doors of the palace, they looked for all the world like people entering a new land world after having been in prison, their faces showing both wonder and a palpable expectation of something new.

The Lady of Lanthor was welcoming them into the courtyard, leading the less certain people by the hand to the huge stone benches that graced the palace yard and letting them sit quietly until they were collected and assured no danger was to befall them.

Though most people were quietly watching the happenings from the streets, a goodly number were belligerent, throwing stones at the King's people and yelling out curses and threats. These were the marauders, the thieves, those that Bythim's reign had not only protected but encouraged. These were quickly silenced and rounded up by the great golden cats, who, snarling and nipping at their heels, herded them in with Bythim's men and let the bears do the rest.

By the time the snow had stopped falling, what could be described as nothing other than a joyful atmosphere had fallen upon everyone and every creature in Cenecal. A good number of the merchants had made their way back to their booths, bringing food and drink to hand out to the vast crowd. Many of the townspeople had done the same, and by midday meal, there was food and drink in everyone's hand, and new acquaintances were being made as everyone broke bread together in the shadow of Bythim's palace.

It was just after everyone had eaten that the sun broke through the winter clouds, making the fresh snow sparkle like crystalline powder, and everyone squint for the brightness of it all. It was also just then that the King came riding in from the woods—Lord Bythim nowhere to be seen.

The crowd hushed, awaiting a word from A'lam.

Turning Brynthall towards the palace steps, he dismounted and stood before the great doors of Bythim's palace.

"People of Cenecal. My name is A'lam. I am the King of Palem, a land of which most of you have no knowledge. I hope to change this. In the meantime, you need to know that Lord Bythim is no longer ruler over Drymac."

There was a long pause before a few brave souls began to clap. The reaction spread until the entire place was filled with cheers and clapping, and shouts of joy. As the noise settled once again, A'lam continued.

"You have been, under his reign, oppressed and abused. Good was suppressed, and evil was glorified. This is not the way in my kingdom." He looked around at all the people and continued. "You have been set free."

The cheer that rose this time was spontaneous and unearthly. It seemed as though the entire crowd, as one, could not contain their joy and relief. People were crying, hugging, and dancing as though they had just been released from the dungeons of Kralek itself. Lanthrea could hear the cheering and joyful noise in the streets and began to weep. It could only mean one thing: the long night had ended, and the dawn had just claimed the darkness.

No one asked about the whereabouts of Lord Bythim. No one particularly cared. It was only much later when Lanthrea had a moment with the King, that she dared ask of him.

A'lam had hung his head before answering her. "He could have been freed that very day," he said, looking at Lanthrea sadly. "But in the end, I gave him what he wanted. A life alone, bending his knee to no one but himself. So, it is to himself that I sent him. He lives now, by choice, in a place where every moment he can only think about himself, speak about himself, until, at last, he will become as small and dark as his own thoughts. Alone, forgotten, miserable, and completely consumed." He looked up at Lanthrea, great sorrow on his face. "Separated from all good, all light, all truth, and all kindness, he will live forever with his choice, with nothing but himself to consider."

Lanthrea felt a sudden, urgent chill run down her spine. Such a horror she could not even imagine, although just hearing his words had been illuminating enough. She shook her head sadly and walked with the King into the palace that was once Bythim's glory.

***

He stood in the midst of the circle, letting the creatures tell him things, their voices mirroring his own small thoughts.

"He is tall and strong," one hag said, voice creaking with sarcasm and venom. "Yes, and so handsome," responded another, its yellow eyes widening for a moment before falling back into the tiny slits that they were. "No one is wiser nor more clever," added in a third.

"And don't forget my unlimited power and authority," he added, fairly spitting the words at the circle of black-robed creatures.

"Of course, of course," they all chanted in unison.

He didn't notice his skin slowly turning pale—a rather sickly gray—nor his hair, what was left of it, falling out in chunks onto the moldy floor, leaving but a few long black strands. He took no notice of the web-like crown that grew from his skull, trapping his head and all his thoughts like a cage. Had he looked in a mirror, he would have seen his eyes had become yellow and milky, but there were no mirrors here, and his eyesight would not have been good enough to see had there been.

After a few weeks, there was no more Bythim that could be recognized. Just another sickly creature, living in the marshes of Nyster, barking at the others in a raspy voice about its fame and fortune as Self alone became its entire universe.

CHAPTER THIRTY-SIX:

Full Circle

The palace that had once been the center of Bythim's rule was slowly, day by day, being transformed into a new place—a town hall of sorts. The opulent materials were stripped from the floors and walls and sold at market, the proceeds being invested into farmland on the outskirts of Cenecal so the city could be more self-sufficient. A suitable mayor for the town was found—Neruk initially being offered the position (but wanting none of it, only wishing to return to his village on the border of the province with his people.) In the end a good man named Galen—the very same that had deduced Rethan's betrayal of them, and suggested a trench during the first battle—was eventually chosen. The people unanimously approved of the choice, and a grand ceremony was held on the palace grounds about two weeks after Bythim's depose. The men and women who had worked for the court had been offered new positions—voluntary this time— and the courtiers had been set free to live their own lives in the city, to marry or not, but the choice would be theirs. The soldiers of the realm were given choices as well: to stay and be part of a defensive force for Cenecal and Drymac as a whole or to return to civilian life with their families. It was found that a few of the soldiers were good men (under bad rule), and these nobly stepped up to be a part of the new Cenecal. The soldiers and citizens who refused to comply with the new rule of order and civic responsibility (the marauders being a good example) were also given options. They could leave Drymac in perpetuity or could be imprisoned in the dungeons of Kraleck until or if they repented of their ways, then returned to city life. Most left, and it was said that they had headed south for the territory of Kress, which had welcomed them with open arms.

In and amidst all the change and celebration and newness, one man was almost overlooked: Rethan, the man who had betrayed his own village of Glanèt. After leaving Bythim's audience the day he had sold out his people, he had stayed on, happily enough, in Cenecal—using his blood money to frequent the pubs and brothels nightly. Having seen Neruk and the villagers march into town, he had gone into hiding in the forest just outside the city. Had it not been for Garanthor and a few of his cousins out digging in the snow for grass upon which to graze, it was unlikely he ever would have been found at all. They had stumbled upon him one day in the forest, shaking from the cold. Thinking he was lost or injured, they had encircled the poor man, who, upon seeing the gigantic beasts surround him, had simply swooned and fallen to the snow. They had picked him up and carried him to the palace for assistance, where he had been recognized by a few of the villagers who were helping rip down the garish tapestries in the Great Hall just as he was being carried in.

At Neruk's request, he was placed in a cell in the dungeons below the palace—in Kraleck itself. The new mayor and his staff would decide what to do with him when the time came. In handing him over, Neruk washed his hands of Rethan's destiny, as Rethan had done to his own people.

One day, after quite a few weeks in this new Cenecal, Lanthrea had been surprised by the Old Towners, who had gathered a veritable small army of people together and had rebuilt her little home outside the merchant quarter. They had blindfolded her one sunny day, and led her there, only to reveal a small house, painted robin's egg blue (Petrul had remembered her grandparent's little home!) with windows all around and a bright red door. Mysta had run inside with glee, squealing about 'the curtains and the soft beds and the big fireplace', and Lanthrea had simply slumped down outside the place and cried. A home of her own. This time, with no glottin to steal her joy, but instead a daughter to bring her nothing but.

A'lam had stayed in Cenecal for nigh on a month before telling the people he had another land in need of his help. A land that had come under dark enchantment—a land with no name at the present time but once called Thetonia. Thetonia: the land of eternal winter where Lanthrea had found Mysta. Thetonia, where Cresta had taken her and Mysta in and taught Lanthrea how to make a cheese pie—her kindness never to be forgotten. Lanthrea could think of no other land in so need or so worthy of his good help.

Azar had stayed behind in Cenecal after the king left, assisting the new mayor, Galen, in learning the ways of Palem insofar as governance. Concepts such as freedom, equality, civility, parity, and goodwill had long been missing from Drymac's courts and civic systems. The Old Towners, Lanthrea, and a few others were now free to speak of Palem and share both illustrations and words from the book, but no one was forced to listen nor believe.

The days passed like a dream, and the winter was mild and easy on everyone. By springtime, just before the Festival of Ciracus, the city had firmly embraced the new order, and an optimism not seen in over a century had settled upon all who lived there. The Prathians had returned to their beloved desert before the winter ended (the snow and cold not appreciated by them at all), and Cla'neen had promised to keep in touch with Lanthrea as best she could, distance notwithstanding. Plaxi, Clink, and the elves had stayed on for a few months, teaching archery and forging skills to anyone in Cenecal who wished to learn. They had been summoned, just before the Winter Solstice, to a Drekken attack in Naganthria, where a group of travelers had been immobilized by their terrors and whisperings to such an extent that they were in dire need of help. The talking animals had felt free to stay in Drymac, unafraid of being hunted, and had sprinkled themselves throughout the countryside, happy to have their Council meet in the open rather than in hiding. Garanthor and his kin returned to the skies of Palem, taking the Lady of Lanthor with them but promising to visit every now and again at first chance. Neruk and the villagers of Glanèt had happily returned to their village within weeks of the battle, Th'rena sending news to Lanthrea by carrier pigeon of the rebuilding of their huts and their joy of being home on Glanètian soil once again.

The men and women of Palem proper had returned home just as the first buds blossomed on the cherry trees in Cenecal. They had stayed over the winter to help the Old Towners fortify some of the gardens and fountains that had long been in need of repair. A handful of them chose to stay in Old Town itself, a fact for which the elders were not only grateful but elated. Younger folk made everything seem new again.

By the Eve of Cirac, Cenecal was a new place; the traditional festival celebrating the spring planting becoming this year a festival of new life altogether.

Lanthrea was lying in her bed (a soft one with pillows and real blankets) staring up at the ceiling of her new home, listening to Mysta's quiet breathing as she slept. A fire was burning low in the fireplace, and she remembered a night similar to this just a year ago: a rough muslin blanket for her shoulders, a glottin curled by the fire, awakening her every so often to warn of 'danger'. Her heart could hardly hold all the changes.

Still, she felt as though something was wrong. It was almost impossible to put her finger on, but it was there, gnawing at her.

Finding it impossible to sleep, she got up, lit a lamp, and pulled the book out from under her pillow. Opening to the page with the illustration of the Courtier, she traced the lovely figure once again with her finger.

Could it be that she, like that lovely young woman, really belonged in this place? That she really belonged to the King? Picking up her crown off the nightstand, she let it sparkle in the firelight. She was his daughter. This crown assured her of that role and honor. But. Did she really *belong*? Had Tenk been there, it would have warned her. *"Warning...danger to believe. You are being tricked. Made a fool. This joy will not last. Danger, Miss."*

How odd. She could almost hear its voice in that darkened room. She shook off the feeling and sat up straight in her bed. Looking up at her shelf on the wall, she stared at the mosaic made for her by the king's own hand. Each stone a reminder of her journey thus far. Each one more beautiful than the last. How could she doubt that she belonged or her own unique loveliness?

"Danger, miss. You are not wanted here. Do not believe you have any worth. None of this will last. Danger will come, Miss. Lies, Miss, lies."

Once again, she could almost hear Tenk's voice in her head, the warnings coming in waves like arrows from a hundred archers.

She closed her eyes for a moment, then opened them and let them fall on a passage from the book.

"Do not remember what is past; instead, move on in truth. For you are not who you once were, and the darkness has no hold on you. Welcome to this new life with joy and blessing."

She let the words sink in, then read them again. And again.

I am not who I once was. She said the words aloud, softly, letting them slip from her mouth like the precious stones in her shield. *I am welcome here.*

She once was alone. But she was no longer. She once thought she was ugly and unwanted. But she knew the truth of that now. She once lived in darkness so great that the terror of it assaulted her heart every night. She once lived only for herself. But all was new now. She was not who she once had been. She was to now remember the king's promises and, just as importantly, *not* remember the past. Not let it take any hold on her.

She glanced over at her sleeping daughter. Just as Mysta was now safe in her love, so was she in the King's. And even though evil yet lived in the world, and though her body was aging still and death one day would come, the King was with her every moment. She had a huge family here and in Palem and one day in the Forever Land itself. She could love them all well, and let them love her *as* well.

She raised her eyes to the moonlit sky outside her window. "A'lam, help me to be who you see me to be. Help me to love those you have given me. And receive love *as* well. It is still so very hard."

The moon winked back at her reassuringly. Her heart calmed, and she slipped the book back under the pillow.

Her impossibly soft pillow in the warm bed with the blankets that she could pull up under her chin.

Tomorrow, she would buy some cloth and paints at the market. And paint her stories for anyone to see. Anyone who lived in the terror of darkness and need of the light.

She fell asleep easily and tumbled into the most lovely dream.

In it, A'lam was riding toward her on his horse, his smile as bright as the dawn. Trotting over, he dismounted and knelt down beside her as she sat in the tall green grass of a lovely meadow—and handed her a rose. A single, white rose whose fragrance seemed unearthly in glory and strength.

"Lanthrea," he said, "it is time you know the meaning of your name."

She gently touched the soft petals of the rose and looked up at him. "It is a lovely name. That's is enough for me."

"Lovely, indeed," he said softly. "But you might like to know why I chose it for you." She nodded in agreement, and he smiled. "Lanthrea means 'peaceful, trusting one'. It is a derivation of another name, 'Lanthor', meaning 'she who believes'.

The rose slipped from her hand. She stared back at him in utter disbelief.

"I was named after the Lady of Lanthor?"

The king smiled. "You were. "For true beauty comes from trusting me, as she does. As you are learning to." She stared at him, her heart full of wonder. He then lay his hand upon her shoulder gently. "But know this. Trust can only be achieved by true humility." Feeling suddenly uncomfortable, she shifted slightly in the grass and looked away. He drew a breath and explained. "Lanthrea, sometimes your desire—and even your resistance—to believe you are loved and to trust me does not come from a humble heart. Oft times, your sorrows and fears are driven by a kind of pride. A desire to control…to make the world revolve around you. My dear child" (and here he lifted her face towards him so as to look into her eyes) "the world, rightly ordered, revolves only around me. Once that is set straight, so will all your sorrows. Let me have control, for, in truth, I have it already. If you can—even in the least —acknowledge this, then your beauty, as with all who humbly trust me, will increase and overflow… pouring out and bringing healing to others." He leaned over and kissed her forehead. "Remember the meaning of your name. And know my love."

With this, he picked the rose up off the ground and handed it to her again, then mounted his horse and turned and galloped away. She lifted the rose and inhaled its sweet fragrance, letting a joy she had never known fill her heart.

And so it was that Lanthrea—daughter of the king, mother of Mysta, member of a new family—slept through the night, as she would for many more, under the brightest stars imaginable in a peaceful town named Cenecal, ruled by good men and women, surrounded by the tall Circacian Mountains in a Kingdom called Drymac.

***

EPILOGUE

He walked past the merchant's booths, uninterested in anything he had yet to see in this town called Cenecal. Why his grandfather had been so taken with this place, he could not comprehend. But then again, his grandfather had been so few places compared to himself, who had been to a great many in his short twenty years… most in the last year alone. For there were rumors that Koth armies were gathering along the border of Mondoria. This, more than his grandfather's encouragement— or even his desire for adventure —had helped him decide to travel north last fall. For the Koth would not be gathering an army for any good purpose. There was little good to be found in the land of Kress.

His decision had thus far been a good one. It had allowed him to see many great sights and meet many good people on his journey to the north. From the great capital city of Nathengard in his homeland of Mondoria, to the great palace and opulent tents of Sha'lin in Prathia —each city was grander than the one before. But Cenecal? He found this town to be completely uninspiring.

Sighing, he wrapped his cloak against the wind, and walked through the Merchant Quarter headed to a place called Old Town. His grandfather had made him promise to visit there, and so he would.

It was as he turned the corner that he noted a booth tucked back against the town wall, run by a very old woman. Something about her (or perhaps the merchandise on the walls) drew his attention. He stopped, walked over and stood for a moment, his eyes going from one painting to the next.

"That one," he finally spoke, pulling the hood off his head. "On the blue cloth. May I see that?"

She smiled, took the cloth off the wall and laid the piece flat on the table before him.

It was a painting of a waterfall, but like none he'd ever seen. It almost seemed alive. He sniffed, unfamiliar with the emotion the thing brought up.

"How much?" He asked, knowing full well he was willing to pay any price for it.

"Three minac," the old woman said, smiling.

Reaching in his pocket, he pulled out a little bag of coins and tossed five of them onto her table and smiled. "For your troubles," he said, winking at her. Rolling up the cloth, he nodded at the old woman, tucked it under his arm and continued on his way.

She watched him go, then turned and smiled at the lovely young woman with the bright green eyes— who was just then returning to the booth with an armful of cloth.

"He'll be back," Lanthrea said with a laugh, motioning toward the man who was quickly being absorbed by the crowd in the marketplace. "I saw the look in his eyes. He has many questions, that one."

She smiled at Mysta knowingly, then turned her attention to the next customer who asked to see a bright yellow cloth with a painting of a deer upon it. A tiny doe, wearing a lacy silver crown atop its head.

"O poor little one, tossed by storms and not comforted, behold I will lay thy stones in order, and will lay thy foundations with sapphire." Isaiah 54:11 (NIV, Douay-Rheims)

Claudette Spear, 2022 "The Crown Amongst Stones"